MIRROR, MIRROR

TIGER FAYE

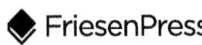 FriesenPress

Suite 300 - 990 Fort St
Victoria, BC, V8V 3K2
Canada

www.friesenpress.com

Copyright © 2017 by Tiger Faye
First Edition — 2017

ISBN
978-1-5255-1545-3 (Hardcover)
978-1-5255-1546-0 (Paperback)
978-1-5255-1547-7 (eBook)

1. YOUNG ADULT FICTION, FANTASY, CONTEMPORARY

Distributed to the trade by The Ingram Book Company

CHAPTER 1

Gleaming abyss

HE HIT THE GROUND RUNNING. SMOKY CLOUDS OF SAND FORMED BEHIND him as he tore a trail through the crowded beachfront. He willed his legs to work faster, ducking under umbrellas and jumping over sun tanners to reach the curve of the coastline, where cliffs of limestone and slate started to tower over the shore. He leapt behind a surfboard rental shack and dove into the tall grass, breathing heavily. Cool bursts of sea air entered his lungs, a welcome relief from the sprinting burn. The sky was a crystal blue, dotted with only a few small clouds and the occasional seagull. He lay back for a moment, gazing upwards. Then the cold shock hit him.

"AAAAAHHH!!" He jumped up and blinked the water out of his eyes.

"That's what you get for trying to pull one on me!" said a voice that was like music to his ears. His vision cleared and he smiled. A pair of mischievous cerulean-blue eyes looked down at him. In front of him stood a petite blond girl holding a neon pink water pail. The contents of which, she had just dumped onto his head. Not that it was really her fault; he had promised not to get her wet and then dropped her into the ocean moments before. Her hair fell in dripping golden strands down her shoulders and her cheeks had a rosy flush from running after him. Her crimson tank top clung to her tiny frame as she smiled in triumph, happily waving the pail back and forth.

"Mavis, you couldn't really expect I'd do anything else," he said, laughing.

"Remind me to punch you in the face before I trust you next time." Mavis threw a light punch to his shoulder. He laughed and shrugged his shoulders.

"Jett Davis is just a really bad boy. Breaking promises and hearts everywhere." He gave her a cocky grin and kissed his bicep. She rolled her eyes.

"Jett Davis is a conceited bastard that doesn't know who he's messing with." She raised an eyebrow at him. "Now before I show my true wrath you're going to buy me dinner and apologize."

"Why do women require an apology for everything? And dinner on top of that?" He hung his arm around her shoulder and both of them started to walk back towards their towels.

"So that you don't ever do that stupid, annoying thing again. Because it will result in a fight and financial loss for you." They approached their scatter of umbrellas, volleyballs and surfboards, where Jett's mildly annoyed twin awaited them.

"You know guys, the next time you decide to ditch me and run a mile down the beach, give me a heads-up. I could have burned my lunch calories with you." He motioned to the burger wrappers they had stuffed into a paper bag, lying amongst their stash of pop, chips and seashells, courtesy of Mavis.

"Come on Adam," Jett plopped down on his towel. "You're telling me you can't spend thirty minutes alone?"

"I actually pray that I can get thirty minutes away from you guys," he said shaking his head. "But when I wait in line for twenty minutes to get you all drinks and perform an acrobatic feat to get them back here without spilling them, I'd rather you be here to take 'em cold and sing my praises."

"I'll have you know," Mavis said as she threw her volleyball in Adam's direction, which he caught with ease. "That I have better things to do with my time than sing your praises."

"Like seducing Jett?" Adam replied as he attempted to mimic what should have been an exaggerated kiss with the ball, but instead looked like he had infected lip injections. Mavis made a gagging noise.

"Dude you're scaring the kids." Jett picked up his wallet and phone from under his surfboard. "Before parents start complaining about inappropriate displays of public affection, let's eat." The trio gathered their things and started towards the parking lot where they deposited their belongings into the trunk of their rental. Once they had artfully thrown everything in to the point where they were sure it wouldn't fall out, Adam slammed the trunk closed and turned to his companions.

"Shall we?" He offered an arm to Mavis who accepted it graciously.

"Glad you decided to start being a gentleman now," she giggled as she looped her arm though his.

The trio strode forward towards what was known as the "Feast Street"; a strip of restaurants, street vendor carts and snack shacks along the far side of the beach. Strings of multi-coloured lights were wound around lampposts and buskers were playing a variety of instruments, ranging from drums, guitars, maracas and castanets. Accordion players strolled up and down the streets, filling the air with wonderful melodic sounds. Jett walked behind Mavis and Adam, left to his own thoughts. The sun was starting to set, lighting the horizon aglow, tinting the sky with shades of coral and pink. A feeling of peace washed over him. There were few wonders as spectacular as a sunset. Especially one over a coastline that stretched farther than his eyes could see. The nightlife had started to come in as the street began to crowd with tourists, laughing and pushing to get to the vacation hot spots listed on the visitor information desk of every hotel in the area.

The restaurants and diners had their extra staff out, waiting to take in the oncoming rush. Mavis and Adam had already gone into to a softly lit diner around the corner. Jett sighed. He hated it when those two decided on stuff without him. They often got so caught up with each other that they usually neglected to take his opinion. Sometimes he let it slide because he knew they didn't do it intentionally and other times he'd put his foot down. They did try to remember most of the time, but once in a while, like now, it'd slip their mind. He wasn't in the mood to fuss so he just hoped that the diner had something good. Jett wasn't a picky eater, but when he was in the mood for something in particular, he wanted it badly. Tonight, it was pizza. He had been in Costa Rica for about a week now, trying wonderfully delicious, and sometimes absolutely weird, delicacies offered by the locals. Though he enjoyed it, tonight he just wanted old, familiar, comforting pizza to give him a little taste of home. He didn't know why he was craving it. Maybe he wanted to remind himself that this was just temporary and he'd have to go back soon and make some choices, a prospect he was dreading. Or maybe because in the back of his mind, he wanted to remember his dad. His hand reached up and closed around a silver disk that he wore around his throat. He felt the cool metal under his fingertips as he toyed with it.

He went through the doorway of the diner, which was framed by palm trees and tiger lilies winding up a wooden arch. Small vines of ivy hung down, brushing his skin as he stepped through and approached the smiling hostess.

Her smile disappeared as he came closer and a look of confusion crossed her face. Jett knew that face well. He got it all the time when he and Adam went out anywhere. Being identical, it took people a moment or two to figure out they had to be seeing a twin and not the same person again. He didn't blame them. The most they could do to look different was to cut their hair at different times, so one had long hair while the other's was short. They both hadn't done it in a while, so now they walked as moving reflections of each other.

He tugged on his dark brown hair. It was starting to curl, a sign that a haircut was long overdue. His mother loved his unruly curly hair, a trait given to him by his father. Ever since he passed away, Jett had kept it short, not wanting to be reminded of his father when he looked in the mirror. It hurt too much. He knew he looked like him, and as he grew older he was becoming even more so. Joseph Davis had given his sons much of his face and slender frame, echoing their distant British heritage. The only significant feature Jett had gotten from his mother was the colour of his eyes. They were a medium hazel, the colour of milk chocolate with the slightest hint of green. His dad's had been a stormy grey.

Jett pointed to Adam and Mavis, who were sitting at a table on the outer deck. The hostess looked back and forth as realization came over her face. "This way…" she said. Jett followed behind her and took his place at the table. She placed down another menu and said, "Ten minutes." Adam nodded to her and she returned to the entrance. Costa Ricans spoke Spanish, but the majority knew enough English to get by with tourists.

"Glad you could join us," Mavis said, stretching her arms back.

"Didn't want to interrupt your quality time," Jett responded as he began to flip through the laminated menu in search of pizza. Luckily, there was half a page with a few different options. He scanned through the toppings list, mentally picking out three or four he'd want.

"I don't call spending time with Mavis, quality time," Adam joked. He pulled on one of the curls that framed her face affectionately. "I call it punishment."

"Such a sweetheart," Mavis said sarcastically. "If I recall, you seemed rather eager to take that punishment."

"No one said Adam was smart," Jett patted his brother on the shoulder. "Go easy on him."

Mavis laughed. Jett looked at her fondly. He loved hearing her laugh. It was soft, musical, and familiar.

"Just shut up and order." Adam flipped open his menu.

"I'm getting pizza," Jett announced.

"Okay. Mavis, what do you want?" Adam said. As the two examined the menu Jett turned his gaze to the ocean. The water was coloured pink and purple, reflecting the dying sun.

"Jett..." Mavis pushed his arm lightly, snapping him out of his thoughts. The two were looking at him. He had been playing with the disk again. He watched their expressions change. Adam gave him a sad smile. He always understood what Jett was feeling. Adam was his other half in many ways apart from his looks. He understood him like no one else did. He didn't know if it was a twin thing, or because they shared a brain at one point in the womb, or because their parents had raised them to be each other's support. Either way, their communication did not require words. *I miss Dad.*

He turned the disk in his hand. On one side was a symbol of a fire and on the other was a wave. His dad had given it to him right before he passed away. His memories must have been tugging at him harder than he had thought. He had ordered his dad's favourite food too. Their father had loved pizza and passed on the love to his boys. Adam's first soccer win, Jett's first A+, his mother's new job, had all been celebrated with pizza. His dad had used it as a way of saying *I'm happy* or *I'm proud of you* or even sometimes *relax.* They would go out in the middle of the night sometimes to get some, and return home to an angry mother who condemned eating junk food that late. The day he gave Jett that disk, Jett had been hand feeding him a slice because he was too weak to feed himself. To some, the disk was a silly thing to be sentimental about. Jett clung to it anyway, desperate for something that would prevent his father's memory from fading.

Mavis put her hand on his arm. She was his other lifeline. They had become friends in their freshman year of high school, shortly before his father passed away. He remembered shy, young Mavis with rainbow hair extensions smiling at him on the first day of geography class. She became his best friend and biggest support through his father's death. She'd come over at night and hug him while he would sob silently into her shoulder. At that time, Adam nor his mother could support him because they were going through the same pain. Tiny Mavis had stepped in and held all his emotional weight, teaching him how to turn his outlook on life positive again. Now here they were six years later, and nothing had changed. She knew that even six years didn't lessen the pain of the blow by much.

"It's okay," she said softly. They placed their order and ate in comfortable silence. Jett felt the warm glow of his memories flood through him. A small smile worked its way up to his lips. It was enough. Being here, with his brother and best friend was enough. He slept peacefully that night.

✂

"Wake up sleeping beauty!"

Jett jerked back and rubbed his eyes. Adam was holding him by his backpack straps, which just so happened to have saved him from slamming face first into a road sign.

"Thanks man," he said groggily. "Mavis," he moaned. "How much farther?" Mavis turned to look at him.

"It's up the cliff side. We're almost there," she said encouragingly. Jett groaned.

"Why do we have to come for this? It's your project! Did it have to be at seven in the morning too?" Mavis sighed. Jett was infuriating sometimes. Especially when he was sleepy.

"Because I was your ticket here. So, we do as I say. I could ask you to climb Mount Everest at three A.M. and you'd have to. I'm your best friend too, so there's no escaping this." Jett mumbled under his breath, but Mavis smiled. She knew he probably would climb a mountain for her. That arrogant smartass would do anything for his friends and family. She was fascinated by how easily his feelings shifted. He could be happy and bright one minute and serious and determined the next. He liked to keep a relaxed, whimsical pretence around himself but she knew that inside, he could be a swirl of emotions at any moment.

She slowed her walk until she fell in step beside him. He was waking up slowly, his eyes becoming alert and his muscles tensing. Out of the corner of her eye Mavis could see his slender profile, with his slim frame and average height. Years of soccer had given him a lean and agile body in addition to speed. If he hadn't stopped running the other day, Mavis would never have caught him.

They were approaching the top of the cliff and Mavis felt excitement thrum through her. She had been waiting to come here for a long time. This place was the reason for her visit to Costa Rica. Her major was in history and artefacts at the University of Toronto back home in Canada. The program often involved researching local folklore and literature. She had, with much difficulty, gotten her professor to approve this trip so she could come and explore the ruins of this country. The areas around the Caribbean had a diverse record of history, from wars to natural disasters to legends to myths. You could find almost any kind of story to gain insight on the land's past.

Jett had begged her to come along and she had agreed readily. She put in a request for a research assistant (a.k.a Jett) to come with her. Who didn't want their best friend to go on an exotic vacation with them? She knew he needed to get away for some time, and hopefully this break would help him out. Jett didn't have the slightest clue about what he wanted to do with his life. He was going to enter his third year of university with an undecided major. He had to make a decision soon. Yet he was reluctant out of the fear that he would commit to something he'd end up hating. One thing he told Mavis he didn't want to do, was hate his life by doing something that made him unhappy or bored. She knew he was still struggling for a decision. He had to decide quickly or else he'd be wasting thousands of dollars of tuition money. Adam on the other hand, had come with her because he had a culinary training program in the capital city, San Jose, that started next week. He loved to cook and hoped to have his own restaurant one day. His culinary school had sponsored him to come and learn a few international dishes.

Mavis sprinted forward, climbing up the path like the howler monkey that was native here. She jumped over rocks and plants blocking her way with agility and grace. Once she reached the top, the land seemed to level out. She took a few steps and then stopped dead in her tracks as she took in the scene before her. Jett and Adam caught up to her, huffing and puffing. She heard them gasp. She could imagine their gaping mouths but didn't bother to look. She couldn't tear her eyes away from what she was seeing. The top of the cliff looked like a sculptor had carved it out. A few feet in front of them, the ground gave way to a massive chasm. It appeared as if someone had hollowed out the cliff side. The ground was a few hundred feet below. Out of it erupted enormous twisted spires of rock that were reaching out towards the sky. Their enormous size and stunning, twisted shape weren't even the most formidable part. The ground, the rock, the chasm itself, was glittering. Glittering and shifting colours in the sunlight. If Mavis moved her head slightly the reflected light would transform from lilac to sapphire to emerald green and garnet red. It was like someone had dumped a bag of nuclear rainbow fairy dust over the entire landscape. It shimmered with an unearthly glow. Mavis' professor had told her there were caves and ruins that she would want to see, but never mentioned anything about this. *It's here. This is actually here.* She still didn't really believe she was seeing it. She shook off her astonishment and looked around. The place was clear of other people. Her professor had told her it was an off-limits research site to the public, and had pulled some strings with her contacts to give Mavis permission to come. Even if it was off-limits, why wasn't there any news about this place? There were no professionals to be seen either. It was deserted.

Jett was still staring at the chasm. Adam walked over to Mavis. "This… there are no words for it. I think even extraordinary is not enough to say how spectacular it is." Mavis nodded in agreement. It's like she had come upon a treasure that she had not planned to find. At least not yet. She thought it would take her several years before she'd come upon something like this. This was a huge step forward for her.

"You see it too. That means I'm not hallucinating."

"Yeah it's almost too hard to believe." Adam shook his head in an attempt to convince himself. They walked over to Jett.

"Can a place like this really exist on Earth?" Jett whispered.

"Apparently so," Mavis said softly. She looked back down at the sparkling landscape. "I want to explore," she said and began walking towards the edge.

"Mavis!" Adam exclaimed. "You can't just go off like that! Are we even allowed to? Why isn't there anyone else here?"

"I don't know. My prof didn't mention anything about a chasm. But there's no one here to tell us no, and we'll probably never get to see this again. I'm going to see as much as possible before someone comes in and limits what I can do."

"It could be dangerous! We should have backup. Someone should know where we are," Adam argued.

"The officers at the base let us through. They know we're up here. If we don't come down after some time, they'll send backup." Mavis was determined. Although it was slightly strange, she was glad the place was empty. No one could stop her from exploring the area to her heart's content. She could do whatever she wanted to do.

"I don't see the harm if we explore a bit," Jett said. "I want to see it up close too." Adam let out a frustrated sigh.

"I still don't think it's a good idea." Adam emphasised the word 'good'.

"Then you stay here and me and Jett will go," Mavis responded.

"Over my dead body. I'm not going to let you go there alone. If you plan on rushing headfirst into danger, at least take some protection with you."

"You count as protection?"

"No, the three of us together are protection. We take care of each other," Adam said defiantly. Mavis wrapped him in a tight hug while Jett smiled.

"Let's go," Jett said. Together, they walked towards the edge of the chasm.

❧

The chasm walls jutted in and out of the main formation, creating a jagged staircase that circled downwards. Jett jumped down to the first ledge, easily finding his footing. The ground was covered in a soft, thin layer of what looked like pinkish sand. The earth itself still sparkled from underneath. He shifted so Mavis and Adam could drop down beside him. Mavis bent down and touched the sand.

"It's so soft!" she said, as the grains spilled through her fingers. The sand felt like silk against her skin. She took out an empty water bottle from her backpack and began to fill it with handfuls of sand. Jett chuckled.

"Want a souvenir huh?"

"You have your desires, I have mine," Mavis replied. Once she had filled the bottle, she carefully put it into her backpack and stood up. Adam and Jett had already gone a few ledges down. She hopped after them, leaving her footprints in the rosy sand. The rock spires began to rise above them, glowing with a magnificent mixture of swirling colours. When she caught up with the twins they were examining a lump in the ground.

"What is it?" she asked.

"I don't know," Jett said as he felt around it. "It's surrounded by rock."

Adam knelt down and began to brush off the sand.

"I think it is a rock," Mavis said. "Just an uneven part of the ground."

"The rest of the ground is pretty smooth all around us. Why would there only be one bump this big?" Jett mused. "It won't hurt to investigate." Mavis got on her knees and helped clear the sand away. Slowly, they began to see that the rock was diamond shaped, unnaturally so. Nature did not cut rocks that smoothly and precisely. Someone must have shaped it. As more sand was cleared Jett noticed he had cleared a hole. He could see through to the other side. He reached to put his hand through it. His fingers came in contact with something smooth and hard. He looked at it curiously. He couldn't put his hand through the hole. *It's glass*, he realized with a start, or some kind of clear, hard substance. He was baffled. This glass was so smooth and clear that it didn't look like glass. It was completely see-through. The trio had cleared away most of the sand to reveal a crystal-clear diamond prism partly buried in the earth. The only way they knew it was diamond shaped was because sunlight outlined the edges. Otherwise it was so clear that you wouldn't have known it was there unless you walked into it. It couldn't be glass either, since it gave no reflection.

"What is it?" Adam asked. "It looks like a big clear rock, but why would there be a huge chunk of it just lying around?" Mavis got up and dusted off her shorts. She turned and gave a quick scan of the area.

"I don't see any more like it," she said. It didn't match the colourful rock spires or the glittery ground. Jett gazed at it thoughtfully. His father had always told him the best way to discover something was by looking at it plainly. A lot snapped into place when you didn't overthink too much.

"The best tools you have are attached to your body. Sometimes," his father said, "you just need to reach for it and it will come to you." *You just need to reach for it.*

Jett reached out and touched the diamond. A burst of blinding white light exploded from within it, completely encompassing the three.

"GAAAAAH!!" they screamed, covering their eyes. It disappeared as quickly as it had come. Jett slowly opened his eyes. Mavis and Adam were staring at him.

"What did you do?" Mavis said, clearly shaken.

"I-I-I don't know, I just touched it. And it wasn't the first time, I had been touching it the whole time we were cleaning it. It just went whack right now--"

"Jett," Adam interrupted. "Look." Jett turned. The stone was no longer transparent. It had turned a milky white. The white colour shifted inside the rock, as if they had trapped some coloured smoke in it.

"What on earth--" A whooshing sound cut him off. The three jumped up and looked around wildly.

"Stick together!" Adam said. They huddled close to each other, trying to locate the noise. It came again, but now clearer, like a vibration from the ground.

"There!" Mavis squeaked. The trio looked up to see a figure on the rock spire closest to them. In a flash, it disappeared and then reappeared several feet down the spire. They started to backup only to hit the chasm wall. The figure was gliding down towards them with incredible speed. As it got closer, Jett realized it wasn't gliding. It was sliding down the rock, almost like surfing the surface. The figure flipped off the spire and landed in a crouch in front of them. Jett could feel Mavis shaking beside him. He was trembling all over too. He felt like he had done something terrible by touching that stone, and now all of them would pay for it. The figure rose and assumed a confident, relaxed stance. Now Jett could see her in full. Standing before him was a girl around his age, head to toe in black. She wore a black, short sleeve crop top that showed off a flat, slightly muscular stomach and similarly coloured cargo pants that hugged her hips. Her skin was a light milk coffee colour with a summer tan on her lower arms. Her hair was jet-black and stick straight, falling below her shoulders. Side bangs covered part of her right eye. The most jarring part about her was her eyes. Just like the rest of her, they were black and emotionless. You couldn't separate the pupil from the iris. They resembled two obsidian stones set in ivory. To Jett it spelled unnatural. She was beautiful, in the way shinning knives or tigers were beautiful. Everything about her screamed danger. Adam stepped forward.

"Look, we don't know what happened, we were just exploring…" He faltered as she took a jagged-edged dagger from her shirtsleeve and tossed casually it from hand to hand. "… We don't want any trouble, we'll leave right away. I'm sorry if we did anything wrong." As he spoke, she eyed them up and down, face expressionless, as if she was judging if they were worth the trouble of mugging. Adam stepped backwards. She looked up, freezing him in place. There was something about her stare that said, 'If you move, you'll *regret* it'. She walked over and touched the stone. It lit up with a fiery orange glow and then returned to its previous white colour. She turned back to them, her expression holding the slightest hint of interest.

"You," she said, pointing three fingers in their direction. Jett supposed that implied all of them. She spoke with a musical accent that he couldn't recognize. "Will come with me."

"What makes you think we will?" Jett challenged. Adam elbowed him, a warning that they probably didn't want to know otherwise. She looked at him with a bored expression.

"Or I could kill you. It won't take long. The decision is yours." She turned her back to them. Mavis tightened her grip on Jett's shirt. Adam evaluated their chances. If they ran, they would most likely be killed. The girl looked like a trained fighter. If they went with her they might suffer the same fate, but they had the benefit of the doubt. What if they all fought her…

"Don't think the three of you could overpower me," she said as if reading Adam's thoughts. "You'll regret it." She still had her back to them. She began to jump down the ledges without looking back. Jett sighed. He clasped Mavis' hand tightly giving it a reassuring squeeze. He could see that she was terrified. He looked at Adam. They came to a silent agreement. With another sigh, they started following her down into the gleaming abyss.

CHAPTER 2
Perceptions can be deceptions

ADAM SILENTLY CURSED HIMSELF AS THEY FOLLOWED THE GIRL DOWN the stone ledges. He should have insisted that they stay up on the cliff platform. Instead he had given permission for the three of them to go down into a dangerous, not to mention deserted, place that they had no idea about, and now they could be walking towards their deaths.

"Don't blame yourself," Jett said quietly. Adam sighed. Sometimes he hated the fact that Jett could understand him so well. Even if he wanted to act brave or confident when he wasn't, it wouldn't help Jett. Jett would see right through it to his fear and panic. Adam couldn't support his brother, unless he truly supported himself. It was easier said than done.

They had reached what seemed to be the floor of the chasm. The earth seemed to glow even brighter here, the sparkling colours moved and shifted with the motion of Adam's eyes. The girl was several feet in front of them, striding forward purposefully. They approached a sloped rock spire, which appeared to bend in an arch. As they got closer Adam heard a rustling sound. Every step they took forward amplified it. *That's water. Flowing water.* Adam took a step back quickly. This chick was going to drown them. He felt a sharp point dig into his back. He spun around. She stood there, dagger out. How had she moved so quickly?

"Forward," she commanded. Jett pulled Adam's arm. He was grateful; he didn't feel like he could move from his spot when she looked at him with those merciless black eyes. She walked in front and turned to face the trio. She pulled out a slim braided rope from her pocket.

"If you don't want to die, tie this through your belt loops. There will be a river below us soon and we have to cross using the spire." She pointed to the bending rock formation. "I'll steer you so you cross safely." *Here's the girl who threatened us with a knife, saying that she'll keep us safe. Going anywhere with you doesn't seem safe to me,* Adam thought bitterly. *Why bother exercising caution here when you'll probably kill us anyway?* She looked at him coldly. "Would you rather I let you take your chances with the sharks?" Adam's eyes widened. "How..."

"No, I can't read your mind," she said, cutting him off. "But I'm excellent at guessing."

"There are sharks in a river?" Jett said dubiously.

"Would you like to find out?" she asked with a daring tone. Jett swallowed. He was sure that she wouldn't hesitate to prove her point.

"I'll take your word for it," he mumbled. The three tied the rope through their belt loops with Mavis positioned in between the twins. Adam took the spot behind the girl. She came over and tied the last parts of the rope the waist of her pants.

"Hold on to the person in front," she instructed. Mavis wrapped her arms around Adam's waist tightly. He could feel the slight tremble that went through her body. He placed his hand over hers and squeezed it. He wouldn't let anything happen to her. He promised himself that he would do at least that much. The girl turned around.

"Hold on," she said. *Great, I get to hold onto her.* Adam nervously reached around and clasped his hands together in front of her, leaving lots of space between them. She let out a frustrated sigh. She grabbed his hands, her nails digging into his skin, and pulled him forwards so he was hugging her around the waist. Adam had never felt more awkward or terrified around a girl in his life.

"Walk," she commanded. They walked to the foot of the spire. He still couldn't see any river but he could hear it for sure.

"Sit," she said. She pushed herself onto the rock, straddling it. The trio followed her example. "Don't let go," she said. Adam barely had time to process what she had told them when she jolted forward, pushing off the sides of the rock with her legs. They went speeding down the rock at the speed of a roller coaster. The wind whistled loudly in Adam's ears, drowning out Mavis and Jett's screaming along with his own. The girl was using her legs and thighs to twist from side to side in order to dodge lumps in the spire as they slid down it like a waterslide. Adam could see that the arch suddenly shot downwards. They plunged down, accelerating faster and faster. They were hurtling towards a huge spike of rock. *How are we going to get over that?!*, his head screamed at him. The girl turned her hips sharply as the spike approached, putting them on the underside of the rock. They zoomed passed it. *I'm upside down*, Adam thought dizzily. He looked down. Under him were roaring rapids of water. The river was huge, stretching out beneath him. The water was a glittering blue. Literally glittering, as though someone had dropped diamonds into it. She shifted, sending them into a spiral down the rock. He could see the water coming up to meet them. *This is it*, Adam thought. This is how he would die. Holding onto some deranged Amazon warrior straight out of his mythology books, and hitting the water at a hundred kilometers per hour. He felt her hands breaking his hold. He was still screaming, now flailing his arms back and forth. She leapt up and jumped off the spire. The rope yanked on them, pulling them off with her. They went airborne. Adam could see nothing but water under them. The rope swung him forward and his knees hit something hard. He landed with a thud. The world spun around him. It took him a few seconds to get his bearings. *I'm alive. Still alive.* She stood over him with a blank face. He struggled to his knees.

"Mavis, Jett!" he called.

"Here!" Jett said. He was helping Mavis up. They were scratched and bruised but otherwise okay. The girl, on the other hand, didn't have a scratch on her. Adam shot her a look of pure anger.

"You could have killed us!" he shouted at her.

The girl calmly gazed at him, not saying a word. Mavis went to his side.

"If she wanted to kill us, she would have done it when she first found us. She wants us for something, so she hasn't done anything yet," Mavis pointed out. "But I think if we don't cooperate she'll change her mind."

The girl nodded. She began to walk on the water. *Walk on the water??* Adam did a double take and looked down. He was standing on the diamond water. It was rushing under him, but he didn't sink, or feel any wetness or pull of the current. It was like he was floating above it.

"It has a layer of the clear rock on it," Jett said. "I felt it when I landed. It's the same material." Adam bent down to touch it. Just as Jett said, underneath him was the hard, smooth feel of the rock that got them into this mess. Just like before, it was almost invisible. They got up and numbly followed the girl down the side of the river. The bank was lined with trim green grass and leafy trees that sprouted violet flowers on their branches. The sweet smell of lilac entered Jett's nose. It calmed him a bit, prompting him to relax his body. The girl began to walk off the river and into the grove of trees. He turned to look behind him. The rock spire they had just slid down hovered in the distance, several feet over the water. He was awestruck. *We jumped from there?* He couldn't understand how all of them weren't dead on impact. *She said she would steer us so we'd be safe, but she couldn't have possibly made that jump. Could she?* She didn't have a mark on her while Jett's arms were scraped and slightly bloody. Then again here he was walking through a sparkly rainbow land with a probably lethal stranger towards an uncertain future. By now, anything should be possible.

෴

They made their way through the trees into a wide opening. A magnificent city rose before their eyes. Jett blinked twice and pinched himself. It looked like most urban cities, with tall skyscrapers and buildings rising upwards. Then the differences kicked in. Everything was polished and smooth, the buildings had exteriors of shining steel, gold and silver. Two enormous bridges were visible between the gaps separating the skyscrapers. There was a ring of shimmery water snaking around the city like a moat, with several garden pathways connecting the surrounding area to the mainland. Each path was lined with various strips of colour, consisting of some of the strangest flowers Jett had ever seen.

They began walking down a path lined with lavender flowers. The stems were normal but the petals formed a long leaf-like shape, curling at the ends. The colour though, seemed to move within the petals, just like the rock had that shifting white smoke inside it. It was like the pigment was humanly alive, but imprisoned inside the flower. They fascinated Jett. He wandered over to the side of the pathway, brushing his hand through a row of flowers.

They felt like normal petals. He looked up. The girl was still walking several feet ahead. Mavis and Adam were trailing behind her. He looked back at the flowers, focusing closely on the shifting colour. He could make out the slightest outline of something traveling up and down the edges of the petals. He pulled on one, trying to break it from the ground. It wouldn't budge. He gave another hard pull, bringing it towards him. It made a crisp snap as it broke from the stem. Searing pain shot through his body. He opened his mouth to scream but instead fell to his knees. The world was fading away from him. Whispers filled his ears and random images flashed through his mind, incomprehensible to his rapidly weakening brain. He felt two strong arms grab him before he hit the ground. The girl's face leaned over him, blurring with each passing moment. She was saying something but he couldn't hear her over the taunting whispers. The whispers in his head started to unify, chanting one sentence. *Kushi ki saihuth.* His thoughts began to unravel. *What? What does that mean?* he thought. The whispers responded. *Happiness. The health of happiness.* The girl was still holding him, easing him down to the ground. Her dark eyes were the last image he saw before he closed his.

⁊

Mavis sat by Jett's bedside. They were in a cream-coloured room, which she guessed was part of some sort of infirmary. It had a pleasant feel, with large windows and vases of, to her relief, normal flowers. Pink and yellow roses, tulips, buttercups and chrysanthemums were placed around the room. The back wall had cupboards with Band-Aids, gauze, and what Mavis assumed to be medicine bottles. Jett's bed had two large white pillows, soft bed sheets and covers that he slept under. Mavis touched his face lightly, running her finger along his cheek and stroking his hair. His face was peaceful and relaxed, as if he was taking an afternoon nap. It sickened Mavis to see him looking like that. Jett had not woken up for two days.

After seeing him fall with the flower in his hand, Mavis' heart had leapt into her throat. The girl had already caught him and had begun to lay him down. Jett's face started to turn the lavender shade of the flower that was still grasped in his unmoving fingers. The girl had placed a hand over his heart and had chanted something Mavis didn't understand. After that, his face return to its normal colour. She and Adam had rushed over, shaking Jett in hopes of waking him. The girl had thrown them off of him, saying they would make his condition worse.

"He's stable for now," she said in a bored tone. "But we need to get him somewhere they can help him." She pulled Jett onto her back and carried him into the city. She had unbelievable strength; she walked up sloped streets and winding roads with speed and urgency while carrying Jett and never tired or faltered once. It puzzled Mavis, how she could be so determined to get him to safety quickly, but never show it on her face? She acted like it was an inconvenience for her to help them, as told by her emotionless expression and minimal communication. No concern for their lives was shown on her part. But she had brought them here nonetheless, where they had hope that perhaps, he would live. Mavis took Jett's hand slowly, locking her fingers through his tightly. *Please, Please, Please Jett. I need you. I've always needed you. You may not know it, but I do. I need you more than you know. Stay with me Jett. Stay with me.*

Adam came in with a plate of sandwiches and two juice boxes. He put them down on the bedside table. He held out a juice box to Mavis. She shook her head. Adam brought it to her mouth.

"You need to eat." Mavis took the box. There was no arguing with Adam right now. He was doing his best to take care of Mavis and himself, trying to hold both of them together emotionally. Mavis could understand. He wanted to feel like he was doing something, even something as small as offering a juice box, so he didn't feel so utterly useless about Jett's condition. Neither he nor Mavis could do anything to help him.

When they first brought Jett to this place the girl had whisked him away, straight to this room where a petite Asian girl was waiting. She laid him down and whispered in the other girl's ear. Then she had quite rudely pushed them out the door and told them to wait so they could do their work. Mavis and Adam had watched through the glass panel in the door. Just like the girl that lead them here, the Asian girl wore a similar outfit but in olive green. She had glasses and short black hair that waved around her face. Her eyes were focused and determined as she worked on Jett. Mavis and Adam couldn't make sense of what she was doing. The room had been dimmed, making it difficult to see. The Asian girl motioned the other girl over. The girl in black started to wave her hand over Jett's body. A vibrant violet colour appeared on the skin of his chest. The girl clenched her hand into a fist and raised it upwards. A trail of purple smoke rose out of Jett's chest. The girl in green started to move her hands, circling them over each other. The smoke followed her command and rolled into a small ball. The girl in black grabbed it out of the air. It floated in her palm and took the shape of a small violet egg. She closed her fingers over it, making her hand into a fist again, crushing the smoke. Out of her hand spilled snowy white powder that dissipated and scattered away into nothingness. Mavis clutched Adam's hand. They were watching what she could only describe as magic. *Magic. It exists.* The lights were turned back on as the two girls nodded to each other. It was only then Adam and Mavis were let inside to sit by him. The girl in black left, leaving the one in green to watch over them.

"Will he be okay?" Adam asked her. She said nothing, standing like a silent guard at the door. "Please," Adam said with desperation, "I need someone to tell me something. I don't know where I am or why I'm here or what happened to my brother or if he will live or not. *Please*," he said pleadingly. "*Something.*" He was squeezing Mavis's hand. She squeezed back, her eyes resting on Jett's motionless body. The girl's eyes softened. She closed the door firmly behind her and then turned to Adam.

"He will be fine. We cannot say when he will regain consciousness but he is no longer in danger of losing his life." She walked to Jett's side and placed a hand on his forehead. Then she went to the cupboards at the back of the room and pulled out small white towels and a red glass bottle. She popped off the top and began to pour the contents of the bottle over the towels. A thick, peach liquid spilled out, staining them. She walked back and placed one on Jett's forehead.

"What happened to your brother is a long and complicated issue that we won't discuss right now. Let's just say he didn't know what he was dealing with. Pulling a flower out here has dire consequences." She looked up at him. Her face was kind and wise, although she seemed to be no older than eighteen. She raised the covers and tucked them over Jett's shoulders. Her movements were precise and controlled, as if she were performing a complicated operation.

"You are not from here, so telling you more will only confuse you right now. Everything will make more sense when you listen with a relaxed mind. As for your other questions, I can't answer. But I may be able to convince someone to answer them for you." She gave them a small smile. Adam felt relief rush through him. Jett would live. They would get answers. It was small progress, but progress all the same.

"Thank you," he said. "Thank you for saving his life, and giving me answers."

"I'm not the one you should thank," she said. "I did save him, yes. That is my job as a healer. But he would have died on the spot if my friend hadn't stabilized him. It bought him time to get here."

"Oh," was Adam's only response. The girl, who had threatened and almost killed them trying to get here, had saved his brother. Even if it wasn't full saving, just buying him time, was important all the same. The thought of her still scared him, even though her hands had salvaged Jett's life.

"I'll leave you for some time. I will be back in an hour with food for you." She said as she turned to walk out the door.

"Wait!" Adam called. She swung her head around, looking at him curiously. "What is your name?"

She smiled.

"I'm Azura."

"Thank you Azura. For everything."

"Like I said I'm not the one you should thank. My friend deserves it a lot more than I do. She will also be the one to give you your answers." Adam's stomach turned. The thought of being trapped in a room with that girl was not something he would look forward to. He would much rather have Azura there.

"Oh, and who is she?"

Azura gave a little laugh.

"Who she is I will let her explain." She turned once again to leave. Before she closed the door, she turned to gaze at Adam. "If you must know, her name is Blaze." *Blaze.* Adam nodded his head. Azura shut the door behind her, leaving the three of them alone.

Now two days had passed. Jett had shown no improvement, and Blaze was nowhere to be found. It didn't surprise Mavis. Blaze probably didn't care enough about them to have the courtesy to talk to them. Azura had told them Blaze was 'a hard one to convince'. Normally, when people were brought here, Azura and her staff were told not to say anything to them until given orders to. Given the circumstances, Azura determined that there should be an exception. She came to see Jett four or five times a day, and brought Mavis and Adam food. Mavis was grateful for her. Azura provided the much-needed warmth and support that she couldn't get from anyone else here. She and Adam were restricted to one hall of the infirmary, unable to leave. Men and women of all ages were seen walking down the corridors. Some carried clipboards and files and others brought boxes of glass medicine bottles. All of them wore the same olive-green uniform as Azura. They would just glance at Mavis and continue on their way, as if no one was there. Even though Azura would only tell them so much, she at least acknowledged them and even smiled, which seemed to be forbidden here.

Mavis wondered why everyone was so cold here. Was it part of their jobs? Or did everyone have an attitude like Blaze? If strangers weren't welcome, why had Blaze brought them here? She pushed the thought to the back of her mind. There was no point in wondering about that.

"Get out," a voice commanded from behind her. Mavis and Adam spun around to see Blaze leaning against the back wall of Jett's room. Mavis was startled. How long had Blaze been here? Why didn't they hear her come in? Her face was blank as ever as her onyx irises came to rest on Mavis.

"Why should I?" Mavis asked. Blaze pushed off the wall and walked towards her. Instinctively, Mavis jumped back.

"You wanted answers, and I came here to give them to you, as a favour to Azura. But I will only speak to him." She pointed at Adam. Adam shook his head.

"Why me?"

"Because I don't like her," she said plainly. Mavis was insulted. The fact that Blaze had threatened them and brought them here had already put Mavis off. She may have helped Jett, but that was no excuse to be rude to her. She hadn't done anything to Blaze.

"That's not a valid reason," Adam said.

"It's my reason. If you don't like it, I'll leave you as clueless as when you first got here. Your choice." Adam was getting angry. Why was she singling Mavis out? He bit his tongue. He wanted to tell her off but that wouldn't be the best idea for any of them. In addition, she had information he wanted. He needed to make sense of what was happening. Mavis turned to him.

"It's okay, I'll wait outside. You can fill me in after."

"No Mavis…"

"I don't want to hear it," her voice softened, "Do it for Jett." She motioned to his brother, who laid unconscious under the white sheets. Adam sighed.

"Okay." Mavis nodded and went to stand in the hallway. Blaze shut the door behind her.

છ

Adam was alone with her now, encompassed in deafening silence. He could feel his heart rate increasing. He didn't trust Blaze, but Azura seemed to have a special bond with her. She had told them that Blaze would give them answers. The fact that Azura had some influence over Blaze was the only thing keeping Adam from bolting out the door. He didn't know why Blaze shook him so much. She wasn't threatening him now, but he still felt like danger radiated from her core. Blaze took a seat in an armchair on the far side of Jett's bed.

"Sit," she commanded. Adam sat. She leaned towards him, her dark hair spilling over her shoulders. Her arms rested by her side. They were slim, but muscular. He could see the outline of her biceps in her shirtsleeves. You wouldn't notice them unless you really paid attention, and right now Adam was trying to focus on anything but her face.

"What do you want to know?" she inquired. Adam squirmed uncomfortably in his seat. He wanted to know everything, but he didn't necessarily want to hear it from her.

"I see. Everything." She shifted from her seat to Jett's bedside. Adam stared at her dumbfounded. He hadn't said a word. How did she know that? "How I know that is not of importance to you right now," she said startling him again. Did she have the power to read his thoughts? It seemed so. He was surprised at the fact that the thought of it didn't surprise him. After what he had seen the past few days, his definition of 'possible' was expanding rapidly. He remembered her telling them she couldn't read minds, but was excellent at guessing. *She's an excellent guesser for sure*, Adam thought.

"Shall we begin with what happened to him?" She motioned to Jett. Adam nodded. "Your brother has a bad habit of touching things he's not supposed to. Though we can't really blame him, as he is a foreigner. But the flowers that line the pathways to Myra are not ordinary."

"Is that where we are? Myra?" Adam asked. Blaze nodded.

"That is name of this city. Those flowers contain memories. Here, you can transfer or copy a memory into a flower to keep, like a time capsule. The ability to see those memories again from the flower itself was lost long ago. The colour you see on the flower is attributed to the type of memory it is. Happy ones are light pink, exciting ones are bright red and so on."

"Jett picked a purple one. What does that symbolize?"

"Love." Blaze turned her gaze to Jett. Before Adam could open his mouth, she spoke again.

"The memory has little relation to what happened to him." She said, answering his unspoken question. "The fact that he broke it from the ground is what caused this. Memories are just a snapshot of a moment in life. But the emotion that is linked with them is what gives them power. In terms you can understand, call it energy. Everyone here knows not to touch them. Long ago, there were people who knew how to remove them safely and extract the memories, and the most skilled of them could use their power. They no longer exist. But if you snap a flower, the power is released and transferred to the holder. Love is a powerful emotion, so Jett here got three times the shock that most of the other flowers would have given him. It was too much for him to bear and he lost consciousness." Adam sat back, trying to absorb all this information. It made sense and it didn't. This was more than he had hoped to get out of Blaze so he didn't push her further. They sat in silence for a while. He knew Blaze was giving him time to accept everything she had told him.

"How did you save him?" Adam asked.

"I didn't. Azura did."

"You bought him time to get here. That's just as important." He looked directly at her face for the first time. Long, thick lashes framed her dark eyes.

"I could stabilize him because I knew what he was," she said quietly.

"What he was? What do you mean what he was?"

She looked at him like he was an idiot.

"Do you think this happened by accident? Why do you think the *ankh* responded to him?" Adam gave her a confused look. "The clear rock you were playing with when I first found you."

"Oh," Adam looked down. She sighed.

"What he is, is the reason I brought you here. What he is, is why he survived that shock from the flowers. Anyone else would have died. No amount of stabilization or healing would save them from any of our memory flowers." She looked at Jett. "By now, don't you think you should have noticed that your brother is different?" Adam looked at his unresponsive twin. A twang of worry shot through him.

"I recognized what he was from his interaction with the *ankh*," Blaze continued. "Only one type of person can do that and withstand memory flowers." Adam slumped down. He was tired. Tired from worrying, tired of hiding it, tired of all the mess he was in and trying to make sense of it. He wanted to curl up and sleep himself into oblivion. Blaze watched him carefully, as if analyzing his thoughts. Her face was still expressionless and cold, as if she didn't care one bit about Adam or what she told him.

"What is he? Why did you bring us here? And what did he do with the *ankh*?"

"What he is, he will be informed of when he wakes. Why I brought you here will become clear then too." She leapt up suddenly, slamming Adam against the wall, pinning him there with her dagger at his throat. Adam's eyes went wide as he took shallow breaths, the dagger's metal cool on his skin.

"One thing to remember," she said in a low whisper as she pressed the flat of the dagger into his skin. Adam was shaking uncontrollably, looking at the door behind Blaze for any sign of Mavis. "This was a private favour. Information is precious and I already gave you more than I should have. No one but Azura and I should be aware of how much you know, or I'll make the memory flowers look like an elbow scrape. Understand?" She was calm and cool as she said this but every word hit Adam with power. He nodded.

"Good." She stepped back, letting Adam catch his breath as he held his neck. She turned to walk out. He watched her retreating form as the door swung shut behind her.

ↂↄ

Blaze came into the hallway where Mavis had been pacing back and forth. Blaze regarded her coldly. Mavis didn't know what this girl's problem was with her. It's not like they had done much together since getting here. What could she have done to earn this? Maybe Blaze was like this with everyone. At least, Mavis hoped she was. Mavis began to walk past her back into the room.

"Love is strange, isn't it?" Mavis spun around to see Blaze tossing her dagger from hand to hand. "It's powerful and crippling. You do anything in the name of love, for it, for lack of it, or loss of it, do you not?" Mavis stood still, watching Blaze numbly. "You know what else is just as powerful? Hate. For all the same reasons." She caught her dagger and pushed it into her sleeve. "Tread carefully, girl. Know that your perceptions can be deceptions. Remember that if you know what's good for you." Blaze turned on her heels and strode down the hall, leaving Mavis frozen in her spot.

After a few minutes of staring after her, Mavis went back to the room. Adam stood by the back wall, looking exhausted. Mavis ran up to him and pulled him towards her, embracing him in an almost crushing hug. He was taken aback at first but then returned it, running his hands through her blonde curls. She looked up at him with concern in her baby blue eyes. He gave her a weak smile. They both slumped to the ground and held each other, taking comfort in the other's embrace. They remained like that until Azura had to shake them awake for dinner. Mavis ate little to Adam's displeasure, but she couldn't get Blaze's words out of her head. *Remember that if you know what's good for you.*

CHAPTER 3
Permotionem

JETT HAD SEEN THIS BEFORE. IT KEPT COMING BACK TO HIM. THE emerald grass. The clear sky. The sound of jazz playing in the distance. He wandered around the open field, following the melody of saxophones and acoustic guitars. There were white tents several yards in front of him. He drew closer and the music intensified, changing from a steady, slow beat to a happy swing dancing tune. Laughter filled the air. He could see a mass of people, milling in and out of the tents, dressed formally, chatting away and drinking from crystal glasses. He entered the first tent. People swarmed around him, carrying gift boxes and plates of delicious food. He could smell the aroma of chicken and rice cooking and the sweet scent of baked goods. He passed a dessert table beautifully set with white china. Pastries, cookies and a chocolate fountain were artfully placed on the table. He continued to make his way through the crowd. No one seemed to notice or care that he had come uninvited. He reached the opening of the largest tent and stepped inside. A band was playing in a corner and about forty tables were arranged around the area, leaving a large space in the middle. People of all ages were dancing in the open space. Small girls and boys chased each other around while the adults were dancing passionately to the beat. Jett looked to his side. Long tables decorated with white and purple linens lined the edges of the tent. Each held several serving trays of food. A circular cart stood in another corner with a marvellous white cake that sported rows of gold and silver balls in its decor. Strings of fairy lights and lanterns adorned the ceilings, showering everything in a soft glow. Everything was so beautiful. It couldn't be more perfect.

Jett looked back on the dance floor. Dancing in the middle were a couple that stood out from the rest. The woman had on a long red dress with a lace belt embellished with white flowers. The edges reached her ankles, where sparkling, cherry red stiletto heels were wound around her feet. The hem was embroidered in a floral design with golden thread. Her long black hair fell down her back, with a white lotus pinning it back on one side. The man was laughing and twirling her around. He had a broad build and kind smile. He wore a black suit with a red tie, matching his partner's dress. The woman smiled up at him. She would never love someone as much as she loved him. There would never be anyone else. She couldn't wait to spend the rest of her life with him. She wanted him to know what she was feeling, but wasn't quite ready to say it yet. What was the hurry? They had all the time in their lives now. Just wanting to enjoy this time with him, she put the thought aside and focused on the beat. She spun around and continued to dance. Jett could now see her face in full. She was stunning. Obsidian eyes that sparkled with mischief. Smooth clear skin and a bright smile. He had seen her before. He was sure of it. She broke away from her partner and started towards him, arms open and welcoming as if she would give him a hug. Her face began to fade. Everything around him was suddenly breaking. Bits and pieces of the scene crumbled before him into blackness. The ground gave out from under him and he fell silently, with no panic and no resistance. He let himself fall, deep down into the void.

Jett. The voice came as distant echo. *Jett Davis.* There was complete darkness. *Son of Joseph Davis and Amira Bloom.* A small light appeared. He moved towards it. *Twin brother to Adam Davis.* He couldn't seem to get near it. It appeared to be the same distance away no matter how much he moved. *Return.* He reached out to it. *Return.*

Jett opened his eyes. Two girls stood over him. A wave of nausea hit him. One of them put something wet on his forehead.

"You're okay," she said kindly. He began to open his mouth but she placed a finger on his lips. "Not now. Rest. You have been in a poisonous coma for a while and must rebuild your strength." He obeyed and pressed his lips together. The other girl watched him, arms crossed. She tilted her head, letting her bangs fall to one side. He stared up at her. She was the one he had seen. The woman in the red dress. The resemblance was clear. But when he saw her before she looked older and elegant. Her figure had been slender and graceful. Now as she stood over him, he could tell she was still slender, but muscular and several years younger. She walked away from him. He heard a door close. His eyelids felt heavy.

"Sleep," the other girl said. He closed his eyes and slept. No dreams, no visions. Just rest.

The next time Jett woke up he saw Mavis. Her eyes filled with tears of relief and excitement.

"He's up! He's up!" Adam came into view, his face etched with happiness and worry.

"Jett… can you hear me? Do you understand me?" Adam asked apprehensively. Jett found his voice.

"Yeah, I can." He tried to push himself up but his limbs were weak. Mavis stopped him.

"Don't strain yourself. Wait a minute. Azura!" she called. "Azura he's awake!"

The girl who had spoken to him when he first woke appeared.

"Good to see you conscious again," she said with a smile.

"How… How long was I out?"

"Four days," she answered. She eased him up into a sitting position. She turned to Adam and Mavis. "Fill him in to the best of your abilities. After that you will need to leave him for an hour so we can give him a proper check-up to see if he's healing properly."

"Of course," Mavis said to her. Azura nodded and left.

The next half hour was spent explaining the strange situation to Jett. Everything Blaze had told them, what she and Azura had done to save his life and their anxiety about him over the last four days. Mavis had kept her conversation with Blaze to herself. It wasn't something she wanted the boys to know or worry about right now. She focused on Jett and the fact that he was still here with her.

"I'm so sorry guys. I really am. I shouldn't have touched anything. This whole mess is because of me." Jett hung his head.

"Hey, it's not your fault," Mavis said. "I was the one who wanted unrestricted exploring and got more than I ever asked for."

"It doesn't matter whose fault it is. What's done is done. From here we just move forward," Adam replied.

"What's next?" Jett asked.

"You need to recover. After that we are getting out of here. I don't care why Blaze brought you here. We will leave as soon as you can run on your feet again."

"Will they let us?"

"We'll think of a way when the time comes. Whether they like it or not, we're going to leave." Mavis was about to speak when Azura and Blaze came through the door. Jett jolted up. It was her. The one watching over him. The red dress. It was Blaze. He was probably too weak to make the connection before. It was undoubtedly her.

"Okay," Azura said. "Time to go out." Mavis gave Jett's hand a reassuring squeeze before following Adam out the door. Blaze took a seat at the foot of his bed while Azura sat down by his side. He gazed at Blaze, trying to recall the image from his vision. Dark eyes without the sparkle. Clear skin without the smile. A beautiful face without the laughter. She was and wasn't the girl from his visions. It was like he'd been looking at an alternate form of her that existed in another world.

"Jett, we need you to tell us if anything happened while you were in the coma. That way we will know how much stress your mind was put through and what severity of treatment you will need." Azura rested her hand on his shoulder. "Please tell us."

"I saw this vision. I think it was of a wedding. It replayed over and over." Azura turned to Blaze. Looks were exchanged between them and then Blaze turned to Jett.

"Did Adam tell you about the concept of memory flowers?" She asked.

"Yeah, he told me how you could trap a memory in them and I'm special somehow because I survived breaking one. I didn't really get that part though." Jett really didn't understand. He had always seen himself as a normal guy. He had no extraordinary talent or skill. He was great at soccer but that was probably irrelevant to withstanding shock from flowers.

"What you were seeing was a memory, that was released from the flower, through the eyes and emotions of the person who placed it there," Azura told him.

"A memory?" he asked. How was that possible, when Blaze was so young? The memory had shown a woman in her mid-twenties. Blaze looked about five years younger. She gave him a piercing look.

"What did you see Jett?" she asked. By the sound of her voice, Jett understood it was a command. He began describing the memory in detail, leaving out the part where he thought Blaze was the woman. Blaze and Azura listened attentively. Blaze's forehead creased as Jett spoke, as if thinking deeply about something. It was the most expression he had seen on her face since meeting her.

"Describe the couple please," Azura urged. Jett obliged. As he spoke Blaze straightened up.

"A red dress? With a flower in her hair?" she asked him.

"Yeah it was a lotus flower on one side of her head," Jett replied. There was a pause of silence. Azura turned to Jett.

"Thank you, Jett. Love is a powerful emotion, so it will take you longer than usual to recover from it. Starting tomorrow we will work on your coordination alright?" Jett nodded.

"Azura?" He asked.

"Yes?"

"Why did I live? Not that I'm ungrateful, but Adam told me it was unusual and explained it was the reason why you brought me here." He motioned to Blaze. Blaze stood up and walked to the other side of his bed.

"I brought you here for two reasons. One was because of what you are."

"What am I?"

"Something that we have not seen for five hundred years." She pushed her hair over her shoulder. "A *permotionem*." She motioned to Azura to continue.

"As you may have noticed Myra is not an ordinary city. We are a city of specialty. We are human but, for lack of a better term, have extended abilities. You are one of us; currently a type we thought had ceased to exist long ago."

"*Permotionem* is Latin for emotional," Blaze explained. "Your emotions are your ability, your power and your weakness. Tell me, do you feel strongly about things? Do you choose your heart over your head? Do things on impulse? Shift moods quickly?" Jett thought for a moment. Every word she said applied to him.

"Yes," he said quietly.

"Emotions are one of the most powerful forces in the universe," Azura continued, "It makes someone like you, very formidable if taught how to use them correctly. Several centuries ago, the *permotionems* developed methods to see memories trapped in flowers. Originally when you trapped a memory, you could not see it, but only use its energy. The stronger the feelings, the more energy it had. They were the only people who could see memories because they could use their emotional depth to create a sympathetic bond with the flower."

"You survived because you have depth to your feelings," Blaze said. "Your spirit drew the shock away from your heart, allowing me to stabilize you."

"How did you do that?"

"A *permotionem's* inner health is directed by their happiness. I gave you a small dose of a happiness illusion to keep the shock energy at bay."

"Inner health?" Jett asked, confused.

"Your outer health is your physical health in your body. Sickness, wounds, and physical strain are a part of that. Inner health is for the stability of your mind and soul, how your consciousness functions. Its needs differ from person to person." Jett was still confused. This was too much to take in.

"How did you know I was a *permotionem*?"

"The *ankh*, the clear rock you touched, responded to you. Only your kind can do that."

"It turned white. What did I do to it?" Blaze sat down beside him, bringing her face close, until it was inches from his.

"You put a memory in it," she said, her voice dangerously soft. "Again, an ability exclusive to your people."

"I thought anyone could put in memories."

"Into flowers, yes. Into an *ankh*? No. That requires great emotional strength. *Ankhs* are like storages for power and energy. We currently use them to send distress signals because it will amplify any emotion you put into it. Their original purpose though, was to store power and were used to be kick-starters for what you would know as spells." Azura gently turned Jett's head towards her.

"You turned it white, the colour of loss. It was also very strong. I assume you lost someone very close to you," she said tenderly.

"My father."

"I see. I'm sorry to hear that. I hope this is making your situation clearer to you." Jett wasn't so sure. He knew much more now, but it had just led him to more questions. Some he wasn't ready to ask just yet.

"Yes, it's helping." He gave Azura a weak smile. She smiled back.

"I do have some bad news though. It will take you about three weeks to fully recover."

"Three weeks? I can't stay here that long, I have to go home! My mom will be wondering about me. Mavis and Adam want to leave as well."

"You're no good leaving if you can't walk," Blaze responded. "For now, you're stuck here. We will send out messages to your families about extending your so-called vacation. You will be able to talk to them shortly."

"You can contact people from here? It doesn't really look like a place for good cellphone reception."

Blaze sighed.

"Our technology and abilities have kept us in touch with the modern world thank you very much. We are much more advanced than you may think," she said coldly. Jett swallowed nervously.

"Sorry, I didn't mean to imply it that way."

Blaze gave him a blank expression.

"Blaze brought you here to be safe." Azura informed him. Jett looked at her with surprise. Blaze cared about his safety? He didn't even know her and she was pretty keen to kill before.

"Don't get a big head. You're not that special," Blaze responded shrewdly.

Oh right, she can read minds. Sort of.

"Then why bother?" Jett asked.

"You are the first of your kind to appear in centuries. Though we love that, you are a danger to everyone if you do not know about your nature," Azura replied. "A *permotionem*'s emotions are stronger than others. Since power can be drawn from emotions, some people may use that against you. With the proper knowledge, they can use you like an *ankh*, to power huge spells or take your energy for their own, most likely burning you out in the process. If you learn about your abilities and how you can use them, you can defend yourself from such attacks. Believe me, there are some people who will stop at nothing for power. Which is why we have kept your nature a secret. Only your recovery staff will know about it."

"Can I tell Adam and Mavis?"

"Yes," Azura said. Blaze flashed her an angry look.

"Azura…" she began.

"They are his family. They have a right to know."

"Adam is his only family here. Mavis is not."

"She's like a sister to me," Jett interjected.

"Blood and like blood and very different things," Blaze said to him. Jett didn't care. Mavis had always been there for him. If anyone could help him get through this, it was her.

"I'll tell her anyways," Jett said boldly. He wished he hadn't. The iciness in Blaze's eyes extinguished any courage he had moments ago.

"So be it," She said. She brought her face near his again. "No one else should get to know about this. If they do, I'll send you back into the coma you woke from. And this time, you'll never wake." Jett trembled under her words. As Blaze turned to leave he called out to her.

"If you don't care about my life, why did you bring me here to be safe?"

"I couldn't care less about your life," she said without turning around. "But if the wrong person got their hands on you, there could be millions of innocent lives in danger. I can't allow that to happen. I brought you here to keep my people safe. Not you." *Well that hurts*, Jett thought. "In fact, we should just kill you and be done with a lot of trouble. But you are the last of the permotionem and are entitled to sanctuary in Myra. But believe me, if you make one wrong move, I'll make sure you won't be able to move again." She shut the door behind her with a bang. Jett looked at Azura wide-eyed.

"Don't worry about Blaze. She's scary as the devil but she won't do anything unless you really screw up," Azura assured him.

"I'm afraid I might," Jett said sadly.

"I have faith in you," Azura told him. "You will start your recovery tomorrow, so rest up. There is a long journey ahead of you."

Azura helped him lie down. Jett stared at the wall until he drifted off into sleep. Once Azura heard Jett's even breathing, she slipped out of his room without a sound.

⁑

A lone figure stood on the highest training platform. Azura stared up at the body's outline from the ground below. The skills center was a large titanium dome, equipped with the latest technology and weapons made by Myra engineers to prepare their armies for combat. Platforms of steel hung from the ceiling at various heights, suspended by cables of platinum wires. The walls were lined with an arsenal of weapons. Azura ran her hand along the glass covers, stopping at a display of throwing knives. She opened the cover and pulled one out. She tied it to her belt, fastening the knot so the sharp edge didn't cut her. She stepped onto a circular lifting disc and shot upward. The disc came to a stop at the highest platform. She jumped down and approached the figure.

"Thought I'd find you here," Azura mused.

"You know me well," Blaze responded. Blaze had seven knives attached to her belt and was throwing them at moving targets. Each one struck a bull's eye.

"What are the chances?" Azura said. "That the memory he snapped would be that one. I'm sorry you had to hear that. It's like a cruel joke."

"My life is a cruel joke," Blaze said. Her voice was empty, void of feeling. She would not allow herself to feel. It would save her from the pain. "I didn't know my mother placed her wedding memories here."

"Lots of us do," Azura said. Another knife nailed the center of a target. Azura watched as Blaze threw with perfect accuracy and deadly speed.

"What did you interpret about Mavis?" Blaze paused and regarded Azura with a calculating expression. Her eyes were sad. Azura's heart went out to her, but she knew Blaze well enough to see that she didn't want to be comforted right now. She'd take out her fury in training first.

"We need to keep space between her and Jett. Her readings are giving me bad conclusions."

"Are you sure? I've spent a lot of time with her. She really cares about him. He feels the same way."

"It's for that reason they have to be kept apart." Blaze insisted. Azura sighed.

"Blaze, I know you know more than you're letting on, so I'm going to trust you. You're almost always right. I just hope in time, everything reveals itself to us as it has to you." She untied the knife from her waist and handed the hilt to Blaze. It had a black leather grip with crystal stones decorating the hilt. An insignia of a flame was prominent in silver. The blade was curved into sharp tips along the sides. On the backside of the blade a pattern of flames was pressed into the steel. Blaze took it from her, pressing the grip tightly.

"The blessing and the curse..." said Azura.

"...United," Blaze finished. The flame insignia turned from silver to orange, to blue and then to white. It glowed brightly, casting an angelic light across Blaze's face. The pattern on the blade lit up with white-hot flames. Blaze let it fly, striking the target. The target was engulfed in flames and then crumbled to ash. Blaze walked over and picked up the knife. It had returned to normal, cool to her touch.

"Your parents would have been proud," Azura said.

Would they? Blaze thought. *Guess I'll never know.*

CHAPTER 4

An Ugly Thing

ADAM WISHED HE HAD A KITCHEN. HE COULD HAVE MADE JETT'S FAVOU-
rite dishes to keep that sadness off his face. More importantly, it would
distract him from the fact he had three weeks he needed to get through.
Cooking always put him in a good place. He had control over what he did
and the food would taste as good as he wanted it to. He could decide how
much effort he wanted to put in and it would be reflected in the result and
in the faces of those who were enjoying it. Here he could control nothing.
Do nothing. He was putting all his effort into Jett's recovery, but the results
yielded him nothing. He was frustrated and he knew it. Adam sat by Jett's
side. Jett was eating a bowl of noodles that Azura brought him. Blaze's harsh
words had taken a bit of a toll on Jett. To be told that you could be responsible for having a civilization destroyed was not a confidence booster. He
was only being kept safe, so others would be too. He knew what Jett had
thought. He wondered that if he weren't special, would they still save him? If
he weren't special would they even be in Myra in the first place? The sad part
was, they didn't know. Adam truly believed these people were good. There
were some exceptions, like Blaze, but there were also people like Azura. She
kept his faith. There was a rapping on the door and a few seconds later it
swung open. A boy around Adam's age entered the room. He had straight
sandy brown hair that angled across the left side of his face and stopped just
below his eyebrows. His eyes were angular and dark. Not as black as Blaze's
but still a deep chocolate brown. He also wore a black outfit like Blaze had.
Fitted t-shirt with cargo pants and fingerless leather gloves. All in black.

"You must be Adam and Jett." He held out his hand. "I'm Joseph. But call me Joe." Adam shook his hand.

"Joseph was my father's name," he said. Joe nodded.

"Azura informed me about him. I'm sorry about your loss."

"It's alright," said Adam. Joe turned to Jett.

"It's time to get you back on your feet. I'll be helping you recover. I have a wheelchair for you outside. Adam can you lift Jett into it?"

"Yeah sure. Come on bro."

Jett swung an arm around Adam's neck as Adam looped his hands around Jett's back and shins. He carried him out the door and placed him into a blue wheelchair that was waiting in the hallway.

"Wait," Jett said. "What about Mavis?"

"Azura already took her to the recovering facility. We will meet them there," Joe informed them. He began to push Jett down the hall. Adam walked beside him. Joe was broad and strongly built, Adam noticed, as Joe towered over him. Muscles were prominent through his t-shirt.

"So," Jett said in attempt to make conversation. "Why does everyone here dress the same?"

"They are our uniforms. Each one is optimized for whatever your job is. I'm in black because I'm a *bellator*, a warrior. My clothes are bulletproof and flexible. Azura is a *sanator*, a healer. That's why she wears green. Her clothes have infection guards and tool belts for her medical equipment." Joe opened the infirmary doors and led the twins outside. Before them lay an acre of open field. The field was divided into sections by short hedgerows. Several people milled around doing different tasks. Around them, the polished buildings and skyscrapers rose towards the blue sky. They went forward.

"How is your shirt bulletproof? It looks like thin cotton." Adam asked.

"Myra technology. Our engineers are the best in the world." Joe pulled on his shirt lightly.

"So, Blaze is a warrior too huh?" Jett asked.

"The best of the best," Joe replied. *That explains a lot.*

"So, can you read minds too?" Adam asked. Joe laughed.

"God no. She was born with that. Just like Jett was born with his emotional ability. But she can't read minds."

"How does she do it then?"

41

"Blaze's ability is that she can read emotions. She can feel what you're feeling and how strong that feeling is. Your emotions are closely related to your thoughts. She can use a pattern of your emotions, plus what's happening around you, to draw a conclusion about what you're thinking. It also allows her to judge relationships between people. She's mastered that technique faster than anyone else like her."

"So, there are more like her?"

"Very few, but yes, there are."

"Wow, she's like, unstoppable then. How can you fight someone who can tell what you're thinking?"

"Technically, she can't. She only guesses, but she's usually right. Besides nothing is perfect. Everything has its drawbacks. For example, she can't use her ability to judge a relationship involving herself. Nor can she tell anyone about what she reads."

"What do you mean?"

"When Blaze reads emotions or relationships between people, her ability blocks her from telling anyone the information in any form. She can only indirectly give hints about it. It comes as part of the power. She can't tell you "I know you're afraid or sad". She would simply guess what you were fearful about and tell you to get over it."

"Sounds like her," Jett said with resentment in his voice.

"I know Blaze is harsh and downright terrifying sometimes. But remember that perceptions can be deceptions. Get to know her better before you label her as a devil spawn. Don't draw conclusions before then."

"Will she even let us do that?"

"Probably not."

"You seem to know her really well."

"More than well. She's my best friend," Joe said with a smile. They had reached a far corner of the field, several yards away from everyone else. Jett could see Mavis and Azura waiting for them. Besides Azura stood another Asian girl. She was tall and in a dark blue uniform. Long, dark, red hair was tied back in a ponytail. She was pretty in an innocent kind of way, with arched eyebrows and shy smile. Her eyes were alive and alert with energy.

Mavis waved them over. They stopped in front of Azura.

"How are you feeling Jett?" she asked kindly.

"As good as I can be in my condition," Jett replied. He gave her a wink. She smiled.

"There's someone I'd like you to meet." She motioned to the red-haired girl. "This is Opal. She works in our security and police department." Opal gave them a wave.

"Hi guys."

Azura turned to her.

"Bring out the equipment."

Opal disappeared. Jett and Adam looked around wildly.

"Where did she go?" Jett asked. She reappeared in front of him setting down two poles and rope. She disappeared again.

"How is she doing that?" Adam asked. Azura and Joe just smiled. They watched as Opal flashed in and out of sight all over the field. Within minutes a full obstacle course had been set up in front of them. The twins stared open-mouthed. Opal appeared in front of them again. "That's amazing!" Jett exclaimed. Opal laughed.

"I forgot you were a foreigner. Everyone here is used to it. Speed is my speciality."

"So, you have super speed basically?" Jett asked, fascinated.

"You can call it that. Comes in handy when chasing down criminals or arriving at the scene of an accident."

"Whoa, why aren't you a warrior then? You'd be unbeatable."

"I'm not a fighter. I prefer to help people and keep them safe rather than knock their teeth out." The twins laughed. "Besides," Opal continued, "Battle requires agility, which I don't have. Depending on my speed, I have to run a certain distance before I can stop or change direction. If you want to be a warrior you need to be able to change direction in the blink of an eye. I do know my battle basics though, as one should."

"Can you teach me sometime?" Jett asked. Opal gave him a sly look.

"Learn how to walk first, and then we'll see."

"You're in good hands. I'll will see you back at the infirmary tonight," Azura said. Jett nodded. Azura ruffled his hair and left. Although Jett found it a little strange, it seemed the people of Myra were normally affectionate with each other. For them, it was a way of showing politeness. Hand squeezing, head patting, leaning on each other, and hugs were very common, even among strangers. It took him a while to get used to Azura doing it. She would hold his hand for no reason sometimes, and it would startle him, even though she was just trying to be courteous. Joe wheeled Jett over to the first obstacle.

"Adam and Mavis, take one of Jett's hands," Opal instructed. They did as they were told. "Now Joe will place two bars under your arms. You must keep your arms above this level." Joe adjusted two steel bars to be about chest height. He walked over to Jett and strapped on two discs to his feet.

"What are those?" Mavis asked.

"Hover pads. Right now, Jett can't support his own weight on the ground. These will help him stand." The discs came to life under him. He could feel vibrations through the smooth metal.

"Stand," Joe said. With the help of Adam and Mavis, Jett stood. The pads pushed him up, until he was hovering a few inches off the ground.

"Does it hurt?" Opal asked.

"A little," Jett winced. His legs were being strained slightly and his balance was constantly being thrown off. Though Adam and Mavis were helping him stand, he wobbled from side to side.

"Relax. The more you worry about falling the more likely it will happen," Opal told him. Jett took a deep breath and calmed down. "Now move your legs forward as if you will take a step." Mavis and Adam held his hands over the bars. He willed his legs to move, shifting his balance and he flung forward. He was caught by someone. He looked up to see Opal's face looking down on him with concern.

"Wow you are fast," he said. She helped him up.

"Try that again. Slowly this time." Jett nodded. He steadied himself. Mavis looked up at him.

"I'm right here," she whispered encouragingly. Jett was grateful. He would do this for Mavis and Adam. Any steps he took today were steps towards getting them all out of here. He began to move. His feet gave out and he fell back. Once again, Opal's arms were around him before he hit the ground.

"It's okay. Try again."

☙

Jett tried over and over. After a few hours, he had taken two successful steps without falling over. "That's good for today," Opal announced. Joe placed Jett into his wheelchair. Jett was exhausted and disappointed. He could take only two steps, and that with major assistance. He felt like a failure. He sulked all the way to the river where Joe had arranged lunch. The river was wide and snaked through the city with regular water. Jett wondered why the other river sparkled. This one was calm and peaceful, unlike the roaring rapids he had slid over on the spire with Blaze. Maple and willow trees lined the banks. A few yards down there was a stone bridge connecting the sides. There was a small clearing where a picnic blanket and food had been laid out for them. Adam helped Jett sit down on the blanket. He, Opal and Joe began to dig in. Jett gazed at the water, mindlessly flipping a sandwich in his hands.

"I know it's frustrating." Jett snapped out of his thoughts and turned his gaze to Opal. "I broke my ankle once. Couldn't walk properly for two months. Trust me, as a person born with speed, it was one of the worst things to happen to me." She leaned over and tapped her left ankle. "I was useless. Couldn't do anything. I felt like I completely let myself down. Security had to run without me while I could only watch from the window. But every recovery takes its time. In the long run, making a proper recovery will be its own reward. It's after falling that you learn to stand on your own two feet. You're on day one. So don't beat yourself up over it."

"She's right," Joe said. "When Opal broke her ankle, she would scream about what she couldn't do. But with the proper support, she's stronger than ever now."

"I guess you have a point," Jett mumbled. He was still disappointed. He began to play with the disk around his throat, thumbing the surface. Mavis put her food down.

"How 'bout you skip rocks with me?" Jett looked up at her smiling face.

"Okay." He smiled back. Adam carried Jett over to the side of the river while Mavis scoured the banks for rocks. She placed several in front Jett and took a seat beside him in the soft grass. Adam returned to his lunch, leaving the two of them alone. Mavis tossed a rock. It skipped three times. Jett took aim and threw one. It made one splash and sunk to the bottom of the river-bed. He sighed.

"Remember the time we fell into that ditch at Mayflower park?" Mavis asked him.

"How can I forget? I thought we'd never get out. Or get eaten by angry squirrels, because we would take their acorns for our slingshots."

"Angering the squirrels was your idea. I was just an innocent bystander who got caught in the crossfire."

"Innocent huh? You suggested that we egg the trees to mark our territory."

"I didn't do it, though."

"Because I stopped you. Or else you were ready to fire."

"Whatever. When we were in that ditch, you didn't stop till someone found us. You did everything from shining flashlights to screaming to shooting our acorns."

"Duh. I didn't want to die."

"Exactly. Even though you need help to get you there, you'll eventually pull yourself out of this ditch just like you did that one."

Jett was silent for a moment. "But what if I can't?"

"Then I'll get a cart and haul your ass out of here. But until you give it your all, that won't happen." The thought of Mavis dragging him in a cart made laughter bubble up inside of Jett.

"Deal," he said. Mavis rested her head on his shoulder. Her hair tickled his face. It didn't bother him in the slightest. They sat there for some time, gazing at the water. Then they heard laughter. On the bridge stood Blaze and Joe. Joe was lifting Blaze up and spinning her in a circle. She had her arms around his neck, her hair flying like a black ribbon in the breeze. She was laughing. Her face had an unshielded happiness on it. Jett gaped at her. He had never seen her like this. Cold, cruel Blaze could laugh? Smile? She looked like an entirely new person. Now she had a striking resemblance to the woman from Jett's visions. Joe placed her down and put his arm over her shoulder. They walked off the bridge together, chatting away and strolling down the riverbank.

"Was that... Blaze?" Adam asked, walking up to them. Opal followed behind him.

"Shocked I see," Opal said giggling. "It's alright, Blaze leaves that impression on people. She's pretty mean most of the time, but once you're her friend, everything changes."

"Why does she do that?" Mavis asked.

"It's her style. Most people like everyone until you give them a reason not to. She's the opposite and hates everyone until they give her a reason not to. Besides as a leader and warrior, she has a certain image to maintain with her armies that she needs to uphold. Blaze may be harsh, but it's for the right reasons. It helps her maintain order and inspire her fellow warriors."

"Inspire them?" Adam said uncertainly.

"For a fighter, there is no greater motivation than being told you're not good enough. It gets them to push themselves in order to prove everyone wrong. Every time they're pushed down, they jump back up and hit harder."

"Warriors are strange," Jett mused.

"Indeed," Opal agreed. "It's time to get you back to the infirmary. Come on." Jett was wheeled away. He kept turning around to watch Blaze's and Joe's silhouettes disappear in the distance.

༄

"You got them scared shitless, that's for sure," Joe laughed. Blaze smiled up at him.

"You know me. Besides, it's better if they see me that way. Can't have anyone thinking I've gone soft."

"You? Soft? Never."

"And don't you forget it." They continued walking along the bank. They reached a spot where sand started to appear on the grass. It was a small strip of beach only a few metres across. It was Joe's favourite place to sit and watch the water. Preferably with Blaze. They plopped down on the sand. Joe reached into his pocket and pulled out a red package.

"Oh, Joe you didn't!" Blaze exclaimed. Joe tore open the KitKat bar and broke off two sticks, handing them to her. "How did you manage to get it?"

"Storm managed to sneak me one. She's got a whole box she's selling out of her room."

"Of course she is. Though she's probably going to keep a few for herself." She bit into the bar. Joe watched her face light up as she took her first bite. He loved making her smile like that.

"Of course. Who wouldn't?"

"Good point," she said, taking another bite. "You're so bad for me. You know we're not supposed to have this during training hours."

"Look at us." He flexed his arm. "We can take a few chocolate bars." He gazed at her. She was striking. So different. She might as well have been a shooting star in a clear black sky for all the attention she got for her attitude and her skill. She had hated him the first time they had met. He wasn't really sure why. But as they got to know each other, things changed. He didn't know what he did, but she began to thaw the ice between them. Years later, here they were, sharing a KitKat bar and throwing sand at each other. Man, did the girl have aim. Almost never missed a shot. But he wasn't going to be outdone. He moved towards the water, taking her hits and backing up towards the shore. She swung to the side, throwing a sand ball at his torso. As soon as the sand left her hand, he grabbed her arm and pulled her towards him. He scooped her legs up from under her and swept her off her feet, as she protested in between laughs. He knew she was letting him get away with it. She could flip him over right now if she wanted to. He carried her into the water a little above waist high and dropped her. She kicked and splashed, shrieking and laughing in addition to spewing some curse words. She sent a tidal wave towards him, drenching him completely. They went back and forth until Joe gained the upper hand, hitting her with wave after wave. She started to run towards the shoreline. He ran after her, catching her halfway and pulling her in close.

He could feel her chest rise and fall with his own. Her dark eyes had an annoyed affection for him and her hair hung over her in a wet mess. Joe liked seeing her this way, with imperfection. Blaze always kept a polished poise around most people, appearing almost perfect. It made her seem inhuman, when she presented herself without flaws. Stunning, strong, confident, unaffected. Kindness was not in that list, but either way, to Joe it was unnatural. Maybe it was because he knew her so well. He wasn't perfect, so he wanted to be with her like this, doing something stupid where they both ended up looking like disasters and not caring. He felt closer to her at times like this, when she would reveal that she was still like him. She could be flawed. She could be silly. She could feel. She could throw him into a river and laugh. Beautiful imperfections. He cleared the hair from her face, softly tucking a strand behind her ear. She had a mischievous grin stretching from ear to ear.

Uh-Oh. She was planning something. Joe took a deep breath. He would not be outdone this time. He put his hands on the sides of her face and leaned down towards her. Her eyes widened with surprise right before he touched his lips to hers. Her lips were smooth and soft as he breathed her in. Sure, they both smelled like river water and sand but he didn't care. He lightly pressed against her mouth. His stomach was in knots. To his surprise, she kissed him back. Her arms came around his neck and his hands slid down to her waist, pressing her closer. She gave a small gasp and kissed him again. He deepened it, breaking contact only to breathe. He felt animated and alive, the knots untying themselves with each passing second. She broke away from him, staggering backwards.

"Blaze… what's wrong?" Joe asked her. He had fear in his voice.

"I'm sorry Joe, I shouldn't have done that."

"Done what?" The hurt was clear in his eyes. "Kissed me back?"

"No. Given you hope for something we don't have." Her words hit him like a slap. She looked at him miserably. "I'm sorry." She walked out of the water and back towards the infirmary, shivering. She left Joe there dripping wet, leaving him to deal with the wound she had pierced his heart with.

❦

Jett walked forward smoothly on the hover pads. It had taken him three days to make the motion familiar to his body again. Opal had moved him to obstacles that required him to change direction around metal spikes and small sets of stairs. After each day, his legs burned with the effort but he went to bed a little happier, knowing that he had improved, even if it was by the tiniest amount. He couldn't stand without the hover pads yet, and that's what they had begun to work on. It was much too painful for him to support his own weight, so Opal switched him to static agility. Basically, he stood on the pads while Joe threw balls at him and he attempted to dodge them standing still. He did his best, because with the power of Joe's throwing arm, they really hurt if they made contact. One nailed him in the chest.

"UGH!" Jett complained as he staggered backwards.

"Time for a break!" Opal declared. Joe walked over to Jett and eased him into his wheelchair and undid the pads from his feet. Jett was alone at recovery today and he felt Adam and Mavis's absence intensely. They were with Azura, contacting their families about a longer stay in Costa Rica. He wouldn't have minded it if Joe and Opal didn't seem so off. Opal was her normal energetic self while coaching Jett but she kept giving Joe troubled looks. Meanwhile Joe was off in an alternate universe. It wasn't like he was totally out of it, but to Jett it seemed that he had put himself on autopilot while his mind was off in the clouds. Jett could tell that Joe wasn't a hundred percent present mentally. He followed Opal's commands without comment and lacked his usually witty humour. Something must be bothering him.

Opal appeared with a water bottle and some ripe peaches. Jett accepted a peach graciously and bit in, savouring the sweet fruit. He had gotten used to seeing Opal's blurred form around the field and her popping in and out of his sight. The super speed was extraordinary to watch. He now understood why having her on a police force was such an asset.

Joe had gone and sat by the riverside, staring blankly at the streaming water. Meanwhile, Jett was observing Opal. She had her hair down today, which added softness to her face as the maroon waves tumbled down her shoulders. Her eyes were attentive and quick as if thinking about a million things at once. *Guess her feet aren't the only things that work fast.*

"What's up with Joe?" Jett ask her quietly. She blinked at him, as if he had pulled her out of the whirlwind of thoughts in her head. After a moment, she shrugged her shoulders.

"I don't know. Joe's not much of a sharing type and I'm not that close with him either. But this is strange behaviour for him." She shook her head sadly. "I'll ask Blaze about it later. If anyone knows, it's her."

"They're really close huh?"

"Best friends. Like you and Mavis I suppose." *Mavis.* He missed her. Even though he knew he would see her tonight, her presence was always a calming one.

"Opal?"

"Yeah?"

"How did they become friends? How did you guys become friends? Blaze doesn't seem like the kind of person you can get to open up easily." Opal laughed.

"Blaze actually hated Joe when they first met, but Joe is persistent. He kept working at it and eventually Blaze warmed up to him or gave up trying to push him away."

"Why did he keep going?"

"Ask him. He probably saw something he liked. Blaze has something special about her. She's like a magnet. You keep wanting to come back and know more about her because she's mysterious and cut off. Although most of the guys here initially try because of her appearance. There's no denying she's attractive but trust me, she puts them in their place right away."

"I'd like to know what he sees in her too," Jett said sourly. Opal raised her eyebrow at him.

"I think you can feel it." Jett began to protest but Opal cut him off. "Don't deny it. If that's not true, why do you keep asking about her?" Jett was silent. Why did he keep asking about her? He was naturally curious to the point it was a fault but he had subconsciously taken an endearing interest in her. He just wanted to know more. This area, these people, had all come into his life abruptly, all because of her. He was intrigued by everything so if he was going to discover more, he might as well start with the one that forced him here with a dagger.

"If you want to know about her there's one way; talk to her. I'm not going to give you the whole story." The thought of asking Blaze about anything made the strength drain from Jett's body. He'd ask Joe once he stopped looking like a lost puppy.

"As for us," Opal continued, "We met in specialty training when we were around fifteen years old. We got put in groups together often, so we clicked that way."

"How old are you now?"

"Twenty." Jett was twenty-one. Blaze was a year younger than him. It sure didn't seem like it, as he always felt minuscule around her.

"She brought me here to be safe, right?"

"Yes."

"Sure doesn't feel like it."

"What do you mean? She saved your life, and you have been given sanctuary here. No one is harming you."

"I don't know what she's even protecting me against."

"Would you like to find out?" Opal challenged.

"No, if she thought it was dangerous enough to bring me, I'd rather not know personally. But I don't know anything. No one will tell me squat. Even Azura only says so much when I know she knows more. I'm not allowed to leave recovery or the infirmary and can't even move without an escort!" Opal looked at him calmly.

"Whose fault was that?"

Jett slammed his hands against his armrests.

"Mine! It was mine…" he trailed off. Opal put a hand on his shoulder.

"Jett, your emotions have not regained balance in your body yet. There's no point in telling you more if your mind is not ready to handle it."

"Then when will I learn about myself? I mean like my ability and how to control it?" He shifted his head to look up at Opal. "I'm being kept in the dark and chained to one part of this city. I feel like a prisoner."

She kneeled in front of Jett making them at eye level with each other. "The journey is never easy. But…"

"But what?"

"I'll see what I can do about getting you a teacher and relaxing your confinement boundaries. I don't guarantee anything though." Jett's face lit up.

"Really? You would do that for me?"

"It might help in your recovery if you maintained a better mood. I guess giving you some slack will help in that. I hated to be contained too. My nature yearns for open space to be free and run wild, both mentally and physically. So, I do understand your anguish."

"Thanks Opal!" He reached out and hugged her.

"Yeah, yeah don't get all mushy with me." She winked at him. "Now, those stairs are waiting for you."

Jett was finishing his last set of stair exercises when Opal popped up beside him. "There's someone I want you to meet," she said. She took his hand and pulled him down the field so fast he thought she would jerk his arm out of his socket. They came to halt at the opposite end of the field. A few yards away leaning against a tree stood a barefoot girl in thin white linen clothing. Loose drawstring pants hung at her hips and a white V-neck t-shirt fitted her shrugged shoulders. Her hair faded from black to light brown tips that were in two braids down her back. She had Aboriginal and Asian features, appearing as a mix of the two with tanned skin and an oval face. Large, honey-coloured eyes seemed to look right through him.

"Jett this is Storm," Opal said. "Storm, this is Jett Davis."

"The *permotionem* right?" Storm said, straightening up. She walked towards them and Opal placed a hand on her shoulder. She held out her hand.

"Heard you got some questions about your nature."

"Yeah, I do," Jett said, slightly confused as he shook her hand.

"Storm will be your teacher. She knows your kind well and can probably tell you more about yourself."

"Oh!" Jett said with pleasant surprise.

"We'll start in a day or two," Storm turned to Opal. "Is he still there?"

"Yup by the riverbank like always," Opal replied. *They must be talking about Joe.*

"Well Jett," Opal shifted and Storm turned to him. Her eyes seemed to look right through him, as if she didn't register he was there, though she was looking right at him. "I look forward to talking to you. It's been five hundred years since someone last asked the people of my family about *permotionem*. This should be quite interesting," she said with amusement in her voice. "Bring him to the Chronicles when you finish tomorrow," she told Opal.

"Sure thing." Storm headed off in the direction of the recovery zone, leaving Jett and Opal alone.

"Oh, I forgot your wheelchair," Opal realized. Jett looked down at his feet. He was still on the hover pads. "One minute." She disappeared and then reappeared with his chair in three seconds. Opal started to wheel him towards the infirmary.

"Will she be a good teacher?" Jett asked her.

"I don't know Jett. It's been five centuries since we've had the need for *permotionem* knowledge. Storm is a good friend of mine and from my experience, I think she will help you understand things better even if she teaches you minimal."

"Okay," Jett said. He was going to start learning. The raging urge for answers inside his mind had soothed itself for now.

⋲⋺

"Mind if I join you?" Storm didn't wait for his answer and sat down beside him. She touched Joe's arm lightly. "What's eating you?" Joe sighed but remained silent, focusing his intensive coffee coloured eyes on the water. The water kept flowing, going for miles and miles around Myra. He wished he could do that with his actions. Let them flow down a river, forgotten. "Affection, is it?" Storm asked. "I should have known." Joe turned to face her. She kept looking out over the river where the sun had begun to sink into the horizon. "Grief and love are closely linked. One is usually the cause of the other. Tell me Mr. Starks, what have you done this time?" She began to move her hand, flexing her fingers in and out of a fist position. A wave of water rose up in front of her, following her hand movements. Joe sat there miserably. After a moment, he spoke.

"I shouldn't have done anything."

Storm relaxed her hand, letting the wave disappear into the current.

"Blaze," she said, turning to him. "About time."

"No, it wasn't the right time."

"Seven years Joe. I'm pretty sure it was about time."

"I blew it." Storm was silent for a moment.

"You're lying, Joe."

"I'm not!"

"You're lying to yourself. I know you and Blaze. What she did is making you blame yourself, am I right?"

"I shouldn't have pushed it."

"You know as well as I do that the implication of what you did scares her. But I also think it's time she learns to break down her walls. You took the first step in that, and that's nothing to be ashamed of," she smiled, "be as you are."

"What do you mean?"

"Don't go around acting like anything's changed, it really hasn't. The relationship is as strong as you want it to be." She tossed him a KitKat bar. It hit him in the head. Joe finally managed to crack a smile.

"How many more of those do you have?"

"Enough to get through a heartbreak. But they're going fast." She turned and strode away towards the trees, her figure vanishing into the leafy grove. Joe put his head down on his knees. He tried to replay the kiss in his head, reminding himself of the good part, where she had responded to him. That image kept slipping away and instead her icy words rang through his mind and replayed on an endless loop. *Giving you hope for something we don't have.* He closed his eyes and inhaled deeply. Hope was such an ugly thing.

CHAPTER 5
Vital and Fatal

"NO," BLAZE SAID. SHE LUNGED FORWARD. HER FIST CAME IN CONTACT with a worn red punching bag, sending it swinging up. Azura stepped back. She knew this wouldn't be easy. They stood in Blaze's personal workout room in the skills centre. Weights and weapons lined the snow-white walls. Light pooled in from tall arched windows, letting in the blinding light of the afternoon sun. The partially tinted glass panes lit the room in a fiery glow, making Blaze appear like a flame with the orange tint glowing off of her skin. One side of the room was lined with mirrors. Under the foam mats, polished mahogany floors extended out to meet the walls. Opal sat on a resting bench across from Blaze, watching her smash the sandbag with her black combat gloves.

"He's taking much longer than he should be to recover. He is still on hover pads. At this rate three weeks may turn into three months," Opal said, stretching her arms back. Azura mentally constructed her argument while judging Blaze's mood. Blaze was in a black cotton tank top and sweatpants. Her ponytail swung from side to side as she moved. She was throwing punches with power. She jumped and swung around, kicking the bag with her leg. Two long scars were visible on the back of her left shoulder. *Here goes nothing,* Azura told herself.

"His energy and emotions are off. I did a scan of his flow streams. They're all intertwined. It's reflected in his behaviour too. The confusion, the struggle, are all being caused by the imbalance in his body," Azura informed her. Blaze stopped for a minute, breathing heavily.

"Then I should be the last person you should be asking. I read emotions well, but I am the worst at dealing with them. You two know that. Besides I'm a horrible teacher. I don't have the patience for it."

"But you understand balance better than anyone. Storm will be teaching him about his abilities but he won't be able control himself if he can't equalize his energy. Injury would be inevitable."

"I said no."

"Blaze!" Azura exclaimed in frustration.

"Cool your jets everyone," Opal said. She looked at Blaze. "You helped me recover for two months. You guided me through how to heal my mental spirit before my physical one. That's what he needs. Look at the wonders you worked on me. Who says you're not good enough?"

"You're a close friend of mine Opal. That's why I found the patience in me to help you heal. It's not a courtesy I extend to everyone. I don't even know if I can help him. I haven't dealt with memory shock before."

"If you want to, you always end up finding a way. It's a part of your nature," Azura said.

"I don't want to," Blaze responded.

"Then you should have let him die," Azura said with tightness in her voice. Blaze spun around and shot Azura warning look. Azura ignored it. "What's the point of saving him when you won't help him regain his strength? He's as helpless now as he was in that coma. That's like helping bring a child into the world and abandoning him right after. He'll die anyway!" Blaze stood there silently with her hands clenched in fists by her sides. A blood-red spiral began to form on her left arm, snaking up from her wrist to her shoulder.

"Blaze," Opal said softly but firmly, "We have a responsibility, to help our own people and others. Jett is one of us. If you brought him here to be safe, you see it through to the end, so he can learn to keep himself out of danger." The spiral on Blaze's arm began to glow.

"Please Blaze," Azura implored gently. Blaze shut her eyes and took a deep breath. The spiral faded and vanished into her skin. She sat down wearily.

"Fine," she said. Relief appeared on Opal and Azura's faces. "But only on my conditions." Azura nodded.

"What are they?" Opal asked.

"My lessons with him will be alone. No one is to interrupt for any reason, except in an emergency."

"Okay, anything else?"

"You guys keep blondie away from him during his days with me. If you don't want me directly telling her to get lost, come up with something to keep them reasonably separated for most of the day." Opal and Azura exchanged looks.

"Blaze, he really puts his effort in when she's around. She has a positive effect on him," Opal said, running her fingers through her hair.

"He needs to learn to have a positive effect on himself. Take it or leave it."

"Deal," Azura said.

"Thanks Blaze." Opal put her hand on her shoulder.

"Don't thank me yet. There no telling if I'll get through to him."

"We all know if he doesn't cooperate, you'll beat it into him," Opal said. The three of them laughed. The tension had cleared and the trio of friends sat down together and chatted away happily, talking for hours, like they always did. After Opal and Azura left, Blaze remained behind in the workout room. She walked to the wall of mirrors and reached out to touch her reflection. Her hand slid down the smooth glass as she examined herself, from bottom to top. She looked like what she was supposed to be. A warrior. An unbreakable force. Powerful and strong. The notion didn't console her, because it couldn't be further from the truth. She was broken. Even though she concealed it, it would never change that fact. She turned and examined the two scars on her shoulder. *Scars*, she thought, *constant reminders of pain.* She leaned against the mirror, the hard glass cool on her skin. There were no scars for happiness. Maybe that was why she didn't remember it much.

෴

Azura came into Jett's infirmary room. Adam was sleeping in a corner on a spare cot and Mavis had fallen asleep in her chair, resting her head on Jett's bed while holding his hand. Jett was also out like a light. Azura quietly walked up to him. His sleeping face had a tense expression on it, as if his dreams were stressing him. Azura waved her hand over his body. His energy flow became visible to her. Not really visible, but more prominent. She felt the different streams with the amount of heat they gave her hand. They were twisted together in an unruly mess, conflicting with each other. She drew her hand away. She backed up, looking at their sleeping forms. She turned and shut the door quietly behind her, leaving the room in silence.

"I have to what?!" Jett exclaimed. It was the next morning and Azura and Opal stood at the foot of his bed, arms crossed and authoritative.

"Jett, your progress is much slower than we expected. It had been five days and you can't stand on your own," said Opal. Azura pointed a finger at his heart.

"Your energies are conflicting with each other. They have thrown off the balance in your body. It's preventing you from achieving your previous coordination. That's why you feel frustrated and disfigured. You need to take care of your mental health first. Blaze is the best one to help you achieve that." Jett's eyes were filled with worry.

"After you're done with Blaze, I will take you to see Storm," Opal assured him.

Jett looked at Mavis and Adam. He didn't want to face Blaze alone.

"Mavis and Adam, I'll need your help today," Azura said. "I need to make some new medicines for Jett. Adam, you can help me prepare the day's meals first, and then Mavis, you will come with me to the Chronicles to find the books I need to reference for the process." Mavis turned to Jett.

"It's for your benefit Jett. We should help Azura in any way we can."

"She's right," Adam added, standing up. "I know Blaze is scary, but if she can speed up your recovery, it's worth giving it a shot." Jett sighed.

"Okay."

"Good. Let's go." Opal wheeled him out. Adam gave him a thumbs up before he disappeared from view.

As soon as they stepped outside, Opal put her legs to work. They shot down the streets of Myra. Everything was a blur to Jett. He couldn't tell whether they were turning or going backwards. He just felt the penetrating wind in his face as they sped along. They slowed to a walk after a few minutes. The world came into focus. They were walking along a green strip of land that stretched out into the distance, decorated with multiple plants and trees. The city buildings rose behind Jett, shining in the sunlight. Opal steered him between two berry bushes that cleared into an opening. A small pond greeted his eyes. The water was crystal clear and reflected the vibrant blue of the sky. Opal sat him down on the soft jade grass. Jett reached for his disk, assuring himself that the cool metal still lay against his skin. It had become a habit lately; the disk was like a calming talisman for him when he was nervous. Blaze appeared a few yards away, walking towards him. Her hair was flying like an ebony curtain in the breeze. She approached them and sat down crossed-legged in front of Jett. She nodded to Opal. Opal gave Jett one last smile and vanished. They were alone.

Jett's heart started racing. She gazed at him with her raven black eyes, as if attempting to stare into his soul. After a moment, she spoke.

"Do you know why you're here?"

"Because my energy or something is messed up." Blaze rolled her eyes.

"From here on out, you're going to listen carefully, boy. I'm not going to repeat anything. Understand?" Jett nodded. "Let's start with your problem. You can't support yourself. This is a manifestation of your inner instability." Jett looked at her blankly. "You must restore balance within your mind before you can balance on your feet. I told you that your emotions are your power, but they are also your weakness. They are conflicting inside you, which is harmful. Partly, because of the memory flower, and mostly because of your denial."

"Denial?" Jett asked.

"You are refusing to accept what has happened. You don't want to embrace the truth we revealed to you; even though you have been given solid proof of your aptitude. You'd rather forget all of this exists and move on." Jett began to argue but Blaze cut him off.

"I know Opal said you wanted to learn about your ability, but I can tell what you really want to do. You want to find a way to hide it. Rid yourself from it. Look me in the eye and tell me if I'm wrong." Jett stared at the ground. He remembered that Blaze could read emotions. There was no point in hiding anything from her. His reaction was all the confirmation she needed to know that she had been right.

"I told you that you could put millions of lives in danger. I wasn't joking. That's the harsh reality. You want to escape it but guess what? You can't. You need to accept it as a part of you. Or it will consume you from the inside." As Jett listened to her, his anger rose.

"How am I supposed to just accept that? You even said it would be better to kill me. Shouldn't I be trying to get rid of it?!"

"It is a part of your soul. There is nothing you can throw away. Yes, it would have been better to kill you when we first met but you were innocent. We don't kill innocents. If you make an effort to embrace your power, you will cease to be a threat. Then, having you alive is something we will all appreciate." Her words were laced with ice.

"Appreciate? If I die, it's okay but if I control myself you'll stop treating me like a nuclear bomb?"

"We don't treat you like a bomb now. You aren't a threat to us. We know how to defend ourselves from your kind of power. You are a threat to yourself and the ones you love most. If someone used you, you would be the first to feel the burn. Quite literally. We are trying to save you from your own destructive potential. You can be used to endanger millions, but we can protect them. But in that case, we can't protect you, so you must learn to protect yourself."

"You said you brought me here to keep your people safe."

"Well protection takes a lot out of you, and I'd rather not have mass scale destruction to deal with. But you are also one of my people, so I will do my duty to keep you safe." She wore a neutral expression as she spoke. It was infuriating. Jett wanted to scream at her but he couldn't. Even though she pulled him into this, she was also the reason he was still breathing right now. He couldn't say that she hadn't done anything. But at the same time, she hadn't helped him like Azura did.

"I'm not like Azura," she said. Jett sighed. He couldn't even have his mind to himself here.

"Pain is a part of healing. The reason you can't support yourself is because you have been taking the positive outlook method. Support, kindness, encouragement. That is only half of the process. The other half involves facing your anguish. Ignoring it won't make it disappear, but just hurt more. No one can help you there. It is solely on you. Which is why once you do it, everything else is easier."

Jett looked down, defeated. He was holding onto the grass, with his hands in twitching fists, ready to tear it out of the ground.

"How?" he asked. "How can I accept that part of me?"

"How you accept it is on you to decide. But what you're failing to realize here is that this is the view of yourself. What your self-worth is to *you*. You need to understand that how you perceive it, is what needs to change." She took a deep breath.

"How am I supposed to look at it differently? It is what it is." Blaze took out a lighter from her pocket. She clicked it and a flame appeared.

"The world has been created in a delicate balance. Everything in it has two sides to it. They oppose each other, keeping them in balance. Look at this flame. It's fire." The flame grew rapidly, expanding outwards in a flash. Jett felt the intensive heat on his face and sprawled backwards. Blaze sat unaffected, looking slightly amused. Jett gritted his teeth.

"Yeah so?"

"Fire can burn. It can be devastating, destroying almost anything in its path if it grows and can't be controlled. It deals agonizing pain."

"No kidding," Jett said. The flame shrunk down back to its original's size, flickering on the tip of the lighter.

"But fire is also life. It gives us our essentials. Warmth and light. When the human body is damaged, we use its heat to heal and give relief. It keeps us from freezing, and gives us the ability to see." Blaze reached for Jett's hands. Her hands were warm and soft as she cupped his around the flame. The heat pulsated in his hands, like small heartbeat.

"It is *both*. It's vital and fatal to our existence. It can end us, or help us thrive. We can't say it is one or the other. We need to accept that it can do both. A spark can start a fireplace fire, or a forest fire. Everything is a curse and a blessing, in equal measure. Now how you choose to give it value is on you. You can choose to see its potential or see its harm. The best thing to do is to see both. Be grateful for all its benefits, but remain cautious of its downfalls. Remember this principle. It applies to all things. Even something as seemingly noble as light, can still blind." She paused letting the words sink in to Jett's head. He examined the flame cupped in his hands. It kept his hands warm, but could still burn him if he got too close. He needed to find the balance between them so he still felt the heat without being burned.

"Yes," Blaze said. Jett looked up at her.

"It applies to everything?" Blaze nodded.

"What about love? Isn't it purely good? Everyone says it's the most powerful force in the universe."

"First off, love is not the most powerful force in the universe but it is a close second. It yields great power, yes. But is it really all good?"

"Of course it is," Jett said, baffled. Why would Blaze think otherwise?

"Think about it carefully, Jett. Love inspires great things. Compassion, companionship, happiness, kindness and bravery. That's all true. But it also inspires all the opposites as well. Love becomes a chain. It can hurt you, which is why many poets compare it to fire. You feel the most agony from heartbreak and fear from the possibility of it. When love is not returned, or when love is lost to death, it's the one that pierces you with the deadliest wounds. If the one you love is in danger, you become helpless. If someone has taken them, you will do whatever they say to get them back, because you love them. People go to unreasonable lengths for this 'force' as you called it, with no consideration for the harm they may inflict on themselves or others. Love," Blaze continued, "is one of the biggest manipulators in the world. As happy as love can make you, it can make you just as miserable. Whatever strength it gives you, it can cripple you with. A man who does not love is the most powerful. Nothing can bend him."

She spoke with tranquility, as if telling him the sky was blue. Her voice had the slightest edge of sadness, as if the wisdom was linked to a memory. As pessimistic as her view seemed to Jett, in a sense she was right. When he lost his father, he felt pain because he had loved him.

"Don't misunderstand me Jett. Just because love can be cruel does not mean you should stop loving. You will lose what's human about you. It's like the fire, you need to find a balance. You can be capable of great devastation but you can also be capable of great power." She flicked the lighter off and stood up, looking down on him. "Stand," she commanded.

"I can't, it's too painful."

"Stand," she repeated.

"Fine then help me up."

"You need to help yourself. Find your own balance. I'm not going to baby you through it." She turned her back to him. Jett growled. He closed his eyes. He saw himself pulling the flower, touching the *ankh* and his brother and best friend's frightened faces. His heart tightened. *A part of you. It's who you are.* He got on his knees. A stinging sensation crawled up his legs. He grimaced but kept his stance. In his mind's eye he imagined himself walking, running and sprinting. He imagined doing all of that, with his father. His dad's face flashed in front of him, warm and smiling. *Don't stop loving yourself, Jett. You can hurt, but you will also heal. You are both.* With an explosive howl he pushed himself up, swaying on his feet. His legs ached, but they held their ground. Blaze turned around, inexpressive as ever. Jett was standing. He was actually standing. Mental celebration fireworks went off in his brain as he smiled widely. He was self-supporting. He began to move forward, but felt his feet gave way and he hit the ground with a thud. Pain flared through his body. Blaze was still looking down on him.

"You stood on your own. That's good enough for today. Don't attempt walking. You're not ready for that yet." Jett felt his disk grow uncomfortably hot. Perhaps it was just the embarrassment burning in his cheeks. He struggled to push himself up into sitting position.

"Thanks for trying to catch me," he said sarcastically.

"I'm not going to cushion you like Opal does. It's only after you fall you learn the value of being able to stand. Now that you know the pain of crashing, you will do your best to avoid it." Blaze turned to walk away.

"Wait! Where are you going?"

"Lessons are done for today. I'm leaving."

"I'm going to be alone?"

"Opal will be here in twenty minutes. I'm sure you don't need a bodyguard for that long."

"But I can't move. If something happens, I'm helpless." Blaze turned to look at him.

"You're only as helpless as you think you are." With that, she walked away from him and turned around the bushes, disappearing from his sight.

ॐ

"So. Many. Books," Mavis stuttered as she followed Azura into what was known as the Chronicles. Apparently, it was the word for magical library. Spiralling towers of books and endless oak staircases rose above them. The shelves and walls were adorned with plants and flowers crawling upwards and intricate designs were painted in gold. It was a circular space with a domed ceiling covered with strange symbols and creatures. There were elegant reading spaces created in different sections of the Chronicles with arm chairs, pillows and reading lamps arranged in small circles. Azura walked her through the twisting maze of shelves until she reached a section that was overgrown with white trilliums. As Azura examined the book titles, Mavis also took a look around. Most of the book titles weren't even in English. The few that were had titles like "Introduction to Herbs" or "Sanator Training Guide." Azura put her hand on a book spine and a soft green light began to pulse around it. She pulled it out and the light died. She continued to do so for several books until a pile of them were loaded into her arms. Mavis watched with wonder. She reached out and touched a book but no light appeared. She ran her hand down a line of them but nothing happened. The books stayed as they were on the wooden shelves. Her brow furrowed with confusion.

"You are an ordinary human," Azura said, coming up to her. She gave Mavis several books to hold while she returned to search for others. "The Chronicles recognize Myra's people. People like me, with extended abilities. Green represents health and healing and since I am a healer, a green light appears whenever I touch a book. Call it an automatic tracking system. They register what kind of person has taken which kind of book. We are in the healing section, looking for herbal medicines."

"So, it matters who takes certain types of books?" Mavis inquired.

"Yes. Knowledge is powerful and can be used to help or harm. We do our best to make sure that there is no harm. No one who is inexperienced, or in a different field, can experiment with the books and end up hurting themselves or others. Exceptions can be made by an adjustment in the system, but that is rarely used."

"Does that mean I can't read anything here?"

"You can read the general knowledge books at the entrance. They have no restrictions. But you can't take any others. Try it." Azura motioned to the shelves.

Mavis placed her stack of books down and walked over, attempting to pull out a slim book with a red felt cover. It wouldn't budge. She braced her foot on the side of the shelf and pulled with all her might but the book may as well have been a tree rooted in the ground. No matter how hard she tried, she couldn't get it out. Then she turned to the stack she had place on the ground. Once the book was off of the shelf she should be able to read it, right? She tried to open one of them but it seemed like the pages were glued shut.

"See what I mean? Now help me bring these out." The two of them started walking back through the labyrinth of books.

"Azura?"

"Yes?"

"Couldn't you open the book for me?"

"Yes, I could, but the system is designed so that even if I did, the book would appear blank to you. Until you have clearance to access them, you can't read anything in here."

"Oh…" Mavis mumbled quietly.

"Is there something you wish to know about?" Mavis paused for a second, determining how to answer. She wanted to know everything about this place. The magic, the history, how all of it worked. Maybe something she learned here she could apply to her own endeavours. That was the one thing she feared saying. She knew most of the time people didn't like their knowledge to be public access for several reasons, many of them justifiable. She yearned to know more, but didn't want to be limited in any way. Given that she was mundane, ninety-five percent of the Chronicles were already off-limits to her.

"I want to know about Jett's kind. What they are and what they can do." It wasn't a lie completely, but it was only part of the truth.

"We'll see what we can do about that. I'll try and bring some books later."

"Thanks, Azura."

"No prob-" Azura suddenly fell over, landing face first on the floor. Books went flying in every direction. Mavis hurried over to Azura's sprawled figure.

"Are you okay?" Mavis said, shaking her. Azura sat up groggily.

"I'm fine," she said shaking her hair out of her face. "What the hell just happened?"

"Oh God, I'm so sorry!" a girl came running up to them. "Are you alright?"

Azura nodded. "I'm really sorry, I left my pile of books here and forgot to move them. I just saw you trip." She gave Azura an apologetic smile.

"It's fine, Jen," Azura said tightly. Mavis looked back and forth between the two. Azura's normal smile was gone and her expression was wary. Jen, on the other hand, held out her hand to help Azura up. Azura waved it away and got up herself. Jen stepped back as Azura dusted herself off. Mavis turned her attention to Jen. She was really pretty, with long tawny coloured hair that ran straight down her back and curled at the ends. Her front locks were braided and pinned into a crown. Her eyes were intelligent and a gentle green. She had on a light-yellow polo shirt and a short, flared, denim skirt. As she leaned over to pick up her books, Mavis noticed a small bird tattoo on her ankle. Jen straightened up and shot her a smile.

"Who might you be?" she asked.

"Mavis Williams meet Jenifer Watson. The chronicle assistant," Azura said, formally making the introduction. Mavis and Jen exchanged a handshake.

"So, you're like the librarian?" Mavis asked.

"No, I'm the librarian's assistant. I do things like organize books and archives and stuff. Checking if the system is working, that sort of thing."

"Cool."

"Come on Mavis, we need to get back," Azura said, clearly itching to leave.

"Right. Well it was nice to meet you." Mavis nodded at Jen.

"Likewise. If you ever want to come by and read something, I'll help you find some good books."

"Sounds good," Mavis said. She and Azura walked out of the building.

They reached Jett's room and placed the books on the back counter. Azura immediately began pulling out glass bottles from the cupboards and flipping through two hardcovers.

"So… I'm guessing you're not on friendly terms with Jen, are you?" Mavis said as she took a seat in the armchair in the corner of the room.

"It's not that," Azura said. "I just don't like her much. I don't know what it is, but I just don't. To me she seems very… manipulating."

"I had no such impression," Mavis said.

"You've met her for five minutes, Mavis. You can't form an opinion on her character yet. I'm speaking from experience. She's not really bad in any way, just has a conflicting attitude with mine."

"Oh, okay." Mavis looked down at her hand. There was blue ink smudged on the side of her palm. *How did that get there?* She turned her palm up. A message was smudged over her hand. She could make out the words if she looked hard enough. *Knowledge is power. Come again. Alone.*

೮⁀ට

Jett stared at the interior of the Chronicles in wonder. Opal had just finished explaining to him how the book system worked. So much information in one place. His eyes scanned the towering shelves of books, taking in the splendour of the building.

"Are you ready for you first lesson?" a smooth female voice inquired behind him. Opal turned Jett's wheelchair around to face Storm. She was dressed exactly as she was before, in white linens and hair in braids. Her eyes shimmered like liquid gold in the soft yellow lighting of the study area.

"Yes ma'am," Jett responded. She smiled.

"Right answer. Opal, we're good from here." Opal hesitated.

"Are you sure Storm? The wheelchair's handles are made of hard plastic and steel. Will you be able to push him?" Jett sat there, confused. Why wouldn't Storm be able to push him?

"The ground is hardened clay. I'll be fine," Storm said. Opal nodded her head.

"I'll be back in two hours to pick you up okay?" she said to Jett.

"Okay."

Opal ruffled his hair.

"Be a good boy," she said teasingly.

"Yes mother," Jett replied with a grin. In a flash, Opal was gone.

"Shall we?" Storm said as she waved her hand towards a long row of books. She started walking forward, leaving Jett behind. He opened his mouth to speak but felt a sudden jolt. He was moving forward. He looked down at his wheelchair in awe. It was stationary but somehow, he was moving. He followed behind Storm as they navigated through the rows of books. Jett followed her for some time, turning to look at his surroundings.

Every section seemed to have a theme to it. Certain plants or symbols would be all over one part of the library and then suddenly switch to different décor. He guessed it was a way of categorizing the sections. They came to the back end of the library, which had shelves arranged in a large semicircle against the walls. Small chunks of *ankh* hung from the ceilings and symbols were scrawled in metallic lavender paint all over the walls and floors. Storm turned around to face him.

"Welcome to the one and only collection of information on your people still in existence today. My family's personal collection."

Jett looked at the rows and rows of books. He suddenly felt ecstatic. He wanted to take all of these books and pour through their contents to unlock all of the mysteries dwelling in his mind. But as he glanced around, he realized almost none of the titles were in English. His heart sank. Storm put her hand out and made a beckoning motion with her fingers, pointing her fingers towards Jett, and then pulling them back towards her. Jett felt himself move and then stopped right in front of her.

"How?" he asked.

"I see Opal didn't speak to you about my abilities," she said with a giggle. "I am a naturalist. I can control water and earth. The ground under us is made of hardened clay, or earth, which is why I can use it to move your wheelchair. She waved her hand and a solid block of earth rose out of the ground, following the motion of her fingers. She made a fist and the earth crumbled, becoming part of the floor once again.

"Why couldn't you just push me?"

"What's the fun in that?" she said with a small smile. He said nothing, waiting for her to add on to it. "I'm also blind." Jett looked at her in shock. She was blind? She moved with confidence and grace, as if she could see everything. She dodged piles of books on their way here and shaped the earth as if she could see it. "Not all skills require sight," she said, sitting down on a sofa by his chair. "I can thank my abilities for that I guess. Being a naturalist, I can sense earth and water, and whatever happens to be touching it. That way, I'm pretty good at building a mental map in my head of my surroundings. Things like your chair though; I would have trouble using, because your handles don't touch the ground and they aren't made of earth or water. I know they are there, but not exactly where, but the rest of it, all the shelves, the walls and decorations I can see, so to speak." Jett looked up into her honey gold eyes. They were aimed at him, but seemed to look right through him, not registering he was there. Beautiful eyes, that couldn't see, but still moved as if they could.

"Well, I will have you know that I am devilishly handsome," Jett said jokingly.

"I shall affirm your physical beauty with Opal later. For now, let's get to your lesson." She turned to him, "*Permotionem*. You are the emotional. The ones in tune with their heart. As Blaze explained to you, you can use your feelings for power and strength." She got up and strode towards a bookshelf and ran her hand along the spines, lighting up the row with a blue light. Opal had explained to Jett how the tracking system worked, but seeing it in person was much more intriguing. She came to rest on a large green text and pulled it out. Striding over to a mahogany study table, she lay the book down gently and turned to some dog-eared pages. Jett's chair was pushed forward until he was beside Storm, looking down on a beautiful illustration. A man and a woman were drawn in the middle of the page, wearing what appeared to be shimmering robes of a translucent white fabric woven together with golden thread. They stood back-to-back, holding hands and smiling upwards towards the sky. The woman had long dark hair and piercing blue eyes while the man was blonde with dark eyes. They stood on a platform, surrounded by columns of flowers in all colours of the rainbow. The purple ones caught Jett's eye. He inhaled sharply.

"Looks like you recognized it," Storm said. "That is the same flower that you pulled."

"You can see the drawing?"

"Ink is mostly water. Besides I've studied these books my entire life. I can literally find them with my eyes closed."

"Oh."

"This is a drawing of Shaneela and Killian. They were the ones who created the method of memory transfer to flowers several centuries ago."

"They were *permotionem* too?"

"Yes, probably some of the most powerful to have ever existed. They could work wonders with the amount of power they could control."

"How did they get that much power?"

"They didn't obtain it in any way. They simply learned how to manipulate energy effectively. There is a mental state a *permotiomen* can go into, called the true eye. This is a delicate and unstable state of the consciousness, but it is when you are at your most powerful. It is extremely hard to enter, and once entered, hard to control. You hand over your mind and body to your heart and emotions so there is no resistance between you and your energy. Shaneela and Killian were one of the exceedingly few who discovered a way to master the true eye, making them the king and queen of spiritual power."

Jett sat silently, staring at the picture.

"There's a downside isn't there? No power comes without a price."

Storm was silent for a moment.

"Nothing comes without a price. Yes, I didn't want to frighten you in the first lesson, but there is a drawback. True eye is when you are at your most powerful and most vulnerable. If you lose a single drop of blood while you are in it, you will cease to exist and your life energy will create a quite formidable explosion, annihilating anything within a mile radius around you. Which is why, for many years, experimenting with the true eye was forbidden. By law, it still is today."

"Whatever strength it gives you, it can cripple you with," Jett mumbled.

"Someone has been talking with Blaze." Storm turned to look at him.

"Yeah. Her words seem to make sense now."

"Blaze imparts great wisdom which indeed rings true. As her friend though, I know she sees life through a very pessimistic glass."

"No kidding. She told me love was evil."

"In a deranged way, she's not wrong."

"But how can you think of it like that? If you see that as evil, what do you hold on to for hope or happiness?"

"You hold on to love no matter what. But Blaze, even while holding on to it, tends to see what pain it's dealing her rather than the positives. Truly though, I don't blame her."

"Why?"

"She's had a complicated life."

"She's only twenty."

"All the more reason to be saddened about it."

Jett looked up at Storm, as her face clouded with genuine worry. He decided to change the subject.

"She also said it wasn't the most powerful force in the universe, but a close second. What's first?"

"Choice."

"Choice?"

"You heard me."

Jett sat back, confused. Storm let out a sigh.

"If you want an explanation on that one, Blaze is the best person to talk to. She knows that better than anyone."

"Why does everyone keep saying that? It seems like she knows everything."

"Experience is the best teacher, unfortunately."

Jett sat quietly. He didn't like Blaze much, but there was clearly more than meets the eye with her. He reached out to touch the illustration. The paper was rough under his fingertips as he traced the flower designs on the page.

Suddenly, he was thrown forward, his chest hitting the rim of the table. There was a sickening crack and pain ripped through his body. The world spun around him. He was vaguely aware that he had fallen out of his chair and was surrounded by chunks of broken wood. He regained his bearings in a few seconds, only to realize the room was trembling uncontrollably. Fissures were starting to appear in the ground, cutting jagged gaps in the floor. Storm stood over him, moving rapidly to seal any cracks that got too close to them. Her hands moved gracefully and fluidly, bending the earth to her will. Her feet always landed in a perfectly grounded stance as she leapt from side to side. Jett could see it was wearing her down; her seals only lasted a few minutes before the fissures sprung up again. The energy was draining from her face as she frantically tried to keep the floor from shattering under them. She stood over him now, holding the ground around them intact as everything else shook with the force of a massive earthquake. She looked down at him and her lips shaped his name. He struggled to move forward, every inch of his body burning with the effort until he grabbed a hold of her ankle. Storm had one hand out and was shaping seals as she leaned down to his face.

"Hold on!" she yelled. She took a deep breath and pulled her arms into her body. They were immediately encased in a solid, hollow ball of rock. He held on to her as she shook from the effort of keeping up their earthen shield. Storm looked like she was going to pass out. *No Storm*, Jett thought,

I need you to be strong. Or we're both dying. She gasped. Jett looked up at her in wonder. Her honey gold eyes slowly turned black. She stopped shaking and stood firmly. Jett could still feel the tremble of the floor beneath him, but it had been reduced to a slight tremor. Storm let out a shout and shot her hands up. There was an explosion. Jett felt the cutting edge of a rock slash him across the face. The earthen shield had shattered, leaving the room looking like there had been a hurricane of meteors inside. He felt the blood drip down his face as he struggled to right himself. Storm collapsed to her knees beside him. She was bloody and bruised but didn't look like she had any serious injury. Her eyes had returned to their normal golden colour. The room had silenced, and the floor was completely intact. Opal and Azura appeared over them. Azura propped him up and shoved a glass vial between his lips. A sour liquid went down his throat, and he gagged. She forced it down and began to wave her hand over his body. The pain dulled to a throb and he was able to think clearly.

"Azura..." he started, but she had moved on to Storm, who lay in an exhausted heap beside him. Opal propped him up against her. He put his head on her shoulder.

"What happened?"

"We don't know," Opal said. "The earthquake shook the city, but we don't get earthquakes." She shook her head. "I don't understand it."

"Is it over?"

"Seems to be."

Azura had put Storm to sleep and was dragging a girl in yellow polo shirt and blue skirt over. She had cuts all over and was barely conscious. Azura began to wave her hand over her and her wounds began to heal. Her eyes fluttered open to reveal beautiful green irises.

"Jen, can you hear me?" Azura said to her.

"Yeah..." she placed a hand on her head. "The world is spinning."

Azura gave her some of the liquid she had given Jett. She took a swig and coughed. "Thanks."

Azura turned to Opal. "This is serious. Have you contacted the heads?"

Opal nodded. "Blaze and Joe should be on their way too. Sent out an emergency flare."

"I'm already here," said a voice behind them. Jett turned with difficulty to see Blaze walking up to them, dagger in hand. She was scratched and bruised all over, and walked with a slight limp. He saw a new feature on her face. Emotion. A mix of anger and sadness was displayed in her expression.

"Joe is gone," she said with tightness in her voice. "And so is Mavis." The words hit Jett like a slap.

"No..." he whispered. Blaze turned to him, her dark eyes cold and merciless. She walked over and stuck the dagger under his chin. "You," she said in dangerously soft tone, "are going to die."

CHAPTER 6
Murderer

THE WORLD WAS FUZZY AS MAVIS OPENED HER EYES. SHE LAY SPRAWLED out on a cold, wet surface. She pushed herself up and attempted to take in her surroundings. A blood red sky rose above her. *Not a sky,* she realized. It was an arched dome that was several hundred feet above her, appearing to be formed from garnets. She was in some sort of cave. Stalagmites erupted from the ground in all directions, curving into twisted and menacing formations. There was a slight rumble to the ground as if the cave was breathing. Groggy and disoriented, she pulled herself up against the cave wall and breathed heavily. The air around her seemed to be fine but with every breath she took she felt like poison was entering her lungs as the intake burned her nose.

Where the hell am I? She closed her eyes. Jett and Adam flashed through her mind. *There you are.* Her eyes snapped open and she jolted forward. *No need to be afraid. I'm here to help* the voice said. There was no sound. The voice was somehow in her head. She could hear it clearly. A smooth, hypnotizing, feminine voice resonated in the back of her mind. *This is what you wanted.* Mavis' heart leapt. She had no idea what the voice was talking about. She was lost and alone with no memory of how she got here. "I...I don't know what you're talking about," she said nervously. Her own voice echoed through the entirety of the cave. *Not now, but you will soon. You upheld your end and now I shall uphold mine.* A sick knot began to form in Mavis' stomach. She was going crazy. *Insanity is not paying a visit,* the voice said consolingly. Mavis wanted to listen. There was something about the voice that was pulling her will to it. It was musical and soothing like a trance. At the same time she felt wrong. *If you wish to remember, you cannot resist. Focus and let go. It will come back to you.*

Mavis looked around her warily. She was alone. Completely and utterly alone. Anxiety began to climb into her heart. *Give in Mavis,* the voice crooned seductively. *Give in.* Mavis lay back and felt her eyes closing. "If... if... I do..." she whispered. *You will know everything. No harm shall come to you. You have already paid the price and now you will get your due. Are you ready to remember?* Mavis sagged against the wall, looking at her surroundings one last time before closing her eyes again. "I'm ready," she said. She let go, and let the memories flood back in.

ᥓ

Adam watched over Jett as he slept. Azura had brought in Jen as well and she was asleep in the bed beside Jett. Azura had done a great job of healing their wounds but she said that the pain would stick around for a while, so Jett had to rest. After pulling a murderous Blaze off of him, Opal had brought him back here. Adam didn't know what had happened with the earthquake, but Blaze blamed Jett for it. This girl was beyond his comprehension. Jett, who could not walk, was being pinned for causing a natural disaster. He did not understand the logic in the slightest. No one else knew anything about what had happened. Blaze was quick to place the blame. Not that it surprised him. She hated all three of them. It didn't help that Mavis was gone too. Adam was exhausting himself with worry. Mavis could be anywhere in any sort of situation. He didn't even know if she was alive. *No, I'm not going to even think about that.* He couldn't afford to. Mavis meant too much to him. Adam laid back in his armchair and put his head in his hands. He was supposed to keep the three of them safe and together and he had failed miserably. Even though Mavis and Jett always insisted that he didn't have to, he always felt like it was his responsibility. Maybe it made sense because he was the most level-headed of the group, or because he had promised his father he would do so. Either way, he took it upon himself to see that through.

"Eat." The command came from behind him. Blaze emerged from the shadows at the back of the room. Though it still freaked Adam out, he had gotten used to her popping in and out of thin air, to the point where it didn't faze him anymore. Stealth was her probably her middle name. Azura had left Adam a dinner tray that had turned cold as time had gone by. He didn't feel like eating, sleeping, or dealing with Blaze. She stood there in her warrior uniform like a bodyguard, observing him with weary eyes. She looked tired and worn, which reflected Adam's feelings. It was jarring, not to see Blaze in her poised, confident stature. He had to hand it to her though; her posture was impeccable, firm and strong, giving no sign of her exhaustion. Her face was the only way he could tell she felt anything otherwise. He sighed.

"Don't want to."

"That wasn't a suggestion. It was an order."

"Why do you care?"

"I don't."

"Right, Azura probably asked you to look after us. That's the only way you would ever give a shit, right?"

"Someone's a quick study," she said sarcastically.

"Forgive me for feeling bitter, you tried to kill my brother."

"And?"

"What do you mean 'and'? He had nothing to do with it. He was there with Storm the whole time, learning about whatever emotional crap he has to deal with. In case you didn't notice, he got cut up pretty bad too."

"And I lost someone just like you did. I know what you're feeling. Tell me, the moment you found out Mavis was gone, didn't that bring a rush of anger so bad that you had to take it out on something? So, did I."

"I didn't take my anger out on an innocent person."

"That's the thing," Blaze said as she walked over to the other side of Jett's bed. "He isn't." Adam opened his mouth but Blaze cut him off. "There's a lot you don't know Adam. There are forces at work here that you can't even begin to comprehend. We don't know all the facts yet. One thing I can confirm for now is that Jett is the cause, whether he knows it or not."

"If he doesn't know it, how is it his fault?"

"You tell me. If your father had died because of a mistake you made, even though it was unknowingly, would you forgive yourself? Would you not blame yourself? Is his death your fault?"

Adam was silent. The truth was he would. He would blame himself for eternity and nothing would change his mind, because in the end, it was his mistake.

"Exactly. Humans by nature, would rather that they get hurt instead of others if it's their mistake. It's one of our better qualities. You can take as much pain as you wish onto yourself, but when someone else pays the price for your mistake, generally it's a feeling you never live down. There are some who are okay with others taking the fall, but if you have any sort of conscience, you probably won't."

Adam ran his fingers through his hair as he struggled to admit to himself that she was right. Blaze was watching Jett's sleeping form with a blank face.

"What now?" he asked.

"I don't know yet. Everything is under investigation."

"So, we're going to sit here and do nothing?"

"Feel free to go out in this totally clueless state and see if you get anywhere."

He clenched his teeth. This girl infuriated him. Her hair swished to the side as she turned to face him, dagger in hand. She tossed it from side to side mindlessly, as if her body was trained to do that on autopilot. The hilt glinted in the soft yellow light, with a silver scorpion prominently apparent on the black hilt. The blade was curved into a slight hook with wickedly jagged edges. He watched it leap like a silver flame from hand to hand, admiring the workmanship.

"I lost my best friend," he said breaking the silence. His voice cracked a bit and, for the slightest second, revealed the sadness and anger he was holding back.

"So did I." Adam detected a slight edge to her voice. There was another pause of silence and Adam put his head in his hands. Blaze sighed. "Being strong for the sake of others is grim, especially when you're bleeding on the inside."

Adam nodded without looking up.

"Your brother thinks with his heart and your best friend marches to the beat of her own drum, which often lands them in trouble. You will do whatever it takes to hold them together, because you never want to experience another tear like the one your father's death caused."

"Don't pretend like you know me," he snapped. She gave him a taunting smile.

"I'm not trying to, but I can figure out more than you think. It's mostly because to some degree, we are alike."

"We are nothing alike. You're an army general with a bad attitude and no heart. All you care about are your own people. I bet if you find Joe, you'll be content, whether Mavis lives or dies," Adam spat. Blaze laughed and gave him a cold, cat-like grin.

"How wonderfully hypocritical of you."

"I'm the hypocrite?" Adam asked in disbelief.

"You say I only care about my own people. What about you then Sir Nobility? All you care about is Jett and Mavis. You wouldn't give a bloody damn about us if it meant getting out of here. You were planning to run, weren't you?"

"I-"

"Don't bother lying. I could feel it. If Jett could run and Mavis was here, you would have hightailed it out of here, leaving us to deal with the destruction of our city. It wouldn't matter to you, would it? You would have left and never looked back." Adam opened his mouth and the closed it. He wanted to spit back at her and justify that he never asked for it, any of it. Why should he have to care about it? But then again, Blaze didn't ask for them to trespass into her territory either. She didn't ask for Jett to cripple himself or for this destruction. He pressed his lips together in silent defeat. Blaze's expression softened slightly.

"Appearances are one of the biggest deceptions, boy. You only see what others want you to see. Don't be so quick to judge." A soft click was heard from the door and Azura appeared, breathless and panting.

"Blaze..." She heaved. Blaze was at her side in an instant, handing her a water bottle from Adam's dinner tray.

"What happened?"

"We... We need you right away. The heads will not let us continue until they hear your input." Azura put the bottle to her lips, draining it within a few seconds.

"You ran here to tell me that? Why didn't you send Opal?"

"That's the other thing. Opal has been arrested." Blaze's eyebrows shot up.

"Arrested? For what?"

"Using black magic." Adam watched Blaze's face transform from doubt to anger and back to her normal blank expression so rapidly that he thought he had imagined it. *She really knows how to hold herself together*, he thought.

"Opal knows nothing about magic, let alone the dark stuff."

"I know that, but while investigating they uncovered evidence that pointed straight to her. It's too much to explain at the moment. That's why you need to go right now." Blaze nodded and turned to leave. "Blaze," Azura said. She turned to meet her friend's gaze. Her eyes were full of pain. "She murdered someone." Adam sat stock still, with Azura's words ringing in his ears. Blaze's mask cracked and the disbelief surfaced all over her face.

"*Murdered someone?* Opal, of all people? Are they out of their minds?"

"They saw her do it Blaze. There were eye witnesses and video footage." Blaze was motionless for a few seconds, then stomped her foot down. "I refuse to believe it until I see it for myself."

"I can't believe it either. But it was her. It was undoubtedly her." Azura reached out and gently grabbed Blaze's arm. There was an unspoken conversation between them. After a few moments Azura let go. "Judge fairly, Blaze. Do not let your own rage blind you from the truth." Blaze sighed and nodded. Quiet as a mouse, she slipped out the door and vanished.

ℴℴ

Blaze's footsteps echoed through the empty streets of Myra as she hurried to the Unity Springs, where all city affairs were run. The heads had ordered a full relocation of the residents to the Cherub Oasis, an emergency safety location, while the destruction was being dealt with. Almost the entire healing staff had been dispatched there to take care of the injured. Azura was still caring for Jen and Jett, but would soon join her team in the Oasis. Blaze's heart was thrumming in her chest as Azura's voice whispered in the back of her mind. *Murder*. She had been friends with Opal for five years, and had had never met anyone as firm on justice as she was. Blaze was ten times more likely than her to murder someone in cold blood if they got on her bad side. Opal couldn't have done it. Just couldn't. It must have been a set up. Self-defence or something. It didn't add up. Part of her didn't even want to entertain the possibility that she could have done it, because if she did, her penalty was death. *A life for a life.* The only way to save her would be to prove her innocence, or have the family of the deceased say that they were willing to spare her life. The latter, was unlikely. Blaze knew that if she were them, she wouldn't be able to.

She sprinted through the main square, making a beeline for the white pavilion that began to emerge in the distance. Joe's smiling face flashed through her mind. Her heart clenched painfully and she slowed to a jog. During training, they would run together for miles to build up their endurance. They'd arrive to the training base exhausted, sweaty and tired, where they'd share a granola bar and she'd tease him about being slower. She had power in her legs, while Joe had power in his arms, so he'd get back at her during upper body combat and lifting. Those moments, where they could just laugh and tease each other were one of the happiest in her life. She felt the stinging burn of tears in her eyes. She took a breath and detached herself from her thoughts. The entryway to the Springs rose in front of her, with a shimmering white and gold curtain pulled to the side of an arched doorway. She tapped into her confidence and strode forward like the warrior she was, dagger in hand. The tears never spilled over.

ം

Azura sat under her cherry blossom tree, sipping her hot chocolate and gazing up at the stars. A large silver thermos lay beside her as she mindlessly picked at the grass. She could see Orion and Ursa Major through the branches towering over her head, but tree bark and pink petals took up the rest of her vision. She had planted this tree when she was four years old with her brother, and it had grown up along with them. She had sown it, nurtured it and rehabilitated it from the start, unlocking her gift for healing. She came here to think, relax, and let her stress go. Many of her memories were tied to it and it always gave her a sense of comfort. *You return to what you know,* she thought to herself. Although she wanted to let go, tonight she was waiting. She had told him to be here by now, and agitation was beginning to show in her relentlessly tapping fingers. His silhouette began to form out of the darkness as he walked into the light of the street lamps. His figure was tall and lanky with angular shoulders and a long neck. His glasses rimmed his dark eyes, partially hidden in the shadow of his fedora. He wore a white t-shirt with a black blazer and jeans, complimenting his lean physique. His skin was the colour of roasted coffee beans and he whistled as he walked with a cocky grin on his face, as usual.

"Hey Hun," he said with a smirk. Azura rolled her eyes.

"Neal, when will you stop?"

"Never, sweetheart."

"Someone shoot me," she sighed. She held out the thermos to him. He twisted the cap off and smiled as he looked at the contents.

"Coffee. Just the way I like it. You must really want something."

"Consider it an incentive or show of goodwill. I need your help."

"I assumed that. What may I do for you?"

"Blaze will need your skill to investigate what she cannot."

"Illegal, under the radar snooping. My specialty," he chuckled. "To think, the almighty Blaze needs aid. This is a red-letter day."

"Neal!" she snapped. "You know if I'm asking for your help, this is serious. Opal's life may be on the line." His smile disappeared.

"Opal? Why?"

"Blaze will explain everything later. I'm begging you, please help. If not for me, if not for Blaze, then for Opal." She untied a red velvet bag from her waist. The jingling of coins could be heard as she undid the knots and placed the bag in his hand. "I promise, you will be adequately compensated." Neal pulled the drawstrings and watched the gold and silver coins spill into his hands. He gazed at their polished surfaces, running over them with his thumb. He returned them to the bag and handed them back to her.

"I owe Opal, so I'm not going to put a price on this. Where's Blaze?" Azura was slightly startled by his sudden change of heart.

"Unity Springs."

"I'll head over."

"Thank you."

"Don't thank me yet Hun." He winked at her and walked right back into the darkness.

☙

Blaze watched as Opal sat before Myra's heads with her head down. She sat on one side of a long mahogany table with her feet tied to the chair supports. Her hands were chained to a golden peg in the snowy marble floor with steel cuffs binding her wrists. Thin lines of blood ran down her hands from the shackles. Blaze winced. The cuffs had a razor lining on the rims. If you struggled or moved too much, you would get cut. They were in the interrogation commons, where suspects were questioned. The large room had glass walls running along all four sides. The glass was made so people on the inside could see out, but the outside could not see in. Blaze watched the employees stride by, completely oblivious to the possible execution being discussed beside them. Opposite from Opal, the three heads, the leaders of Myra, were positioned in their respective seats. Maya Aequo, a tiny but loud woman with snowy white hair, was furiously typing on a holographic keyboard. She was probably forty at best, but her hair had turned white at the age of twenty-five, giving her the illusion of being much older.

Beside her sat Jay Khan, who happened to be one of Blaze's trainers during her initial years in the army. She had hated him the moment they had met and was quite positive the feeling was mutual. It wasn't that he was a bad person. In fact, he was one of the most honourable people Blaze knew, and a great fighter. The thing was that their personalities clashed a lot. With both of them being alphas, there was always a struggle for authority. Blaze was not one to be commanded; she would be the one to command and that drove Jay crazy, since an army's discipline was based on listening to authority. He was also the reason she was a junior general now. He had told her that if she wanted to continue being the way she was, she'd have to move up in the ranks or shut up and listen. Once he was promoted to head she had barely seen him, but now he sat in his leather jacket and black turtleneck, staring intently at Opal. He wore a single silver hoop earring on his right ear, under which a faint scar was visible on his neck. Blaze smirked slightly. She had given him that when she was fourteen, after he had fought with her about the form of her spin kick. He had gone on to insult her and claimed, that she just "couldn't handle it." She had, in turn, performed the best spin kick of her life and had stamped in a permanent reminder of how good her form was on his neck in the process. It was a fond memory, for her at least.

The last head was Jackson. No one knew his last name. He didn't share and no one really cared enough to ask. He was flipping through a pile of police reports and photographs. Jackson had a photographic memory, so he could go through an entire pile of documents in minutes and remember them all, which was what Blaze assume he was currently attempting to do. Blaze could not see Opal's expression but she felt fear, exasperation and confusion rolling off of her in waves. Blaze had soundlessly slipped inside and stood by the back wall. Everyone was so absorbed with what they were doing that, to her pleasure, they didn't notice her. She preferred being able to observe when she was hidden. People only revealed their true self when they thought no one was watching. Blaze understood that well; she was no exception to the rule. Jackson leaned over to show Jay some of the reports. She felt his surprise, doubt, and then sadness and disappointment. *Shit. They think she's done it.*

Blaze tapped on the wall behind her. All of their heads shot up.

"Blaze," Jay said with slightly alarmed expression. "How long have you been there?"

"Long enough. It has been a while Commander Khan." Jay leaned his head on his right hand and sat back in his chair, gazing at her thoughtfully.

"It has. Let's ditch the pleasantries, shall we? How much do you know?"

"You may assume I know nothing." Opal couldn't turn to see Blaze, but she felt the exasperation change to relief.

"That would be a lie, wouldn't it?"

"We have a real genius on our hands here, don't we?" Blaze's voice dripped with sarcasm.

"Still a smart mouth I see."

"Does it surprise you?"

"Not in the slightest."

"Then why don't you cut the crap and tell me what's going on?" Jay was going to fire back when Maya stopped him.

"Enough, Jay. Get to business." Jay gave Blaze a poisonous glance and cleared his throat.

"We will address the earthquake first. At three o'clock today, a massive, unnatural earthquake shook the city. We know it's unnatural because it only shook Myra and none of our surrounding land. The cracks ended at the entrance paths. There were a great number of injuries, but to our knowledge, no one has died. During this time Joseph Starks and Mavis Williams disappeared, with no trace, except for a small smear of Joseph's blood found in the men's change room in the skills center. Would you know anything about who or what might have caused it?" Blaze shook her head. Jay raised an eyebrow at her. "Please elaborate on your relationship with the two." While standing at perfect attention, Blaze groaned on the inside.

"Joseph Starks has been one of my closest friends for about seven years now. You know the rest Commander Khan, considering you saw us train together. There's not much more to say." Blaze gave him an icy look, daring him to inquire further. He saw the challenge in her eyes and lowered his gaze. *Good Boy.*

"And Ms. Williams?" Jay asked.

"She is the close friend of a patient at the infirmary that I had helped Azura save. She is supporting him while he recovers."

"Who is this patient?"

"His name is Jett Davis."

"Who else is at the infirmary with Mr. Davis?" Maya interjected.

"His brother, Adam."

"Would you know of any reason that Ms. Williams would flee Myra willingly?"

"No Ma'am."

"Then we will have to assume she was taken by force." Maya straightened up and examined Blaze with her stormy grey eyes. "We know of your astounding abilities Ms. Darkfire." Blaze flinched slightly. She hadn't used or heard her last name for a very long time. It had always been just Blaze. "We want to know what you picked up about Ms. Williams," Maya continued. "The same would apply to Joseph, when you last saw him."

"Ma'am, don't you know? My power prevents me from telling you. Telling anybody."

"Directly? Yes, I'm aware. But you may hint at it indirectly. Do your best, as your input will be the most crucial to this investigation." She leaned back in her chair expectantly. Blaze felt her soul putting an invisible hand over her mouth, not allowing what she really knew to be spoken. That force clenched her hands, so she could not write it. The pull was familiar to Blaze, she had experienced it since birth. It would allow everything to pass, except for what her abilities let her learn about other people. She struggled within her mind, to find something that she could say and that they would be smart enough to decipher. She really wanted to get on with what had happened with Opal, but she'd have to give them something before she could do that.

"All things come with a price, and many times we don't see what that price truly costs us." Jackson was observing her silently; she could feel his gaze follow her as she slowly paced the room.

"Is that all you have to say Ms.Darkfire?" Maya asked.

"Yes." Maya leaned back and sighed. She was probably hoping Blaze would have given her something more to go on. Blaze had given her a lead, but it was only a fraction of what she knew. Partly because her soul prevented it, and partly because she didn't want to reveal it. This case involved Joe, and she would not let someone limit what she could do based on their suspicions or conclusions. Blaze would find him and bring him back home.

"Now, please explain to me why one of our best officers is in chains." Blaze motioned to Opal.

Jay leaned forward to rest his chin on his hands.

"Today, Opal Dystar was witnessed murdering the Chronicles leader, Kaitlin Greens, through a chain chokehold. We have video and eye witnesses' reports of the incident."

"Play them."

"As you wish." Jay snapped his fingers and a projection appeared on the wall in front of Blaze. It was the security footage of Kaitlin's office in the Chronicles. She watched as Kaitlin sat at her desk reading papers when Opal entered the room. Opal was swaying as she walked, as if she was drunk. A rusted chain was in her hands as she strode towards Kaitlin. Blaze watched in horror as Opal threw Kaitlin against the desk and wrapped the chain around her neck, pulling tight. The other people browsing the Chronicles had rushed forward to stop her, but were stopped by something that formed a small circle around Opal. *Snakes.* They had red eyes, shimmering blue scales and dripping fangs, causing the floor to sizzle wherever their venom dropped. Kaitlin's face went red as she gasped for air before becoming still. As soon as Kaitlin hit the floor, Opal collapsed beside her, both bodies lying motionless beside each other. The snakes crumbled to ash and people rushed forward, trying to wake them both. Jay closed the projection. Blaze stood stock-still. The girl was Opal. Same uniform, same hair and even the same birthmark on her arm. Blaze could feel Opal's fear and confusion still. There was no guilt. She hadn't done it.

"I assume the snakes were why you pegged her for using black magic," Blaze said as evenly as she could. Her mind was running at whirlwind speeds, trying to come up with a plausible solution to explain what she just saw.

"Not only that. When we examined Kaitlin's body, the healers could sense black magic radiating off of her. Opal had the same response but hers was much stronger, meaning she was the one who used it," Maya said.

"No offense Maya," Maya narrowed her eyes at Blaze. Blaze hadn't used her last name, which was taken as a challenge of authority. Blaze didn't care. Defying authority was a hobby for her. "You're no expert in black magic. It has vast applications. In fact, no one here is, since the knowledge was out-lawed. The Chronicles though, still have books on it in the Seal."

"What are you suggesting Blaze?" Jay asked.

"I personally don't believe she has done it. Think about it. Criminals, especially ones who deal with magic, are much smarter about not getting caught. Opal knows how their minds work. You think if she'd want to commit a crime she'd leave so much evidence?"

"You're saying she's been framed?" Jackson asked incredulously. "How can she be framed when you saw her doing it?"

"I don't claim to have all the answers Jackson. But I request that you give me access to the Seal so I can look into it. Grant a grace period please. I have some insight into magic and it can be used to influence actions, and if there is an answer to all this, I am the best person to find it."

"How do you happen to have this insight?" Maya inquired.

"Family gift," she snapped at her.

All the heads exchanged glances. Jay looked down, embarrassed. They knew the basics about her family. It was stupid for them to ask.

"Very well," Maya said. "We will give you two weeks to investigate. You know what will happen otherwise."

Blaze clenched her teeth. Two weeks? What did Maya think magic was? It could take months to decipher spells or trace them to their casting points. She felt Opal's relief and hope. Blaze couldn't disappoint her.

"Fine. I'd like to speak to Opal now. In private."

Jay nodded. The three collected their papers and walked out, shutting the door softly behind them. Blaze could see them huddled outside, discussing the situation. Blaze ran over to Opal.

"Blaze!" Opal said with relief. Blaze looked her over, checking for injuries. Opal looked exhausted, with her maroon hair in tangles and dark circles under her eyes. "I'm fine, physically, for the most part." Blaze kneeled in front of her and met her gaze.

"What happened?"

Opal's face clouded with worry.

"I don't know. I don't remember anything. I woke up in these steel cuffs. My own pod of officers, had taken me down." There was a slight quiver to her voice.

"They were questioning me and I didn't know anything. The last thing I remember is dropping Jett off at the Chronicles, going home for lunch, and going to take a nap. Nothing after that. They showed me the footage and I couldn't believe what I was seeing. I didn't do it, I swear. But the chain was in my hand. It looked horrible."

Blaze couldn't argue with her. It did look awful for her.

"Look Opal, I believe you didn't do it consciously."

"Consciously?"

"There are streams of magic that can be used to control another person. It takes some serious power, but it can be done. I think that's what happened to you. The only part I'm struggling with is the fact that you were probably asleep when it happened, since you don't remember waking up. Normally, it can't be done while you're asleep."

They both sat in silence for a while, mulling over the matter.

"Jen!" Opal exclaimed. "She's a *hyponos*, a dream stretcher. Maybe she can help." Blaze thought about it. She didn't know Jen that well, but it was worth their while to try.

"She's healing with Jett in the infirmary. She was cut up pretty badly in the earthquake."

"Yeah they told me about it. I don't remember that either."

"Okay I'll go and talk to her." She put her hands on Opal's shoulders comfortingly.

"You and I both know what's at stake here. We will find a way, so be ready to brave it."

Opal nodded and gave her a weary smile.

"Whatever it takes," she said.

"Whatever it takes," Blaze echoed.

Blaze stepped out of the room and nodded her head at Jackson. He went in and brought Opal out. Jay took Opal's other side and together they led her down the hall. Blaze watched until she could no longer see her friend's figure. Maya stood beside her, watching Opal go.

"I hope your friendship doesn't block your better judgement."

Blaze didn't even bother looking at her.

"It never has before. You're quite aware that I'm a capable judge."

"Even so, are you ready to handle the truth, if your efforts fail to prove anything?"

"I've handled more bitter truths than you know. Don't question what I can and can't handle."

"Very well. It's unfortunate to see someone so young in so much pain."

"It wasn't Opal's fault."

"I wasn't talking about Opal, I was talking about you." That got Blaze's attention. "Blaze, nothing becomes strong without upholding adversity. Your strength is unparalleled, which also implies, your burdens are too. I'm not going to pretend like I know anything about it, but even the mightiest steel can break, when hit at its weakest point."

"What are you implying?" Blaze said with a razor-edged voice.

"To put it plainly, you will break soon. You have endured so much that almost nothing can affect you now. But everything has a weakness, and soon yours will be exploited and you will fall." *The nerve of this woman*, Blaze seethed in her mind.

"Only time will tell, Maya."

"Time is not on your side, my dear."

"I'm counting on that," she responded. With that Blaze strode off down the hall, leaving Maya alone.

℘

Maya sighed and began to walk to her office, running her hand along the rosy copper walls. She closed the door behind her and went to sit at her desk. She leaned back in her chair and closed her eyes, calling the vision to come to her again. It reappeared in her mind bright and clear. She saw Blaze down on her knees, bloody and bruised, with tears streaming down her face and a look of absolute despair. The scene switched and Blaze was running towards something as if her life depended on it. It switched again to show her screaming in pain and hitting the ground with two ugly scars fresh on her shoulder. The vision went black. Maya opened her eyes slowly. Glimpsing was a difficult power to have. Maya would see random clips of the past in her mind, most of which were irrelevant. Very rarely, did she ever get a glimpse of the future. That vision was a combination of both. Maya's power also came with what was known as Apollo's curse, where no one would ever believe her about anything to do with the future, based on the story of the maiden that the sun god Apollo had cursed with the same dilemma. Maya, in a strange way, felt the way Blaze did. Being unable to tell, or in her case, not being believed, meant you carried a lot inside that only you could know. No one else could, and you would have to sit there and wait for it, knowing it will happen, unable to do anything about it. They were right when they say ignorance is bliss. Not knowing, for the most part was a blessing. Knowledge on its own could be one of the heaviest burdens. All Maya could do was pray for Blaze. Pray for Myra's dark angel.

CHAPTER 7
Darkfire

"I DID WHAT?" JETT ASKED. STORM SMILED. SHE HAD COME TO VISIT HIM in the infirmary while Azura was out. Storm had given him some vague details about Opal's situation but refused to discuss it further until she had all the facts. Jett's heart ached for Opal. She had spent so much time trying to get him to stand and walk again, not to mention calm him down about Blaze. He hoped she'd be free soon.

"You amplified an emotion in me," Storm said, stroking his hair playfully.

"It's something *permotionem* can do. If they are physically touching someone, they can send a current of energy that will amplify any kind of emotion the person is currently experiencing. You amplified my bravery, my strength, so I could protect us both. That's why my eyes went black, since it's the colour of strength. I'm very impressed that you managed to tap into that without any help."

"Well," Jett said jokingly, "It was a life or death situation. Is that why the army uniform is black?"

"Indeed. Luckily you didn't amplify my fear. That would have been the end for both of us."

"How did I do it?" Storm laughed.

"I don't know Jett. That's on you. You can't exactly train yourself to use it. It's like an impulse, it comes and goes without you noticing."

Jen moaned and turned in the bed beside him. They both watched her toss and turn for a few minutes before she became still again. Adam had told Jett about her when he first woke up, right before Adam had to leave to work in the kitchen. Jett examined her sleeping form as her body curled up into fetal position. Her long tawny hair fell in delicate waves around her face.

"Earth to Jett," Storm snapped her fingers at him.

"Yeah?" he said, not taking his eyes off Jen.

"Open up." Jett turned to see that Storm had twisted the water from his glass into a stream. He opened his mouth and lightly touched her hand to tell her he was ready. Storm motioned her fingers towards him and the liquid followed her command, going directly into his mouth. He swallowed. "Good boy," she said teasingly. "I'll be back with your lunch." Storm began to walk out the door.

"Okay, Thanks!" he called back after her. Once Storm had left, Jett shifted to his side so he could look at Jen. She was so strangely captivating to him. Her sleeping face was innocent, kind and free of worry. He had the oddest urge to reach out and stroke her hair. He couldn't get up at the moment or else he probably would have. The white hospital blanket had fallen off of her shoulder slightly where the bruises from the earthquake became visible. He wanted to tuck it back in under her chin. Her eyes fluttered. Jett pushed himself up into sitting position, staring at her intently. She opened them to reveal beautiful green irises. She looked around, confused for a moment and then realization came over her face.

"Hi," Jett said. She turned to look at him. "I'm Jett." Jen smiled and nodded. Then with a loud yawn she turned her back to him and went back to sleep. Jett was a little disappointed, but he couldn't help but smile.

⁊ℬ

Blaze ran her hands across the maple wood stalls of the stables. Horses leaned their heads out to nuzzle her as she walked by, but reared back and whined loudly when she came near. She was used to it; most animals had never liked her. She couldn't blame them; they could probably sense her tainted blood. She heard whistling behind her and smiled. Just the person she was looking for. A small Asian girl with long black hair and silver uniform was carrying a bag of apples to the stables. She stopped at the first stall and held one out to a snow-white mare who snapped it up immediately and nuzzled her shoulder lovingly. She stroked the horse's snout, smiling while she fed it.

"You can come out Blaze," she said. Blaze walked up to her. The horse reared back. "No, no, it's okay," the other girl said as she attempted to calm the horse. The horse backed up apprehensively.

"Don't bother Scarlett," Blaze said wearily.

"Long day huh?" Scarlett asked as she moved to the next stall. "I'm sorry to hear about Opal. Is that why you're here?"

"Yeah. Why didn't you relocate with the others?"

"The heads determined that there weren't enough resources to relocate the animals. I stayed to tend to them. Tell me, which one would you like?"

"I need mine." Scarlett raised an eyebrow at her.

"You're not referring to…?"

Blaze nodded.

Scarlett's smile disappeared.

"It's that bad?"

"Joe is missing."

"Oh god…" Scarlett stammered. She saw Blaze's exhaustion and composed herself. "Follow me." As she turned to leave the horses neighed. Scarlett smiled.

"Neal came by to see you. He said he'll meet you at the bridge tonight."

"He told you that?"

"No, he told Crystal that."

Blaze sighed. Leave it to Neal to pass a message through a horse. Crystal was the white mare that Scarlett had been feeding. Since Scarlett could understand animals, there was almost always a way to get a message to her. She couldn't speak back to them, but she had calming effect on them, and most were very friendly to her. Blaze had seen the girl make friends with polar bears and cobras. To Blaze it seemed a lot more useful than her own ability.

The two walked around the stables to the gigantic fields where the horses ran for their exercise. The pasture was tinted in a light orange glow from the dipping sun. Scarlett came to a stop in front of her, held out her arm and let out a piercing whistle. Blaze heard powerful shrieks coming from the horizon. Two small brown dots appeared in the sky. As they drew closer Blaze could make out the enormity of their wingspans as they raced forward. Scarlett had put leather guards on both arms, preparing for the birds to land. The two hunting falcons landed in a perch on her arms, squawking at Scarlett. She stroked their wings while looking into their beady yellow eyes.

"Your hair, Blaze," she demanded. Blaze broke off a single strand and handed it to her. Scarlett waved it in front of the birds. The falcons studied every movement her hand made, committing the strand to memory.

"Bring him to me," she commanded. With that she let them fly off again into the distance.

"Thank you," Blaze said.

"Not a problem. What are friends for?"

"I need to ask you for one more thing."

"What's that?"

"Help Neal. I know he's good at what he's doing, but he needs someone to keep him in check to make sure he doesn't cross any lines he can't come back from."

"Neal doesn't like others interfering with his work. You know he's a lone wolf."

"He's about to get a partner. Whether he likes it or not. This is too important."

Scarlett nodded. She turned her head suddenly, motioning for Blaze to stop speaking. A faint bird's cry was heard in the distance. She grinned.

"They're coming."

For the first time that day, Blaze genuinely smiled as the sound of pounding hooves became audible. A brilliant black stallion came into view, thundering across the field towards her. Blaze held her arms out in welcome. The horse slowed to a trot and Blaze embraced it with full force. She hugged the horse's neck, stroking its back and sides. The stallion neighed happily, resting its head on her shoulder. Scarlett had stepped back to avoid being burned. Blaze ran her fingers through the horse's mane. The thing was, the mane wasn't made of horsehair. It was made of blue fire. As was its tail and the areas around the hooves. The flames were long and bright, licking their way up the length of his back. This kind of fire didn't affect Blaze. It was the same fire that burned through her veins. A symbol of the curse they both shared. A fire ignited from her scars and a whip of white–hot flames began to appear and spiral down her arm. It didn't burn this time. Not while she was with him.

She looked into the stallion's large ebony eyes, the very ones that mirrored her own dark irises.

"He's beautiful," Scarlett said in awe. "What's his name?"

The horse whined. Scarlett smiled.

"I see," she said. "Hello Darkfire."

&

Opal sat in her holding room, staring up at the worn grey ceiling. Once Jay and Jackson and left her here, she had cried silently for a few minutes. She couldn't believe that this was happening to her. She had to be the most loyal officer in the force, with the best track record. Then again, they did have video evidence against her, so she couldn't exactly blame them for not believing her. She probably wouldn't have either. It was infuriating, not being able to pin the blame on something. She had tried for hours to meditate in an attempt to remember something. All she could remember was the blackness of sleep when she had started to drift off into her nap. She could feel a whisper tugging at the back of her mind, but try as she might, it would not reveal itself. She had kicked the wall in frustration, leaving a crack in the already crumbling concrete.

Now she lay on the bed, exhausted and depressed. Blaze had assured her she would do whatever it takes. Opal winced at the thought. Blaze had already lost so much doing 'whatever it takes'. She would never be able to forgive herself if Blaze had to go through something similar for her. Despite that, she knew Blaze would do it, and nothing would stop her. It was something she both loved and hated about her friend. She was positive it would get Blaze killed one day if her sass didn't. Yet, Opal was here, staring death in the face. If Blaze couldn't pull through, Opal was counting down to her last days on Earth. It wasn't a scary thought to her, but it wasn't a pleasant one either. She would like to live, because she would only get one shot at doing that. After death… there was nothing. No pain, no suffering. In the words of Storm though, there was no happiness or pleasure either. Just a blank oblivion. Unless she chose to believe in heaven and hell, which she wasn't quite sure that she did; the future was slightly bleak. She closed her eyes and willed her unsettling thoughts to silence.

"Bit early for a nap don't you think, Hun?" Opal rolled over onto her side and lazily opened one eye. Neal tipped his fedora at her. He was a few feet away from her, behind the invisible force field that kept Opal caged inside. Anyone who got too close would be shot backwards into the wall. Surprisingly, there was nothing magical about it. It was just a strong network of powerful, polarized magnets and some electricity, where opposing poles were forced towards each other to create a repulsion force formidable enough to seriously harm a human if they got too close.

"How did you get in?" she asked.

"I gave the guard a lollipop."

"You're hilarious," the annoyance was prominent in her voice.

"Don't tell me what I already know," He gave her his signature cocky grin. "I told them I was doing a tech check. Then it was just a simple security override. I did help design it you know. Not much, but I know my way around."

"We should all be grateful you're not a felon," Opal said sarcastically, even though she was only half joking. Neal was a computer and technology genius. Thanks to Blaze's hobby of hacking when they were thirteen, he could get through almost any firewall at that age with her instruction. While Blaze only bothered learning as much as she cared to, Neal had taken it on as his passion. He was now even better than she was and could build incredible networks and computer-controlled devices. He could also destroy them with vicious viruses. His principle was that you should know how to destroy everything you can create, because that way you'll know its weak spots and how to guard them. In more practical cases, if the wrong person got a hold of one of his viruses, they would all be screwed if he couldn't stop it. If Neal was going to do something despicable, Opal wasn't sure they could stop him, or even link him to it. He was untraceable.

"You flatter me, Opal." He laid back against wall in a relaxed stance, his slim figure outlined by the dim fluorescent bulb in the hallway. "I'm here to offer my services." Opal shifted to face the wall beside her bed, turning her back to him.

"I don't have anything to offer you Neal. I know your price."

"I'm willing to negotiate on this one."

"Lucky me. I'm not interested."

"Then I'll have let Blaze know she'll have to find someone else."

Opal's muscles tightened. She refused to show her apprehension.

"She's paying the price, isn't she?" Her voice came out as a low whisper. Her mind began to whirl with emotions.

"Opal, I promise you, I'm not taking anything from you, or Blaze. Consider it a repayment for a personal favour." Opal sat up and walked the force field, locking eyes with Neal.

"Personal favour huh? From whom? You take no debts from anyone."

"Before I decided on that, I made the sorry mistake of doing so. So here I am."

Opal was silent for a moment. She gazed at the mask of confidence and arrogance that stood before her. Neal was an admirable deceit, but Opal knew better. Her mind could work at light speed to track the changes in his body language and facial expression. There was something dark hidden in the flash of his smile and in the ease of his posture. She decided to let it go.

"I'm listening."

"You'll find an earpiece attached to the underside of your bed. This way Blaze and I will be able to speak with you. You can hear us, but you can't speak to us. It was too risky giving you one with a microphone. There will also be a wave pad there. Place it under a section of hair. It'll monitor your brainwaves, so we can tell if you're in danger, stressed, or worried."

"Where did you get them?"

"Oh honey," he said smoothly. "I designed them. Managed to put them there before they brought you in." Opal raised her eyebrow in grudging respect. Only Neal.

"A pleasure to see you Opal," Neal said before vanishing into the shadows.

✂

Neal smiled at the guards as he strode through, giving them a quick thumbs up for passing his 'tech check'. The night air was cool as he walked out of the Springs, whistling as he went. The moon was a pale silver bone in the sky, giving Neal the cover of darkness that he longed for. He headed towards the bridge to meet Blaze and seal their deal. He reached into the pocket of his coat and pulled out a cherry blossom. It was soft and delicate under his fingers as he stroked the petals. He remembered the bitter taste in his mouth after lying to Azura. He always avoided debts. He didn't owe anything to Opal, but she didn't need to know that. Azura's desolate face floated in front of him every time he closed his eyes, making him clutch the flower tightly in his hand. He began walking faster down the grassy fields towards the rushing sound of water. Blaze was leaning against the side of the stone bridge, staring down at her reflection.

Blaze's dagger hung low on her hip, the silver scorpion glowing eerily in the moonlight and the wicked edges gleamed through its sheer sheath. Neal remembered when she and Joe would practice fighting with their training weapons. That dagger may as well have been a part of her arm with the frightening accuracy she used it with. He hadn't seen it for years.

"As you requested Blaze." He held out a small, clear earpiece to her. She took it gingerly and nodded her thanks. They stood beside each other quietly, following the movement of the rapids under them.

"Why did you lie?" Blaze asked. Neal sighed.

"The same reason you do." She turned to him, leaning in dangerously close, commanding his attention with all of her deadly, threatening beauty. From here she could kill him or kiss him. It would most likely be the former. Neal didn't find her that desirable, but there was a compelling pull from the blackness in her that he couldn't ignore. It called out to his own.

"I lie for many reasons Neal," she whispered in his ear. "Which one are you referring to?" Neal felt the malevolence tug at his mind. He took a deep breath and met her gaze. "To show that I don't care." She nodded.

"Illusion of emotional detachment. One of the best."

"Best contradiction I've ever seen," he mumbled.

"In its own way, it is painful too. But would you rather expose your vulnerability?"

"I think about it sometimes."

"Well that's your choice. Let me tell you why I love and despise the illusion." Blaze toyed with her dagger as she spoke to him, as if she was twitching with anticipation to throw it. It was making Neal slightly uncomfortable. He motioned for her to continue.

"We have a strange thing in common that we've bonded over. That's our desire to appear emotionless. When they don't know you care, they can't use it to hurt you. If they do end up hurting you, you don't give them the satisfaction of knowing it. Our principle is, in your words "to guard our weak spots" so we appear unbreakable and unaffected. Reality wise…" Blaze ran her hand over his arm and across his chest, stopping right over his heart. He felt the tingle across his skin. "…We care the most, and it scares the shit out of us. When we do something for a loved one, we perform it in silence, so we can pretend like it never happened." Neal placed his hand over hers, holding it there. He leaned into her, brushing her hair back so he could speak into her ear.

"Then tell me," he said softly, "Tell me why I hate myself for doing it."

Blaze sighed, letting out an exhale of hot air that rushed by Neal's cheek. She patted his chest.

"Because of that little guy right there." Neal could feel his heartbeat thrum against her hand. "One day, you will lose them. The people you love. Whether that be to death or another human is irrelevant. If you never show them how much you care, they will go to the grave or into the arms of another believing that you never loved them. That regret will stay with you for life. You also deprive yourself of a chance at happiness. If you admit to your feelings, they may be returned, and that is one of the best feelings in the world. But there's always a chance of pain that looms over you. Which is why we don't take the risk. Don't ask for happiness, don't ask for pain." Blaze dropped her hand and leaned back, returning her sights to the rapids.

"There should be no price for taking a chance," Neal muttered dejectedly.

"You're naïve Neal. You'll find out soon enough, that everything has a price, and taking a chance is the ultimate expense."

✂

"Canada huh? I heard it's a really beautiful country," Jen said as she swirled her spaghetti with her fork. Jen sat cross legged on her bed, facing Jett as they ate dinner together in his recovery room. Fading purple bruises still decorated her arms and legs along with parts of her neck. Jett looked no better, with healing cuts all over his upper body. He watched her take small forkfuls of their seafood pasta while silently admiring her. They had spent the last few hours getting to know each other while Azura routinely checked in on them.

"Yeah we have some great landscapes. Our lakes and mountains are stunning. I live in a city though, so we don't have too much of that."

"You still get to see it."

"Well Myra is plenty beautiful too. There's nothing else like it."

"When you live here long enough it starts to lose its wonder. The nature here though is enchanting because of the…" She proceeded to explain to Jett the cause of Myra's strange and splendid natural beauty. She covered plants, water and weather, speaking passionately about the subject. Jett loved it when her eyes became animated when she spoke. Being a Chronicle assistant, part of Jen's job was going through enormous volumes of books. She had gathered small bits of knowledge on almost every subject known to man and always had something to say about everything.

She's really intelligent, Jett thought to himself. He instantly felt bad. Mavis was missing and here he was, occupied with another girl on his mind. He missed Mavis even more now. She would've been the one he'd open up to about Jen. He was the worst friend ever.

"Jen, it's time for your exercise," Azura said, popping her head out from behind the door.

"Okay Azura." Jen stood up unsteadily, taking a minute to regain her balance.

"See you later Jett," she said before slowly walking across the room to the door.

"See ya Jen," he called after her. She gave him a small wave before turning to leave, her bouncy tawny hair swaying from side to side. Jett had the urge to gently tug on one of her loose curls.

"Jett, you're going to choke if you add any more spaghetti to your fork," Azura said, amused. Jett looked down to see that he had be continuously twirling his fork in his pasta bowl and now had a giant lump of noodles twisted around the tines.

"Sorry," he mumbled. Azura suppressed a smile. Jett looked up at her innocently with curious eyes. Azura couldn't read emotions, but she was smart enough to know what that look meant.

"Jen is a *hyponos.* Dream stretcher. She can send messages and appear in people's dreams while she is also dreaming. Her abilities extend to any kind of sleeping, when the mind is unguarded. She can help people out of nightmares or remember lost memories. Though memories are really tricky, and she's not that developed in her skill."

"Is it a rare one?"

"No, it's pretty common. The art of dreams is really delicate and complicated so very few bother to master it, though many are born with it. Learning the basics is good enough to get by."

"Oh." Jett looked down at his feet. He still couldn't walk or even stand for too long, or he would have done his exercise with Jen, maybe gotten the chance to talk to her more. Frustration rumbled at the back of his mind. Blaze has gotten him to stand, but he was far from recovered. Ever since the earthquake, she had been nowhere to be seen, much to Jett's disappointment. Not that he enjoyed her company, but he was hoping she'd be able to help him walk by now. Azura had told him that she was working on proving Opal's innocence. Jett didn't quite know what Opal had done; it was all hushed up, but it must have been serious for her to be held for interrogation. Still, a selfish part of him wished Blaze was here, working her magic on him so he could be free again.

"Azura..." he said. She looked up from her book and gazed at him expectantly. Her glasses sat low on her nose like they always did when she was reading, giving her the appearance of a clever college student.

"Will I ever be able to walk again?" he said, not even bothering to hide the desperation in his voice.

Azura gave him a weary smile. He hadn't noticed it before but she was exhausted. Her eyes had dark rims and her motions were slightly sluggish, as if she had been up for days. Jett knew she took care of him for most of the day, but didn't have the faintest clue about her time off. She knew a lot more about him, than he knew about her. Maybe it's because he never bothered to ask, he thought with a guilty knot in his stomach.

"Jett, honestly, I don't know. You're a special case that we haven't ever had the chance to deal with before. Being a *permotionem*, getting shocked *and* surviving. It's really a one-of-a-kind situation. I want to say yes, I really do, but I won't give you false hope."

Jett felt like his soul was being crushed into powdered dust. He didn't trust himself to speak.

"Jett..."

"I want to be alone," he said in a low voice. "Please." Azura looked at him with genuine concern in her eyes. She began to stride towards him, reaching out to take his hand.

"GO!" he shouted. Azura flinched and jumped back. Hard. She was holding her palm tightly. Jett felt bad for scaring her but this was what he needed. He laid down and buried his face in his blanket. He didn't look up until he heard the door shut with a bang. *I'm sorry Azura.*

Azura stood out in hallway and released her palm, wincing in pain. Marks of despair were burned into her palm. They were interconnecting spikes that formed menacing patterns across her hand. She bit her lip to hold back the stinging burn and began to chant. She took out a small green square and placed it on her ring finger. The square began to expand and move, wrapping around her hand, creating a green-gloved bandage. Relief coursed through her body and she sighed with contentment. Her content was short-lived and quickly turned to worry. Jett didn't know he had burned her, and he may do something more reckless if his emotions weren't kept in check. Jett could seriously harm someone he loved, like Adam. She had to end this, once and for all. Gulping down her hesitation, she walked to the small chunk of *ankh* that hung in the side of the corridor. *I'm doing it for him,* she told herself. She touched it and concentrated. The *ankh* lit up green and pulsed for a few seconds before winking out. It was done. There was nothing she could do now. Regret hit her instantly. She knew what she had done was far from right. But it may be the only way for Jett to ever get back on his feet.

☙

Mavis was stumbling down the tunnels of the ruby red cavern. She was still disoriented and confused, with memories coming back to her in choppy bits and pieces. Her green shirt and jeans were torn and dirty. The dry air seared her lungs. The voice was directing her, guiding her down the ashy pathways of the rocky dome. She turned a corner to find herself facing a dead end. She fell to her knees in defeat. *This is what I get for listening to you,* she hissed in her mind.

Patience Mavis, the voice crooned, *You are so close.*

Yeah, she thought sarcastically. *To a stone wall.*

There is more than meets the eye. This is a special place. One you've been looking for all your life. I have brought you here, as agreed in our deal.

WHAT DEAL? Even the memories that I do have give me no recollection of this!

All in good time. Now, take out that vial.

What vial?

The one around your neck.

Mavis looked down in surprise. Sure enough, a small seashell shaped vial hung on her neck. It was literally hanging there. There was no cord to hold the tiny glass vessel. The glass was a sheer black and as light as a passing breeze. Mavis could see a dark liquid swishing around inside. She reached for it tentatively. It shot into her hand. She sucked in a gasp. There was no mistaking the shimmering maroon fluid. It was blood.

Wha-What is this??

A key. Soon you will understand everything. Now chant! the voice commanded.

Mavis felt herself walking forward to the wall and chanting words she didn't even recognize, but had apparently memorized by heart. Her lonely voice echoed in her ears as she spoke. Her body was no longer under her control. She felt herself grip the vial in one hand as she continued to chant and raised it up. With a yell, she smashed it against the ground. For a moment nothing happened, the blood just pooled out of the shattered remains of its container. Suddenly, it spread out, racing towards the wall with alarming speed. It rushed up the side and zipped around, forming a sinister glowing pattern in front of her. The ground gave way from under her and she fell swiftly, her screams lost in the void.

Mavis woke on a white marble floor. The stone cooled her heated body, and she clutched it for respite. She felt a rush of energy and managed to push herself up. She heard cold, cruel laughter resonate in her ears. She sat there agitated, as the laughter horrified her. It was her own voice.

CHAPTER 8

Ambush

JETT WAS LYING IN BED WHILE HIS DINNER SAT COLD BESIDE HIM. JEN was out recovering with her trainers so he had to eat alone. Guilt churned through his mind. Ever since he had yelled at Azura, she only came by while she thought he was sleeping. He hated the fact that he was so harsh with her. He didn't mean for her to take his words to heart. Jett wasn't good at apologies. He didn't like to admit he was wrong, or that he hurt someone. It was easier to pretend like he didn't do it, so he could will the remorse away. Azura had done nothing but help him, so he was trying to muster up the courage and words to apologize to her. He stared up at the ceiling while he let his imagination play out his future conversation. He heard a loud swish and thump beside his ear. His peripherals picked up the silver edge of a knife. He shot up, petrified by the scene in front of him. She stood there with a wicked gleam in her eyes and an evil smirk, flipping another knife in her hand. The other one was lodged in his pillow and had been shot just a hair's length away from Jett's face. Blaze stood by the back wall that faced Jett's bed, eyeing him with cruel intentions. All he saw was her irises that paralyzed him like devastating black holes, gazing at him with a malicious glee. She flung another one at his head, and Jett barely had time to breathe before flinging himself off the bed. The knife struck the wall with a crack. He hit the floor hard, sending waves of agony through his chest. His eyes were wide with fear as she laughed diabolically, taking a moment to enjoy his misery. He couldn't find the words to ask what the hell she was doing. All he felt was his heartbeat rise as he saw the next knife appear in her hand. She

104

moved towards him slowly, like a deadly black panther cornering its prey, as he struggled to catch his breath.

"Finally," she said with anticipation. Jett pushed himself away from her advancing form, only to hit the wall. Dread gripped his heart.

"No one's around to protect you anymore, little boy. I have you all to myself."

"AZURA! ADAM! SOMEONE!" Jett screamed.

"They can't hear you sweetheart, I've taken care of them. No one's going to get in my way today."

"You're a monster."

"I am, aren't I?" she said with a chuckle. "Funny, how you saw it all along. You know you were right from the beginning. I wasn't to be trusted. I'm dangerous. Thought I was killer too. Congratulations smart guy, today I'll prove to you just how right you were."

"Joe told me to give you a chance. He told me that my perception was a deception. Looks like he was the one who was deceived."

"Sweetheart, I deceive everyone. It's one of my mastered arts. Joe was just another one I played."

"You didn't fool me. Not for a second."

"Aren't you lucky then?"

Blaze aimed the third knife over his heart, giving Jett a predatory look with her soulless eyes. "I'm going to enjoy this. Prepare to die, Davis." She brought the knife down.

☙

Scarlett watched Darkfire as he rested under an apple tree in the open fields. Blaze had told him to stay until she needed him. Scarlett had no idea what that meant, or how Blaze would let the horse know when to come, but she didn't dwell on it too much. There were many mystical alliances at work in Myra, and trying to comprehend even half of them would take a toll on anyone. Scarlett knew not to pry in Blaze's affairs. Azura had told her a long time ago that she was mysterious and complicated, and it was best not to ask. Scarlett could feel the dark magic radiating off of Darkfire even from this distance. He was a good twenty meters away, and when he came any closer than that, the other animals would go wild. *Danger. Darkness. Evil,* the animals' voices had vibrated through her mind. Darkfire had simply said *I will keep my distance,* and trotted away to the apple tree. She truly sympathized for the stallion. Forced to be an outsider. He was beautiful, with his glossy black coat and blue fire mane. He seemed to be made for Blaze. Dark and stunning, with a knack to burn. Scarlett had seen Blaze ignite her fiery whip once before, when she had used it to kill a serpent that had cornered them in the Dias River. It had gripped Joe with his tail, crushing the life out of him. Never had she seen Blaze so angry. The flames coiled down her arm and she lashed out with it, cutting through the serpent with a deadly, searing ribbon of heat. Scarlett couldn't forget Blaze's eyes that day. Their normal night sky noire had been replaced by leaping blue flames. The serpent had backed up out of fright. Blaze had dropped in exhaustion afterward, while Scarlett and Neal pulled Joe out of the glittering water. She hadn't seen her whip since. Not until yesterday. She started walking across the grass towards Darkfire. He lifted his head as she drew near, gazing at her with calm, yet curious eyes. She felt the heat of his mane and tail as she drew closer. The fire didn't seem to affect the grass or plants around him. She stopped a few feet away from him and sat down cross-legged. It was the closest she could get without incinerating herself.

Human. Why have you come? Scarlett wished she could speak back to him. Instead she took an apple out of her pocket and rolled it towards him. He leaned down and sniffed the fruit before biting in to it. *Many thanks, but I know your presence is not to feed me, listener.* Listener. The horse knew what she was. A twang of admiration shot through her. Animals knew so much more than what people gave them credit for. *Speak human. I am connected to Blaze and thusly I share in her power. I will sense your emotions. That will suffice as communication for now.* Scarlett was taken aback at the moment. The stallion met her gaze evenly.

"What are you?" Scarlett asked.

I sense curiosity. What do you wish to know about? Scarlett pointed at him. His blue tail swished from side to side in acknowledgement. *To your mortal eyes, I am a black stallion. In reality, for lack of a better word, I am fashioned from Blaze's darkest impulses, memories and am tied to her soul, manifesting in this form. It is why any living thing will fear me. They can sense the chaos and the feeling of wrongness.*

"So... you're not alive?"

I am by all means alive, considering the fact that I am essentially a part of Blaze that gives her life.

"But you're dark..."

Dark does not mean not living. Life is not a pure, benevolent force that most mortals make it out to be. It is an existence, a balance, between dark and light, both as forms of energy. Life is the ability to do both, to be both. One cannot exist without the other. You are familiar with it, listener.

Scarlett swallowed. Darkfire was tugging on a buried memory, one she wished to keep buried. She framed her next question carefully.

"What is death then? If living is both?" The horse neighed loudly. Scarlett could sense it was laughing at her. She was slightly offended but didn't want to provoke him. She stiffened her expression.

Death in it of itself is just the counterbalance to life. It is neither good nor bad. It is what we associate with death that has many linking it with evil. It devastates, because we love. It makes us despair, because we remember. As it is with all things, you learn their true value when they are taken from you. That is not a consequence of death. It is of human nature.

Scarlett sat there, picking the grass by her feet, pondering Darkfire's explanation. They sat in silence, watching the sun slowly move lower into the sky.

I sense your apprehension listener. You have yet to speak your mind.

"If you are a part of Blaze's darkness..."

Why have I not burnt this field down or eaten you? Why am I not urged to cave to it? Simple, human. I am the urge. I am the memory. I do not fall to myself. Evil and darkness have always existed. But they can do nothing until a human uses them. I can do nothing, until Blaze calls upon me. Good and bad are both forces that need to be exercised in order to have effect. I am the glove, but I bend to Blaze's hand. I cannot do harm, until I am pushed to, or given permission to.

Scarlett paled as her heartbeat quickened. "Blaze is going to call on you..."

I do more than destroy, human. Scarlett sensed the anger in the horse's voice and backed up. *I may be her worst, but I also serve as motivation, a reservoir for power, and if necessary, a line of magic. I am a reminder as much as anything else. Blaze's chooses what she wants to do with me, not I.*

"Magic has a price."

A terrible price but she had already paid it long ago. I am part of it.

"You?"

Indeed. As are her scars.

"What could she have possibly wanted in order to be willing to receive scars for it?" Before the horse could respond, they heard a thump as an arrow struck his side. Darkfire jumped up and reared back. *Ambush,* his voice echoed in her head.

C/D

Opal was staring daggers at Jay, who was slowly pacing in front of her force field. He fit his position as a head and a commander with his military-style posture and strong build. He was not muscular, but toned and agile, and still had immense strength. He had fought his way to the top of the army, building a notable reputation for himself. Opal despised him. Although he was an honourable fighter, he was also arrogant and conceited. Blaze had put him in his place once with the scar on his neck as a reminder, but that hadn't put him in line for anyone else except her. Even with Blaze he was still questionably hostile.

Opal's eyes followed the shadows that moved across his angular face as he paced in and out of the light.

"You know you can go off guard duty," Opal quipped. "It's not like I can leave." Jay ignored her and kept walking. Opal sighed in frustration. Fine. If he was going to give her the silent treatment, she wouldn't pry. It was still a mystery to her as to why he was here. He would glance at her every now and then with a condescending expression. She turned on her side to face the wall and began to pull threads out of her thin linen pillowcase. She could hear Jay's footsteps echo behind her. A second set of footsteps joined his. She rolled back over to see Jackson shaking hands with Jay. Jay nodded to him and left. Jackson began pacing the same way Jay had. Opal couldn't understand it. It was like they were taking turns watching her like she was child they had to babysit. The force field itself was enough to keep her in, she didn't need a bodyguard too. Jackson's side bangs swept over one eye, making it difficult for Opal to see his expression. She didn't care enough to try. She wanted to see Blaze, inquire about if any progress had been made. She couldn't talk to her but she could send Blaze her brain signals. She closed her eyes and thought of herself climbing up a cliff's side, where she could lose her balance at any moment and plummet into the sinister waves below. Her heartbeat picked up slowly as she began to stress and give off warning signs of panic. That should be enough to get through to Blaze.

"I knew it!" Jackson hissed. Opal jumped. He was right beside her bed, his grey-blue eyes clouded with anger.

"Jackson what..." before she could finish he yanked her by the hair, forcing her up. Opal cried out in pain and threw a jab to his pelvis. He grabbed her hand and twisted it so he was holding it behind her back while he continued to hold her hair. She was right up against him, with her back against his chest. She could feel his breath on her neck as he held her immobile.

"What the hell Jackson?!" Opal winced as he gave her hair a hard tug. She couldn't see him as he was behind her, but she felt him tense up all over.

"Think we wouldn't figure it out huh?"

"Figure out what?!" Opal struggled against him. He only tightened his grip.

"That Blaze would bend the rules again. See this beauty here?" He let go of her hair momentarily to flash a blue and white ring in front of her. He pulled her head back again. "That lets us track any transmission that goes out of the area. We knew Blaze would give you one. We just had to wait for you to use it."

Shit. He must have used his clearance to disable the force field when I tried to contact her. Opal thought. She felt his arms relax slightly and took her chance. She elbowed him in stomach, letting him double over before spinning around and nailing him in chest with a kick. He flew backwards, hitting the ground on his back. Opal ran for the opening of her cell. The force field was still disabled, and she'd be able to get out. Jackson tackled her from behind, bringing them both down with a sickening thud. He attempted to get on top of her to pin her down. Her fist hit his face, splitting his lip and bruising the surrounding area. He growled and threw his weight down, pinning her hands own with one of his, and using the other to pull her hair back to reveal the wave pad.

He was breathing heavily as he loomed over her.

"We'll just have to cut this off now. Cooperate with us Opal, we just want the transmitter. It'll be less painful." He yanked, making Opal cry out. Opal was terrified, but fear was giving her strength. She saw every twitch in Jackson muscles and the slightly change in his expression. She was fast, but only in one direction. She had to corner him somehow. Opal relaxed her body as if she was giving up. She felt him tighten in surprise. She waited, staring into his eyes as she anticipated his muscles releasing. She saw his biceps flex to relax, and then threw her hips up, throwing him off of her. She rolled over rapidly and pinned him underneath, his eyes wide in shock. She aimed for a knee to the groin but hit the side of his thigh instead as they struggled against each other. He hit her in the throat and she gasped, blinking the tears out of her eyes as she attempted to breathe. He threw her off and stood up slowly, with blood dripping from his lip and the side of his face. "*Bitch!*" he hissed at her.

Anger flowed through Opal's weakened muscles. She pushed herself up into standing position. "That's right you bastard. I am a bitch. Bitch for defending myself. Come and get it." It was like waving a red flag in front of a bull that was incredibly fast. He lunged at her. She waited for the last moment and then stepped to the side with her unnatural speed. He crashed into the wall. *Perfect.* She began to nail him with lightning fast punches until he dropped to the ground. He was still and unmoving on the cold-pewter floor. Opal exhaled. She turned and walked to her exit. Just as she was about to pass through she heard a roar. She turned to see Jackson's face just inches from her as his hands were leaping out to grab her. A loud clunk resonated in her ears and Jackson dropped to the floor, with a gigantic red welt beginning to form on his head. In front of her stood Neal, holding a fire extinguisher which, she assumed, was the reason for Jackson's welt.

"Honey," Neal said with his regular, smooth demeanour. "Why do you keep attracting the crazy ones?" His tone had an underlying current of tension that they both knew was there. Opal just shook her head at him. "Not the best time to joke huh?" He grabbed her hand. "Come on, we're getting out of here."

"Where to?"

"To the person you want to see. Blaze."

"Thank God."

"Well we might have to wait a bit. She's currently trying to commit a murder."

"What?!"

Neal smiled at her coyly, amused at her horrified face.

"Didn't you know? Jett Davis is getting throwing knives flung at him as we speak, from our own knife master."

"Neal are you out of your mind? We need to get there. Now. Wait… Azura! Azura's there, she will stop her. She has too."

"Oh honey," Neal winked at her. "Azura's the one who asked her to do it."

❧

The knife cut through Jett's shoulder as he flung himself across the floor. A fresh stream of blood began to trickle down his arm with a stinging sensation. Jett barely noticed the pain. Keeping himself alive was all he could think about. Blaze turned lazily, relishing in his struggle.

"Aren't you a disappointment," she mocked him. She kicked him square in the chest, sending him sprawling on his back. He felt the fire in his lungs as he coughed and fought for air.

"Maybe it was a good thing your father died when he did. He won't have to know that his son had to die like a coward. Cowering in fear." She tossed the knife from hand to hand, still stained with his blood. "His poor baby couldn't learn to walk on his own. Glad he was spared the embarrassment. Adam on the other hand, won't be. Don't worry though," She kneeled down and cupped his face with one hand, running the flat of the knife against his cheek with the other. "I'll make his death quick so he doesn't have to think about it for too long." Jett's eyes widened again.

"That's right little boy. He's next. As soon as I'm done with you." Jett shut his eyes as Blaze's voice continued to taunt him. Adam. He was innocent. He was against coming here in the first place. Jett couldn't let Adam die because of him. He had already lost Mavis, he wasn't about to lose him too. His mind went on autopilot. He saw his hand lashing out to twist her wrist, forcing her to drop the knife. It clattered to the floor. He took the moment to aim an uppercut at her. Blaze dodged it easily, but it had forced her to back up, granting Jett the few precious seconds he needed. The door was just a few feet left of him. He used the wall to propel himself up and threw his dinner plate at Blaze before he ran. He was about to turn the knob when Blaze grabbed his collar and swung him around, pinning him to the door, knife right at his jugular vein. His breaths were shallow as he attempted to swallow, preparing himself for the worst. Blaze held it there, tightening her grip if he made a single movement. They stared at each other and to Jett, time seemed to have stopped moving. Blaze let go and backed up. Jett caught his breath slowly, clutching his shoulder as he leaned over to inhale.

"What are you waiting for?" he rasped at her, "Do it." Blaze took out a maroon cloth from her pocket and cleaned her blade. Her expression was clear; her black eyes reflected her calm and collected posture with none of their previous maliciousness.

"As much as you'd like to believe it," she said as she sat down on his mess of a bed, "I didn't come here to kill you."

"Then what was this? An early birthday present?" he spat at her.

"Somewhat. Consider it a gift."

Jett was bewildered.

"Fat lot of good that did me. How dare you…" Blaze cut him off by holding her knife to her lips.

"Shh," she whispered. "Didn't realize you were taller than me until now. Not by too much though, which is good."

"What…" Jett stopped himself. He was taller than Blaze. How would she know that unless…

He stared down. He was standing, full weight on his feet. He remembered running to the door. He gave his legs a slow push forward and took a step. A faint sting ran through his muscles but nothing else. He took another, keeping his balance perfectly.

"I…I…you…"

"You're welcome," Blaze said. "Bandages and antiseptic are in the top cupboard at the back. I'll send Azura in to make sure you don't bleed to death. You'll have quite a bit to tell her."

Jett just stared at her, trying to comprehend what had just happened. Blaze pushed him out of her way and swung the door shut behind her.

ℰ♫

Azura waited at the end of the hall. She watched Blaze stride towards her. The knots in her stomach were tightening as Blaze drew closer. Passing medical staff gave Blaze a quick bow of their heads to show their respect. The girl commanded attention wherever she went. The only time she didn't was when she didn't want it, and she would pass in and out as silently as a shadow. She came to a stop across from Azura. Her hair was dishevelled and her knives were unsheathed. Azura looked up at her hopefully. Blaze nodded. Azura breathed a sigh of relief.

"Thank you Blaze. Thank you."

"That boy gets no more favours from me," she said. Azura nodded.

"He's my problem from now on."

"Good." Blaze turned to leave.

"Wait, I got you something." Azura threw a small silver object at her back. Without turning around, Blaze reached out and caught it in her right hand.

"Neal, right?" Blaze inquired.

"Yeah, he managed to make a duplicate. We know the heads would take too much time."

Blaze turned her head and smiled. Not her cocky, confident smile, or her evil one. The genuine one that most people thought didn't exist anymore. Even Azura didn't see it at as much as she would have liked to. For the smallest sliver of time, it created a window that gave a small peek at the girl she used to be.

Azura watched her disappear with the key to the Seal in her hand. She hoped she had played her cards right by having Neal duplicate the one to the Seal doors. All the dark magic archives were heavily guarded there. Maya and Jay would have never delivered the access on time, wasting the majority of the two weeks they had to get Opal free. Azura walked into the recovery room to find a white-faced Jett, standing in the middle of a wrecked room. Shatters of a ceramic dinner plate littered the ground. The walls and pillows had cut marks in them. Jett was bleeding from his shoulder. He looked up at Azura with absolute confusion. "I…I…" he sputtered.

"Jett!" Adam and Jen had walked in behind Azura and were taking in the scene. "What the hell…"

"Blaze told me what happened," Azura said evenly. "You need to sit down."

"Blaze did this?!" Adam half shouted. "God that woman is…"

"No," Jett cut Adam off. "She got me to walk."

Jen stared at him open mouthed. "Walk? You can walk now?"

Jett stepped towards her in confident strides. Azura could see his muscles weren't fully recovered; there was a strain to his steps.

He had gotten half way to Jen when she ran over and gave him a hug.

"I can't believe it," she whispered. Jett wrapped his arms around her tightly. "I can't either."

Azura got him to lie down and made him drink some sour liquid to steady his heartbeat and calm himself down. As she tended to him, Jett relayed the story to the three of them. Azura was mildly impressed with how much Blaze had restrained herself. Jett only had some bruises and a very shallow cut.

"There are other ways to heal people," Adam said, still in dismay. "You don't go around and start throwing knives."

"Fear is a huge motivator Adam," Azura informed him.

"Still. We could have worked him up to it. I don't know why she thinks she has the right…"

"I asked her to do it," Azura said, cutting him off. Both twins stared at her.

"Why… would you do something like that?" Jett asked in a small voice. Azura could hear the slight sense of betrayal in his words.

"Because of this." Azura unwound her green bandage off her hand and held out the fading burn marks towards Jett. "The day when I told you there was a chance that you may never walk again, you were so emotionally over-whelmed that you burned me. These are marks of despair. If I couldn't get you to walk soon, you might have burned or done worse to someone you care about. Like Adam."

"I… burned you?" Jett was guilt ridden. "Azura, I'm so sorry, for blowing up at you, what I said, I hurt you…" Azura put a finger to her lips.

"The past is in the past. But now you see why I did what did. I don't always approve of Blaze's methods, but she gets the job done. You weren't responding to anything else. I have to hand it to her though, she wasn't too hard on you."

Azura saw the disbelief written over Jett and Adam's faces. She half-smiled.

"Blaze is legendary with throwing knives and daggers. If she really wanted to hurt you, she wouldn't miss any targets. She intentionally missed so you weren't hurt too badly."

"I swore she wanted to kill me. Her whole face, body language, the way she spoke, I was convinced the knife would go through my heart," Jett said, shaking his head.

"Blaze is great at radiating fear. She knows what strings to pull. Study a person long enough, and you can pinpoint what makes them tick. Acting becomes second nature when the majority of your job requires you to do so. As a general that's what she trained to do. You can't rally your soldiers if you can't show them anything but strength."

"I have very mixed feelings about whether to thank her or to hate her for what she did," Jett mumbled.

"It doesn't matter. She won't care either way," Azura said truthfully.

"She never does, does she?" Adam said.

"Nope," Azura said, wiping off the last bit of blood from Jett cut. "Not ever."

CHAPTER 9
The Seal

AS SOON AS BLAZE STEPPED OUTSIDE SHE BROKE INTO A RUN. HER HAIR whipped back behind her as she sprinted across the deserted cobblestone streets. In no time, she had reached the side of the first bridge that spanned the Dias River. The river broke off into smaller streams when you entered Myra but all of them converged into a huge, snakelike canyon again in the city centre. Unlike on the outside where the rapids roared, the Dias was calm here, still and unmoving like tinted blue beach glass. The shimmering water nearly blinded her in the late afternoon light. She stopped her stride where the two bridges met in the middle. She knelt and placed her hand on the ground, creating a small circle of orange light. She could feel the rumble beneath her palm as she heard the grinding of gears and clicking of metal locks. The sides of the bridges were held together with beams that formed a crisscrossing triangular pattern, but now the ones in front of her moved apart to shape a star. She climbed onto the edge, staring down at the Dias. She took a breath and stepped out over the edge.

Her foot landed on something hard. She breathed a sigh of relief. The *ankh* pathway under her faintly pulsed with her signature orange glow. *Ankhs* would always glow the colour of a person's gift. Blaze was a *lectora*, a reader, and the colour orange identified her. Azura was green as a *sanator* and Storm was blue as a *huria*. People like Jen, who were *hyponos* emitted black light. Sometimes it was confusing with Myra's uniform code, because black was also the colour of the army and blue was used for the police force. Blaze also had a third colour set to track, which was the one of emotions.

116

When memory flowers held their respective emotions, they followed their own colour scheme too. Love being purple, strength being black, loss being white and so on. Blaze liked the idea of that. Even though their jobs and gifts divided them, their emotions would always be something they all shared. They all loved, hated, gained and suffered loss. Inside, everyone was rainbow. She chuckled at the thought.

It was a little disorienting as Blaze walked, as the *ankh* was transparent, giving her the illusion of walking through the sky. The Seal was located over the water in a gigantic glass sphere. It was made of the same material the integrations rooms were fashioned from, except it was next to indestructible. People could see out of it, but no one on the outside could see in. It appeared as a large curved mirror to anyone who approached. As she drew near she saw the imprint of an intricate lock on the otherwise smooth glass. She pulled out the key from her pocket and pressed it into the matching outline. The key was a small circular disc that ran some code and entered a sequence of laser commands to open the doors. As much as Myra was magical, dabbling in magic was dangerous. They had reverted to using technology to achieve things like high-level security and science in order to keep the magic to a bare minimum. When she and Azura had healed Jett, it was the first time they had used magic in years. Her gift may appear like magic to ordinary humans, but it was an innate ability that she had been born with and therefore did not classify as magic. It could do no harm to others. Magic was magic because it made the unnatural happen. There was always a price to pay, and it was almost never worth the cost.

She quietly slipped into the main lobby of the seal, securing the door behind her. The domed room was empty, leaving Blaze to stare out at the river surrounding her on all sides. The floor gave way to steps that lead to a slightly elevated marble platform. She went and sat down in the dead centre, closing her eyes to focus. *Black magic, witchcraft, sorcery. I call out to you.* Blaze opened her eyes to see piles of books surrounding her. The Seal had responded to her. *Thank God.* She chose to start with an old felt cover that looked like a diary. Suddenly a near silent whoosh of air passed by. Her eyes became alert and alive, her body ready to attack. Someone was here. Blaze looked up to see Opal and Neal coming through the door.

"Made a third one for yourself, did you?" Blaze asked, amused.

"Of course I did. Couldn't let you have all of this to yourself," Neal said.

Blaze locked eyes with Opal, widening as she took in her appearance. "What on earth…"

"The heads were tracking transmissions. Used my tracker design for it too. Opal tried to panic to contact you and they picked it up," Neal explained.

"I don't get it. Shouldn't they have detained you?"

"They would have, if Neal and I hadn't knocked Jackson out cold," Opal said bitterly.

"What?" Blaze turned her head back and forth between them.

"He attacked me, trying to rip the wave pad out of my hair."

There was silence. Blaze could feel the tension in air that roped them together getting thicker by the minute.

"Attack you…" Blaze mulled. "So, you're on the run right now?"

"Considering that we beat a head unconscious, yes," Neal retorted.

Blaze twitched. They would come after them any minute. Her mind went on autopilot.

"Destroy the keys," she commanded. Neal took both keys and smashed them against the ground, shattering them into metallic fragments. "Redirect the lasers so their key can't unlock the door. That should buy us enough time." Opal grabbed several books while Neal used his security clearance to open the locking mechanism. While they worked together to deflect the lasers off of book covers, Blaze went scouring through the piles to find anything relative to Opal's situation, scanning the texts as fast as was humanly possible. Her mind was a twister of thoughts. Blaze had bent the rules before, but never did it warrant this type of reaction. The heads were trying to intentionally sabotage their efforts. Granted that Opal was under suspicion of murder but what major harm would have come from their communication? Blaze narrowed it down to the possibility of her try to play it in favour of her friend, or her assisting Opal in escaping. The latter of which, was now true. A sudden jolt went through her as she doubled over in pain, dropping the manuscript in her hand. *Ambush*, Darkfire's voice resonated in her head. *No*, Blaze thought desperately. He should have been safe with Scarlett. No one else except for Azura and Opal knew that he existed. The day she got her hands on the bastard that dared harm her horse… she grimaced. Opal was at her side in an instant, holding her up.

"Blaze!"

"Darkfire..." Blaze managed before wincing again. She felt her horse's anguish and fear spiked through the blood in her veins. Opal was trying to tell her something. Blaze could see the concern written all over her face but couldn't hear her over the thrum of adrenaline rushing through her ears. Her mind struggled against the panic. She took a shaky breath and yelled, letting her fire flow through her. She brought back every dark memory, impulse and fear to fuel her flames. The darkness in her responded, sending a twisted chill through her body as it embraced it. She was emotionally compatible with Darkfire now, and she willed him back to her. *Return as my dark fire.* She felt her scars light and Opal let go. Black flames wound down her arm just like her whip did, but these flowed off of her fingers, creating a burning cloud of smoke in front of her. She held on as his form began to appear amidst the smoky shroud. Once Blaze saw the wisps of his blue fire mane she let go, dropping in exhaustion. She had willed him to come through as energy, as fire, to bring him to safety. Despite that, she had pulled him through as his true form and every piece of darkness she had unburied burned her soul, metaphorically speaking. The strain of it was causing her physical weakness, but the mental scars it brought back stung more. It hurt to remember. Blaze knew that more than she'd like to admit.

She felt Darkfire's muzzle against her, feeling the horse's distress as he nuzzled her face. She pushed herself up on her knees and let out a rattling cough. The ground around them was charred black and grey. Opal and Neal kept a safe distance, wary of Darkfire's incinerating heat. She looped her arms around his neck and he pulled her up gently until she could hold onto his back.

"Neal, Opal!" She pointed to the pile of books she had made. "We need to get those out of here."

"There's too many!" Opal said. She had gone over to collect the books but could only get six or seven in her arms. Neal was collecting them too but couldn't achieve much more.

"Teleportation spell!" Neal exclaimed. Blaze shook her head.

"No, the price for that is to leave someone behind, it's not worth it!"

"If we don't do something all of us will stay behind, and get caught!" Neal shot back at her.

Leave me Blaze, Darkfire urged in her mind.

"No. Not after what I did to get you here."

You can summon me again.

Blaze didn't respond to him. Darkfire was silent for a moment, and bowed his head.

I'm sorry I hurt you. I understand.

"It was my decision. I took the chance and accepted the consequences that came with bringing you here. But I won't suffer for it again if I don't have to."

Can we afford to do that?

"Until further notice, yes."

"Blaze!" Opal called. "Look." Opal pointed to a small band of soldiers marching down the pathway. Jay, Maya and a beaten Jackson were making their way down to the Seal. Behind them marched the *jaculus aspis,* the five elite fighters of Myra, each specialized in a different style of battle. Literally, their name translated to viper snakes, because they fought and lashed out like them. Quick and deadly. Their symbolic golden snakehead shone on the sleeves of their uniforms. Blaze felt a small twang of apprehension. She was the most confident in combat but even she couldn't take on five of them. Even one was a tough match.

"The *jaculus,*" Neal seethed. Opal also frowned. Generally speaking, they were the most hated group in Myra. While Blaze admired their skill, they used it to oppress others. Somehow, they thought being a *bellator* entitled them to superiority. Just because if they could protect others, they could harm them too. Since Blaze was also a respected warrior they didn't bother her, but on several occasions, she had to stop them from ganging up on innocent people. They were powerful and they knew it. Just like she did. It sickened her to think that she was like them in any way, but she had been told multiple times that she would have fit right in. She pushed the revolting idea to the back of her mind and tried to collect her thoughts.

She watched Reed, their archery expert, lift his bow and fire. The first arrow hit the door with a light thud and then calmly dissipated into ash without so much as a scratch. He fired again, this time nailing the lock straight on.

"No!" Neal scrambled over to the door to close the mechanism. Without the glass casing the arrows would burn through the clasps.

A third one struck its target, sending Neal flying backwards. The lock snapped and lay in sizzling heap on the marble floor.

"Shit!" Blaze exclaimed.

"Took the words right out of my mouth," Opal mumbled.

Opal ran over and yanked Neal up. He winced, but didn't complain. They both stood beside Blaze. She could feel her friends' fear and anxiety. She looked at them both.

"I'll hold them off. You guys take Darkfire and as many books as you can and go." She mumbled a quick chant and Darkfire's flames minimized.

"He can't burn you now. Hurry! That will only last for a little while, so go!"

Before they could protest, Blaze pushed them onto his back.

"Blaze don't…" Opal's voice died as Darkfire smashed the door with his hooves and took off. Maya and Jay had to dive to either side of him to avoid being stampeded. Blaze whipped out her throwing knife and dagger. The first *jaculus* charged at Blaze, metal whips at her side. She lashed out and Blaze barely had time to deflect the slash off of her face before the other whip came and wrapped around her arm, yanking Blaze forward. The *jaculus* had a gloating smile on her face as she roped Blaze in. As soon as she was close enough Blaze slashed upwards to force her back and then dropped to kick her legs out from under her. Blaze pinned her down, delivering a punch to her face. They went back and forth until Blaze felt someone kick her side, sending her sprawling. *Combat expert,* Blaze thought weakly. She rolled over quickly, avoiding a jab to the throat and flipped herself up and kneed him in the stomach. In the distance, she heard Darkfire's distraught neigh.

She grabbed the *jaculus* by the collar and slammed him into the ground. Out of her peripheral vision she could see the heads going through the books and Neal and Opal fighting the metal whip master and the sword fighter, trying to shield Darkfire. Blaze went back and forth with her *jaculus.* She nailed him with a jab in the eyes and as he reeled back she tackled him to the edge of the pathway. Without a second thought she spin kicked him in the chest, sending him tumbling over into the Dias.

Blaze looked around wildly. Her eyes landed on a dark red patch on Darkfire's side. A wound. An arrow wound. *Reed,* she fumed. Nobody messed with her loved ones. No one. A cold, cruel detachment came over her. She felt her fiery whip ignite and surge power through her. The white-hot flames coiled down her arm. Her darkness ran like oil through her blood, the wickedness waiting for a spark of her anger or pain to ignite and grow beyond her control.

She lashed out, hearing the whip master scream as it latched onto her leg. Blaze's vision became tinged with red. She flicked her wrist and sent the *jaculus* flying into the back wall of the Seal. The heads turned to look and backed up in fright. Blaze couldn't tell what they felt, since the feelings were directed towards her, but she knew fear when she saw it. Her eyes landed on Reed, who had another arrow notched at Darkfire. Blaze's flames were around him in a flash, as she watched him screech from the burns. Neal grabbed her non-burning arm.

"Blaze, stop!" his words just echoed off her. Reed would pay. They all would. She would make them suffer for it. The darkness was pulling at her and she was more tempted to let it take over.

Neal swung around in front of her, forcing her to look at him. Her whip let go of Reed who dropped and withered in pain on the ground. Neal took a breath and wrapped her in a tight hug. Her anger flared for a moment and then was tugged down. It flared again and then calmed again. She felt Neal's heartbeat pulse against hers until they synchronized. *He's pulling my anger into him.* She realized. She tried to push him away. Neal held on tighter.

"Come on Blaze..." he said with a strained voice. Blaze felt her flames extinguish as she slumped down, exhaustion taking over her. The heads all looked at her in terror.

"You... you're a slave to darkness?" Maya asked in disbelief. Blaze was too winded to respond. Opal was still engaged with the sword fighter. She was blur but he knew his stuff as he pushed her back and deflected her blows.

"Kill her," Jackson commanded the remaining *jaculus*. Blaze and Neal were still kneeling, holding onto each other. The last one was a knife master like she was. He prepared to throw his first. Darkfire leaped in front of her, kicking the knife out of midair. He sneered.

"Your little pet can die first." The knife left his fingertips a millisecond before a wave of water hit, sending the knife clattering down beside Blaze. Two huge waves roared up from either side of the pathway, towering over all of them. They smashed down, sweeping away the heads and the *jaculus*. Blaze watch them fall into the Dias. Their shrieks were lost in the wind as they disappeared into the water. Blaze lifted her head slowly, looking into a pair of familiar golden eyes. Storm helped her up with one hand while bringing Opal back up onto the pathway with a wave using her other. It bent and obeyed every twitch of her fingers.

"How..." Neal started.

"Later," she said. "Let's go." She ran to the marble platform with all the books and began to move. The marble twisted to her command and began to break off the glass platform. Blaze jumped onto Darkfire's back and pulled Neal and Opal up with her. Darkfire took off and jumped onto the marble platform.

"Hold on!" Storm yelled over the wind. They all knelt together in the middle against Darkfire's body as Storm broke the marble out and raised a wave to lower them into the river. They fell quickly as the water could only cushion their fall so much. They hit the river with a splash, drenching them all. Storm created a current to push them forward. They sped off into the distance, with only the dying sun to light their way as the Seal lay destroyed behind them.

☙

Storm guided the platform to a grassy bank outside of the city limits. Blaze recognized the spire that towered over them. This was the same spire she had brought Jett, Adam and Mavis on when they first arrived in the chasm. She had taken quite the enjoyment in their shock and astonishment. The memory seemed so distant now. They all stumbled into the grove, their clothes sticking to them as they struggled to move into the protection of the trees. They all stood shivering. Blaze began mumbling under her breath.

"Jal-lo," Darkfire's flames heated and flared on full blast. Everyone else jumped back due to the intensity, but their clothes dried within seconds.

"Thanks," Opal said. Blaze nodded at her and turned to Neal and Storm.

"Books first everyone. We have to get them. Neal, Opal, start bringing them here. Storm, can you make us an earthen tent?" Storm frowned.

"The earth here is very loose, mostly fine dirt. There's no rock or anything. I would have to hold it together."

"Leave that to me."

"Okay Blaze." Storm set her stance and breathed in. She pulled her arms up and streams of dirt shot up and followed her hands, patching together a domed tent.

"I can't hold this for long," Storm said. Blaze motioned for Darkfire to follow her. She put one hand in Darkfire's mane and the other on the wall. "*Masbooth*," Blaze commanded. Blue flames licked up the walls and in a flash the earth had been baked into solid clay.

"You can let go now Storm." Storm gave her friend an impressed smile.

"I assume that's clay?"

"Yeah. They won't be able to track us so long as we're in this. They'll be looking for traces of black magic and the earth will mask anything of the sort for the time being." Neal and Opal had brought in the last of the books.

"They're all pretty soaked," Opal informed them. Blaze pointed two fingers at the ground and said, "*Aag.*" A small white flame of fire started in the middle of the tent. Neal shook his head.

"This is most magic I've seen used in my lifetime. Is it safe to be drawing from it so much?"

"This is nothing," Blaze informed him. "These are small feats, small enough so they remain untraceable. Don't worry though, I won't use more than what's necessary. We all need to talk, but first everyone get some rest. I'm going to send a few messages." Her friends didn't bother arguing with her. They all lay down around the fire and shut their eyes. Blaze walked out of the tent with Darkfire trotting behind her.

Master...

"Don't call me that," Blaze said. They walked back to where the marble platform drifted in the water. Blaze nodded at her horse. Darkfire used his rear legs to kick the platform into the rapids. It traveled swiftly downstream and out of their sight.

Blaze...

"In a moment Darkfire, I need to focus." They were standing on the layer of *ankh* that bordered the Dias here. Blaze knelt and pictured Azura and

Scarlett. She had a screenshot of her location in her mind. The *ankh* quickly glowed orange and winked out just as fast.

"What is it Darkfire?"

There is something eerily familiar about the dark residue that radiates from Opal. I think one of your memories is trying to link to it.

Blaze raised an eyebrow at him, "Let's see." She looked into Darkfire's eyes while placing her hand on his forehead. Their thoughts began to merge and flow as one. Blaze saw his time with Scarlett and the arrow that hit his side. She stole through more recent memories and found the energy pattern that Darkfire sensed around Opal. Now she dove into her own mind, trying to make a match with one of her memories. She felt a small pulse, but it vanished too quickly. She went through her memories again, slowing down this time. An image of the Chronicles, after Storm had almost fainted trying to save it, flashed before her eyes. She saw herself stick the dagger under Jett's chin. The energy pattern matched the one that had pulsed through the Chronicles the day of the earthquake. The day Joe and Mavis had gone missing. Blaze broke off the connection with a gasp.

It seems that the same person who influenced Opal also caused the earthquake. Their situations seemed to be linked.

"It doesn't make sense though. How does an earthquake that caused two people to disappear be linked with a murder?"

No spell I know of requires anything of the sort. Perhaps the books will provide more guidance. An image of Joe tugged at her mind. Blaze pushed it away.

It's okay Blaze. He is a source of your fire too. Not like me who feeds off darkness. He provides you with life's flame, the one that keeps you going. The warmth that surrounds your otherwise hardened heart.

"I don't need anyone to keep going. My own willpower is enough for that."

It may be for now. But life calls to life. You cannot ignore that. Lo…

"Don't."

You are human Blaze. Therefore, you feel. It is not possible for you not to.

Blaze sighed. Darkfire was a part of her, so it was like arguing with her own conscience. She would have made the same argument in her mind. She had quite enough of this for now.

Darkfire's laughter echoed through her mind. *As you wish.*

Blaze's ears picked up a rustle. She swung around with her knife ready and the point of dagger landed a centimeter away from Scarlett's throat.

"I come in peace," she said holding her hands up in surrender. Blaze sheathed her blade.

"Good, you got my message."

"So did I." The voice came from the far edge of the grove. Azura stepped forward with Jett, Adam and Jen trailing behind her.

"Why did you bring them?" Blaze asked.

"They city has been evacuated Blaze. It's not like another healer was available to look over them. I couldn't leave them. Besides, I got enough food to last us awhile." She opened her over the shoulder bag to reveal tons of canned food, wrapped sandwiches and water. Blaze's stomach grumbled, reminding her that she hadn't eaten since this morning, and now the stars were out.

"Thanks for thinking ahead."

"You're welcome. I know you put things like your personal health on the back burner a lot,"

Blaze half-smiled.

"Is that… a flaming horse?" Jett asked, astounded. Blaze looked at him incredulously.

"What else does it look like? A firework?"

"Sorry I asked," Jett mumbled.

"Well then, everybody it's time to get some sleep. We'll talk in the morning."

They all nodded and went into the tent, leaving Blaze and Darkfire alone.

Was he worth saving? Darkfire inquired. Blaze sighed sadly and stroked his back.

"I don't know Darkfire. I don't know."

❧

Jay sat in his appointed seat around the heads' discussion table. Maya and Jackson sat with him, as did three out of the five *jaculus* warriors. The other two who had been burned by Blaze's whip had been immediately sent to the evacuation location where healers could treat them. After dragging themselves out of the Dias, they had only seen the edge of the platform as it disappeared in the distance. Jay had not even seen who had hit them. None of them had. There were several *huria*, naturalists, in Myra and Blaze was linked to many of them. He, for the first time, had truly felt fear while watching her today. Even as his student he had felt threatened by her skill and attitude. He always pushed her down harder than others and she kept leaping back up and hitting just as hard. He was, in a way, responsible for her frighteningly advanced skill. The fact did not console him. He may have taught her, but she had learned from more experts than just him. But today, when her eyes lit up with demonic flame and her whip was burning Reed, he had felt truly afraid. There were waves and waves of darkness that radiated off of her. He had never known that she was a slave to the very black magic her father used to teach about. She was an imminent danger to everyone. He could tell she was losing control with Reed. If it weren't for Neal she would have killed him. There was no telling what Blaze would do next, especially since she helped a murderer escape. The other heads shared his sentiment.

"Jay," Maya said. "Have you ever had any idea about the darkness that possesses Blaze?"

Jay shook his head. "If I did, I would have said something years ago."

Maya looked around the table.

"Any idea how she happened to come across it?"

"Dark magic is normally forced onto someone Maya. No one in the right mind asks for it. Blaze may have had something happen to her that we don't know about," Jay pointed out.

"That is the general consensus Jay, but there are exceptions; people can obtain dark magic willingly. It provides immense power," Jackson said. He was massaging the back of his head where he had been hit in Opal's cell.

"He's right Jay," Maya said. "If there was some kind of forced incident we would have felt it right away. If it is taken willingly, it can be masked."

"Blaze did not always live here, Maya. It could have happened beforehand," Jay reminded her.

"For argument's sake let's say it was forced on her. Why wouldn't she have told anyone? Her own father was an expert on the subject and there are ways to remove it. If anyone would have known how, it would have been him."

"I don't claim to know her motives Maya. All I'm saying is that there's probably more to the story than we think."

"Either way," Jackson began, "she's used her darkness against us and is now on the run with a wanted criminal. She has to be stopped."

"I agree," Jay said. "But let's think rationally here. She's an intelligent girl and will be ready for most of the moves we could think of. I don't know where that horse came from either. We will need a solid plan. Something that will catch her by surprise. Blaze is a general in our army. She knows strategy and she knows how to attack. That being said, she will also know how to defend well. Too well. We can't use our normal approach to deal with her." Jackson turned to the *jaculus*.

"Bring up all records of Blaze Darkfire and her family and friends. Check the stables for missing horses. If she has a weakness, we're going to find it." They bowed and left the room.

"Be prepared everyone," Jackson said. "We're going on a demon hunt."

ॐ

Neal watched Blaze lay back against the curved wall of the dome, her gaze resting on the fire as it flickered and sparked while her friends slept. It cast long shadows on her face and her sombre expression made her seem much older than she was. The rage he had taken from her earlier had dissipated, but at that moment he had felt what she was feeling, and he had wanted to kill someone too. He shuddered at the thought. Blaze had to live with that gnawing urge every single day.

He got up and went to sit next to her, casually throwing his arm around her shoulder. He felt her shoulders tense and then relax as she leaned into him. Blaze always had that reaction to someone touching her. It was like she was always ready to nail someone if they tried anything. She wasn't comfortable enough with anyone to not have that wall of defense pop up, even with the lightest brush of the fingertips. Being this close to her took a good portion of Neal's courage. Even though he had done this God knows how many times before, every time a twang of fear shot through him. It was like holding a scorpion. She could attack for no reason or leave him in peace if he didn't push her. She didn't seem lethal right now, so he took it as an encouraging sign.

"I hate you," she said in a low voice.

"You're welcome, honey," he retorted. "Thanks to me you didn't kill someone."

"Not what I meant. But yes, I suppose I'm grateful for that. I hate you for taking my anger. It could have consumed you."

"I've been dealing with my own darkness long enough to understand how much I can handle."

"I'm poisoned by some powerful maleficence Neal. You might as well be an angel compared to me." Neal was silent for a moment. Blaze was right. Her pull was nothing like what he had experienced before.

"How did it happen?" The iciness in Blaze's eyes made him sorry he asked. She turned to look at the fire and didn't say a word. Neal sighed.

"I was sixteen," Neal said. Blaze's gaze didn't waver from the flames. "I didn't know how much they wanted my brother."

Blaze looked down. "Marcus," she said.

"Yeah, Marcus."

"Is he still alive?"

"I don't know. You know how it goes with the *jaculus* recruiting. When we were on the run from them we split up and I ended up trespassing on a *yue-jung's* territory. He 'punished' me. That's how I got this." Neal took Blaze's hand gently and squeezed it. Blaze could feel his dark urges pulling at her from under his skin. The same sense of wrongness and anguish, but it was much weaker than her own. "I woke up alone and never saw Marcus after that. My sisters found me and brought me back to Myra quietly so I could heal."

"A *yue-jung*? They still exist?" Blaze questioned. The *yue-jung* were an ancient lineage of Myra's people specializing in stealth magic. They were ghost-like and mysterious, with varying additional abilities. Like *permotionem*, modern day Myra assumed they had died out.

"Only one I've ever seen and that was in the northern edges of the chasm. I don't know if he's still around. I don't want to find out." They sat in silence for a while.

"I'm sorry about Marcus," Blaze mumbled. Neal sighed.

"I know he escaped the *jaculus*. That's enough to keep me going for now. So long as he's out of their clutches, I can live with myself." Blaze was quiet for a moment. Another vile aspect of the *jaculus* was that when they found someone they wanted to join their ranks, they would have them by any means necessary. They would threaten, oppress and blackmail *bellators* into joining them if they refused. Blaze remembered when they had wanted her join. The only reason she escaped them was because she had nothing to lose. They didn't have anything they could threaten her with. She didn't fear death and had no family to be held for ransom. She remembered one of them holding the knife to her throat, and Blaze had laughed. Cold, menacing, laughter. *Do it*, she had taunted them. *If I'm going to Hell I might as well take you with me.* She had then ripped the knife out of the *jaculus's* hand and aimed the tip over his heart. *You can't break me and you can't beat me, and that's why you want me; because I am unstoppable. Because I scare you, and believe me, I know it.* Blaze let the memory settle at the back of her mind. Becoming one of the *jaculus* used to be one of the highest honours in Myra. It had now degraded to the point where new members had to be forced into loyalty. It was a long way to fall.

"Why are you telling me this?" Blaze asked. Neal didn't respond. Absentmindedly, he traced a pattern on the back of Blaze's hand with his thumb. He could see the angry red scratches and cuts that ran down her arms. His other hand was only a few inches away from her scars. The ones that could summon demon flame.

"Today, I felt a fraction of what you fight with daily. I know you won't tell me your story. You never tell anyone. Still, I want you to know that I get it. It's excruciating to bear that kind of experience alone. You're not the only one."

Blaze resumed eyeing the fire. "That's where you're wrong Neal. I am alone." He raised his eyebrows in surprise. "I took the darkness willingly. Yours was forced on you," she said quietly.

Neal's heart tightened in his chest. *Willingly?!*

"I can feel your disbelief Neal. Like you said, I won't tell you my story. You were right about that. It's better that you don't ask. But don't assure me that you know what it's like. Because you don't. You never will. No one will."

"If you took it willingly, you brought it on yourself. I would have no sympathy for you. You know the consequences of magic."

"Better than you, that's for sure. So, you should realize something. I wouldn't have done it if I didn't have to."

Neal shook his head. "The price for your level…"

"Is one I'm still paying," Blaze said sadly. Neal didn't know what to feel about Blaze right now. It was one thing to have darkness forced on you. It was another to take it willingly. Whatever situation Blaze was in, must have been dire for her to pull such a reckless move. He didn't believe any situation justified doing that.

"The line between good and bad is a blurred one Neal."

Neal tipped his fedora at her. It had somehow managed to wash up with them on the shore of the Dias.

"You're a ticking time bomb you know that?"

"Yeah," Blaze agreed. "I do."

℃℈

Azura woke up to smell of eggs and toast. Adam had started to prepare breakfast over the fire, cooking the eggs on a tin plate she had brought. He was focused and engrossed with the task at hand, for the most part anyways. She watched his eyes periodically flick up to look at a sleeping Blaze, who was curled up on her side, and back down to the food. From here she couldn't tell if he was looking at her with disdain or fascination. Azura assumed he was staring because Blaze looked young, vulnerable and innocent when she was sleeping. It was the only time she was unguarded and would have a peaceful look on her face. Neal was asleep beside her, his fedora covering most of his face and one hand on his stomach. Azura silently admired his sculpted face. High cheek bones and a sharp jawline brought a unique definition to him. His long, lanky form seemed to match his personality. Relaxed and carefree and at the same time sly and mysterious. Neal's body structure gave him the ability to do just that. He was tall and flexible, and due to his slender frame, he could disappear easily. Azura hated it when he pulled that on her. Vanishing into thin air when she was arguing with him was quite rude she felt. Yet she was drawn to him. His carefree attitude was infectious. She craved it more lately. It was probably due to the fact that in her profession, she had to be serious all the time. You couldn't exactly joke around and laugh when you were trying to stitch a wound closed, or consoling someone after their loved one had died. Such were the joys of being a healer. She was sure

131

mundane doctors shared her struggles. Though most were probably much older that she was.

She wondered what Opal had done for Neal that would have caused him to help without payment. Neal was talented and he knew it. As a result, he made sure he was compensated accordingly. A free favour was rare. She made a mental note to ask Opal later. His smooth, dark skin had a subtle shine to it in the flicker of the firelight. His white shirt was torn and tattered from the hem and his jeans were covered in a smattering of marble dust, making him appear like a chiselled statue.

"Hope you like eggs." Adam handed her the tin plate.

"You should eat, you'll need your strength." Azura pushed the plate back towards him.

"Could you stop being a healer for a bit and worry about yourself? You're going to need your strength too."

Azura was taken aback.

"Adam…" He shoved a forkful in her mouth before she could protest.

"You worry too much about us." Azura was still chewing so she couldn't respond but gave him a supportive pat on the back.

"It's my job," she said after swallowing.

"Then you're never off duty. We only know you as our healer. Not as a person. You've done so much for us. Can we not at least be friends?" Adam had the next forkful ready in his hand. Azura gave him a pained look. She leaned back on her hands, letting the soft jade grass interlace with her fingers while staring up at the terracotta dome above.

"No."

"We can't be friends?" Adam's question was laced with a mix of confusion and slight offense.

"Adam, healers never make any kind of emotional attachment with their patients. It gets in the way of proper healing, which requires a neutral state of mind. Besides, if we did, I might have gone insane with grief by now according to the number of deaths I've seen. If I hated you, I wouldn't want to heal you, and if I loved you I would be too afraid of making a mistake. Therefore, no emotions whatsoever."

"You healed Blaze and Opal before."

"Those are small exploits that can be done in any given situation. I tend to rely more on my medicines for my friends anyways. But, if it came down to a serious injury, I could not help them. My feelings would cloud my judgement and my healing would be unstable." Adam pondered that for minute.

"Well Jett is basically healed now." Adam poked his eggs as he spoke.

"Thanks to Blaze," Azura chimed in.

"Still don't know how to feel about that, but yeah. So, we're no longer your patients. Can we start over?" He stuck out his hand. "Hi, I'm Adam. I go to culinary school in Toronto, Canada. I have no idea what I'm doing here and why I'm still around. But out of this entire whack job of a situation I got to meet a really cool healer. Want to be friends?" Azura took his hand and shook it, amused by his gesture.

"Do you start all your introductions that way?"

"I've altered them slightly to accommodate my current circumstances."

"It's a start." Azura got to her feet and stretched. "I'm going to wake Opal. She'll sleep straight through the day if I don't." Azura had just turned when Storm pushed her from the side, sending her flying face first into the ground.

"What the..." the words died on her lips as she saw what Storm was shielding her from. Staring down at Storm was a massive wolf. Its fur shone with a whitish-blue hue, like a blistering-hot star in the emptiness of space. It was more blue than white, giving it an unearthly guise, its gleaming cerulean irises glowing like pulsars. It was cold, intelligent and possibly murderous as it stood with regal beauty and a predatory stance. Gleaming white fangs flashed between its jaws, ready to bite anyone of them in half. Azura didn't understand how it got inside; Storm and Blaze had sealed the entrance last night. After hearing Azura's thud against the ground, everyone suddenly was up and alert. Storm held out one hand, a signal for no one to move.

"Scarlett," Storm said softly, "What does it want?"

"I can answer that," Jen stood up a nodded at the wolf. "I summoned her."

CHAPTER 10
Temptation

MAVIS WAS STARTING TO LOSE HER PATIENCE WITH THE VOICE. IT HAD gone silent a while ago and she could no longer call on it, even though she still had million questions and some colourful insults for it. She had to find Adam and Jett. They would be able to help her, but she had no way of contacting them and leaving this infernal place. The white marble shone beneath her feet. The room was large enough to host a regulation rugby match, while the bloodshot ceiling sparkled about two hundred feet overhead. A design had been patched into the marble with rose-gold stone, forming the same symbol that the blood had formed on the wall before she fell through. The thought made her shudder. She didn't know whose blood it was, or how she had obtained it the first place. She had wanted to retch when she realized what the vial was holding but couldn't control her own limbs. The voice had taken over and the words had flowed over her like honey, smooth, sweet and perilous. How did you fight something that was in your mind? She had considered knocking herself out cold, but passing out would probably do her more harm than the voice. More of her memories had patched together but the crucial puzzle pieces were still omitted. Like why she was here, what deal had she made, how she got here and why she was listening to a voice in her head. She leaned her head back against the wall and shut her eyes. Jett and Adam were probably frantically searching for her right now. All she wanted to do was get out but what would she do then? Mavis didn't know the area and had nothing but the clothes on her back with her. The voice had answers, and she wanted them, so she was biding her time.

Her hands were white at the knuckles and dry from the heat in the cavern. She had been counting the lines on her palms to pass the time. Suddenly a small pulse went through her, an indication that the voice had returned to invade her mind.

"I want answers!" Mavis demanded. She could feel the tremble in own her voice.

I suppose you do. You have been obedient.

"*Didn't* have much choice in the matter."

Oh, but you did Mavis. If you truly wanted to resist me you could have. But your clouded memories call out to your subconscious. You wanted this to happen. I am only trying to help you.

Before Mavis could consider running head first into a wall to end her misery, the voice's laughter echoed through her skull.

As you wish. Prepare yourself. Conmemini!

Mavis sunk to her knees as a powerful warmth flooded through her. A whirlwind of images raced before her eyes, disappearing within seconds into a flash of white. Her hands were clenched into fists and she was heaving for air when she opened her eyes. Her strength returned slowly and she rose up, blinking at her surroundings. All of the memories had snapped into place, forming a complete picture.

Now then. Are you ready to proceed?

Mavis followed the intricate stone pattern on the floor around the room. She held back the tears that had begun to form at the corner of her eyes.

"I want... I *need* them back. Jett, Adam..."

It's difficult Mavis. To watch yourself lose the ones you love. To be unable to protect them. Don't lose hope, they will come to you.

"How can you guarantee that?"

I will make sure they are sent on their way. I have very persuasive connections that will push them in the right direction.

"Very well. I'd like to be left alone now." Mavis felt the connection sever, like a snap that left her thoughts alone. She could think only of the twins. Her heart ached so badly that it was causing her physical agony.

"We'll be together again," Mavis whispered tearfully, "I promise."

☙

"You summoned a wolf?" Blaze was ready with her dagger in hand, not taking her gaze off of the beast. Jett had woken up, petrified to see a colossal canine looming in front of Storm. The wolf was majestic and terrifying as its tail swished behind it patiently. Jett got the feeling it was waiting for something or someone, probably Jen, to give it instructions. "Could have given us a warning."

"I summoned her in my dreams a little while ago and didn't have enough time to exit the dream phase to wake up and tell you."

"You can do that?" Jett inquired.

"I am a *hyponos*. It's within my realm of power." *Dream stretcher. Right,* Jett thought. She nodded at the wolf. It came by and nuzzled her hand, rubbing against her affectionately. It sat down with her and lay quietly while Jen stroked its fur. Blaze frowned.

"Wolves are not that friendly, not even to their masters."

"I freed her from torment, Blaze. You and Scarlett understand the exceptional bond with your animals. He is my Darkfire, so to speak."

"I highly doubt that."

"Doesn't matter. She's a free wolf but will always return to me and is at my service as thanks for saving her." The wolf whined.

"She-wolf. Leader of a pack." The girl addressed as Scarlett moved closer to her. The wolf snarled initially but then become docile when Scarlett approached. Jett watched with captivation. She could talk to animals? While the ability in itself was pretty awesome, Jett wasn't sure he wanted to know what a hundred and twenty-kilogram predator had to say. Scarlett scratched it behind the ear and stared into its hypnotizing, glowing irises. A series of grunts, growls and whines came from the wolf. Scarlett listened intently, brushing her long black hair off to one side to hear clearly.

"Wolves are great trackers. Fang here is a great huntress, she'll be able to locate Mavis and Joe." Jen continued to comb through the wolf's fur with her hand. Scarlett shot her a sideways glance.

"Fang is a short form, isn't it?"

"Yeah," Jen replied. "She probably introduced herself as *Odiv Sun-konyee*" Scarlett nodded.

"Ice Fang."

Jen seemed mildly surprised.

"You know Korean?"

"No, but I can interpret wolf. She told me." Fang's glowing eyes seemed to be everywhere at once, enveloping everyone in a transfixing stare.

"Blaze, you might want to keep your distance from Fang," Scarlett advised. Jett turned his head in confusion. Why would she have to stay away? If this thing went feral, Blaze was probably their best chance at besting the beast. Blaze just nodded.

"Duly noted," she said. Blaze's flaming stallion flicked its tail uneasily. Jett didn't blame him, since Fang looked like she could bite the doors off a car without breaking a sweat. Then again, he didn't think Fang was eager to get a mouthful of horsehair infernos either. Blaze shifted her attention to Jett, nailing him down with her eyes, gleaming like two glossy pools of shadow. It was enticing and horrifying to watch her watch him. Her expression was sombre and calculating, as if she was formulating a battle plan in her head. Storm stepped between Fang and Blaze.

"How about we discuss this after breakfast?" The suggestion was welcomed by Jett's rumbling stomach.

"Control your dog Jen," Blaze warned. "Or I'll be the first to cut her down." Fang growled at her and then yelped as a knife flew by her ear. Jett had barely seen it leave Blaze's fingertips. It lodged itself in the dome wall right behind Jen. Jett was amazed that she had managed to not hit Storm, who was still between them.

"That was a warning for your mutt. The next one won't miss." Jen mumbled to Fang and the wolf bowed in reluctant submission, snarling. Jen's expression was hard and cold, watching Blaze with contempt. As much as Jett hated seeing Jen upset, he was secretly grateful that Blaze had the courage to declare her strength over a wild animal in close quarters.

Breakfast was eaten half-heartedly as everyone talked in groups of two or three. Jett spent his time with a fuming Jen, trying to get friendly with Fang while Adam and Azura chatted away beside them. Scarlett and Neal were swapping stories and while Storm and Opal brought each other up to speed. Blaze was on her own and apparently speaking to her horse. Jett would glance over occasionally and see her nod in acknowledgment or give a small smile like Darkfire was making a joke. Burning steed or not, Darkfire was a cool name and it suited Blaze to have her animal companion named as such, in Jett's opinion. Thankfully for Jett, Jen got over Blaze launching a blade at her wolf pretty quickly, and was guiding Jett on how to pet Fang properly. He did not have the nerve to try yet, but listened as she demonstrated. Fang showed him no hostility, but that was probably due to Jen relaxing her at the moment. Jett knew what it was like to have a knife thrown at him, so he could share in the canine's sentiment for being agitated.

"It seems everyone is refreshed and full now, so let get down to business," Azura said. She motioned Jen. "You may have what we need to find our two missing friends." She then turned to Blaze and pointed to the stack of books that were stacked by the fire. "And you have the means of finding out what plagued Opal, which we need to decipher immediately considering that we're all fugitives right now." Jett held up his hands.

"Wait what? Fugitives?" he asked.

"Long story," Opal said. "I'll explain later." Jett wanted to protest but the sullen bags under Opal's eyes kept him from inquiring further.

"First, we'll send Fang out to start tracking them and then work on figuring out Opal's situation," Storm said.

"They're linked," Blaze interjected.

"What?"

"Darkfire and I figured out that energy patterns that flowed off Opal matched the ones that pulsed through the Chronicles the day of the earthquake."

"How did you figure that out? How did you even sense it?" Jen asked.

"I'm very familiar with dark magic."

Jen frowned. Jett sighed. As if he needed another reason to fear Blaze. Not only could she murder him in cold blood, she might be able to magically draw all the air from his lungs if she so pleased.

"Practicing dark magic is forbidden, Jett, so you don't have to worry. I'll stick with my daggers." Jett cocked his eyebrow in annoyance. This mind reading thing was getting tiresome. "So, Kaitlin's murder has something to do with the disappearances?" Storm shook her head.

"More like vice versa."

"It means the caster would be the same," Blaze said, "and that they are using the same line of magic. Which is quite risky on their part."

"Hold up," Jett was more confused than ever. "There was a murder?"

Adam looked down. Jett caught it immediately.

"Adam, you knew about this?" Jett was surprised and a little hurt his twin hadn't mentioned something that big to him.

"You weren't in the right state of mind to hear that kind of news, Azura had just run into Blaze and told her that Opal had been arrested…"

"Opal killed her?!" Jett exclaimed. His head spun with a million questions and an intense hurricane of mixed emotions. Blaze had the nerve to look amused.

"Before Jett spontaneously combusts with questions, perhaps we should summarize the situation for him."

Opal and the man who introduced himself as Neal, gave a condensed version of what had happened and what their suspicions were. Jett locked gazes with Adam. They would have a long discussion later, but for now he tried to absorb as much of the information as he could. This entire time, Opal had been arrested, attacked, rescued and dumped into a river and he had been none the wiser. He was also alarmed with how much Blaze was a part of this as well. Neal was describing their fight at the bridge and Opal would jump in occasionally to express her admiration for Blaze's fighting skill. Blaze apparently kicked, punched and swung her way to Darkfire before Storm had shown up for the finishing blow. Jett could see the silent conversations between the members of the group, giving him the feel that they were hiding something or leaving details out. He didn't particularly care at the moment; they were getting the point across.

Once they were done overloading Jett's mind with recent events, all attention turned back to Blaze. Jett and Adam had a silent conversation, both of them acknowledging that they had to go along with whatever Azura did. While he didn't want to be in this mess, the twins couldn't be alone in Myra right now, especially with Mavis missing. They were deeply intertwined with this group, and they weren't about to escape any time soon.

"Let's get the search party started, and we can work on going though these books," Blaze said as she knelt in front of Jett. "Do you have anything of Mavis' that we could track her with? Something that would have touched her or have her smell on it."

"I do," Adam reached for a blue drawstring gym bag lying along the sidewall.

"This is Mavis' backpack. The one she wore into the chasm." Two identical bags, one green and the other orange, were beside it, reminding Jett that he had a pair of clean clothes that he had bought with him. He smiled, grateful he could change out of his hospital gown. Blaze took the bag and tossed it to Jen. Jen held it out for Fang to sniff. The wolf inspected it carefully, tracing her nose over the surface. After a few seconds, she barked.

"Your turn Blaze," Scarlett said, "She's asking for Joe's scent."

Blaze reached into one of the pockets on her cargo pants and pulled out a silver chain. She slowly walked over and held it out to Fang. In her hand glittered a necklace with a single dragonfly pendant. It was crafted from what looked like diamond, the light twinkling off of it as it shone like clear glass. Jen's eyes widened in surprise.

"There are no diamonds here... that thing must cost a fortune."

"Calm down princess," Blaze said. "It's moissanite, a lookalike to diamond. Not nearly as expensive." Jen was not pleased that Blaze had called her princess. At least that's what Jett picked up from her facial expression. Blaze cautiously snapped the chain around Fang's neck. Fang growled but didn't move.

"Joe will know that we sent her when he sees this, instead of trying to fight her." Blaze informed them.

"I didn't know Joe was into jewellery," Jett whispered to Azura. She looked at him like he was an idiot.

"He made it for her, not himself. Since he worked on it long enough, it would still have his scent on it. Enough for Fang to pick it up." Now Jett did feel like an idiot. Of course, the necklace was for Blaze. He had never seen her wear it, but maybe she wasn't sentimental about that kind of thing. Then again, it was conveniently in her pocket for Fang to track him with.

Jen nodded at Fang. "Storm, if you would be so kind," she said. Storm nodded and thrust her arm forward. An opening large enough for Fang to fit through was punched through one side of the dome. Fang bowed her head before turning to dart through the hole. Storm raised her hand and the earth crawled back up to seal the entrance behind her.

"Fang can find Mavis... right?" Jett asked. Jen put a consoling arm around him.

"If she's anywhere on this continent, Fang will. Don't worry."

Easier said than done, he thought.

"Time to do some research everyone." Blaze started distributing books to several of them. Jett was not surprised when he and Adam didn't receive any.

"I don't assume you'll be needing our help?" Jett said, miffed.

"Not unless you know how to read any other languages besides English."

Blaze had a point. All the covers were inscribed with Latin, Greek, Chinese and Arabic letters along with several others he didn't recognize.

"Wouldn't we not be able to read them anyway? Because of the whole knowledge tracking system?"

"These books are different from the ones in the Chronicles. They don't follow the same system and they can't be tracked. Anyone can read them, which is why they were so heavily guarded."

"Why can't they be tracked?"

"Because of this." Blaze turned the spine towards him, tracing a symbol that was printed near the top. It was a series of interlocking triangles that formed what looked like a ninja star. Azura and Opal also held theirs up, pointing to the identical symbol on their books.

"It's the symbol of black magic, sorcery or whatever you want to call it. It's there as warning, but also an image of power that prevents the books from being tracked, hidden or altered in anyway."

"So, you could draw that symbol on any book and it'd be untraceable?"

"Just drawing it isn't enough. There is some enchantment involved that I'd rather not explain to you right now." Blaze was clearly tiring from his insistent questions. He decided not to probe further.

"Then what are we supposed to do?" Jett asked. Glances were exchanged.

"Why don't you practice walking and running outside? You're not at a hundred percent yet. Adam will help you," Jen suggested.

"We can't let them go by themselves. The heads are after us as it is," Opal countered.

"I will," Storm said. She walked over to help them up. "I can't read anyway." Before everyone could protest she held up her hands. "I'll come back and provide my input on whatever findings you have later. Do a preliminary search without me."

"Okay… be careful," Opal advised. Storm nodded.

"Come on you two." Jett and Adam dutifully followed Storm into the grove outside.

❦

Once Storm had left with the twins, everyone got down to some serious reading. Since Jen knew several languages by working in the Chronicles all these years, she worked on dividing the books by their topics. Everyone had a few languages they could understand so they grabbed them accordingly. Blaze was thumbing through a Spanish manuscript, trying to find any mention of possession or unwarranted control. Opal and Azura worked on earthquakes while Scarlett and Neal searched for blue snakes. Blaze let out a sigh of frustration. All the texts that mentioned possession clearly stated that the one being possessed had to be awake in order for the spell to take hold. Opal had been asleep at the time, which didn't add up. It was infuriating. She tossed aside book after book.

"Blaze look at this," Scarlett plopped down next her with a large encyclopaedia written in Latin. An illustration of a cobalt serpent with lava red eyes stared back at her.

"That's not the same snake."

"I know, but it says here that they can appear in various shades of blue, and the smaller ones often take the shape of cobras. They can be summoned as part of a spell, to protect the caster or their companions while the magic is at work." They shared a silent moment of understanding.

"So that's what they were doing around Opal. They were protecting her while she was under possession." Blaze said.

"Yes. Unfortunately, the caster was using them to make sure no one interfered with their plan,"

Blaze pondered for a moment.

"Any particular spells they can be summoned with? Or can they be called upon with any?"

"According to this, they can only be summoned when the caster's magic is being split, when they are in a vulnerable state," Scarlett responded.

"Invoking two bewitchments at once? You need to have one hell of a power source or a godly amount of stamina." Blaze traced her fingers over the snake's body, the yellowing paper crinkling under her fingertips. "I'm afraid Jett was used to power them."

"Wouldn't he have felt something? You can't exactly take energy from people and not expect a reaction."

"And you can't control people when they're asleep but here it's happening anyway. I'm telling you, he was involved whether he knows it or not."

"If that's true, then what two spells were being cast? One was possession. The other couldn't be the earthquake, there was too much time in between."

Blaze tried to remember her dad's lessons on fuelling spells and maintaining their power. There had been tons of his research notes on the topic as well as several books in his personal library. She mentally grasped for something, anything that would ring a bell. Something clicked in Blaze's mind.

"Unless... the earthquake was being used to power the possession spell!" Scarlett gave her a confused frown. "Guys come here, I think I know how the situations are linked!" Blaze yelled. Her mind whirled as the group formed a circle around her. "These snakes can only be summoned when the caster's magic is split, which means two spells were being done. One was controlling Opal and the other was the earthquake, even though they didn't happen at the same time, they were still cast at the same time. Some spells require a warm up, or time to collect enough energy to be used. So, the caster did split their magic, but put in the majority of their strength into the earthquake, while feeding whatever was left to the possession spell as a power up. It wasn't enough obviously, so they set up so that when Mavis disappeared during the earthquake, Jett's emotions would be on an all-time high. Being as he is, he would have been the perfect target for someone trying to piggyback off of his feelings and provide the remaining power needed for possession. The sole purpose of Mavis disappearing was to get a rise out of him!" Blaze focused as the pieces fit together in her mind. "Still don't know how they did it while Opal was asleep or why Joe vanished as well. But with Jett being so emotional, he wouldn't have noticed a slow sapping of energy. He had also fallen heavily asleep afterward, which was probably from the exhaustion of the entire ordeal."

"So ..." Opal mused. "It's not Joe and Mavis they wanted, they just used them to get to Kaitlin. Their real goal must be something Kaitlin had or knew."

"Exactly. We were all so worried about the direct consequences of the earthquake we didn't consider it being a stepping stone to something else."

"That theory has holes in it," Azura closed the book in her lap. "It's the best one we've got though." Blaze was silently thankful for all her father's work on powering magic. *Some spells are like a car on a cold winter day*, he had told her. *They need time to warm up and generate heat before they can run. If they can't do it on their own, another car that's already running can give it some of its power to get it going. You know how the jumper cables work. The same kind of thing can apply to starting a spell or several spells.* Her father's eyes had lit up whenever he talked about the workings of magic and its properties. She could recall his smile, warm and loving as she would study alongside him. The memory faded as soon as it came. Blaze was relieved. She didn't want to be reminded of the family she no longer had.

☙

Storm listened for the sound of Jett's footsteps hitting the ground as she created obstacles for him to dodge. She pulled her arm in and thrust it towards him, sending a rock about a foot high for him to jump over. She felt his feet leave the grass and touch down again and she readied herself to send another his way. Storm vaguely remembered what the world looked like, but she had never had any trouble navigating it and building a picture of it in her mind. She had lost her sight at three or four years old, but her naturalist nature allowed her to sense earth and water and anything that was touching it. She was eternally grateful for that, as it allowed her to stay independent and self-reliant. She rarely felt the pain of her handicap, unless she wondered about what someone looked like, or mulled over the desire to witness a sunset. As Jett dodged her rocks, she slightly longed to know what he looked like. Her family had studied Jett's kind for centuries and she was the first to meet one in about five hundred years. She was sure he looked like a normal guy, and with the help of Azura and Blaze's descriptions she had formed a mental image in her mind. Still, she wanted to actually see Jett as he was, and not as a half-baked image in her head. She couldn't sulk about that now, she knew nothing good would come out of it. She created a beam out of dirt and commanded Jett to walk on it. Adam stood by his side, encouraging him. He mentioned Mavis a lot, which implied to her that Mavis was a great source of motivation for Jett. Why Blaze condemned their friendship, she didn't understand. Obviously, there was more that Blaze was aware of to make her say such a thing, but Storm was doubting her friend's instinct here. Blaze was usually dead on with her interpretation of people, but she had, on rare occasions, made mistakes. Storm was starting to think this would be one of those times.

Jett was a strong but unstable *permotionem* she had discovered. He had been able to give her his strength when she needed it but also burned Azura with some deadly marks that hadn't faded yet. She feared for him, knowing how naïve and inexperienced he was with his power. If word ever got out about him, there would be a line of savage magicians just waiting to use him for their own witchcraft. Myra was not without corruption, like any other country on the planet. Even though black magic was outlawed, there were always those who snuck under the radar to build their knowledge about it. They were there, watching and waiting, seeing what they could grab a hold of to work their spells. Blaze, on several occasions had tried to explain to the heads that outlawing magic all together was not a solution to the problem. If they banned it completely and someone went under the radar, they would have no idea how to stop them. In her words, to understand something was, in turn, knowing how to defeat it. You had to know how a spell worked in order to halt it. Yet, the heads had refused to lift the law. Storm understood why they didn't want to lift it, but at the same time, they did have the power to fashion it so only authorized individuals would be able to dabble in that kind of information. She knew Maya feared an abuse of power if someone was given privilege to those books. That is after all, how her daughter died.

Jett lost his footing on the beam and crashed into the ground.

"Ugh," he winced.

"Here, take my hand," Adam said.

"No, I'll get up on my own."

"Are you sure?" the uneasiness in his voice was clear.

"Yeah, give me a second." After a few grunts and groans, Jett stood back up on his feet.

"Do your legs still hurt?" Storm inquired.

"Not as much as they used to, but yeah after a while the ache comes back." Storm nodded in agreement.

"It will take some time. Lucky for you Blaze knocked two weeks off of your recovery by getting you to walk now." There was a moment of apprehensive silence.

"I guess she did," Jett said finally.

"Jett you're shaking." Storm could sense the vibrations through the ground. She pulled him down to sit beside her in the soft jade grass and put her hand in his. The tension in his palms was prominent as she intertwined her fingers with his. "What's bothering you?" She felt Adam sit down on the other side of Jett.

"Blaze I'm guessing? How she healed you?" Adam said as he nudged him. Jett sighed.

"Yeah. Not just that though. It's everything about her. How she brought us here, how she carried me to Azura, how she tried to kill me in order to get me on my feet again..." he paused. Storm gave his hand a small squeeze. "I just don't know what to feel about her. Part of me is furious at her, for dragging me here, putting me into this mess. If she didn't, Mavis may never have gone missing. Now at the same time, I feel so guilty for pegging her as a monster. I even said that to her when she was supposedly trying to throw a knife at me, while in reality she came to give me the one thing I wanted most. My ability to walk again. What was worse was that for the sake of me getting better, she agreed with every terrible thing I said. Then on the flip side, she blamed me for causing the earthquake. I just don't know what to *feel* anymore." He put his head in his hands.

"Jett," Storm began gently. "No one is perfect. You can't immediately paint someone as a villain or a hero, it doesn't work like that. Not everything Blaze did was right, but she did what she had to do. If she hadn't brought you here, and you kept exploring the chasm unmonitored, there are worse things that could have happened to you. All three of you may have been separated and subjected to God knows what else. Just like you lost Mavis, she lost Joe. Did you, for even a moment, think about how she was feeling? How she was coping with the pain? Even though lashing out at you on her part was wrong, you lashed out at Azura too. Then again, she would have never have tried to help you walk if Azura hadn't asked her. She did it as a favour to her. Everyone has their ups and downs."

"So basically, we're both awful," Jett mumbled.

"Everyone is awful sometimes. But you have to let that go. What's in the past, is in the past. Focus on the now. You can walk, and we have a top-notch huntress on the search for Mavis." Jett nodded.

"Storm!" Opal's voice resonated in her ears. "Get in here!"

"Do we have any development?"

"Major advancement. Now we've got to decide what to do next, and do it quickly."

"Why?"

"According to Neal's trackers, the heads' locator drones are getting close to homing in on us. The may not be able to detect magic, but a giant dirt tent will definitely catch their attention."

Storm helped Jett to his feet. She strode towards the tent, not noticing the twins standing frozen behind her.

❧

Jett found himself in a hazy trance. Everything around him was cloudy, with the exception of Adam who was standing beside him, sharing his confused look. He grabbed the disk around his neck nervously, fidgeting with the cord. He stared at the side with the flame stamped into it. It almost seemed like the metal was glowing. *That's strange*, he thought. A light flickered in front of them and a holographic image of a young Brazilian man slowly appeared. He was tanned and rugged, with sharp blue-grey eyes and dark brown hair. He wore an all-white suit, with the initials J.P. stitched on the chest pocket with black thread. He smiled at them warmly, putting Jett at ease.

"I assume you are Adam and Jett Davis?" The twins nodded in awe. Jett couldn't comprehend what was happening. Storm and Opal's voices seemed so far away. "Nice to finally meet you."

"Pardon me," Adam interrupted. "Who are you exactly?"

"Silly me, where are my manners? My name is Jackson. I am one of the heads of Myra." Heads… heads… Opal had said something about heads. Jett's head was cloudy and disoriented and couldn't grasp the details he was looking for. Adam straightened up.

"You're a head. You're hunting us right now."

Opal's warning clicked in Jett's mind and he backed away from the projection. Jackson shook his head.

"We are not hunting you right now. We are going after Opal Dystar and Blaze. You must know that Opal just committed a murder."

"She was framed… or possessed or something. She would never do something like that. They're trying to prove her innocent as we speak." Adam grabbed Jett's arm. Jett knew they had to leave but his legs didn't seem to want to move.

"Is that the story they told you? My boy, it was no accident. You see, Kaitlin Greens, who was murdered, had keys to the Seal. All those books your so-called friend have right now were stored there."

"They're using them to figure out what happened," Jett squeaked.

"On the contrary, they're diving into black magic, which is forbidden here. Give us your location, and we can save you from them."

"No. They have done nothing but help us. We don't betray our friends," Adam said adamantly.

"Then perhaps I should show you what your friends have been up to lately, and what they've been hiding from you." The image changed to an office in the Chronicles. The twins watched Opal strangle Kaitlin with a rusted chain and then collapse, the snakes dissolving alongside her. Jett's heart leapt into his throat.

"That was from our security footage, which is why we put out orders to arrest her," Jackson's voice narrated. "She also escaped from prison after knocking me unconscious." The video changed to show Opal striking Jackson across the face and hitting him with punch after punch. Jett didn't want to believe what he was seeing. Opal had told him that the head had attacked her. He didn't see any of that here.

"As for Blaze, she helped Opal escape by giving her a transmitter. She's the biggest threat to us as of this moment. Here's what happened when we tried to stop her from taking the books from the Seal."

The image changed yet again. Jett wanted to scream. Blaze's eyes were lit up with flames and a fiery whip coiled down her arm. He watched in horror as she flung a soldier into the Seal wall and all of the horrified faces that looked on. She kicked another into the river before her whip coiled around the archer. Jett resisted the urge to retch when he saw him cry and wither from the whip, his skin shrivelling and turning an angry red from the burns. "She is a slave to black magic. What she has there is demonic flame, one of the most lethal types of fire. The burns need special treatment and often take months to recover from. She nearly killed Reed, our archer, with no just cause. That's how powerful she is now. Imagine what she would do with the information in those books."

"I...I..." Jett stammered. Adam jumped in for him. "I don't believe you. This has to be some sort of deceit."

"She is the one deceiving you. That's what she's best at. They probably hid this all from you so you would cooperate with them. I know your friend is missing. You really think they'll help you find her? Let me help you, we can find her together. We have all of Myra's resources at our disposal."

"No," Adam said with finality. Jackson's smile didn't waver.

"I'm sure when your friends stab you in the back you will want my help. So, whenever you want to talk, touch an *ankh* and think of me. I'll be waiting for that." His smile turned sympathetic, as if he knew they would be hurt soon.

"If you don't believe me about Blaze, try putting her horse in danger or Joseph if you find him first. Those flames will appear faster than you can scream."

Jackson's image faded out and the haziness dissipated from Jett's vision.

He looked up to see Storm still striding towards the earthen tent. It was as if time had slowed down when they had been talking to Jackson. Both he and Adam were rattled by what Jackson had said.

"We have to tell Azura," Adam pulled his arm. "Come on!" Jett fell in step beside his brother.

"Do... do you think he could really have helped us find Mavis?" Adam was quiet for moment.

"I won't lie, I did consider it, that maybe he would be able to find her faster than this group can. But Azura is our friend; she raised us up when we hit rock bottom. We can't take a stranger's offer for help, especially one she's warned us against."

"The video though..."

"Could have been fake. He was trying to bait us into giving away our location anyway." Turmoil was running through Jett's stomach. He wanted so badly to believe that it was all a joke. It seemed too real though, and the group had been hiding something from them, he could tell. The anxiety sat in a pit at the bottom of his stomach.

"I need to know for sure. I can't handle the distrust anymore."

"How do you plan on doing that? If it was true, it's not like they would tell you."

"I'll do what Jackson said. Put her horse in danger." Adam's eyes widened.

"Jett…" he said in a stern voice. "Under no circumstances are you going to do that, do you hear me?!" Jett was taken aback by his brother's fury.

"Why not? Don't you want to know if they can be trusted?"

"Not by doing that. It is low and vile to place someone they love in danger in order to get a rise out of them. Blaze will kill you for doing just that and you might hurt Darkfire."

"But if it's true…"

"Then we will deal with it when the time comes. We're not going to sink to that level to weed out someone's loyalty." Jett decided to keep his mouth shut and avoided arguing further. Deep down, he still wanted to do it, because he was sick of not knowing what to believe. He just wanted Mavis back and Jackson would probably be able to find her faster. He suppressed the temptation and pushed the thought to the back of his mind. Azura had warned him about the heads, so for the time being he was going to listen to her. He knew his emotions would cloud his judgement, and missing Mavis had just made it worse. It would probably do him some good to listen to his twin.

CHAPTER 11
Demon Flame

IT WAS NO SURPRISE TO BLAZE THAT HER SUGGESTION WAS MET WITH A chorus of disapproval. As her group argued amongst themselves, she placed her chin on her knees and waited. With her right hand she stroked Darkfire's back, as he nuzzled his head against her leg. Once she felt the arguments had gone on long enough she cleared her throat.

"Would you all shut up already? This is going nowhere." She continued to run her fingers through her horse's glossy coat. "It's the best option for us. We have to split up."

"Blaze…" Opal started. Blaze held up her hand to silence her.

"Trust me. It would be ridiculous to travel together. We're a huge group. In addition, Opal and I can't risk going back to the city. But the rest of you, they don't know that you were involved. You can go and investigate the Chronicles for whatever Kaitlin had."

A sudden wave of uneasiness and doubt hit her. She scanned the faces in the group. The emotions were radiating from Jett. She narrowed her eyes at him. She sensed a lack of trust. She would force exactly why out of him later. For now, she turned to Opal. Opal brushed a strand of maroon hair behind her ear. Her jaw and neck had fading purple bruises from her fight with Jackson. Her shirt collar was torn. Blaze looked down at herself. She didn't realize how beat-up she looked as well. Her uniform was made to withstand fights, but bruises and cuts decorated her limbs. She was sure her face didn't look much better.

"Who's going to do what then?" Opal asked.

"Here's the plan," Blaze pointed to Storm and Jen.

"You two take Neal and Scarlett to search the Chronicles. Jen knows the place best and can probably get into Kaitlin's files."

"That's true," Jen said. "Her clearance would have been passed to me now that she's... gone." There was an acknowledging moment of silence.

"I want any update you get from Fang about Mavis or Joe." Jen nodded. "Azura, take the twins back to the infirmary. Opal and I will find cover in the chasm. They won't be able to trace us there. Call us or use an *ankh* to let us know what you find."

"I don't like this," Storm stepped forward. "Will you two be able to fend for yourselves in the chasm?"

To be honest, Blaze didn't know. She had been in the chasm several times. She knew what to look out for. But where they had to go to avoid detection wasn't a place she dropped by frequently. She didn't know what would come, or if she could handle it. The chasm was uncharted territory that Myra had explored for centuries. It was vast and unyielding, with several expanses that no one had ever set foot on. Blaze hated the uncertainty with a passion. She liked things to be definite and clear. This would not be going in her favour, but she didn't have much of a choice.

"We'll be fine," Blaze said. She could tell that Opal was having the same doubts that she was. She squeezed Opal's shoulder supportively. "I got your back," Blaze insisted. Opal smiled.

"It's settled then." Azura handed her a small backpack of food and water. Blaze nodded her thanks. She motioned to Storm's group.

"Go. Take the books with you. Don't let the heads find them." Storm stomped her foot and punched downwards into the ground. The dome came shattering down around them. Rocks tumbled and bounced around them, spraying bronze dirt everywhere.

"Run," Storm said. Blaze shared one last interlocking glance with Neal and Azura. She took Opal's hand and felt herself fly forward. Opal took off with her full strength, dragging an almost flying Blaze behind her. The wind whipped through Blaze's hair and she struggled to hold on. Her arm felt like it might dislocate from its socket. The world was one massive blur. She felt Opal run up the rock spire she had slid down on with the twins. She felt the brush of the chasm's pink sand against her cheek as Opal left a blazing trail of flying dust and sand particles behind her.

"Where to?!" Opal yelled over the wind. Blaze tried to focus.

"We need to go to the tunnels!"

"Roger that!" Blaze felt Opal slow down and then veer right to take off again at breakneck speed. They raced across the glittering landscape, bolting past the rocky spires as they made their way toward a mountain range in the distance. She felt Opal slow down again as they approached the base, and Blaze's feet managed to touch the ground again at a sprinting pace and then slowed to a halt. She turned to look for Darkfire, who should have been following them. She saw the flicker of a blue flame on the horizon and sighed with content. He would arrive soon enough. She turned back to face the several tunnels that protruded from the mountainside. The range itself consisted of about twelve interlocking peaks that were each two to three kilometers high. They glowed and glimmered with a pinkish hue against the afternoon sun. The tunnels, as far as Blaze had explored them, went into the hollows of the mountains. Some snaked all the way across the range. At least that's what Storm had told her; she had never gone that far into them. Perhaps it was a mild case of claustrophobia, but the idea of going underground with six hundred tonnes of rock overheard did not sit well with Blaze. She would do it if she had to, but would, very much, prefer not to.

"Here." Blaze walked towards a smaller, coral coloured entrance a few feet above them. She flicked out her dagger and throwing knife to serve as hand holds. She stuck them into the rock and began to scale the wall. Once she reached the platform in front of the tunnel, she tossed her blades down for Opal to use. Upper body strength was not Opal's strongest suit, and Blaze had to pull her up the last foot of the wall. They ducked into the tunnel and plunged into darkness.

The darkness lasted only a few feet before the glittering rock reappeared on the tunnel walls, providing enough dim lighting for the duo to find their way. Light appeared in the distance and Opal raced towards it, leaving Blaze behind her. Blaze squinted as she stepped into the light and joined Opal. It was just as she remembered it. The tunnel lead into a hollow cove that was ninety percent clear crystalline water about two feet deep. This was regular water, unlike the Dias, but still had a strange shimmer to it. Blaze determined that it must be the reflection of the glittering rock that shaped the walls. A white marble basin shone back at her when she stared into the pool. Strips of rock randomly jutted out, providing some walking and resting space. Blaze hopped from rock to rock until reaching a fairly large one near the centre of the cove. Opal followed her lead and sat down beside her.

"This is the basin you were telling me about," Opal looked around in wonder. "It's beautiful."

"We'll be safe here for the meantime. I really hope Azura uses an *ankh* to contact us, because I doubt I have cellphone reception here."

"True. She probably will, the Chronicles are covered in *ankh*." The clip clop of hooves interrupted their conversation. Darkfire peered his head through the doorway.

"It's alright Darkfire. You can come to us." Blaze mumbled a chant and the stallion's flames minimized. He leapt easily from rock to rock until Blaze felt him settle behind her. Opal turned to pet him, carefully avoiding the flames. Normally Darkfire's heat was so intense that no one except Blaze could be within a five-foot radius of him. Even though Blaze had reduced the heat, the fire would still burn if Opal touched it. The tip of his flaming tail swished back and forth in the water, letting steam rise from the surface of the pool. Opal watched him with curiosity.

"His fire can burn under water?" The flames were unwavering, remaining their normal white-blue colour as they swayed under the water.

"Demonic flame can do that. It's fitting, considering it's a fatal substance. Fire that can burn under water."

"So, your whips would still work if you were submerged?"

"Yeah they would. Never tried it, but I'm sure something as petty as H_2O can't stop demon fire."

"In the old stories, it's referred to as Lucifer's chains, the eternal fire that binds him to the depths of Hell, right?"

"Nope. The story said that the fire that binds him is Heaven's, the one he can't escape. This fire is the one he uses to fuel humanity's, darkest and vilest desires, actions and impulses. It's just a story, though. The fire I have, I guess, is some altered, reduced form of it. I've never been completely sure. All I know is that it's wicked."

"It there any way to extinguish it?" Blaze was silent. Opal waited patiently for her answer.

"I don't know. I wish I did. If we are going by the laws of magic, then something as benevolent as the fire is abhorrent. I'm not sure there is such a thing. Love, perhaps, but it must be unprecedentedly strong."

"Like family," Opal said softly. Blaze shifted her gaze down to the water.

"Yeah. Like that."

"I know there's no chance of that for you now, but if you just let your guard down a bit, someone will walk in and shower you with more love than you could possibly imagine. You don't let anyone in."

"If you're talking about Joe, I don't want to hear it."

"Blaze, he's been crazy about you for seven years." Blaze looked at her friend with disbelief. "I'm not exaggerating. I know you can't feel the emotions directed towards you but take it from me, and the rest of our circle, we've been watching this the entire time we've grown up together."

"Seven years? I didn't think it had been that long. Why didn't you tell me before?"

"Knowing you, you would have been scared off and would have gone about ruining a completely good friendship and that would have torn Joe in two. He knew you would never do anything of the sort with him."

"Because he's my friend. I don't see him as more than that. He even encouraged my temporary romances."

"He did that because it meant more to him to see you happy. Both you and I know that it's not because of that. It's because you won't let it happen. You were afraid that if you let Joe in, it would become real. Everything you fought to avoid would spring out at you. You've always been clear about love being a weakness."

Blaze clenched her hands in frustration. Joe had always been that constant in her ever-changing life that grounded her to this world. She knew they shared a special connection. That resolute bond of friendship, laughter, tears, fights and compassion was irreplaceable. She didn't think she could make a bond that strong with anyone else a second time. She feared losing him. If she allowed him to be anything more, she would open herself and him to the possibility of pain and heartbreak, which is something she could never allow. She couldn't take that risk.

"I know you fear that the relationship would not work out. But you've stayed great friends with a lot of your ex-boyfriends."

"I wasn't particularly invested in those relationships. It was all for fun, something to experiment with and both of us understood that. I couldn't do that to Joe. He means too much to me."

"Then why don't you show him that?"

"I do. As his best friend, I do it as much as I can, but I can't be held down by love's chain. It does make you weak. Above everything else, the thing I despise most is being weak, in any form."

"Joe might be dying Blaze," Opal said solemnly. "If tomorrow you had to say your last words to him, would you let that selfish desire keep you from telling him that you feel something too, or might feel something one day? He will go to the grave, without knowing how much you care for him. Are you prepared to live with that regret?"

"Selfish desire? Is it selfish that I don't want to be hurt?"

"By doing so you are still hurting yourself and you know it. I don't know much about relationships, but I can tell you that's where you're wrong. You're depriving yourself and Joe a chance at happiness, letting the uncertainty eat away at the both of you. All so you can stay within this emotional safety net you've created for yourself." Blaze looked at her friend with a grudging admiration, annoyance and shock. Normally she was the one who constructed all the good arguments. Opal had just used her own style of arguing against her. Dammit. If Joe really was dying… could she tolerate that regret? She couldn't bear to let the thought finish.

"I'm sorry if I made you seem like the villain," Opal said.

Blaze shook her head.

"No, it okay. That's why we're friends. We tell each other everything straight up, like it is."

Finally, someone got through to you, Darkfire's voice resonated in her head.

"Shut up, Darkfire." Blaze gave him a glare. Opal laughed.

"Guess he agrees with me," she said.

Blaze gave a wary smile.

"Yeah, yeah whatever."

Opal's smile slowly disappeared.

"Do you think there's a way to unravel all of this? The murder..." Opal choked on the word. "...The magic... will we ever be able to return home?"

Blaze turned to sit crossed-legged in front of Opal, looking her directly in the eye. To be honest Blaze hadn't thought about that. She had been so wound up in recent events that she hadn't mulled it over this far.

"We are going to do everything we can. We're among Myra's top talented personnel. Either way we're going home, in either prison chains, or in victory but not until we've exhausted every option." Opal sighed and leaned over to put her head in her hands.

"At least you don't gloss over the fact that failure is a possibility," she said.

"It always is, my friend. It always is."

∾

Neal always took a moment to appreciate the grandeur of the Chronicles when he stepped inside. Storm had prevented it from being reduced to rubble (with Jett's unintentional help of course). Neal was grateful that hundreds of years of architecture and knowledge had been spared destruction. He respected the beauty of creations that could withstand the test of time, and the Chronicles were the oldest standing example of such a thing that he was aware of. Jen, Storm and Scarlett walked ahead of him, with Jen leading the way to Kaitlin's office. They all carried several of the Seal's books with them, to be stowed away under the floorboards of the office. The heads had already scoured and cleared the crime scene so there would be no reason for them to return to it. They approached a nook in the general section where Jen's information desk stood. She pushed past it and walked to an oak door that almost blended into the wall. If you didn't pay attention you would miss it entirely. It was arched and sturdy, with emerald leaves sprouting from the branches that framed it. Jen shifted her pile of books to one arm as she placed her free hand on a carved symbol of three owls in the centre. They glowed with a black hue, the colour of a *hyponos*. The door swung open silently.

Kaitlin's office was a modestly large room, as it also doubled as a reading circle and research station on occasion. All of Kaitlin's personal notes and belongings had been kept at a russet redwood desk along the back wall, as far as Neal was informed. After neatly stacking the books under loose floorboards along the edges of the room, the four of them split up to investigate. Neal went through Kaitlin's desk, while Jen used her newfound clearance to search through Kaitlin's accounts and the library's catalogues for missing books, scripts and the like. Scarlett went through the bookshelves near the research tables while Storm explored the walls and floor to see if she could detect anything below or behind them.

Neal flipped through note after note, all of them scribbled in Kaitlin's loopy cursive. Book orders, system access checks and inventory counts filled the pages. In her drawers sat classic books such as *Pride and Prejudice* and the *Tale of Two Cities*. Shakespeare and Sherlock Holmes also lay about. He assumed they were her favourites. Looking at it made him feel oddly sad. He had not known Kaitlin personally, but her office held endless reminisces of her life. If he looked long enough, he could probably piece together what she was like by sorting through her stuff. He reluctantly cleared his head. Neal always preferred working with technology than with humans, since the former did not come with emotions attached. He could bend it, change it or shift anyway he wished to and feel no remorse. Humans were not like that. Azura had always chided him for trying to analyze people like he did his computer programs. *There is no one algorithm that would make a person behave or feel the way you want them too. It simply does not work like that*, she had told him. He had realized that soon enough, but still found it difficult to connect with anyone on an emotional level. He liked to keep up his whimsical demeanour as his way of hiding or avoiding it. Blaze saw past it of course; it was impossible for her not to, considering she could basically read his mind. Azura on occasion cracked into his pretence as well, but not the way Blaze would shatter it.

Azura. His chest constricted for a moment. They had a terse goodbye when they parted ways after reaching Myra's entrance. She turned and left with a wave, not looking back once. Although he was partly relieved, as it allowed him to watch her walk away without judgement, it hurt that she hadn't turned around. He was sure she saw him as what he pretended to be; an opportunistic smart mouth that sold his talents. Not that there was anything wrong with his enterprising, but he feared that she saw him as someone who exclusively looked for a profit in everything because of it. Not that it was her fault in any way; he hadn't made an effort to do anything that would make her think otherwise.

Neal didn't fear emotion like Blaze always had, but he did fear what Blaze did not. Failure. In Blaze's slightly twisted world, she was generally pessimistic to the point it was uncomfortable. She gave no one, not even herself, false hope of any kind. She always expected failure, never ruling it out. He feared he would fail with Azura. Azura, who was intelligent, kind, and had a great sense of humour. Only Blaze could tell how he truly felt and Neal was immensely grateful she was unable to tell anyone about his feelings. Yet, she didn't annoy or torment him about it, like they normally would in their love-hate relationship. Neal knew she personally believed Azura would not return his feelings. That did not encourage him.

Neal was so lost in thought that he barely noticed a notebook laying at the back of the drawer he was searching through. He blinked a few times, clearing his head and reached for it. In Kaitlin's handwriting on the cover it said *Seal Roster*. As Neal began to flip through the pages he realized it was a written account of all the books in the Seal.

"Hey Jen, why does Kaitlin have a written catalogue of Seal books?"

"We don't keep an electronic catalogue in the system for those. It's too easily hackable. You would know that." It was true. Neal could easily override the library system if he wished. "The written account is a safety precaution. If someone wanted that information they would have to break into here to get it, which is a lot harder than passing a security firewall from the comfort of your laptop." Neal continued to thumb through the pages. Eventually he saw titles highlighted in green. Frowning he continued to flip seeing all sorts of colours highlighting different books until he reached the back cover where a small legend was scrawled. Green were titles about spell preparation, orange were encyclopaedias of plants and potions, blue was research journals e.t.c. He came down to the last colour, pink, labelled as experimental. There was a star beside it that said *protect*. It had been scratched out and the word *missing* was written beside it.

"Guys… I think you should see this," he called. The three girls crowded around him to look over his shoulders. "Apparently some books that were supposed to be protected are now missing."

"Missing?" Jen exclaimed. "No books have ever gone missing from the Seal until yesterday, when you ripped the main floor out of the ground. Kaitlin did inventory every week. She would have noticed and alerted someone if there were any disappearances. The only people who have keys are the heads and her."

"Let's check when she was last there. Do you know where the key is Jen?"

"Yeah, here. She went to the opposite wall and placed her hand on one of the bookshelves. It glowed black and a small rectangular compartment opened. Jen reached in and pulled out the circular disc with two fingers. She handed it to Neal who swiped it across a sensor in front of the Kaitlin's catalogue computer. A spreadsheet opened with several columns trailing down. Neal went to the most recent entry and stared. It didn't make sense.

"Kaitlin died in the evening, right?" he asked quietly.

"Yes, what's the mat…. Oh God." Jen's hand came over her mouth. The day Kaitlin had died, someone had been in the Seal, three hours afterwards. It couldn't have been Kaitlin. Nor could it be Opal, considering she was arrested immediately afterwards. Someone had gone through the effort to murder Kaitlin to get access to the Seal.

"How did they even know where the key was?" Jen wondered out loud. "Only the library staff knows where it is, and even then, they couldn't touch it. The only reason I could get it now was because I got her clearance. And I was in the infirmary that night."

"Neal duplicated the key from the blueprints in his lab, since they designed it. I don't think anyone else has access to that." Storm pulled on one of her braids in agitation. Neal nodded in agreement.

"The second last entry said Kaitlin had visited the Seal that morning. Maybe she left it out on her desk or something?" Scarlett suggested.

"Maybe… but it's unlikely. Kaitlin was pretty good about keeping it locked up. The heads have the security tape, so we can't even check." Jen's face clouded with worry as she twisted a strand of her tawny hair. Storm placed a hand on Neal's shoulder.

"Neal, what are the titles that are missing? Maybe it'll give us a clue as to what this person was after." Neal gave the notebook a quick scan.

"They're research journals on different topics that were written a century and half ago..." he translated from the Latin on the page. "There's blood magic, energy bindings, amplifying spell strength, necromancy..."

"No wonder those are to be protected," Storm said. "Experimental magic is something that has not yet proven to work. If someone started messing around with that, they may not succeed in what they're trying to do, but could cause a lot of damage in the process. Considering the topics too, those are all under dark magic, which comes with a terrible price."

"All magic comes with a price," Jen said.

"The ones for dark magic are devastatingly steep," Storm took a shaky breath. "I have a bad feeling about this."

"At least we've confirmed someone else is behind this. I'm sure Opal is innocent." Scarlett took the book from Neal. "We still don't have enough evidence to prove it though," she turned to Jen.

"Blaze said Opal was being controlled while she was asleep. Though to our knowledge that's impossible, maybe you could go through Opal's thoughts while she's sleeping. See if you can dig up any answers out of something in her subconscious," Storm said.

"I can try," Jen said. "But I'm not too good at dream stretching. The most I've been able to do effectively is communicate to others. I haven't tried going through thoughts or memories. A little invasive."

"Desperate times call for desperate measures," Neal pointed out.

"I'll try, but I make no promises."

"That's all we ask," Scarlett assured her. Storm turned around sharply, whipping Neal in face with her braid. Her golden eyes darkened.

"Someone's coming," she tossed Jen the key. "Hide it. Neal, Scarlett, put everything back." The four of them worked rapidly to reset the room to proper order. A loud knock came from the door. Neal sucked in his breath.

"Guys!" Azura's voice rang out. "It's me!" The group let out a collective sigh of relief. Neal's heart had started beating faster, but he took in a deep breath to compose himself.

Jen opened the door to let Azura walk in with the twins trailing behind her. Jett had changed out of his hospital gown into some jeans and a black hoodie over a fitted black t-shirt. He occasionally winced as he walked but he was in much better condition now than he was a few days ago. Neal smiled. There was nothing like a knife in your face to get you on your feet again.

"What are you doing here?" Storm asked.

"These two wanted to help. That's half the reason, the other half is that commander Khan was at the infirmary, interrogating the cooking staff about Blaze's whereabouts. They're getting suspicious about our involvement, since Blaze came by a lot, upon my request," she looked guiltily at her feet.

"That's not your fault Azura," Storm assured her. Azura just sighed.

"The staff was forced to tell him that she came to see Jett. I got the twins out of there before he could come by to question them, but I'll have to take them back at nightfall." Storm gritted her teeth.

"We're running out of places to relax in. It probably won't be long until they come here too. Blaze came to the Chronicles often."

"They've already checked out this office so they won't come in here. For now, you all can stay." Jen said.

"Thank you, Jen. That means a lot," Storm smiled at her. "Azura, we need to give you an update." Storm and Azura walked over to one side of the room, where Storm proceeded to explain their findings to her. Neal watched as Azura listened intently, pushing her glasses back on her nose as sign of concentration. Jen, Jett and Adam talked quietly in another corner. Scarlett headed towards the door.

"I need to go back and tend to the animals," she said. "Let me know what you find."

"Are you sure you can't stay?" Azura asked.

"No, I didn't leave anyone to care for them. They need to be let out to exercise and be fed. Drop by if anything develops."

"Will do," Storm said.

Scarlett nodded and slipped out the door. Storm motioned Neal over. He joined her and Azura by the sidewall.

"Unfortunately, since this is a matter of black magic, no one in the city can help us decipher any of these." Storm pointed to the pink titles in Kaitlin's notebook.

"Can't Blaze?" Neal inquired. Azura shook her head.

"Blaze's knowledge may be the most extensive out of all of us, but even hers is limited. These topics are too advanced," Azura explained. She shifted her gaze between him and Storm. "I can't believe I'm going to say that we do this, but we have no other choice."

"What would that be?" Storm asked.

"We need to pay a visit to someone who's an expert. I promised Blaze that I would never see him, but…" she looked down. "I have to break it. Opal's life is on the line here. Joe and Mavis' too. Too much at stake."

"There's no one in Myra who knows about this. It's been illegal for years." Neal pointed out.

"You're right. No one in Myra." Both Neal and Storm looked at her, confused.

"He doesn't live in Myra. He travels the world. Which is why I'll need your help Neal." She gazed up at him, making his heart flutter. "We need to locate him."

"Azura…" Storm had a warning tone in her voice. "How can you be sure this man will help us?"

"He knows me. He will I promise." Neal tried to conceal his doubt. Azura was being unexpectedly vague. He could tell Storm felt the same way, but she didn't push. Azura was normally very open and clear. If she was leaving out details, it was for a reason. He admired that Storm and Azura's friendship was strong enough that they still trusted each other even though one of them was refusing to give the other all the details. They had faith that any concealment was for the right reasons.

"Very well. Neal, take Azura to the lab and help her locate this man. I'll arrange supplies for your journey in the meantime."

"Thanks, Storm." Storm nodded gingerly. Neal could tell she still was not in favour of the idea. Azura turned to Neal.

"Shall we?" she said in soft voice. Neal put up a self-assured smile.

"After you, honey."

℘

They said their goodbyes to Jen and the twins before shutting the oak door behind them. They fell in step beside each other while Neal whistled a catchy tune. Azura was strangely quiet. Normally they had pretty fun conversations.

He stopped whistling and nudged her. The brush of her arm against his sent shivers up his spine that he attempted to obscure.

"What's wrong?" he asked. She smiled sadly at him.

"I'm going to break a serious promise to one of my closest friends. I feel like a traitor."

"You're doing what you have to do. Blaze won't even know about it until you're back anyway."

"Still, I've never seen myself as that type of friend."

"You're not. It's just the circumstances."

"I guess…" They walked in silence for a few blocks. Neal took her hand lightly. She regarded him with mild surprise on her face.

"Honey, who are we after here? If I'm going to find him, I need to know who he is." Azura slipped her hand out of his and turned to walk again.

"We… we're going after Benjamin Darkfire. Blaze's father." Neal stopped dead in his tracks. Azura turned around, showing him the pain of betrayal she hid in her expression. Admitting that had taken guts, but Neal was still transfixed over one crucial detail.

"Blaze…" Neal started. "…is an orphan."

"She is, and she isn't. It's complicated. But he was one of the greatest professors and researchers on magic. He will have copies of the experimental journals, and probably vital information in figuring out what plagued Opal. It's our best shot."

"Her parents died when she was seventeen. The accident…"

"Neal, I'm telling you as much as I can without betraying Blaze's trust more than I have to. Will you help me find Professor Darkfire or not?"

"Of course, I will, but Blaze…"

"…is an orphan. Will always be," Azura finished his sentence miserably. She clammed up after that, stopping Neal from probing her further.

They walked in pin-drop silence the rest of the way to Neal's lab.

❧

Storm had taken Adam to help her collect supplies for some journey as far as Jett knew, leaving him and Jen alone in Kaitlin's office. Jen had brought him up to speed as best as she could, but most of the magic component flew over Jett's head. He just hoped whatever they had found would bring them closer to proving Opal's innocence. He felt quite useless, considering he couldn't do anything to help her. He couldn't read foreign languages or understand the workings of magic. All he was doing was waiting. Waiting for a breakthrough, waiting for Fang to return, waiting for his legs to heal completely. It was agonizing. He wanted to kick a wall in frustration. He restrained himself, as that would only prolong his recovery.

Jen was mindlessly fiddling with the stationery on Kaitlin's desk with a desolate expression. Her emerald irises held a note of sadness, framed under her coppery lashes. She must have been close to Kaitlin, considering she worked with her every day. They had talked about her for some time, fond memories Jen had with her and her amusing quirks. Jen avoided any discussion about her anger or sadness on the matter, claiming she didn't want it to be at the forefront of her thoughts. Jett didn't push her. Jen had returned to wearing her yellow polo and blue skirt uniform. Azura had brought them for her the day after the earthquake, though she hadn't put them on until yesterday. The yellow of her shirt offset her eyes beautifully. He listened quietly as she talked about Kaitlin while she ran her fingers through her long wavy hair. He wanted to say something, do something, to take her pain away. She had masked it well in front of everyone else, but coming back to a space that was like a mould of Kaitlin's life had taken its toll on her. He had zilch that he could do. Just like with everything else.

"Are you going to run the Chronicles now?" Jett inquired.

"I'm not sure. Most likely yes, but that will be determined after the evacuation order is lifted off of the city. Not really the top priority right now."

"Yeah, hunting Opal and Blaze seems to be the goal here."

"Unfortunately, you can't blame the heads. In their eyes Opal is a murderer and Blaze helped her escape. What else are they supposed to think? But the fact that they tried to intentionally waste the grace period they gave Blaze was a mistake on the heads' part." Jett mulled that over for a moment. It seemed like everyone was doing the wrong thing for the right reasons. Who was good and who was bad was becoming increasingly difficult to identify. He did have one concern that loomed over the others. It had been haunting him since his talk with Jackson.

"Can we trust Blaze?" his voice died as the last word left his lips. Jen put a hand on his shoulder and gave it a squeeze.

"To be honest, I don't know Blaze that well. I only know her reputation. Strong commander, intelligent, frightening, pessimistic, stunning... I can't think about what she's like because those are most of the things that I'm not."

"You're gorgeous," the words slipped out of his mouth before he could stop them. Her eyes widened in surprise. "And super smart," he added hurriedly. "You know so much about everything and are so passionate about it. Non-judgemental too." She smiled shyly. Jett could feel his body starting to heat.

"I appreciate that, but my point was that I can't give you a straight answer on that. She's working on figuring out what happened to Opal. I'll support her if it means finding out who's really behind Kaitlin's murder. There's no alternative. If they're going to execute the death penalty on someone, it better be the person who's actually guilty." Jen's tone was definite.

Jett had a nervous energy thrumming through him. His eyes lingered up the curve of Jen's collarbone at the base of her throat up to her lips and then those stunning green eyes. He admired the way she had refused to make a judgment call before she actually had all the facts. She acknowledged both possibilities and chose to give Blaze the benefit of the doubt. That was more than Blaze had ever done for him in that regard. A strange desire raced through him, like an ocean wave that crashed against the shore again and again. He leaned back against Kaitlin's desk and gently pulled Jen towards him, until they were centimeters from each other. Her breathing was slow even as she tilted her chin to look up at him. He couldn't tell what she was thinking; he had lost all ability to reason properly at the moment. He slid his index finger up her left arm and shoulder stopping at the lower portion of her cheek. He felt her tremble as he worked his way up, which only made his heart beat faster. She wasn't pushing him away. He didn't know what that meant. His gaze shifted down to her lips. She was pressing them together. She let them part when she saw him focusing on them. The silence stretched out between them. She shifted and put her arms around his neck. That was all the approval he needed. His hands went around her and rested on her back as he pressed her gently against him before brushing his lips against hers. He felt her hands run through the hair at the nape of his neck softly and slowly. He tugged on her bottom lip delicately before intensifying the kiss. She responded to him, tightening her grip around his neck. Jett could feel her heartbeat hammering away along with his. He could only focus on the sweet sensation of their lips together as the rest of the world spun around him. She smelled like a clean ocean breeze, her hair brushing against his cheeks, her lips soft as clouds. He couldn't get enough. Kiss after kiss, each one sweeter than the last, he lost himself in a trance where he knew nothing else. She pulled away for a moment to catch her breath. Jett was breathing heavily, but that couldn't stop a grin from taking over his face. She rested her head against his chest. They held each other for a while until Storm's voice interrupted their lovely silence.

Jett could hear it resonate through the walls. "Hello Maya. Can I help you?" Jen stiffened in his arms.

"A head," she whispered. Jett nodded in acknowledgement. The two of them stood stock-still as they strained to hear the conversation.

"Why have you not evacuated with the rest?" came an older feminine voice that Jett assumed belonged to Maya.

"I'm on direct orders to patch up any damage done to the city property. I was working on the entrance pathways this morning and came here for a break," Storm replied.

"Wonderful job on the Chronicles my dear. They are as they should be."

"Thank you Ms. Aequo." Jett heard the pacing of shoes on the floor. "Why don't you tell me why you're really here?" Storm asked.

"You're a frequent acquaintance of Ms. Blaze Darkfire correct?" Jett stifled a shocked squeak. Her last name was Darkfire? Jen put a finger on his lips. It would explain why her horse was named as such. Perhaps he was a family pet. He didn't know if Myra had pet stores that sold flaming stallions, but what did he know?

"Yes ma'am."

"Have you spoken to her in the past two to three days?"

"Can't say I have, the last time I talked to her was when she was on her way to the Springs to see Opal."

"I see. Are you aware of the situation regarding those two?" There was a pause.

"Yes," came Storm's answer.

"Then I hope you will let us know if you have any information about their whereabouts, or if they try to contact you."

"Of course, Ms. Aequo."

"Very good then. I heard she came here often."

"Yes, she loves to read. It's how we formed our… acquaintance."

Another surprising fact to Jett. Blaze did not seem like the type to curl up by the fireplace with a good book. Then again, he didn't know if the Chronicles carried novels. They all seemed to be informational.

"Did she read anything in particular?"

"Not really. She would read anything and everything she found remotely interesting. As far as I saw anyway."

"Very well then. Thank you for your time, Storm." He heard her take a few steps and stop.

"My dear, if Blaze is any way a friend to you, do her favour."

"What would that be?"

"You know I am a glimpser correct?"

"Yes ma'am."

"I have seen that she has suffered much, and perhaps, will suffer more. Make sure she doesn't have to endure more agony than she can stand. I do not wish her any ill, Storm." There was another pause.

"Yes ma'am."

"Until we meet again." Jett listened as Maya's footsteps receded into the distance. A second set of footsteps entered the room.

"So that's a head?" It was Adam.

"Yeah. Always be wary of them."

"She seemed genuinely concerned for Blaze. What is a glimpser?"

"Don't be fooled Adam. A glimpser is someone who can see clips of the past, and very, very rarely, the future." There was silence.

"So, we can't trust them at all?"

"Not even if your life depended on it," Storm replied coldly. "Trust me on that."

CHAPTER 12
Joseph

BLAZE WAS LOST IN THE ENDLESS EXPANSE OF HER DREAMS. SHE SAW herself twirling in field of purple and blue flowers. Violets, blue roses, lavender, clematis and bellflowers tickled her feet as she ran through them. *My favourites,* she thought. The sky was clear and the air was crisp, ruffling her dress in the breeze. *Dress?* She looked down to realize she was in a fitted, sky-blue spaghetti strap gown. It was strange. She hated dresses. They blocked her ability to move freely. At the moment, she apparently didn't care. She went about her way, taking in the beauty around her. *Magnificent,* she thought. A hazy figure appeared on the horizon, striding towards her purposefully. As it drew closer she could make out sandy hair, soft brown eyes and broad shoulders. He was wearing a loose, light blue shirt made from thin cotton, accompanied with crisp white trousers. His smile was warm in the buttery light, making Blaze want to melt. *Joe.* Her heart hammered away in excitement. She ran towards him and he held his arms out, ready to embrace her. She hugged him tightly, resting her face on his shoulder and collarbone, feeling the tightness of his muscles under his shirt. His skin was smooth and unscarred and she held on to him for dear life, afraid to let him go. He put a hand under her chin and angled her head so he could look at her. His side bangs swept over one eye, while the longer sections of hair curved slightly around his neck. There was a serene feeling about it all. He leaned towards her and whispered, "Why not me?"

"Huh?" was her only response. He was still smiling at her, that heart-warming grin lighting up his face. He pulled off the clip that tied her hair back and tossed it aside, letting a curtain of her black hair fall around her.

"Do you love me?" he asked, his eyes full hope.

"I do! Of course, I do." He ran his fingers through her hair.

"I know you do Blaze. But this is what I've been dying to know for seven years. Are you *in* love with me?" The words hit her straight in the heart. She put her hands on his chest, creating distance between them. He gazed at her adoringly, as if what she would say wouldn't affect him at all. Time stretched out between them, as she stood stunned in his arms.

"Oh Joe, if you could only understand. I can't seem to fall in love with anyone. Nothing's tugged at me that way." Blaze felt a relaxation come over her. She had admitted it. It was true like Opal said, Blaze would never allow such a thing to happen between her and Joe. But that was exclusive to them. She had dated countless other guys, and even tried a few times to find reasons, or reach for a non-existent feeling that would make her fall in love. Nothing had worked. No matter how sweet, caring or suitable any man seemed to be for her, try as she might, Blaze could not form that connection. At first, she thought it was her darkness, but quickly ruled it out as it had been happening for years before she agreed to take it.

She couldn't stand to put Joe through that process, where in the end he would just realize she couldn't love. Or if by some miracle she did, Joe was so close to her that the fear of losing him or having her heart broken was too much for her to handle. Any other man she could bear. Not Joe. She needed him desperately in her life, and if the best way to keep him there was to keep him distanced from her heart, then so be it. All her options were bleak, but at least one of them kept Joe by her side with certainty and that was something she refused to pass up.

"No then," he murmured in her ear. She felt his breath rush by her face when he spoke. Tears began to burn behind her eyes.

"No Joe. I don't." He pulled her back into a tight hug. She ran her hands over his back gently.

"I'm sad," he whispered. "I'm so sad that I can't handle it anymore." Blaze felt wretched. Her heart ached to hear him say that.

"Joe please…" He let go of her and began to back away slowly. Blaze gasped. The front of his shirt was stained with blood and it was dripping steadily down his chest. She could see the strength leaving his body. She reached out to grab him and screamed. Her hands were covered in blood. His blood. And in her right hand she held her scorpion dagger whose blade was also coloured in red. *NO!* she shrieked internally. Blaze wanted to go after him, but her feet seemed to be stuck to the ground. His smile was as perfect as ever as he drew further and further away.

"No! Joe, wait!" Blaze struggled to move, to no avail.

"Dark angel," he said as he retreated, "My wickedly dark angel." Like that he was gone. Blaze dropped to her knees in misery. She looked up at the sky in hopes that he may come hurtling back to her. A wave of darkness overtook her and everything went black. She was floating in the blank oblivion of her own mind.

"Blaze!" a voice came from behind her. She turned to see Jen standing there. Jen's eyes widened when she turned around. Blaze looked down at herself to realize she was still in her dress with the dagger in her hand. "What…were you dreaming about?" *It's a dream,* her subconscious screamed in relief. *Just a dream. Jen could only visit me if I was dreaming.* Blaze just shook her head, implying that she shouldn't ask. "Alright then," Jen said, concerned, but didn't prod. "I have news from Fang."

"And that is…"

"She found Joe." The words rang in her ears. *She found Joe.* Blaze felt like she might cry from relief. Joe was coming back to her. "But he's unconscious, and Fang could only wake him up a few times before he stopped responding completely. She says he's injured and fever is probably taking over him. She's carrying him back to Myra, but probably won't get through the limits without being noticed. I'm going to send her to you instead, and also send Azura on her way so she can heal him."

"Yes, of course. We're in the tunnels on the easternmost point of the mountain range."

"Be good to Fang, Blaze," Jen requested softly. Blaze stared at her for a moment and nodded.

"Thank you, Jen. For everything. Words can't express how grateful I am."

Jen smiled sadly. She turned around and vanished from Blaze's mind. Once again, Blaze floated in the darkness, alone.

ભ

Azura and Neal sat in front of Neal's main computer in his personal lab. The lab was one of several that were connected together in a beehive formation with the main control centre in the middle. His room had doors to his colleagues' labs. Each of their names was engraved in gold on the frosted glass doors. The lab itself appeared like an optical illusion, with random sections of the room painted black and the others a blinding white. Gadgets of every kind were neatly hung on the wall by type. From computer chips to humanoid robots, Neal had it all. Several of which Azura couldn't even recognize. A sleek, modern, white worktable stretched across one wall, scattered with mechanical parts, laptops and coffee mugs. Of course, there were coffee mugs. This was Neal they were talking about. The main computer had a screen that took up most of the other wall. The computer itself was a small but insanely powerful laptop that wirelessly connected to the wall display. Neal started to activate Myra's locator software. It beeped, and a holographic projection of the earth appeared behind them. The two walked over and Neal began to rotate the sphere. "Find Benjamin Darkfire," he commanded it.

"Confirm: Find Benjamin Darkfire?" the computer responded.

"Correct."

"Searching now." Photos of Mr. Darkfire appeared on the wall screen that the software used for facial recognition. Blaze didn't look too much like her father. Azura supposed she had the same sort of strong shoulder build and straight hair but that was about it. She resembled her mother much more.

"You know this will only give us where he has recently been? If he's not wearing a Myra uniform, we can only track him through recent satellite images."

"I know. Let the computer do its job," Azura responded. All Myra uniforms and clothing had a tracking system built into them. They could be located anywhere on the planet, unless they were obscured by magic, a location of power or strong nature. The chasm radiated powerful auras of magical potential, which is why Blaze and Opal had taken refuge there. It was also why Storm's earthen dome blocked them from being tracked. Blaze, after succumbing to darkness, could not be tracked, since the black magic in her veins was too strong. Neal also could not be. No one had really tried to track them before, so it never came up with the heads. Now that was going to be a problem. *We should really go into the city and buy normal clothing,* she thought. However, Myra had next to invisible camera drones that flew all over the earth as well, pulling video feeds from all corners of the planet. The recognition software would be able to tell them where Mr. Darkfire has been recently. Which meant the heads would be able to as well, once her friends were on the run again. They would have to be careful.

"Location results for Benjamin Darkfire," the computer spoke. Red dots appeared on the globe.

"Narrow results to last twenty-four hours," Neal commanded.

"Search refined," the computer responded. Several dots disappeared off of the globe. Neal zoomed in on ones that remained. Europe came into view with all the dots clustering in one country.

"Spain," Neal said.

"Where exactly?" Azura asked. Neal zoomed in further.

"Zaragoza." He pressed on one of the dots. A photo had been taken of Mr. Darkfire walking on a bridge. Another showed him by the city's church, sitting on the rim of a fountain. In another he was in the city centre clinking glasses at a corner café with people they didn't recognize.

"Seems like he's on vacation," Neal pointed out.

"No kidding. At least he seems like he will be there for a while. We need to see him immediately." She watched him stride over to his worktable and lean forward on it, turning his back to her.

"How exactly do you plan on getting there?" he asked. She sighed.

"I'm not sure. We can't use any of our usual transportation; it would have to go through approval before they let us use it. If there was only some way we could get a hold of something else..." She heard the scraping of metal and clicking of gears. She watched as Neal tinkered with something on his workbench. He began typing out a program on one of his laptops with his other hand.

"What are you doing?"

"I might be able to make something that can help you."

"Neal, you couldn't possibly build a car in the short amount of time we have."

"Not what I was thinking of."

"Then what on ear…" Azura was broken off by her cellphone ringing. Neal continued to work as she answered it. It was Jen. She listened to her speak, her eyes getting wider with every sentence.

"Okay, I'll be there as soon as possible." She hung up and clutched her phone tightly.

"Who was it?" he asked without turning around.

"Jen. Fang found Joe." That got Neal's attention. He spun around.

"What? They found him?"

"Yeah but he's badly hurt and can't be brought into the city. Fang's taking him to the chasm. I have to get there, before it's too late." She looked around wildly. "I need my medicines a-an-and my fever towels, herbs…" she stammered. Azura was nervous. She didn't know why. She was prepared for this kind of situation. An emergency call, not knowing what to expect when she arrived. It was her everyday job. Neal walked over to her and held her by the shoulders, lowering himself to her eye level. "You keep emergency bags in the infirmary. Go get them and then get out of here. Help Joe." He repeated it again slowly for her and her eyes came into focus.

"Yeah… I will. Thank you, Neal." She hugged him unexpectedly, startling him. It was a little awkward, considering how much taller he was. It was only for a moment and then she let go and took off through the doors.

Neal had watched her retreating form dart off. He went back to his workbench and continued to type out his program. His coffee maker sat at the end of the table, which he had already set to prepare a fresh cup for him. Beside it lay the cherry blossom he had taken from Azura's tree, sticking out like a sore thumb amidst the metal junk on the table. It was a wonder that she didn't notice. He reached for it and rubbed the petals softly between his fingers. *One down,* he thought, *one more to go.* A girl named Mavis was also still missing. A friend of Jett's apparently. Hopefully Fang would be able to find her as well, because if she couldn't… they weren't in a position where they could ask for the city's help in resources. They would have to manage on their own. *Blaze,* he thought, *I hope you know what you're doing.*

Blaze sat outside watching the horizon, hoping to see a flicker of blue-white wolf fur in the distance. No such luck yet. She didn't know when Fang would arrive. She had sent Darkfire and Opal to retrieve Azura from the edge of the chasm, where Azura would be waiting to meet them. Opal would run her back here, while Darkfire would carry any supplies she brought with her. Blaze's internal clock was ticking dangerously. She didn't know what kind of state Joe would be in. Jen had told her that he was now unresponsive. The only thing that mattered to her now was that she would be able to somehow wake him. Where he had been and why, she would worry about later. The afternoon sun was at its zenith, showering the chasm with rainbow light. She couldn't care less. Her mind was too preoccupied to enjoy anything right now. She hadn't wanted to eat or sleep since Jen spoke with her. All she had been able to do was wait impatiently for the wolf's arrival. She held her knees against her chest and began to breathe deeply. Her darkness was raging inside of her and she had to calm it down. It pulled at her and tore away at her mind, whispering evil and maliciousness. She wouldn't cave to it, she had promised herself. Joe's impending arrival made it hard for her. She wanted to cut down whoever took him and burn the place he was held to ashes, destroying it until there was nothing left. *Breathe,* she told herself. After a few minutes, her heartbeat evened out. A quick movement was caught in her peripheral vision. She whipped her head around, throwing knife ready at her fingertips. The flame insignia sparkled against the black hilt as she wielded it in front of her. She heard a howl and it echoed through the chasm, replicating the sound over and over. She jumped to her feet. It was the howl of a wolf. From her left, she saw the tiny figure of a racing canine with something odd riding on its back. As the glare from the sun lifted off it, Blaze could tell it was Fang. She waved and shouted to get the wolf's attention. Fang noticed and came toward her. Fang ran in leaps and bounds, covering several feet in each stride.

As soon as Fang reached the base, Blaze prepared to swing herself down. That proved unnecessary. She had barely moved when Fang leapt up and pushed off the side of the cliff as a boost to reach the tunnel. Blaze ducked and Fang jumped over her onto the platform. Lying on her back was Joe.

Fang darted inside the tunnel and Blaze had to sprint after her. The wolf had leapt to the center rock where Blaze and Opal had slept the night before and sat down. Blaze joined her, quickly dragging Joe off of her back to lay him down on the ground. She cradled his head in her arms while pushing his hair out of his face. His body was covered in a light sandy dusting from being carried through the chasm. She placed two fingers against his jugular vein and breathed a sigh of relief. His pulse indicated he was alive. His head ran hot with fever and his fingers were stone-cold. Dried blood ran from one corner of his mouth and scrapes and bruises wound up his arms and neck, as if he had been choked. No amount of shaking or yelling would wake him. *Azura should be here soon*, she reminded herself. His left hand was clenched in a fist. Blaze gently undid his fingers to see the damage. His palm opened to reveal her necklace. She stared at it quietly. The dragonfly shape was pressed into his palm from being held so tightly. She pulled him close and trembled. Trembled from the thought of what could happen.

"Joe…I'm so sorry," Blaze didn't know what she was apologizing for. For neglecting his feelings all these years. For pushing him away when she became dark. For running away when he kissed her. Now, for failing to protect him. For allowing such a thing to happen. She was remorseful for all of it. Fang regarded her silently with her glowing eyes. She placed Joe down gently and turned to her.

"Thank you," she said, even though she knew Fang couldn't understand her. Fang was covered in sand and her paws were slightly swollen from running for so long. She was sure the canine would not appreciate a hug, especially from her. Blaze slowly stepped into the water, and made her way around to Fang. She looked Fang straight on, keeping her hands up where Fang could see them. She sent small waves towards her, indicating that she should drink from the pool. Fang seemed to understand and lowered her head to lap up water from the basin. Blaze stood silently and didn't move until Fang was done. When her eyes came to rest on Blaze again, Blaze approached her slowly and steadily. A low growl came from Fang but the wolf made no sudden movements. Blaze gently took her front paws and lowered them into the water. When Fang didn't object, she rubbed them gently, cleaning away the dirt.

176

"Blaze!" Azura's voice rang out. She and Opal stood at the end of the tunnel.

"Quick! Joe is here!" she yelled back. Azura and Opal jumped their way to Joe. Adam and Jett appeared carrying the emergency supply bags that were kept in the infirmary. Blaze sighed. Azura just *had* to bring them with her. Blaze didn't appreciate their presence, because she was on the verge of breaking down and now could not. Not in front of them. Joe's body was hidden by Azura and Opal as they leaned over him, talking back and forth nervously. Azura called for items and the other three would bring them to her. It had been a long time since Blaze had prayed for something specific, but today she had something she desperately wanted. Blaze moved to take handfuls of water and start rubbing Fang's side. She closed her eyes and mentally begged that God would answer her today. *Dear God, if you are listening, please, please let Joe live. I ask for nothing else.*

Fang stood up and shook her fur, spraying water droplets everywhere. She met Blaze's gaze and the two held it there for some time. Blaze felt like Fang understood that she was trying to say thank you. Fang turned and ran out of the tunnel, leaping over everyone like they were ants. *Probably going to see Jen.* Blaze pulled herself out of the water and onto the rock platform, cleaning off her hands. Blaze didn't dare interrupt Azura while she was working. She sat there watching the commotion with her hands clasped so hard together that her knuckles turned white. Jett and Adam also sat to the side now, whispering amongst each other.

Azura's voice got louder and louder, which meant she was getting nervous. That did not console Blaze. Joe's bruises were disappearing slowly but he showed no sign of responsiveness. Opal brought Azura a book and some yellow liquid with crushed herbs floating in it. Azura flipped through the pages at an alarming speed while mumbling to herself. Now Blaze was starting to get scared because Azura was never this nervous when healing before. Was it because Joe was in such a bad condition? Azura had dealt with worse, but it may be that she couldn't figure out what was ailing him. Blaze looked up to see the twins staring at her. They looked away when their eyes locked. *Good*, she thought. Azura had injected the liquid into Joe's arm. Her alarm seemed to fade as she began to bandage his wounds. Blaze ran over to Joe's side.

His cheeks were regaining their colour and his temperature had cooled slightly. Azura's was expression was grim.

"I'm keeping the fever at bay right now. His body will heal," she let the last word hang there, like an unfinished sentence.

"But?" Blaze asked.

"The medicine will only last for a few days, and we can't give him more. If he doesn't wake up soon…he can die." Azura might as well have stabbed her in the heart. The word *die* echoed through Blaze's head. Azura looked miserable.

"Die?!" Blaze exclaimed. Her voice lowered to a quavering whisper, "he could die?" Azura nodded slowly. *No.* The darkness was pulling Blaze under, washing over her in unsteady waves.

"I'm sorry Blaze, there's nothing I can do." Blaze could feel Azura's helplessness, Opal's panic and the twins' confusion and pity. She needed to escape from it all. She dragged together whatever stability she had left and composed herself.

"I need to clear my head. I'll be back sometime in the night. Take care of him." Before anyone could say anything, she bolted out of the tunnel.

Darkfire was resting at the base of the mountain. The rest of Azura's supplies were unloaded onto the ground beside him. As Blaze came flying out, the horse stood up in alarm. She jumped onto his back without a second thought. "Take me somewhere far!" she commanded. Darkfire reared up and took off, stampeding through the desert-like landscape that lay around them. He could feel what Blaze was experiencing, so he remained silent as his hooves thundered across the ground. Blaze didn't want any consolation right now. She focused on the sheer power she was riding forward with and the wind cutting through her skin. Her grip on Darkfire was unyielding and she urged him on as the mountains shrunk into the distance behind them.

After some time Darkfire began to slow and his gallop became a steady trot. They had come to this area often before, when Blaze initially started to scope out the chasm. Smaller rock spires twisted up from the ground here, about twice Blaze's height. Coves of rock and larger dunes surrounded them. Blaze slid off and sat down against one of the spires. Darkfire settled beside her. Blaze barely noticed. Her mind swarmed with thoughts, emotions and a sense of agony. She had suffered before. She had come to terms with her painful reality, but if Joe left her, she would lose everything. Joe brought out the best in her, the version that was capable of fighting with her own darkest form. If she lost him, would she have a reason to fight it anymore? Opal's words made sense now. *If tomorrow you had to say your last words to him, would you let that selfish desire from telling him that you feel something too, or might feel something one day? He will go to the grave, without knowing how much you care for him. Are you prepared to live with that regret?*

Blaze was not prepared, she realized. It would burn her from the inside out. She wasn't *in* love with Joe, but she did love him. Something she had never said to him. The darkness swelled up, drowning her underneath. She couldn't fight her anger anymore. She screamed and sank into the urge. Her scars lit up and her whip coiled down her arm. Her vision tinged with red once more, the demon flame laughing diabolically in her mind. *Helpless you are*, it whispered. *Helpless you shall remain.*

☙

Jett watched Opal set down Azura's requested supplies beside her as Blaze ran into the tunnel.

"Go after her!" Azura yelled at Opal. "I'll take care of things here." Opal got up and pulled the twins to their feet. "You're going to help me," she said determinedly. Before either of them could object, she grabbed their wrists and pulled them along with her. Opal put on her full speed once again and tore across the chasm. Soon Azura had disappeared and they were heading well into uneven ground. Jett barely felt his feet have any traction, but the way Opal bobbed up and down he could tell the earth wasn't level. He mainly tried to focus on not getting his arm dislocated from his shoulder. They halted and Jett went flying forward, face first, into the sand. The sand here was smooth and soft, but still made him cough like crazy as he attempted to get up and wipe it off of his face. Adam was luckier; he had only slid a few feet on his back.

"Darkfire's prints go all over the place here. Blaze must be close by. Look around, holler if you see her." Opal was all business as she roamed around yelling Blaze and Darkfire's names, running up and down dunes in the blink of an eye. Jett and Adam began navigating through the spires, keeping an eye on Opal for their own peace of mind. They picked their way around spires and boulders, hoping for a glimpse of Blaze's raven hair. Suddenly, a loud crash came from behind them.

They froze. Opal was beside them instantly. Jett had a bad feeling about this. He really didn't want to find out what made that noise. Opal dragged the twins in the direction of the sound. They had just made it around a rock spire when they saw the unmistakable flames of Darkfire's mane. Opal dragged them all the way around and stopped dead in her tracks. Jett couldn't believe his eyes. Blaze stood in middle of the gathering of spires with violet flames in her eyes. The same serpent-like whip that Jackson had showed them was wrapped around her arm. She lashed the whip out, sending a lethal blade of heat straight through the rock. The spire vaporized where the whip touched it and the rest tumbled, shaking the ground like a landslide. She swung her arm back and cut through two more, bringing them down just as fast. She was destroying the landscape. Jett had heard of anger management problems, but this was too much. Fear bubbled up inside of him as he held onto Opal, making an undignified whimpering sound. Adam grabbed his arm, compressing it tightly. He was feeling the same way Jett was. *It's true. It's all true.* The horror only continued to build as spire after spire was demolished. Opal had put herself in front of them in case anything came flying their way. Blaze yelled and sent her whip flying out in a circle. The heat was so intense that Opal had to turn around to shield the twins. She tackled them down and hugged them against the ground. The hair was singed off of Jett's forearms. He felt his necklace being crushed against his windpipe, as it grew hot from the heat of the sand. All was still for a few minutes. They got up slowly and turned to assess the damage. Broken chunks of rock from the spires littered the ground like a battlefield. Blaze was on her knees in exhaustion. Her eyes had returned to normal. Darkfire was completely unharmed and went over to nuzzle her. Blaze rested her head against the crook of his neck.

Jett couldn't get over the fact that everyone had hidden this from him and Adam. Jackson had been right. Opal pulled them away from the scene.

"She'll be fine," she said tightly, "Let's get back." She might be, but Jett didn't know if they would be. He didn't even have it in him to ask Opal what had just happened. It had shaken both he and Adam badly. As they raced away, Jett pondered what he should do next. His trust in this group had been lowered to next to nothing. Jackson's offer loomed over him, like a taunting gesture. Jett still wanted to trust Azura, but getting Mavis back meant more to him. When they got back, he didn't care what would Adam say. He was going to look for an *ankh*.

હ

After Opal had filled Azura in on Blaze's episode, Azura had given the twins some drowsiness medicine to put them into a deep sleep. It would help them deal with the terror of what they witnessed. It also gave them to time to think about explaining the situation in a way that wouldn't reveal how Blaze came across her deadly powers. Jett was sleepy and droopy, but still awake by Azura's side. Adam had already caved to the drug and was snoring quietly behind her. Azura was scanning Joe's energy streams with her hand. They all seemed clear, which was a relief. To her horror, his heartbeat was getting weaker, and there was nothing that she could do about it. She began to wave her hand over his skin to heal any nasty bruises or cuts that remained. Jett watched her half-heartedly. He mumbled things like "what are you doing?" or "that's cool" or "where did it go?" He was making less and less sense as the medicine began to take hold. She was healing the bruises on Joe's chest when Jett grabbed her other hand. "You're a superheroooo!" he warbled. She smiled.

"Go to sleep Jett."

"You can do it," he smiled innocently at her, his eyes closing. "Save him." She felt an electrifying shock go through her. Jett had fallen asleep, his hand still holding hers. Azura's eyes turned a dark shade of green. Her determination soared. She felt like she could run a hundred miles. She felt her palm grow hot with power and she put all her energy into her healing hand. The feeling faded just as fast as it had come. A steady thump pulsed under her fingers. It took her a moment to figure out that it was coming from Joe's chest. His heartbeat had returned to normal. She dropped her hand in shock. His fever had reduced significantly and he let out a quiet moan. Azura wanted to scream in triumph. Joe was responding, which meant he would wake up soon. She shifted her gaze to Jett's sleeping form. Somehow, he had amplified her determination just like he had increased Storm's strength. Without him… would Joe have been able to wake up at all? Azura let the thought go. The only thing that mattered was that Joe would be okay, and she hadn't failed her friend. Whenever Blaze got back, they would have a lot to talk about. She replaced the wet towel on his forehead, wiping away the sweat on his temples. Opal lay asleep beside Adam, curled up on her side. Azura carefully made her way around her to grab her supplies, doing her best not to wake them. She pulled out two thin blankets and draped one over Adam and Opal and the other around Jett. As she tucked the blanket around Jett, she gently stroked his hair.

"Thank you, Jett. Thank you."

Two hours later, Blaze still hadn't returned. It was well past dark and Azura was getting restless. *Where on earth is this girl?* She knew that Blaze needed to let her fury out, but she had already done so, according to Opal. What she could be doing for so long afterwards was beyond her. Joe moaned. Azura went to sit by his side, holding his hand. He moaned again and turned on his side. Azura's excitement grew and she shook his shoulder, hoping he would wake up. After ten minutes, she gave up. Joe continued to mumble incomprehensibly. Suddenly, she felt his hand tighten its grip on hers. His eyes flew open as he woke up with a gasp, as if waking up from a nightmare.

"Joe! Joe can you hear me? Do you understand me?" Opal snapped into consciousness from the volume of Azura's voice. Jett and Adam were still out cold from the medicine. They wouldn't be getting up for a while. Opal was on the other side of him, shaking his arm.

"Earth to Joe!" Opal exclaimed. He blinked slowly, taking in his surroundings.

"Azura… Opal…" he managed weakly. "Where am I?"

"We'll explain that to you later. Right now, you need to eat."

Azura had her herb infused meals ready in the emergency kits. She spoon-fed him his meal, while Opal soothed his nerves by assuring him everything was okay. He was quite dazed and bewildered. After an hour or so, he began to regain control of his senses. The last thing Azura wanted to do at the moment was bombard him with questions that they all wanted the answers to. It wouldn't be good for his state of mind. She also made sure Opal didn't do anything of the sort. He spoke in broken sentences and half completed thoughts, which didn't reassure her. She patiently fed him, as he would occasionally take only half a bite or not notice her holding the spoon at his mouth altogether. She had just wrapped a blanket around him when he said his first full sentence. "When can I see Blaze?" Azura and Opal exchanged glances.

"Whenever she returns," was all Opal said. Joe seemed to be satisfied with that answer. He curled up and went back to sleep. "Have you thought about what you're going to tell the twins?' Opal asked. Azura shook her head. She was beginning to feel the exhaustion settle into her bones.

"One battle at time, Opal. One at a time."

CHAPTER 13

Lady Scorpion

BLAZE STROLLED THROUGH THE PINK SAND WITH DARKFIRE BY HER SIDE. They were making their way back to the tunnels. After she had finished letting loose, Darkfire had pressed his body up against hers, providing her with the support she didn't want to admit she needed. They had sat there for hours, letting Blaze drain away the last of her anger. Instead of riding him back, Blaze walked beside him. She didn't want to return so soon and she took solace in the crisp night air. Now they were almost back to the tunnels. She was too tired to think anymore. She trudged along, longing for her bed. She would be sleeping on rocks again tonight and for many nights to come. She would have to come up with a game plan tomorrow morning. Mavis was still missing, Opal was nowhere close to free, and neither was Blaze. At the moment, they had no idea what to do next and they couldn't hide forever. Something had to be done. As she approached the base of the mountain three figures stood in wait of them. They stepped forward slowly, supporting the figure in the middle. Confused, Blaze made Darkfire's flames brighter to illuminate what was in front of them. After a few seconds of staring she sprinted away from Darkfire to tackle Joe with a fierce hug. Azura and Opal let go of him from either side, smiling as she and Joe stumbled backwards from the impact. Blaze couldn't speak. Joe was back. He was alive. He wasn't going to die. The walls she had put up when he had vanished came crumbling down. She couldn't resist it anymore, she realized, as she clung to him, the real Joe, not some dreamt up fantasy. He was very much warm and alive. A dark cloud had been lifted off her. She leaned her head back to take in his full face. His eyes reflected the bluish hue of Darkfire's mane, crinkling at the corners as he smiled. That beautiful, tranquil, heart-melting smile. His bangs fell partly over his eyes like they always did, as he looked at her between strands of auburn brown.

"We'll leave you two alone for now," Opal winked at them and turned to scale her way back up the mountainside with Azura. As soon as they were gone Blaze punched him in the shoulder. Hard.

"OOWW!" he yelled. "What was that for?"

"Joseph Starks, do you know what kind of heart attack you gave me disappearing like that?!"

"It was my fault? I don't even know how I got there. It wasn't my idea to disappear off the face of the earth." Blaze hit his arm again, lighter this time and pulled him back into a hug, winding her arms around his neck as his arms clasped her around the waist.

"We can fight about where you were and stuff later. You could have died in the state you were brought here in. Somehow Azura managed to wake you," her voice quavered. "Do you know what it felt like? Being told I could lose you?" she whispered. She ran her thumbs delicately over his cheekbones. "You were dying before my eyes. I could do nothing to save you. I could only watch. Watch and pray," she paused. "When I sat there, watching Azura working her hardest to keep you alive, I felt like I experienced what Hell was like."

"Blaze," Joe whispered tucking her hair behind her ear. "I didn't mean to hurt you. I'm sorry." She let out a little laugh.

"I know it's not your fault Joe. There's nothing you have to be sorry for. But whoever did this, will be." The malice in her own voice alarmed her.

"Not tonight Blaze," he said softly.

"What?"

"Don't let your darkness interfere tonight," he pleaded, "Please." Blaze nodded reluctantly. She steadied her nerves for what she was about to say.

"I love you Joseph." His eyes widened as the words left her mouth. "Don't misunderstand me," she added. "I've never told you how much I loved you as a friend." He nodded in acknowledgment.

"I understand. I know I've told you that before on multiple occasions, but it's nice to hear you say it back to me, finally," he joked. "There's a little piece in your stone-cold heart for me too."

She laughed.

"You, unfortunately, do hold a teensy piece of it. But..." she caressed his cheek. "That's the only part of me that's warm anymore. Otherwise I'm made from stone." Joe held back a faintly pained expression because they both knew what she said was true. She had turned her heart to stone. His muscles twitched against her back. "Joseph..." she said quietly.

"Yeah?"

"It's funny, isn't it? When death is staring you in the face, how it straightens out your priorities. You figure out what really matters to you." He cocked his head to one side.

"What are you trying to say?"

She took a deep breath.

"I know I can get hurt. I know I can become weak, and how I *despise* that but..." She looked up at him, eyes shining. "I want to try. Try it with you."

"Are... are you serious?"

"I'm not one to give out false hope Joe, you should know that by now. When I thought you would die, I couldn't function properly..." she was cut off by Joe lifting her up by the waist and attempting to spin her around. She shrieked as he stumbled, since he was still fairly weak. He held her against him, catching his breath and caressing her hair lightly.

"You don't know," he began, "how long I've waited for you to say something like that. I might be a dazed wreck right now, but I'm probably the happiest dazed wreck on this planet."

"Don't get ahead of yourself. There's no guarantee it'll work out."

"Always the pessimist."

"I prefer to think of myself as a realist."

"Worst case scenarios aren't that realistic," he pointed out. "Blaze, you will forever be a part of my life. Losing you would be like losing the air I breathe. Whether it works out romantically or not, if you ever need me to kick someone's ass for you, I will be there. Though you could probably do it yourself, but you know what I mean." He leaned down to whisper in her ear. "I know how hard this is for you, after everything that's happened. I won't ever push you. Are you sure you want to do this?" She was silent for a moment.

"Yes, I'm sure." With one hand on the back of her head and the other at her waist, he lowered his head to the base of her neck and kissed her gently against the collarbone. Her heart fluttered as she stared up at him.

"Was that okay?" he asked softly.

"Mhmm…" she mumbled. She shivered as he did it again, pressing herself closer to him. She heard him laugh gently. He continued to brush his lips up her neck and then trail kisses along her jaw until he worked his way to her lips. This time she didn't push him away. She welcomed the bliss with open arms. *Joe, you've always been like a sunrise to me. I had lived in shadows for so long that I had forgotten what light was. Burn my shadows away Joe. Burn them away.*

℘

Opal couldn't be happier than Joe had woken up. It was now the next morning, and she was handing the twins their breakfast. Blaze had returned to her normal self. Actually, a little happier than her normal self. Joe was also in unexpectedly bright spirits and was gaining strength fast. That spiked Opal's interest. Sure, they were all ecstatic that Joe survived, but she sensed something special going on between those two. She would grill Blaze about it later. Azura was also in better shape especially after the scare that Joe caused, and was finally relaxing to Opal's relief. She always pushed herself too hard, as the perfectionist she was. Her efforts had finally paid off. On the other hand, the twins were still slightly traumatized and wary of Blaze. Opal didn't blame them. Seeing demon flame for the first time was scarring. She remembered being terrified herself. Since Blaze was in a good mood, they were at ease for the time being but the tension was still evident. She had probed them to remain silent on the matter, until she and Azura would have a chance to talk to them. One problem had been solved. Now they faced the ones that remained. She was still guilty of a murder she kind of committed, and Blaze was still under fire for helping her. She still shuddered at the thought of her fight with Jackson. He had been unusually aggressive. She didn't know how much of a threat they thought she was, but she was well aware about how much of threat they thought Blaze was. Even more so after the incident at the Seal.

There was no report of Mavis from Jen or Fang. Her disappearance bothered her the most. Mavis was unknown here. No one would have carried a motive for kidnapping an ungifted human. They may have used her to get a rise out of Jett, but what use would she have been after the fact? They couldn't track her, and she was nowhere to be found around Myra and the surrounding areas. Neal's locators would have found her otherwise. All had returned empty handed. Opal wanted Jett to find his friend. The twins couldn't stay too much longer before their family would start worrying about them again. The how was escaping her. She faded out of her own thoughts and focused on the conversation in front of her.

"Zaragoza?" Blaze asked. "Why?"

"He's a rare book collector from our part of the world. If anyone has those missing titles, it's him," Azura replied.

"Who is he?" she asked. Opal caught her breath. She had talked to Azura about this the night before, after they had left Joe and Blaze outside. She felt seriously uncomfortable for hiding their true intentions from Blaze. Blaze could only vaguely sense it, as their guilt was directed towards her.

"Can't say. Confidential terms. You know how under the radar collectors are. I would risk losing my contact with him if I was to say anything."

"I can respect that," Blaze tossed her dagger from hand to hand. Opal let her shoulders relax. "If we're going to Spain, I have a friend there we might be able to visit for some extra help on searching for Mavis. He lives in Barcelona. It's about time that we see each other again." There was an underlying tone of sadness to Blaze's voice that made Opal question if visiting this friend was worth their time.

"Sounds like a plan. Just one question," Joe said, leaning his head forward on his hands. "How are we getting there?"

"Leave that to me," Blaze said. She stood up, dusting of her cargos. "We need to get to San Jose. I can arrange for a ride there, and we can stock up on supplies and get out of these clothes so they can't track us anymore."

"A good hour from here. We can get back into the city through the chasm, but it's not like we can hail a taxi for all of us," Azura pointed out.

"I'll teleport us," Blaze assured them. Joe stood up immediately.

"Blaze, no! Using magic…"

"Is something we have to do. Or would you rather we spend an hour escaping the heads as they chase us through the city?"

"Who are you going to leave behind?" he shot back.

"I'm aware of what the spell requires, Joe." She shot him a warning look. "I will leave Darkfire. He can't come with us anyway. I'll tell him to go back and stay with Scarlett." She turned to Azura. "The residue from the spell will last about half an hour. That's all the time we have to ditch the uniforms so the heads won't know we're gone. When we land, I'm going to be tired, so get what you need as fast as you can."

"Sorry to butt in," Jett started. "But if you can teleport us to San Jose, why can't you just bring us straight to Zaragoza?" Blaze sighed like Jett was a child she had to explain the same concept to over and over again.

"*Because*," she said pointedly. "Magic has limits. I can only teleport within a certain distance. The maximum would have dropped us somewhere in the Atlantic. In addition, the effort to travel that far would have killed me. Now do you understand why?" Jett looked down and didn't say a word. To Opal's ears that was typical Blaze. She was used to it, but she could see that Jett had taken it a little harshly. She wished Blaze wasn't so tough with him either. He wasn't from Myra and he didn't know anything. He was within his right to ask questions.

"Gather the supplies together and throw out the things you don't need. I'm going to talk to Darkfire and give him a few messages." Blaze strode out, and at the last moment, Opal made the snappy decision to follow her.

☙

Opal landed in a crouch beside Darkfire as she jumped from the tunnel platform. Blaze was stroking his back slowly. She had tied rolled up pieces of paper to the horse's front locks, explaining to Scarlett, Storm, Neal and Jen, where they were and what they'd be doing.

"Stay out of the heads' sight. Only come out if you need to protect someone. Scarlett will help you stow away somewhere safe," Darkfire bowed his head in agreement. He was probably talking to Blaze in her mind.

"I'm sure," Blaze said. After a moment she smiled and said, "yes." She hugged him around the neck, as he nuzzled her back and shoulders with his snout. "I'll miss you."

"I'm sure he will too," Opal said. Blaze craned her neck slightly to meet her gaze. "Thank you Darkfire," Opal added, "For everything." Darkfire trotted over and nuzzled her too.

"Let's go," Blaze said half dejectedly. Together with Darkfire behind them, they trailed back into the tunnel. The others stood ready on the center rock with the supplies packed at their feet. Opal followed Joe's gaze back to Blaze, his concern clearly displayed. Opal was nervous about teleporting too, considering magic was dangerous and how much energy it would actually take out of Blaze to transport six of them. They joined the group and Darkfire settled on the ground. Blaze took a deep breath and traced a small spiral in front of him. Blue light lit up wherever her fingers touched the ground. She indicated for everyone to be quiet so she could focus. The twins watched with amazement as Blaze worked her magic. Blaze sat down cross-legged and closed her eyes. After a minute or two, a glowing blue circle surrounded the group. Blaze was mumbling the words of the spell under her breath. She touched Darkfire's forehead and everything began to become gray and hazy. Opal felt like her stomach was free falling. She clutched it queasily. The world faded into a stormy cloud, with Darkfire's neigh echoing in the distance. Wind pushed at her from all directions, causing her to squint her eyes as she watched her hair fly everywhere. After what felt like forever, the sensation dissipated and the cloud faded. A polished white marble building came into focus. Gardens lined the sides and to their left was a magnificent fountain with stones stacked on top of each other, imitating the layers of a flower in polished cerulean and royal blue tile. An angel statue stood at the top the building, reaching a hand into the sky. She struggled to regain her bearings, scanning for her friends. They were all dazed and lay a few feet away from her. Blaze slumped against Joe, barely awake. They all ran to her. She waved them off and pointed to the right.

"Mall. Now." She reached into her pant pocket and produced a golden credit card, giving it to Azura. "Go," she whispered.

"You guys go, grab something for the two of us. I'll stay with her," Joe commanded. Opal never paid much attention to it, but Joe could also be a leader when he had to be. No one questioned his order. It was so authoritative and definite that Opal was naturally urged to comply with his voice. Maybe it was the army training. Everyone linked hands with Opal and she took off, stopping them in front of the mall in a matter of seconds.

"Thirty minutes start now everybody," she said. "Make it count."

❧

Joe held Blaze up by her shoulders. "Blaze, are you okay? How much strain did you put yourself through?"

"I'll be fine," she managed, "Need sleep." The fatigue was taking over, and he could feel her sagging his arms.

"Get me to the lobby," she said, turning to face the white building. Joe complied. He had her put her arm around his shoulders so he could support her as they walked. Blaze stumbled more than she walked, shifting the majority of her weight onto Joe. They pushed through the front door to enter an elegant hotel lobby. The ceilings were two stories tall and painted with clouds and cherubs. Mahogany supports and pillars lined the walls along with vases of poinsettias. Bellhops and wait staff hustled by, carrying luggage, towels and the like. "Front desk," Blaze murmured. They approached the desk and the receptionist's expression changed from a smile to worried frown.

"Is she alright?" she asked. Blaze righted herself and nodded weakly.

"I'm fine, just need to get some sleep. I'd like to book a room for tonight."

"Of course. Which one would you like?" Blaze pulled her dagger out of her belt chain and pointed the hilt towards her, facing the scorpion insignia face up. Joe wanted to yell at her for pulling a dagger of all things out at the hotel reception. They would surely get kicked out now. The receptionist was taken aback for a second and then regained her composure, to Joe's disbelief. She began to type away at her keyboard with her long red fingernails. "We'll get you set up right away. I'll show you to your room personally." The receptionist produced a key card and came around the desk to meet them. She motioned towards the elevators with her hand. "This way please."

Joe still didn't have the faintest idea of what was going on, but Blaze was drifting in and out of consciousness so he remained silent for the time being. He would take care of her first. The elevator stopped with a ping and they began to make their way down a long hallway. They stopped at the third door and the receptionist slid the card through to unlock the room. She led Joe inside to an incredibly fancy suite. She showed him quickly where the bedrooms and showers were. Joe would focus on the grandeur of the room later. The receptionist helped him flip back the covers on one of the beds as he lay Blaze gently down on it. She was asleep in a snap. He tucked the blankets around her tenderly and then turned to nod his thanks to the receptionist.

"If you need anything else, just call the front desk."

"Thank you," Joe said. She smiled and turned to leave. "Excuse me miss," he called after her.

"Yes?"

"Do you know her by any chance? You gave her a room with no questions asked."

"I do not know her personally, but everyone here recognizes the symbol of the Lady Scorpion. This is her personal room here." *Lady Scorpion? What the hell?*

"We are more than happy to serve her here, so do not hesitate to ask if you require anything." She bowed her head and left. Joe sat by Blaze's side, stroking her hair gently. Blaze showed no signs of anything but exhaustion, which comforted Joe. She would be okay once she got some rest. He placed a quick kiss on her forehead and got up to scope out the suite. It was easily the size of two standard rooms, complete with a full bathroom and living room style area. Beige and black sofas and chairs were placed around a large glass coffee table, in front of which, was a large flat screen TV. One side of the living room was entirely glass, with a sliding door that lead out to a balcony overlooking the courtyard. The room itself was bathed in soft yellow light and had sections of black carpet alternating with white marble tile. A mini fridge and breakfast table were along the other side. A welcome basket sat there, full of coffee, sweets and gum. Joe helped himself to some gum.

He went out onto the balcony, fishing out his cellphone from his pocket. He sent Azura and Opal a quick text about where they were, telling them to let him know when they made it back to the lobby. He looked out over the city, which was blooming with summertime greenery. Tall palm, coconut and fig trees rose up, towering over roads and homes. Ivy hung down in threads over building doorways and windows. Joe leaned against the rail, pushing his hair back. The Lady Scorpion comment was bothering him. He and Blaze were very close, and he had made the notion to assume that they shared a great majority of their lives with each other. Everyone was entitled to his or her secrets he supposed, but he hoped that she would have shared the more significant portions with him. How she was related to this scorpion issue was beyond him. He knew that was a dagger her mother had given her, crafted to suit Blaze's hand only. Perhaps her mother held ties to it. He went back to the bedroom, stepping softly to avoid waking Blaze. Her dagger lay by her side, partially under her blanket. He eased it out gently, and examined the blade. There was nothing especially unique about it, with the exception of the curved and jagged edges. The grip and weight were suited to fit Blaze's hand, with the silver scorpion symbol glittering against the black metal.

Blaze had three knives that she personally owned. The throwing knife, which was the smallest and had the flame insignia, the scorpion dagger and her flame channel sword, which had a fire pattern stamped into the metal. The last one she used in the skills centre mostly, and could set it ablaze before throwing it at her targets. He and Azura had gotten that made for her from a tinker in Venezuela, to help her focus any fire power she had into the weapon so she could keep herself under control. The dagger though, was her most favoured by far, always hanging by the chain at the side of her hip or up her sleeve. He could see his reflection in the polished metal as light glinted off the edges. He put it back by Blaze's side, slipping it under the covers.

He still couldn't believe the fact that Blaze had agreed to try a relationship with him. It was something he had only dreamed of for years. More than once today, he had to remind himself that this was real. He hesitated before placing a kiss in her forehead again, her skin hot and smooth under his lips. He had been holding back for so long that it had become a habit.

He remembered the girl before, the girl that still surfaced from time to time on a good day. He cared for her as much now as he did then, perhaps more. She kept her sweet side hidden away and only showed it to those she thought deserved to see it. She would still bake his birthday cake by herself every year, and go out of her way to find the video game or book he had been wanting forever. In her own little ways, she showed that she cared. His phone buzzed, letting him know that the others were waiting for them in the lobby. He glanced at Blaze one last time before shutting the door behind him.

☙

Storm paced the Chronicles in distress. Scarlett had arrived a few minutes ago to read her Blaze's letter and then go back to help Drakfire stow away where he'd be safe from the heads. The fact that Blaze was using a teleportation spell did not bode well with Storm. Neither had her conversation with Maya. Storm would sooner run and live as a fugitive than sell out her friends to the heads. Maya had seemed tired but determined to find out where Blaze was. Her apparent concern for Blaze had thrown Storm off, saying that she wished her no ill. It was quite contradictory with the fact that they had warranted a manhunt for her. Storm knew Blaze would not be one to surrender and come in easily. She wondered why they even bothered offering that as an option. Storm was back in her family's section of the Chronicles and books about *permotionem* surrounded her. She started collecting them and organizing them on the table and occasionally shelving them to clean up the space. She hated being messy, and when she was stressed, she liked to plan and organize things. It would help her organize her thoughts.

She was lucky the heads didn't realize she was the one who had almost drowned them during the fight at the Seal or she would have had to take refuge in the chasm too. She couldn't deny that it had felt good to do that, knocking away the people she despised so much. The *jaculus* especially. Blaze was a *bellator* and Storm was not, which was all the *jaculus* seemed to consider when they choose who they wanted to oppress. They intentionally picked individuals they knew couldn't fight back. While the majority never dared to challenge Blaze, Storm had been challenged several times. Many assumed that because most naturalists were blind, they had some kind of advantage over them. If a naturalist was trained properly, that couldn't be further from the truth. Storm had happily stood in triumph over most of her opponents and quickly established a no bullshit attitude about herself. If you wanted to fight, you should be prepared to have a chunk of rock or a cannon of water shoved down your throat. That didn't stop the *jaculus* from taunting her from time to time, but it was enough to keep them at a distance and wary of provoking her. She was just as lethal as Blaze, but instead of attacking like a fire, she attacked silently, like a poison. You would be down before you knew what hit you.

Maya kept coming back to Storm's thoughts as she tried to decode the head's motives. Maya was a hard one to read. Taking into account what Storm knew about her past history gave her several possibilities of what could be going on inside her mind. None of them made too much sense, or had enough evidence to draw a conclusion from. She sighed and continued to put her books back on the shelves. Storm felt Jen's footsteps come up from the side aisle.

"I think the space is clean enough Storm. It looks spotless," Jen joked. Storm managed a small smile.

"Just been… thinking, that's all."

"Well if you insist on organizing, you can help me sort out the books at the front desk. Perhaps it will help you think better." Storm shrugged in agreement. She wasn't doing much else at the moment. Storm turned to follow Jen and stumbled forward, landing on her knees, catching herself right before face planting into the ground.

"Are you okay?" Jen asked her worriedly.

"I'm fine, just klutzy," Storm laughed. For some unknown reason, she was blessed with grace and coordination when it came to fighting, but when she had to perform simple tasks such as walking, her grace abandoned her. It was a running joke among their group of friends that she was undoubtedly the clumsiest among them. Storm didn't mind. It was pretty hilarious most of the time. She got up and brushed herself off.

"Let's go," she said. Soon she was separating books into even numbered piles for shelving according to Jen's instruction. They made small talk in the meantime, offering polite inquiries about the other's life. Storm wasn't too familiar with Jen since their interaction was solely limited to when Storm was out and about at the Chronicles. It was a little bit of a forced conversation, but nothing too awkward. She learned that Jen was an only child, and that her favourite colour was green. Her book taste lay in old classics such as *Pride and Prejudice* and a *Tale of Two Cities*. Storm had always been more of fantasy novel girl herself, old English didn't really appeal to her. Their conversation was interrupted by Storm's phone ringing. Joe was on the line. After speaking to him Storm ended the call and motioned to Jen.

"Joe asked for a favour. We need to research something."

"And that would be?"

"Do you know anything about the Lady Scorpion?" Jen frowned.

"I vaguely remember that being the name of the leader of some sort of elite mafia. Give me a second," Jen typed away on the library system. "I'll be right back." A few minutes later she returned with a small book and began to flip through the pages. "There's not too much about them or the Lady Scorpion, she was pretty secretive. She was the leader of a group called the Shadow Swarm, an organized criminal association. They were huge about twenty to thirty years ago. They went underground after that and there's been no suspected activity for decades. No mention of why or how. This was their recognized symbol all over the world. A silver scorpion with a curved stinger." Storm's stomach dropped. Joe had told her that was the symbol on the hilt of Blaze's dagger. She had gotten that dagger from her mother...

It seemed impossible to Storm that Mrs. Darkfire had anything to do with a mafia, let alone be the leader of one. Maybe she had fought the leader and taken the dagger? It had been crafted for Blaze's hand though... something was clearly missing from this puzzle. Another fact also didn't fit. Storm had heard of the Shadow Swarm before. In the death reports for Maya's daughter, Alana, it had mentioned something about the Shadow Swarm, how the place she was killed was an old meeting place of theirs. A pit of anxiety was settling in the bottom of her stomach. The date of her murder fell shortly after Blaze had turned dark, at a time she had trouble controlling herself. One of the causes of Alana's death was a knife wound and according to the reports, some kind of dark magic trance. Storm didn't want to think there could be a correlation between the two, but the possibilities were uncomfortably matching each other.

"Storm, you're white as ghost. What's wrong?" Jen asked.

"There's a possibility that's really bothering me. It's lining up a lot of the evidence, but I don't want to believe it."

"A theory is just a theory until proven true. Don't over analyze it. It's quite possible that many of the events you are thinking of are coincidences. Until you have hard proof, it's better for your peace of mind not to mull over the possibilities."

"I know. I can't help it though. I'm used to doing that."

"I've noticed."

"Really?"

"Yeah. When you meet people for the first time, or talk to them, it's like you try to read them like a book. I feel like you notice things like tone and word choice to try and draw a conclusion about them and their motives."

"That is true," Storm admitted.

"You need to ease up a bit. People can't be understood that easily. It takes time and several interactions before one can infer an accurate reading of a person. People present themselves how they want you to see them. More often than not, you end up thinking what they want you to think, not what they really are."

"You seem to know a lot about this."

"I read into psychology occasionally. A few betrayals have also ingrained that into me too," she said sadly. Storm didn't know what to say. As much as she wanted to comfort Jen, she wasn't quite sure how to. She tended to be more logical when she was consoling her friends, providing a detailed explanation as to why they felt the way they did, rather than comforting them. It was just her style. She felt Jen would not appreciate that sort of sentiment right now.

"I'm sorry to hear that," she managed. Jen waved it off with a flick of her hand.

"What doesn't kill you makes you stronger," she stated. Storm thought of Blaze. She thought of Neal. She thought of Jett. Did it really make you stronger? Or just serve as a reminder of how close you came to going under?

What didn't kill you scarred you for life. And scarred areas never become stronger. They just hurt when they're pressed over and over again. If not physically, then emotionally. She nodded at Jen and went back to sorting her books. A broken bone would become stronger after it's mended, she thought. But there was no healing on this earth that could take away a scar.

CHAPTER 14
Benjamin Darkfire

SCARLETT TWIRLED IN THE BALLROOM OF THE SKILLS CENTRE. WHILE the majority of the centre was designed around the army, Maya was adamant on diversifying the facilities for the arts, such as music, dancing, singing, painting and pottery. Although the sections were much smaller than the combat areas, Scarlett was grateful. Dancing sometimes was the only thing that would melt her sorrows or frustrations away. Baby pink slippers were wound around her feet and her black leotard and skirt spun out like a flower at her waist. Soft jazz played in the background as she moved across the mahogany floors, giving herself away to the music. She felt a hand cover hers smoothly and spin her around. She landed hand and hand with Neal. He smiled at her mischievously, tipping his fedora back.

"May I have this dance?" He didn't wait for her to respond and pulled her into a two-step waltz.

"Really Neal, you wait for the lady's consent first before taking her hand. Didn't anyone ever teach you that?"

"Guess I missed that lesson in the little gentlemen's academy." Neal was much taller than she was, and being short herself, Scarlett had to tilt her neck up to look at him. He moved smoothly and gracefully, to Scarlett's surprise as he led her around the room. She could see herself in the reflection of his glasses, sweaty and pink from the exercise.

"Honey, you really need to work on your footwork. I feel like I'm dancing with a novice." Scarlett rolled her eyes.

"Just because you know one dance Neal doesn't qualify you to be an expert." She spun out and back in, facing him again and stepping on his foot intentionally.

"OW!" he winced.

"Oops," she said innocently. Neal grinned.

"Clever little cat, aren't you?"

"Nah I just don't take your shit. What do you want?"

"Well I was hoping to dance with a beautiful lady, but I guess I could settle shuffling around with you."

"Sorry to disappoint, I'm not Azura."

"Who said I was talking about Azura?"

"Who said you weren't?" she gave him a knowing, catlike grin.

"Let's not talk about that, I come in peace." Scarlett motioned for him to continue. He let her go and walked over to the side of the room where two tin containers and plastic wrapped cookies lay on the floor.

"Join me," he said. Soon they were digging into some homemade *chifrijo*, with Scarlett savouring the flavour of salsa and smoked meat in every bite.

"Thanks," she said between mouthfuls. "I was starving."

"There's no time you aren't starving," Neal joked. Well half joked, because it was true. Scarlett was usually hungry all the time. Neal and Azura often teased her about it, saying she loved food more than people. To be honest, who wouldn't prefer a pizza over a conversation? That was her opinion anyway.

"Cookie?" Neal asked holding one up. Scarlett could smell the sweet aroma of baked flour and chocolate, making her mouth water, but the other smell that came along with it held her back. Peanut butter.

"You know I'm allergic to nuts, Neal." Neal's face went blank temporarily and then realization took over as he put it down quickly and shifted the pile to the other side of him.

"Sorry," he said, embarrassed. "I completely forgot." Scarlett enjoyed moments like that. It was rare to see a crack in Neal's composure. It was so unusual that it was funny.

"It's all good," she reassured him. "You could have killed me, but it's okay." His pained expression made her laugh out loud.

"I'm kidding Neal. Lighten up." She nudged his shoulder playfully.

"Don't do that to me Scarlett."

"Sorry, I couldn't resist. So, what's on your mind?" She knew he wouldn't have come here without a reason. She and Neal had grown close because Azura was a mutual friend of theirs and often times the three of them would hang out together on a regular basis. Now that Azura was on her way to Spain, she figured he didn't come by just to say hi. Perhaps he would, under normal circumstances, but they both knew this was a high stress time. That's why she was in the ballroom and he had been cooped up in his lab.

"How is Darkfire?"

"Safe for the time being. He's in the cedar grove enclosure, when the nature is strong and will block off his aura."

"I never thought I'd be indebted to a horse. Life is strange."

"He did play a crucial part in saving your life. He was following Blaze's orders though, I suppose. Even now she's ordered him to protect us if the need arises."

"Let's hope it doesn't get to that point. I don't want the heads getting their hands on him. Who knows what they would do to him, and then they would have leverage over Blaze. The least I could do is spare him that fate."

"You take your debts that seriously?"

"Of course. Plus, I'm not an idiot. I know how cruel the heads are and the *jaculus* too. So, I've made this for the horse." He took a delicate silver chain out of his pocket, with a plain, circular, silver pendant hanging from it. "It's a temporary light shield," he said, answering her unasked question. "Any time it feels Darkfire's heartbeat rise to panic levels, it'll let out a blinding burst of light, buying a good minute and a half for him to get away." He handed it to her. "Put it around his neck the next time you see him." It was as light as a dime as Scarlett turned it in her hand, thumbing the surface. "That's not why I'm here though. I need you to help me deliver something." He took out a small rectangular box and opened it. Inside lay a small remote like device, made from polished metal with two buttons on it. It was about the length of Scarlett's ring finger, with rounded edges.

"What is that?"

'Something that'll help Blaze and Azura out of tough situation if need be. It's like a universal remote, but for motor vehicles of any kind. It will hotwire a car, motorcycle, truck, you name it. They'll be able to get transportation if they need it." Scarlett gazed at it in wonder. Neal was good at his technology, even she knew that. He was known for creating software and hacking more than building chip controlled devices. But something like this… that was new, at least to her.

"Wow… how did you manage to do that?"

"A little innovation and playing around with universal remotes for TVs. Do you think one of your falcons could get this to them while they're in San Jose? They already recognize Blaze."

"Yeah not a problem. Come on, let's send it now." She changed into her running shoes and they walked down a few blocks to get the stables. Scarlett whistled and waited, getting her arm guards on in the meantime. In no time, there two magnificent birds were perched on her arms. She put the both down gently on the ground stroking their brown and grey feathers. One of them was spotted with white specks while the other was a solid brown with a whitish underbelly. She slid a strap with a small harness around the spotted one and secured the box on to the falcon's back. Falcons were deadly hunting birds, but around Scarlett they became almost playful and eager, flapping their wings for attention. She couldn't help but smile at her birds, thinking back to the time that she had played with them as chicks. They were grown and powerful now, but still carried that loving attachment that they had with her as young birds.

"Take this to Blaze," she commanded them. She made a clawing motion over her chest. The two perched on her arms once again and Scarlett stood up, balancing them on either side. "Go."

She pushed her elbows up and the falcons took off, crying out as they raced up towards the sky. They watched them go, fading out sight.

"Thanks Scarlett," Neal said, shoving his hands in his pockets.

"You're welcome. I hope you don't have anything else to deliver, because I'm all out of falcons."

"That is all I require as of right now," he winked at her.

"Do you have any more *chifrijo* on you?" she asked as they began to make their way back. Neal laughed.

"It never ends with you, does it?"

"Nope. So, do you have more or what?"

"Make your own." Scarlett shoved him to the side.

"Hey!"

"You do have more I know it. You're just being stubborn."

"What if I don't want to share?"

"Then you shouldn't have come here," she laughed. She examined him thoughtfully. "You could use it though, you're so skinny. Some weight wouldn't hurt you."

"And give up this body and compromise my muscles? Never."

"What muscles? The nonexistent ones?" She yelped as he pushed her lightly to the side. He ruffled her hair and she swatted him away, annoyed. "Skin and bones doesn't count," she taunted him.

"I'm perfectly happy in my skin and bones, thank you."

"Whatever you say." They had come back to the skills centre entrance and Neal bid her goodbye with a tip of his hat.

"I will leave you to your two left feet now."

"Gentleman indeed," she replied sarcastically. His smile was as haughty as ever.

"As always."

"No argument there," she said. With a bow of his head he turned and left, disappearing around the corner of the street. Scarlett made her way back to the ballroom. As she entered the door she saw a man standing in the middle of the room, his back facing her.

"Can I help you?" Scarlett asked as she approached him.

"Yes," he said. He turned and rested his chilling grey eyes on Scarlett.

"Jackson," Scarlett said. The unkindness failed to hide itself in her voice.

"How are you Scarlett?" he inquired politely.

"Don't waste your breath on me. What do you want?" Jackson pretended to look hurt.

"Is that anyway to treat your former lover?" he asked nonchalantly. Scarlett seethed silently inside her mind.

"Former for a reason."

"You never told me that reason. You abandoned me, left me with no answer and a broken heart."

"Like you have one," she retorted. Jackson's expression turned to grief for a moment and then he composed himself, as if it never happened. Scarlett noticed though. Inside she celebrated the fact that something she said could still hurt him. In a way, maybe it was a beginning in taking revenge for the pain he had caused her.

"You know very well why I left you. There was no explanation needed."

"There was kitten, there was." Scarlett flinched. Kitten was the nickname he used to call her when they were together, before everything had gone to Hell.

"Don't you dare call me that."

"Funny, isn't it?" he said as he walked around her slowly. "You never told anyone about us. Kept it hidden away. Then you abandoned me, leaving me to come back to an empty room and cry about why you could have possibly left me. That was cruel, Scarlett. But I suppose it runs in your genes. Your parents did the same thing to you, no?" That comment flared Scarlett's anger. She grabbed him by the collar and squeezed, making it hard for him to breathe. He just smiled and looked at her smugly, knowing he had gotten to her. She cursed herself for falling for it but kept her grip. "You were lucky you were adopted into your currently family. But I bet it burns you every day to think about why your birth parents left you. Just like you left me."

"Don't you even try to bring us to the same level," she snarled at him.

"Easy on the collar kitten." He reached up and tugged her hands away from his neck. "Don't you think it's time we discussed us again?"

"There is no longer an us to discuss, Jackson."

"I have a deal to propose to you."

"I'm not interested."

"It won't cost you much, just a discussion over tea."

"You have nothing I want, so if you could kindly get lost, that'd be great."

"Don't underestimate me kitten. I know where Mavis Williams is." Scarlett stared at him. He flashed his haughty smile. "Got you there, don't I? All I want to do is talk to you, and in exchange I'll give you her location. Fair deal, right?"

"Nothing is ever a fair deal with you. It's like bargaining with the devil."

"Only your little friend, Blaze Darkfire can tell you about dealing with the devil. She has experience. I assure you I'm much kinder."

"Would you stop talking nonsense? How do you even know about Mavis?"

"Do you want her location or not?" he countered. Scarlett tensed. Azura had told her how they were desperately searching for Mavis. If they found her and got that out of the way, they could focus on Opal, who was running out of time. All he was asking for was a talk. She sighed. She knew it was never black and white with Jackson, but he had something her friends needed. She nodded reluctantly. Jackson beamed.

"This way." He motioned for her to follow as he took her hand and lead her out of the ballroom. She let him drag her along, wondering just what she had gotten herself into. Her heart constricted as she gazed at him with regret. Regret that she wasn't enough to stop him from turning into what he was now. A monster.

❡

Jett sat on a black leather sofa facing the balcony. Joe, Azura and Opal were talking in hushed voices in one of the bedrooms and Blaze was asleep in the other. Adam was in the shower, so Jett sat alone in the living room with his thoughts. They had arrived with armfuls of supplies and clothing, and everyone was now decked out in new outfits. It was strange to see the others without their uniforms, but Joe had explained that any clothing from Myra could be tracked. Azura and Opal had done most of the shopping, Opal zipping from store to store in no time flat. She now wore some denim shorts with a loose, colourfully printed tank top. Joe had an olive-green button up, which he rolled up and wore open over a white graphic t-shirt and dark jeans. Azura wore black jeans and a white zip up over a red V-neck. Everyone wore converse high tops for shoes. They looked almost normal, which was a little jarring for Jett. He was so used to seeing them professional and poised that it didn't occur to him that they were a lot more like him than he thought. He and Adam had gotten new hoodies in black and blue and some underwear. He closed his eyes and leaned his head back. He was almost back to normal when it came to walking now. Occasionally he would still feel a strain but the feeling was fading fast. Once he had taken a shower and changed, he felt like he was ready to run a hundred miles. With Blaze still asleep though, they couldn't do much for the time being. Jett still shuddered at the memory of Blaze tearing down spire after spire with purple flames in her eyes. Opal said she would explain it in due time, but really, what was there to explain? They had lied to him, or hidden it, depending on how you looked at it. He knew for sure that Mavis was a second priority to them, and it was eating away at him on the inside. Jett was not a patient person and this whole trip to Spain, in his opinion, was time taken away from finding Mavis. He had to stick with Azura though, and that was becoming increasingly more difficult as time went on.

He loved Mavis like a sister. His father had loved her like a daughter. In his dad's final days, she would come over every afternoon after school and make him tea and read him the sports section from the newspaper or watch the game with him on television. She would hold Jett up when he broke down, piecing him back together. She was just as much family as Adam was. Blaze had gotten her best friend back, but he was yet to find his. Jett took a deep breath. He could feel himself getting overly emotional, something he was now aware of since he realized he was a *permotionem*. Storm had explained that he would be, by nature, impulsive and yielding to his emotions, and that was something he had to keep in check. He did what he felt like in the moment, and often regretted it later. Now he knew why. His power seemed to mock him, appearing like a twisted and confusing set of talents. He could amplify emotions in other people or burn them with his own. His energy could be used to start spells. He could see into memory flowers and survive breaking one. Not that he was in any position to attempt that again. That part intrigued him, but the rest seemed like a burden he had to carry. It lay in front of him like a tool he was supposed to use, but had no idea how to. He felt useless. Jett hated feeling useless. Everyone else was using their power or knowledge to achieve something. To help Opal. To find Mavis. He had no knowledge and a crappy power that he could use as well as he could do a backflip, which was not at all. He was glad Mavis and Jen weren't around to see what a failure he felt like right now.

There was some shuffling from the other side of the room, and he saw Blaze come out the bedroom. She came out in a black leather jacket with golden zippers and a black-silver belt, wearing it open over a fitted cream-coloured shirt. Dark skinny jeans were paired off with long black leather boots stopping an inch or two below her knees. Her dragonfly necklace glittered at the base of her throat. She looked like she could be a stylish college student. Blaze seemed to pick up the fact that Jett was staring and made eye contact with him, giving him a pointed look. He quickly shifted his gaze away, focusing on the coffee table in front of him. She walked around to the breakfast table and grabbed coffee grounds from the welcome basket. He could hear her starting to prepare a few cups. He sat in uncomfortable silence as she brewed the coffee, fidgeting with his hands. He started fidgeting with his disc after a second, twisting the faces to show him the wave and fire stamps in the silver. After another ten minutes of antagonising silence, she walked over and placed a cup in front of him and sat on the armchair across the table. Jett didn't really drink coffee, but he took it anyway to sooth his nerves.

"Thank you," Blaze said.

"What?" Jett asked, confused. "Thanks for what?"

"For healing Joe. Azura told me that apparently you amplified her determination and healing strength. Accordingly, she was able to wake Joseph up."

"I did?" Joe couldn't remember doing that.

"You fell asleep right after," she informed him. "So, either way, intentionally or not, thank you." *Wow*, Jett thought. He never expected those words to come out of Blaze's mouth and be directed at him.

"Uh… you're welcome. Just don't count on me to do it again, I don't really know how it happened."

"I don't keep any such expectation of you, so don't worry." She was staring at him intently, her black eyes gleaming in the light. It was slightly frightening, but he had sort of gotten used to it now.

"So how are we getting to Zaragoza?" he asked.

"Plane," she said, "We leave in about three hours." There was a brief pause.

"This friend of yours, how is he going to help us find Mavis?" he prodded after a moment.

"He's a specialized detective with a talented workforce. They find missing people for a living."

"Is he from Myra too?"

"He's never stepped foot in Myra, but if you mean does he have an ability, then yes, he does. He's a *hyponos*, like Jen. Doesn't really use it too often though."

"You guys go way back then?"

"Childhood friends. Haven't see each other for years though, although we still talk from time to time." Jett twisted his hands together. It seemed like this was more of a reunion visit than a mission to help Mavis.

"We're all working to find Mavis as we speak, Jett. There's a lot of activity going on that you don't know anything about. Don't jump to conclusions so quickly." Jett wondered what it was like to be able to read minds like Blaze did. There wasn't much that could surprise you. He didn't know if that was a good or bad thing.

"Then why don't you tell me what's going on then? What effort you're putting in?"

"I don't believe in giving people false hope. I'll tell you something when we have a breakthrough and not before. I don't need you getting emotionally unstable over something that's just a possibility. You're not the greatest at controlling your despair." Azura's burned palm flashed through Jett's mind and a twang of guilt shot through him. He knew Blaze could sense it. For a moment, she actually looked sympathetic. It didn't last, and her blank mask was up once again. Jett wondered if he had imagined that moment. He was still uneasy about what Jackson had showed him, and if he should believe what she was saying about searching for Mavis. He hadn't even told Azura yet that Jackson had talked to them. He was debating if he even should. He didn't have time to finish that thought. Azura, Joe and Opal all came out and joined them around the coffee table. Blaze got up and went to pass out everyone else's drinks.

"How did you manage to arrange for tickets so fast?" Opal asked Blaze.

"I know someone who works for the airline. I called in a favour." That sounded incredibly vague to Jett, but everyone else nodded like she had given them a fully detailed explanation of the situation. "The plane will drop us off in Barcelona, and from there Azura can take the high-speed train to Zaragoza. We'll meet back in Barcelona for the returning flight."

"One problem though," Azura interjected. "I can only take one other person with me on the train. Both twins can't come."

"Hold up," Jett said. "I'm going to be separated from Adam? Not a chance."

"Not your choice," Blaze said. "Azura, take Jett with you. He would be the one needing your abilities the most in the worst-case scenario. Opal can take care of Adam and he's pretty comfortable with her."

"Wait a minute! I'm not leaving my brother! We're a package deal. Someone else can go with Azura, why does it have to be one of us?"

"You're too unpredictable, and there's no knowing what kind of situation we'll find ourselves in. If you get hurt, or injure yourself or others, we can't help you. Azura is your best chance at survival." Jett was about to argue when Azura placed a hand on his knee.

"It's our best option Jett. I'll watch over you, I promise." He wished he could tell Azura that his safety was the least of his worries. He would happily go along with her. What he was worried about was leaving Adam alone with Blaze. Joe and Opal he was okay with, but under no circumstance did he want his brother to be going along with someone who could vaporize rock. Azura's face was genuine and earnest, convincing him that he would be all right. He caved against his will.

"Okay fine," he said tightly. Blaze didn't say a word. He felt like she knew what he was thinking, but decided to stay silent about it for the time being.

"Great," Opal said, "Everyone pack your bags. We have a plane to catch." There was a sudden ruffling sound at the glass doors. Blaze already had her dagger out, approaching the door cautiously. As she got closer her body eased up and she sheathed her dagger.

"What is it Blaze?" Joe asked her.

"Looks like Scarlett sent us a present." She opened the door and Jett ducked as two predatory birds flew in, circling around the room. Blaze whistled and pointed toward the coffee table. They swooped down and landed on the table like it was a runway. The birds' chests puffed up and down, showing the strain from their trip here. Jett watched them with wonder, taking in their regal beauty.

"Opal if you could be so kind..." Blaze asked. Opal stepped forward, gently rubbing the birds under their beaks with her index finger. Then she set to work on undoing the harness that was attached to the bigger of the two.

"Why couldn't you do it?" Jett asked Blaze.

"Animals don't like it when I get too close to them," was all she said. Jett shrugged it off. Maybe Blaze had a thing against birds, or animals in general. Opal tossed Blaze a small rectangular box and a rolled-up note. She read the note, her smile getting bigger as she made her way down the page.

"Looks like Neal came through for you, Azura."

"Huh?" she said, confused. Blaze held up a small remote.

"This," Blaze said, "is our ticket anywhere."

Jett watched the countryside of Spain go by from his seat beside Azura. The train raced along the track, initially pressing Jett back into his seat. Rolling green and brown hills, along with miles of power lines and telephone poles whipped by them. The train was going too fast to catch much of anything else. When they had touched down in Barcelona the others had dropped them off at the train station and hailed a cab to take them to Blaze's friend. Both Azura and Blaze could speak Spanish fluently, which was a huge help when navigating the station and the airport. The knot of guilt in Jett's stomach was growing. Before their flight, Opal had pointed out that the San Jose airport had once been under Myra's control. Their symbols and structures were still constructed into the building. Chunks of *ankh* were scattered through the floor, causing it to appear like glossy marble tile. In case of emergencies, she told him, to send out a flare for help. Jett had made an excuse to go to the bathroom, and separated from the rest of the group. Once he was sure he was well out of their sight, he sat down against one of the walls and placed his palm on the floor. He closed his eyes and concentrated. He tried to remember every little detail about Jackson. The way he looked and held himself, along with his way of speaking. If this really was *ankh*, he should be able to use this to contact him. His hand was growing hot. He focused and brought back the exchange they had the first time. He opened his eyes to see himself surrounded in the same white haze. Jackson's projection slowly faded into view a few feet in front of him. Jackson smiled and waved.

"Jett Davis. A pleasure. I suppose you're reconsidering my offer?" Jett took a deep breath. "Can... can you really find Mavis?"

"Of course. We have the best locating technology in the world, and professional trackers. I guarantee we can find her within a week, safe and sound, no matter where on the planet she happens to be. The crowd you're running with, they're only in it to set their friend free. They will not help you, at least not in time. I suppose you figured out how they've been lying to you?"

"Yeah, you were right. I saw firsthand what Blaze is capable of."

"Terrifying, right?" Jackson's voice was as smooth as honey, warm and coaxing as he continued to talk. "It's a terrible thing to witness, and I'm sorry you had to find out that way. Now I hope you believe that I'm on your side.

Let's discuss business, shall we?" he grinned at Jett. "In exchange for finding Mavis, you tell me where Blaze Darkfire and Opal Dystar are so we can come and apprehend them. You will be placed under witness protection, so you need not fear any backlash from them." Jett's heartbeat sped up dangerously. Despite everything, he truly believed that Opal was innocent. Flashbacks of Opal training him to walk on his hover pads tore through his mind. Catching him and encouraging him every time he fell over. His heart was torn between an opportunity to find Mavis, and a desire to protect the girl who had put in her best to get him to walk again. Then again, how well did he really know Opal?

"Jett," Jackson said. "Those two are wanted criminals. You understand why I have to ask you for this, right? I am only asking for a location. You don't have to worry about anything else. We will execute the arrest on our own."

"On one condition," Jett offered. Jackson raised an eyebrow at him. "You give Opal a fair trial, time to prove her innocence. I don't think she was behind Kaitlin's murder in all honesty." Jackson thought about the proposal for a bit. Jett waited tensely for his response. He still wanted Jackson's help. Jackson eventually gave him a slow nod. "Deal. I will give Opal a full six months to prove herself innocent. Does that suffice?"

"Yes, that's fine," Jett said, his muscles relaxing. Opal would have more than enough time to figure out her situation. She would be okay. That eased his conscience.

"Do we have a deal then?" he asked. Jett took a deep breath. "Yes. We do." A slow smile spread over Jackson's face. "We will start looking for Mavis right away, and I will update you with progress. In the meantime, you owe me a location."

"Blaze and Opal are in Barcelona, Spain right now, visiting a detective. That's all I know."

"A detective you say? I know just the one Blaze Darkfire will go to. That's more than enough information for us. Thank you, Jett."

"Just hold up your end of the deal," he responded.

"Of course. I am a man of my word. You will see that proven shortly. It's best if you keep this deal between us. We'd like to have the element of surprise on our side."

"Uh…sure," Jett rubbed his eyes. Jackson's image was flickering and fading into the white mist.

"Until we speak again, Jett." Just like that, Jett was once again sitting on the floor of the airport. Rushed tourists and businessmen walked around him briskly to catch their planes. Jett swallowed, gathered himself together and started to walk back towards his group. He felt horrible for revealing their location to Jackson, especially since Opal had done nothing but help him since he woke up from his coma. He had struck a deal with Jackson though on her behalf, and his burning desire to find Mavis elapsed any feeling of betrayal he had.

Sitting beside Azura now, the guilt was working its way back up. He couldn't reverse what he had done now. There were only two things stopping him from breaking down and spilling everything to Azura. One was the guarantee to find Mavis under a week, the other being the memory of Blaze. Anytime he thought about how they had hidden that from him, his guilt suppressed itself. He steeled his nerves and gazed out at the passing landscape. Azura held out an egg and cheese sandwich.

"Hungry?" she asked. Jett took the sandwich gingerly and nodded his thanks.

"So, who is this book collector we're going to see?" Jett asked between bites. Azura sighed. "He's not a book collector. Although he will have the ones we're looking for. He's a former professor of black magic. If anyone can figure out what's wrong with Opal, it's him." Jett frowned. It wasn't like Azura to lie.

"Why did you say he was collector to everyone else then?"

"The only one who I actually lied to was Blaze. Everyone else knew."

"I thought you two were good friends? Why..."

"It's hard to explain. I had promised her I wouldn't see him, but the circumstances are such that I have to go back on my word this time. I couldn't risk telling her, she wouldn't forgive me for it." Azura looked wretched. Jett didn't blame her. Here he was debating his inner guilt, when Azura had an incredibly more pressing issue of integrity tearing her between her two friends. One whose life was on the line, and the trust of the other.

"Who is he?" Jett inquired. Azura pushed her glasses back on her nose.

"Benjamin Darkfire. Blaze's father." That stunned Jett to silence. A million questions flood his head. Why didn't Blaze want Azura to meet her father? How was he a professor on black magic and how did he know so much?

Why didn't Blaze ask him for help herself? He must be phenomenal at what he does if it was enough for Azura to risk her promise to Blaze. It wasn't adding up. Seeing how miserable Azura looked, he decided to withhold his concerns for now. He squeezed her hand reassuringly. Azura just stared off into the distance until their stop arrived. They got off to find themselves in the city square, where streetcars ran through the roads and little shops lined the sidewalks. Black metal balconies and arched windows were on almost every building, alternating from brick to cement to wooden walls. Buildings were coloured light yellow, reddish-orange and creamy white. Potted plants hung from the lampposts, bringing in a touch of greenery. It was a serene and peaceful setting, even though the streets were busy with people. Jett followed Azura through the crowds, struggling to keep up with her as her head disappeared occasionally in the masses. She approached a small corner café at the end of the street and leaned against a nearby lamppost.

"He comes here often around this time. If we're lucky we can catch him," she explained to Jett.

"He doesn't know you're coming?"

"Nope." Jett didn't know Blaze's father, but Jett knew he hated being surprised like that. He hoped for their sake, that her father wasn't like him. If he was anything like Blaze, he didn't know what he would do. He and Azura had been waiting for twenty minutes when a man in his mid-forties went into the café. He came out a few minutes later with two croissants and two coffee cups, making himself comfortable at one of the patio tables. As soon as Jett could see the man's eyes he jumped. He had seen this man before. He was an older version of the man that was dancing in the visions from his coma. His black hair had streaks of grey and there were small wrinkles around his eyes. He was still broad shouldered and confident, carrying himself with power. The woman in his vision had looked like Blaze… but older. It hit him there. She must have been Blaze's mother, which meant this was Mr. Darkfire. Jett had seen an episode from their wedding day. While Jett was still reeling from this information Azura approached him. Jett saw the recognition in Mr. Darkfire's eyes as Azura drew close.

"Azura!" he exclaimed. He put down his croissant and got up to meet her. "What are you doing here?"

"Ben! Who are you talking to?" came a voice from behind Jett. He turned and did a double take. The woman who had spoken was undoubtedly Blaze's mother. The resemblance was uncanny. While her mother wore glasses, Jett could still associate her facial features with Blaze. Dark eyes, same jawline and cheekbones and the long straight raven hair mixed with grey strands like her husband. She was poised for an older woman, and rushed over to see Azura.

"Azura! It's been so long!" she hugged her. "What a weird coincidence seeing you here! What bring you to Zaragoza?"

"I was just asking her that," her husband told her.

"It's no coincidence Mrs. Darkfire. I came looking for you. Oh, this is Jett Davis, a friend of mine." She motioned Jett over. Jett joined her nervously.

"Hi," he said. He shook hands with both of them.

"I need your help. Opal's life is on the line if we can't figure out what kind of dark magic possessed her. Is there somewhere private we can talk about this? I'll explain everything there," Azura said quickly, looking around like they may be watched. Blaze's parents exchanged concerned glances.

"We'll take you back to our hotel. That will have to do for now, and you better be ready to explain all of this Azura." Azura nodded. Jett concealed his mild surprise. Azura had barely said anything about what was going on and Blaze's parents had just taken it as is, not inquiring further up front.

"Come along." Mrs. Darkfire walked on one side of Jett while Azura walked on the other.

"You look a lot like Blaze." Jett told her. She looked at him, confused.

"Sorry?"

"You look a lot like your daughter, Blaze," he repeated. Azura pinched his arm. He turned to look at her. She was shaking her head no. Now Jett was confused.

"I think you might have me confused for someone else. I have two daughters, but neither of them are named Blaze."

"Are… are you sure?" Jett asked, bewildered. Mrs. Darkfire looked at him like he was an idiot. It was the same look Blaze gave him often too.

"I'm quite sure Jett. I've never heard of anyone named Blaze."

CHAPTER 15
Ace Ryder

ADAM HAD STARED OUT THE WINDOW IN FASCINATION FOR THE ENTIRE taxi ride. He would probably never have the chance to come to Spain again, so he was taking it all in now, the city, lights, architecture, and environment. When he was younger and had initially discovered his passion for the culinary arts, one of his dreams was to do a European tour and cook in some of the world's most renowned cities. Madrid, Spain had been one of them. He was about an hour away from Madrid according to Opal, but Barcelona was still stunning to experience. They pulled up alongside an elegant entranceway strung with fairy lights and lanterns. Blaze paid the driver and ordered everyone to get out. They stood facing a massive door that was mostly frosted glass with a wooden frame. Engraved in gold on the frost, in steady cursive, were the words 'The Lapis Serpent'. Blaze threw open the door and strode inside. They were immediately stopped by two security guards about three feet into the doorway.

"Where do you think you're going?" one of them asked in a deep, gruff voice.

"I'm here to see Ace Ryder," Blaze said.

"He has a private party tonight. No walk-ins welcome."

"Oh, he'll make an expectation for me, I assure you." Blaze flashed her dagger at them. The two guards were briefly stunned before turning to stumble down the hallway. Leave it to Blaze to scare her way into and expensive hotel or banquet hall or whatever the heck this place was. Adam was glad that Blaze could handle people like that for their safety, but at the same time it went against his morals. Threatening someone to do something, by violence or by show of it, was low and oppressive in his opinion.

"Couldn't she have just asked them to bring him out?" he whispered to Joe. "Instead of threatening them with a knife?"

"She didn't threaten them, Adam. She was showing them the symbol on her dagger. It carries a lot of weight around here." Joe's response carried a concerned undertone, like he was wary of Blaze doing such a thing.

"Oh," Adam said, embarrassed. The two guards came back and waved their hands at Blaze.

"This way Miss." Adam noticed that the guards' entire demeanour had changed. They were now polite and courteous, speaking clearly and softly to Blaze if she asked them a question. Apparently, a scorpion was highly treasured here. After several twists and turns they arrived at a doorway covered in shining blue tinsel that served as a curtain. The guards bowed to Blaze and left, returning to their post at the front door.

"Let's go," Blaze said. She looped her arm through Joe's and strode in, leaving Adam and Opal to trail behind her. On the other side of the curtain, a full-blown party was underway. There was a light-up dance floor in the middle of the room, full of moving bodies. The main lights were off and red, blue, green and white strobe lighting pulsed and shone in varying patterns across the walls and floors. There was a bar and a few tables along the far side and a small, circular concert stage was set up with a grand Steinway piano and microphone. The music was so loud that Adam could feel the floor vibrating underneath him. They made their way to the edge of the concert stage by skittering around the edges of the room. Blaze pushed back a black curtain that was hung over an opening in the wall. Adam ducked in behind her, leaving the music and lights behind.

The immediate light hurt his eyes, and he had to blink a few times before focusing on the room. It was a softly lit lounge area with sofas, a snack bar and one wall with floor to ceiling mirrors. Blaze made herself right at home, taking some chips and pop from the bar and tossing them out to the others before cozying up to Joe on one of the sofas. Adam had noticed the change in behaviour from those two. Blaze was always happy around Joe as far as he had seen, but now she seemed even more so, and Joe would smile at her every now and then when she wasn't looking. He pushed the thought aside quickly

and mentally prepared himself to meet this detective Ace Ryder. Adam
had no idea what to expect and that made him nervous. He hated offend-
ing anyone for the most part, or serious confrontation. He liked to know
what he was up against so he had time to prepare. With the spontaneity of
recent events, he had been thrown off completely for the past week. Adam
was halfway through his packet of Doritos when a man, who he assumed
was Ace, entered the room. The first word that hit Adam was *striking*. Ace
had stunning electric blue eyes, framed by dark lashes with brownish-black
hair against rosy, slightly sun-kissed skin like a surfer. His hair was styled
up, with layers that spiked over each other on the left side of his head and
three or four small bright blue streaks were scattered between them. He had
unshaven stubble around the majority of his angled jaw and a black earring
glittered off of his right ear. As he stepped further into view, Adam saw he
was wearing a worn, black leather jacket over a white V-neck that went low
enough to give a peek at his pectorals. Black jeans were held up by a spike
studded belt. Polished combat boots and a silver Rolex completed the look.
While Adam stared in awe, Blaze got up to greet him. When Ace's eyes
landed on her, a smile took over his face and he reached out to hug her. Blaze
came forward and punched him in the stomach. Adam and Opal both shot
up, watching tensely as Ace doubled over. To Adam's surprise, Ace laughed
weakly while holding his stomach.

"Guess I deserved that," he said.

"No kidding," Blaze responded with a grin. She grabbed his hand and
straightened him up before tackling him with a hug. "It's been a long time
Ace." Ace squeezed her tightly. Adam turned to see how Joe was reacting. Joe
seemed to be the only one of them who wasn't surprised at all, and a small
smile played on his lips as he watched the scene unfold.

"Too long."

"And whose fault is that?"

"Guilty as charged," he held up his hands in surrender. "I'm sorry babe,
but you know how busy I am."

"You can't be so busy that you couldn't visit your friend for the past
five years."

"Hey, I call you often!"

"Not anymore! Now it's like once every few months."

"Too many girls. Hard to keep up with them all." He flinched back as Blaze faked another punch at him, laughing. She clearly didn't mind that Ace didn't call her often.

"Whatever makes you happy, Ace. There are some introductions in order here." She waved her hand out, gesturing to Adam, Opal and Joe. "This is Joe, Opal and Adam."

"This is the Joe I've heard so much about. Nice to meet you bro." He gave Joe a fist bump.

"Glad to meet the infamous Ryder after all this time," Joe said.

"You know about me?"

"I've heard a lot of stories from Blaze. You two were quite the terrifying duo."

Ace covered his face with his hands. His fingers were long and slender.

"Oh God... I swear I'm not as bad as she makes me out be," he joked. "She was the devil in the pair, not I."

"Don't worry, I can believe that," Joe winked at Blaze. She rolled her eyes at him.

"Anyway... I didn't come to see you out of the goodness of my heart," Blaze said. Ace nodded in agreement.

"Of course," he mocked her playfully. "I was wondering what brought you here."

"It's very serious, and I need you sworn to secrecy." Blaze's change in tone was not lost on Ace. His expression darkened.

"What's wrong?"

"We have a missing person we need to find. Adam here, is a close friend of hers. Adam could you please give a full description to Ace?"

"Uh..." Adam stammered. He had not been prepared to be addressed directly. Ace reminded him a lot of Blaze and Adam found him a little intense. He had thought Blaze would do most of the talking and sort it out with him personally. He did know Mavis better than all of them though, so he supposed it made sense.

"Her name and physical appearance would be great for starters," Ace said objectively.

"Right. Her name is Mavis Williams. She's Caucasian with long, blond, curly hair, light blue eyes and is slim and short, a little over five feet. The last time I saw her, she was wearing a cropped jean jacket, and black shorts and red crew neck top."

"How did she disappear?"

"I'll answer that one later. It's complicated," Blaze interjected.

"How is she related to you?" Ace inquired.

"She's my best friend, we've been close since the beginning of high school."

"I see," Ace turned to Blaze. "If you need a missing person found though, why haven't you used the locators in Myra?"

"She's ordinary, the locators wouldn't be able to track her. And… we're kind of cut off from city resources at the moment."

"What?" Ace asked, confused.

"It's a long story."

"One I want to hear," He turned to face everyone else. "If you all don't mind, I'd like to speak with Blaze alone for some time. Feel free to relax here, or join the party." Opal and Joe nodded at him. Ace took Blaze's hand and lead her out of the room. Adam wrung his hands together. He was beginning to panic internally. He felt like everything was taking too long. He wanted to drop everything and go and search for Mavis at this very instant, scouring the country, leaving no stone unturned. He was aware it was highly unrealistic; he knew he would need help. He just didn't want to sit around and do nothing. With every passing moment, Mavis could be getting more lost, or sinking into deeper trouble. Joe clapped him on the shoulder.

"I know it sucks to do nothing Adam. But right now, there's nothing you can possibly do that would help Mavis. It's better that you let yourself relax and rest up for when we do go out to find her," Joe said.

"It's not that easy. Blaze didn't show it much, but I bet she was just as upset over you."

"I can only imagine. But she knows which battles she can and can't fight. When she couldn't do anything for me, I'm sure she didn't go around in a futile attempt anyway. There will always be times, when the best and only thing you can do is wait." He stood up and walked towards the party. "Come on, let's take a walk."

"What about Op…" Adam turned to see Opal curled up on the sofa, asleep, clutching a pillow to her chest.

"Let her rest. She has a lot on her mind anyway." It hit Adam again that Opal was on trial for murder. He couldn't imagine what she could be feeling, on the run to avoid a death penalty for a murder she didn't really commit. They were all in dire straits. Adam shrugged of his hoodie and placed it over her gently before following Joe out. They made their way out of the party and began to roam the first floor of the building. Long, almost endless, hallways provided tons of walking distance. Adam had to work a bit to keep up with Joe even at a walking pace, since Joe's strides were much quicker.

"Joe..." Adam began.

"Yeah?"

"Where did you go when you disappeared? Do you know? What happened to you?" Joe slowed down to match his pace with Adam.

"Did I know where I was? No, I didn't. I could describe it to you though. When I woke up initially, I was in really bad shape. The last thing I remember was practicing in the skills centre before a sudden wave of dizziness hit me and I fainted. I woke up in some kind of quartz mine, underground. I was beat up pretty bad, but had no memory of how I got there or what happened. I wandered through the mine for a bit and found a small freshwater stream flowing between the cracks in the wall. I drank up and cleaned up my cuts as much as I could. Without food though, I lost consciousness again shortly after. The next thing I knew the wolf, Fang, was standing over me, pawing at me to wake up. I'm glad Blaze had put her necklace around her, because I was much too weak to fight Fang, and I didn't waste my time or energy freaking out. I used the last of my energy to get on Fang's back and then passed out again. Then I woke up to Azura. I have no idea where that mine was. Maybe Scarlett can try and get it out of Fang. I know for sure though that Mavis wasn't there with me. If she was, Fang would have found her." Adam looked down at his feet. Another dead end for Mavis. He had hoped that since they had disappeared at the same time, Joe and Mavis would have ended up in the same place. "I told Blaze and Azura on the plane. They didn't have any idea where I was either. It's a mystery to all of us."

"Do you have any idea why whoever did this chose to take you? We know for Mavis, they wanted to get a rise out of Jett. But why you?" Joe shrugged.

"I don't know to be honest. I'm not connected to many power players in Myra. I suppose it could have been to poke a finger at Blaze, if they didn't like her. The amount of power it takes to work that kind of spell though doesn't seem worth it for something as petty as that. I think there's an ulterior motive, just not too sure what."

They walked silently for some time and Adam calmed down. He discovered talking to Joe was strangely soothing. He felt like Joe was pretty understanding of most situations, so he felt inclined to open up to him more. He had understood his frustrations about Mavis and didn't push them aside as unreasonable. Adam often thought he was overworked about many things, which was probably true, but Joe had put him at ease by assuring him his concern was valid. He turned to look at Joe, whose expression was unusually peaceful. Adam wished he could feel that way right now.

"So, you and Blaze..." Adam prodded. Joe chuckled.

"You noticed?"

"To be honest, I'm sure everyone noticed." Joe rubbed his arm gently, lost in thought for moment.

"Part of me still can't believe it. For the longest time, I thought I would never get past being just a friend to her. It wasn't even that she didn't return my feelings. She did, but refused to act on them. I think that hurt more."

"Why?"

"If you haven't noticed, Blaze is quite pessimistic. She probably expected the worst to happen between us, and couldn't deal with the possibility of that."

"What changed?"

"I'm assuming me disappearing and coming face to face with death had her re-evaluate our relationship."

"I suppose the possibility of death tends to do that to people," Adam joked lightly. "If you don't mind me asking..."

"Asking what?"

"Why do you like her?" Joe stopped and leaned against the corridor wall. Adam joined him.

"Before I answer that, can I know why you want to know?"

"Because... lately I feel like I've been missing something. My impression of Blaze is not a good one, and yet she has a group of solid friends who, despite the exterior I've seen, stand by her unwaveringly. There has to be something you guys see that I don't. You told me perceptions can be deceptions, so I want to know your side of things."

"Quite mature of you, Adam. As for why I like her..." Joe sighed, "There was a time when she wasn't as cold as she is now. She was still somewhat cold, but not cut-off like you have seen. She loves adventure, and once you get to know her, she is bold, daring and strong. Sure, she's stubborn and hard-headed too, but it all completes her. I was exposed to a whole new world with her, doing things I hadn't ever dreamt of doing. I'm pretty laid back, relaxed and live life comfortably. Sometimes that was boring. She was like a firework, explosive and always reaching for the sky, pulling me along with her. She went through a horrible tragedy, and that changed her forever. She became cold, distant and emotionless. Despite that, I fell for her more. Because even though she suffered, she picked herself up again and stayed strong. Every day she fights that memory and none of us blame her for becoming cold. Under that rough exterior though, is still the girl who will let no one put her down, who will destroy anyone who harms her friends and family," Joe took a deep breath.

"She... can be cruel and insensitive sometimes. She's hurt me before too, being like that. I get along with others really well; I know what offends and what doesn't and am empathetic. She's not. She won't realize how sharply words can sting. She understands pain in physical and emotional agony, and for the most part words don't affect her. To her they're meaningless unless they're accompanied by action. Sometimes she forgets that they affect others. She will always correct her wrongs though, once she realizes it. All of us still see the fire that burns in her, fierce, but warm. Everyone had their flaws and despite hers, I think she's someone worth standing by." Adam and Joe shared a long pause of silence while Adam absorbed what Joe had said. He was beginning to see how someone could love someone like Blaze. Perhaps not a newcomer into her life, but the old friendships she had kept and maintained with steel bonds. "You're easy to open up to Adam," Joe said. "I didn't expect myself to tell you that much." Adam gave him a weak smile. He didn't know that about himself.

"What happened to her?" Adam asked finally.

"That's not my story to tell," was all Joe said. Adam didn't prod further. Adam had never thought of himself as judgemental, but often times he did take things at face value, because there wasn't much more he could look into. If someone doesn't give you anything to go off of, what is one supposed to think? Then again, Jett always asked him if it was necessary to have an opinion about everything. Without all the facts, why bother drawing a conclusion? He let the notion slide. Either way, he felt a little closer to Joe now, and in turn, a smidge more to Blaze.

☙

Scarlett sipped some orange pekoe tea from a delicate china cup. She flipped her hair to one side so it wouldn't get in her mouth and drank away. She couldn't deny it, the tea was delicious. She still had a bitter taste in her mouth though, since Jackson was sitting across from her, drinking as well. They sat in his office at the Springs, where he had the kettle ready for them. Scarlett was still in her leotard and running shoes; feeling uncomfortably underdressed in Jackson's presence. Jackson always dressed to impress, and today was no exception as he rocked a fine tailored black suit and tie.

"Just how you like it, no?" he asked.

"I've had better," she said curtly. He smirked.

"Whatever you say. I know you don't want to admit it." Scarlett sighed and pressed herself back into the sofa.

"What do you want to say to me Jackson? Get it over with." Jackson leaned forward and took her hand softly, running his thumb over the back of her fingers. Scarlett resisted the urge to snatch her hand away. His face morphed into a desolate mask, with a painful longing in his eyes.

"Kitten, I need you. I want you. I can give you everything you desire."

"Jackson there's no way..."

"Let me finish," he said. "I...I've thought about you constantly. Every day since you left me. They say time heals all, but they're wrong. Time only heals what you allow it to heal. It's been two years, Scarlett. No matter how hard I try, I can't let the wound close." Scarlett's heart wavered a bit. For a moment, she felt like Jackson was sincere. She quickly chided herself. She would not be fooled. Not again. Perhaps he was sincere. That wouldn't change what he had done, or how she felt about him.

"Doesn't that suck for you," she said pulling her hand away.

"Don't be like that," he said softly.

"What gave you the Goddamn right to tell me how I should or shouldn't be like?!" she exploded. Jackson was taken aback, looking at her wide-eyed. Anger simmered in her blood. Two years of effort to supressing these feelings burned away and the rage boiled over. She had left quietly the first time, without saying anything to anyone about why she left. Not him, not her friends or family. Now she was ready to spit that poison out at him, the one she had bottled up for so long.

"What gives you the right," she seethed, "to ask me to come back to you?" She slammed her fist on the table, making the tea set clatter and bounce. "After everything you did, you have the audacity to think you should be forgiven?! How dare you…"

"I never did anything so bad that I couldn't be forgiven for it! I did what I thought was right!" he shot back.

"The fact that you don't even think you were wrong sickens me. How…" she was desperately trying to hold back angry tears, "How could you think that it was possibly okay to give me Lilith's curse?" Jackson stood stock still, the shock written over his face. Scarlett was red eyed and furious. He didn't know that she had discovered what he had done.

"It's that revolting *jaculus* mentality. You think you're so superior to everyone else. Torturing, oppressing and hating anyone who's not a *bellator*. I was stupid enough to think you were different. The sweetness and so-called acceptance you gave me was just for show, wasn't it? Didn't want my blood to taint you or your children, so you took away my ability to have any!" The shame was written all over Jackson's face. He came towards her.

"Kitten…" Scarlett slapped him so hard she could feel his cheekbones move under his skin. He went tumbling backwards, holding his face.

"I've wanted to do that for two years, you lying piece of shit. Ask me again to come back to you. Just try it. That was for what you did to me, and for all the other women you've done that to." She got up and hurled her teacup to the floor, spraying shards of ceramic glass everywhere.

"You never wanted to have children, Scarlett."

"At the time, I said that at the moment I didn't. I was nineteen! Of course I didn't. That didn't mean in the future I wouldn't change my mind. It doesn't matter if I did or didn't want them. That was my decision to make, not yours!" She stood over him, her eyes alight with fury. "You two-faced bastard. Hunting Blaze and Opal for using black magic, when your own hands are tainted with it."

"Opal killed someone Scarlett."

"Don't act like you haven't," she said. He flinched.

"How could you say that..."

"Leaving someone to die, or standing by doing nothing while they die, is just as bad as killing them. In my eyes, you're a murderer." She looked him straight on. They both knew what she was referring to. Her anger had passed its climax, and she was starting to simmer down.

"I'm done talking to you. Give me Mavis' location."

"Scarlett..."

"NOW!" she shouted. Jackson slumped in defeat. He knew she wouldn't listen to him now, no matter what he said. He took a small folded piece of paper out of his suit pocket and handed it to her. She grabbed it and turned to leave.

"I wasn't the one who cursed you Scarlett." His voice came from behind her, miserable and weak. She clenched her hands into fists.

"Did you let it happen?" He was silent. "Did you do it to others?" Not a word from him.

"I thought so," she said. She let the door shut with a bang behind her.

✂

Jett was beyond confused as he followed Azura and the Darkfires to their hotel. *I've never heard of anyone named Blaze.* Ms. Darkfire looked exactly like Blaze, and Azura had said they were going to see her father. So, what on earth was going on here? Azura had told him to stop, so he had, but he would definitely get it out of her afterward. They settled around a coffee table in the hotel room that was littered with books, papers and pens.

"I apologize for the mess. As you can see I'm not really here on vacation, I'm still working."

"That's quite alright," Azura said. "We'll probably need your notes."

"Okay, start talking. What is going on?" Ms. Darkfire asked. Azura filled them in to the best of her abilities. When she got to the fight with the *jaculus* both of them grimaced. Apparently the *jaculus* were universally hated, Jett realized.

"We need to know if there's some way to control someone while they're asleep. If so, how we can trace it back to caster? Opal doesn't have much time."

Mr. Darkfire rubbed his forehead.

"Possession magic... delicate stuff. Also needs a powerful start-up. I'm curious about how they obtained enough energy for that." Azura stiffened momentarily. Jett recognized her hesitation. She was debating telling them that he was a *permotionem*, because he had been used to collect that power. Guilt shot through him. He didn't know why. Why should he feel guilty about something he hadn't done intentionally? He was used. So why did he still blame himself? *Because if you weren't there it wouldn't have happened,* whispered a small voice in his head. *Shut up,* he told it.

"We are too, but there are various ways they could have achieved it. What's important is how they managed to work the spell." Azura rested her head on her knees. Mr. Darkfire grabbed a laptop that was on the TV stand and started clicking through documents.

"Give me a second, Azura, to pull up my research on it. Here we go." He turned the laptop to face them, showing them a page with various diagrams and notes that Jett couldn't decipher. Azura seemed to understand some of it as her eyes scanned the page. "Possession is most effective when brain waves are at an active state. Since the brain is focused on other tasks, invasion of the mind is easiest at that point. Being awake is enough for possession to take hold because of how strong it is, but if you're asleep, your subconscious is on its guard." He leaned back, thinking deeply. "Unless..."

"Unless what, Ben?" Ms. Darkfire asked.

"Unless it's done during the dream phase, when brain waves are reactivated. I think dreams can generate enough activity to create a distraction for a possession to take hold. But that would just be a theory; it isn't proven. There's also a hole in it. A possession also requires a visual aspect, sort of like a small hypnotizing before control can be taken. Usually it's by looking at the caster, or the caster uses a symbol of significance for the victim. If one is asleep, I don't know if the victim would be able to see that."

"Perhaps it's not a possession spell at all?" Azura suggested. Mr. Darkfire shook his head. From what you described, it has every attribute of being one. "The collapsing, the no memory, are all very standard in that kind of witchcraft. It would be quite smart of the caster to run the two spells at once, using one to power the other in order to summon the snakes as protection."

"Any way to know who cast it?" He shook his head.

"Not by any typical means. Since two spells were cast, the line of magic would have been split. There would be no way to follow it back to the source like that." Jett's stomach dropped. Was there really no way to find out? He had been promised six months for Opal. Here they were playing Azura's trump card, and it seemed to be getting them nowhere either. If Mr. Darkfire couldn't help them, then six months or not, could anyone? Azura rubbed her temples.

"Oh, I almost forgot," she said, taking a piece of paper out her pocket. "Do you have any of these titles?" She handed him a list of missing books from the Seal. Mr. Darkfire glanced over the titles.

"I do have most of them. Very dangerous and experimental magic though. Why would you need them?"

"They've gone missing from the Seal. We think whoever did this is trying to do something with them."

"There are several topics in each one," Ms. Darkfire said. She clapped her hands together. "Is there a reoccurring subject in each one? Or complimentary spells to another?"

"Maybe… I'd have to take a good look through them," Mr. Darkfire said. "They're at my temporary office a few blocks away. Tell you what, Ayesha and I will go and study them for a bit and come back in a few hours to let you know if we notice any patterns. In the meantime, you two should rest up, you look quite wrecked." Ayesha Darkfire nodded.

"I'll make you guys some food before we leave."

Azura inclined her head to them.

"Thank you for your help," she said.

"Not a problem."

The Darkfires got up and began to pack their bags while they talked amongst themselves, leaving Azura and Jett alone in the living room. The laptop was still on, displaying Mr. Darkfire's research. It blinked out and the screen saver came on. It was of the Darkfires, with three children sitting around them on a beach with the ocean in background. Two small girls and a slightly older boy were sitting in the sand, smiling up at the camera. There was a small caption at the bottom saying *Ben and Ayesha 2015 with Jax, Sabrina and Phoenix.* The two girls seemed to share Blaze's physical appearance, the youngest one with her dark eyes and jaw set, and the older one with her straight black hair and broad shoulders. The boy seemed to be in his early teens, but resembled Mr. Darkfire.

"Blaze's siblings," Azura whispered. "She's the oldest out of the four of them."

"She's not in the picture," Jett pointed out. Azura sighed.

"Yeah."

"Azura, Ms. Darkfire said she only had two daughters…"

"Let them leave first Jett. I'll explain after."

After bidding them goodbye, Azura and Jett set down the sandwiches and coffee Ms. Darkfire had left for them. Azura was going through the notebooks and papers that were on the coffee table. Jett watched her hands work at light speed. Azura was quick and precise when she was focused. She didn't miss a single page even when she was going that fast. Her hands came to a sudden stop at a page in a red leather notebook. She carried it gingerly back to Jett, as if she was holding a sensitive explosive. She set it down lightly on the table and lay it open for Jett to see. The pages were blank with two dried white flowers pressed flat against the paper like a bookmark. The white colour seemed to be tricking his eye. He thought he saw it move. He glanced at Azura.

"Look familiar?" she asked. Jett focused on the flower petals, trying to make a connection. Had he seen this before? The white seemed to shuffle and move inside the petals, like something was trapped in it. *Trapped…* he thought. He gasped.

"A memory flower!" he exclaimed. "Right?" Azura nodded. "They're white… so it's a memory about loss?" he asked. Once again, she nodded.

"I want to you access the memory," she said.

"Are you crazy? The last one nearly killed me!"

"That because you tore it out of the ground. While anyone can put them in, only *permotionem* can access memories. You need to create a sympathetic bond with the flower. Hold it and call out to your own loss. The flower will respond to you."

"Why do you want me to see it?" Azura patted his hand gently.

"It's the best explanation I can give you for what's going on. Now try it." Jett sighed. Azura was being cryptic and vague again. Whenever he wanted a straight answer from her he couldn't get one. He picked up one of the flowers and closed his fist around the stem.

"Now focus on a memory of loss. Remember, the emotions you went through and the resulting actions from it," she commanded. Jett thought of the day Blaze told him Mavis was missing. The shock, dejection and fury he had felt. The anxious state he entered after and the hole her absence had left for him. The flower grew hot in his hand and then cooled again.

"Hmm..." Azura said. "Perhaps what you're thinking of isn't a strong enough memory. Can you recall a more... significant one?" To Jett, losing Mavis was pretty devastating. The only thing that could have been worse was his father's death. He brought back all the days leading up to it. Mavis giving his dad tea and watching sport matches with him. Jett, Adam and their mother trying to keep each other together while they watched the life drain away from his father. Jett had felt like his world was slowly falling apart, piece-by-piece, into a void of despair that he couldn't escape from. The final moment, when his dad's hand had gone limp and his chest ceased to rise with breath. Jett didn't think that there was anything that could compare to the anguish he felt that day. It hadn't been a shock, like Mavis' had, but a slow building of fear that grew over time. A little part of him had always hoped for some kind of miracle to reverse the process, even though he knew it was next to impossible. He had still hoped, that if there was still life in his father, no matter how little, it could be salvaged. Consequently, his hopes had been crushed. The day Joseph Davis had died, Jett knew that everyone felt like a part of them had died too. The stem grew hot once again and began to glow. The light pulsed and then flashed brightly, swallowing Jett in a sea of white.

CHAPTER 16
Cursed

JETT FLOATED IN THE WHITE VAPOUR FOR A WHILE, WATCHING IT SHIFT and move like a cloudy, smoking serpent that was enveloping him. The cloud dissipated and he was standing along a pink sand beach with stunningly clear water. Blaze appeared in front of him, walking with her father. She was laughing, holding her flip-flops in one hand. She seemed younger, around sixteen or seventeen years old. Her genuine smile brought a new air of beauty to her face that made her appear much more striking, and Joe's dragonfly necklace was sparkling around her neck. This was so cool. She would get to relax here, away from army training with her family and help out her father with his research. They walked along the coastline until a thick expanse of tropical growth began to appear in the distance. She headed straight toward it; this was nothing she hadn't seen before. Her father had taught her well enough to know how to navigate and travel her way through a jungle, and what tools to use to make a path for herself. Soon they were making their way through the palm trees and long grass, stepping lightly over quicksand and mud. She didn't mind getting dirty. It wasn't like there was anyone she cared about impressing anyway. They got through to a small clearing that was at the base of a hillside. The hill climbed several feet upward and was covered in rich black soil and emerald green plants. Her dad winked at her. She knew what that meant. A race. Both of them sprinted to the hill and began to climb. She felt the familiar burn in her muscles, just like when she scaled the climbing walls in combat training. She was so used to the burn that she often associated it with the adrenaline rush she had as she went up higher and higher into the air. Heights were something she loved and she happily raced up the side, using her powerful legs to beat her dad to the top. A woman should be, above all things, strong she believed. Physically, emotionally, intellectually, because strength stayed with you forever. You could be self-reliant, if you were strong. You would never need anyone else.

They had reached their destination, a small cave on the top of the hill. They were looking for tropical gemstones, different variations of *ankh* with special properties. Traders in the black market dealt these out for powerful magicians, like portable spell enhancers. Her father wanted to study them and figure out a way to cut off the power at its source, or see if it left a traceable energy path. They worked the day away, tapping and mining stone samples out of the rough rocky walls of the cave. They came back to the main beach by late afternoon where the rest of her family was waiting for her. Sabrina and Phoenix wanted to play volleyball, so she and Jax got to work, setting up the net while their father took the stones into his workstation. She smiled as she watched her little sisters fumble with the ball. Her father called her over and she left the ball in the sand and ran towards him. He held out a necklace to her. It was a polished, beautifully cut, obsidian and violet stone that had the two colours spiralling around each other.

"What's this?" she asked.

"One of the stones we mined today. It's a rare one; usually they're not multi-coloured. You know how *ankh*s power spells right? These are altered *ankh*s, the colour representing what emotion it will power up to."

"Love and strength...." she said turning it in her hand, letting the light glimmer off of it. "This must be insanely powerful."

"Yes. If the traders have found this and have it on the market, there's no telling what someone could do with them. Though all of my informants have told me they have only been able to find it here, on Rehma Island. It appears untouched though, so they may not know it exists yet. We have to take extreme measures to hide these ones, because they have demon flame in them. You don't see it now, but it can be summoned through the stone, since both love and strength are represented by fire."

"Why would we have to worry about it though? How would someone access it? The spell would only respond to the emotions, right?" Mr. Darkfire scratched his head.

"I haven't had enough time to study them to figure that out. But if it's there, it can be accessed. It's just a matter of time before someone figures out how. I want you to have that one though."

"Me? Why?"

"Because," he said "I want you to remember just how dangerous black magic is. It can take something like love and strength and morph it into evil and despair."

"Magic cannot do what it does not have potential for. That's a law of magic, Dad. If it can morph it into those things, doesn't it mean love and strength have those aspects to begin with?"

"Out of the laws of magic, that is probably the hardest one to understand. Others are simpler, like no bringing back the dead, no forcing love or hate. Potential though, is very flexible, and it often times depends if the user sees it as such. I know how pessimistic you are and sometimes and I'm glad you're not a magician. Because if you can see love as an evil, that is what it shall become." He put the stone around her neck, resting it under the dragonfly. "Wear it and remember that power is a responsibility. Just because you have it sitting at your throat, doesn't mean you should abuse it. Black magic is black because it involves hurting others. You can take as much pain as you want onto yourself, but when it affects another, that's something else. Do you understand?" She nodded. She understood most of what he had said. She returned to play volleyball with her siblings before her mother called them for dinner.

Later that night she was walking about knee deep in the water while her family sat around a bonfire on the shore. Jax was roasting marshmallows while her sisters were playing cards with her parents. It was so peaceful and quiet that she became lost in her thoughts as she walked along. A movement in her tent caught the edge of her eye and she whipped around to see a man running out with the bag of stones.

"Hey!" she yelled. "Stop him!" Before she knew what she was doing, she was thundering after him, closing the distance between them. She could hear her father's voice yelling in the background. The thief turned to tread into the water, attempting to go around a jetty of rocks. Blaze leapt up and landed on the jetty, running forward to catch him by the collar. She struggled to pull him towards her as he splashed in the water. He turned and grabbed her hand unexpectedly, yanking her forward as she plunged face first into the ocean. *No*, she thought. There was only one thing on this earth that Blaze Darkfire could not do. *Swim*.

She attempted to move her arms and bobbed to the surface for a quick second to take a breath and then plunged under again. She could still feel the thief's hand grabbing her wrist. She twisted his arm back, forcing him to drop the stones. The bag fell from his hand and she grabbed it and kicked her way up to the surface again. She could see that her whole family was in the water, with her mother in the lead, swimming towards her frantically. Water pulled her under again. The thief appeared in front of her, holding a milky white stone. *Dammit, he got one.* The stone was glowing, which was an indication of a spell starting. It illuminated the thief's face; making his wide jade eyes and sandy hair visible to her. He pushed her down and began to go towards her father. *Over my dead body*, she thought. She was slowly beginning to lose consciousness as the air she had been holding in her lungs ran out, but he wasn't getting away that easily. She held on to his ankle, pulling him down with her as they sank into the depths of the ocean. The stone exploded, sending a powerful current through the water. Blaze realized it was too late. The spell had been cast. Powerful waves of water hit her, spinning her around. She glanced up to see that a whirlpool had formed above her. Caught in the middle of it, was her family. Her mother was holding onto her three siblings, as she clung to the jetty rocks with one hand. Her father was trying to reach her, but had gotten stuck in the spinning vortex. The thief ripped his foot away from her grip and swam upward, giving her a gloating smile as he left. She watched in horror as her mother's grip slipped and they all tumbled into the current. Blaze wanted to scream. Her family was going to die in front of her eyes and she would too. She couldn't move up to save them, so she watched them flail helplessly in the fatal waves as she sank further away from them. All because she had fallen into the water. She gripped the stone her father had given her. *It's not going to end like this.* She would fight fire with fire. *I'm sorry Dad. I have no choice.* With the last bit of her strength she clenched the stone and channelled the love for her family into the stone. She had used magic in small doses before, so she knew how to channel her emotions but the stone required her all. She held it to her heart and with every ounce of her remaining strength, crushed the stone.

Blaze shot like a torpedo out of the water. She no longer was in control of herself. All she could feel was anger. Pure, raw fury. Everything was tinted red. She was at the top of a column that was thirty feet of water high, looking down at the scene around her. She saw the thief, trying to swim away from her.

"*He will pay!*" she shouted. The water responded to her rage. An enormous wave crashed into the thief and wrapped around him like a chain, bringing him up to her eye level. He was choking as the water tightened around him, his face turning blue from the lack of oxygen. "*This is what you deserve for going against me. Going against my family. How DARE you!*" The water flung the thief with such force that he created a crater in the sand where he landed. Blaze then noticed her family still trapped in the whirlpool. Phoniex screamed as her hand slipped out of Jax's and she was pulled under. Agony hit her and everything came to a frozen stop. The water stood completely still and her family stood unmoving beneath her. *Well, Well,* a voice echoed in her head. *What do we have here? Why do you summon me human?* Blaze looked around wildly. There was no one, just her.

"I didn't summon anyone…" she said.

Oh, but you did. I am the spirit of the demon flame. When you crushed that stone, it meant you wanted to get to me, to use my power to work magic.

"I did want to use magic, but not use you! I need to save my family!"

Yes. A pity they have to die like this. Unfortunately, the only way you can save them is by using me. That is why you crushed the stone in the first place, no? I will warn you though; I am the devil's weapon. Your request will come with a heavy price. Not like you have a choice in the matter. She could sense that the voice was laughing at her, maniacally. She could see little Phoenix's fingers still popping out above the waves. Her eyes swelled with tears.

"What do you want?" she said.

It's not what I want. You are the summoner, you decide what your sacrifice is. It must be equivalent to what you are receiving from the spell. You are asking for five lives. In return, you must give five lives, or the equivalent. Tell me human, are there another family's lives you wish to exchange for yours? Blaze closed her eyes. She would not slaughter or sacrifice other humans, no matter what the stakes were. She would rather die five times to pay the price. This situation was her fault, she couldn't pin that expense on anyone else.

"Is there no other way?"

Something that would have the same effect as five of your family members dying can also be accepted. Something that would cause the same, or higher level of despair and anguish. Blaze's heart constricted. The tears spilled over, leaving salty streaks down her cheeks. She knew what she had to do.

Blaze swallowed, looking at her family one last time.

"I can't bring pain to anyone else, so deal the pain to me. All of it. Take away their memory of me. Have them forget my existence, but let them remain in mine. That pain will be like they all died for me. In exchange, you save them and assure their well-being." She went silent, holding back her sobs. The voice laughed cruelly, echoing in in her mind.

Excellent deal, human. You understand what truly causes human agony in this world. Your pain for their safety. An ideal devil's bargain. This deal will come with a side effect though. Demon flame will be exercised through your body to save them. It will remain there for all time, as a reminder, a stamp of your deal.

"Why?" she asked.

A punishment for making a deal with Hell's forces. Nothing I can do about that I'm afraid. There may be an upside to all of this though. The grief you will experience might kill you, so the demon flame will extract the majority of the darkness from your body and place it into another living form. We can't let you die now, can we? Who would be around to feel that despair then? Letting you die would be much too kind.

"You're despicable," she spat.

It is your choice, and your deal, my dear. I am laying it out clearly in front of you. Remember that after this, you can blame no one but yourself for your misery. This is the price, the true price, of magic. Blaze's tears flowed freely now as her lips quavered.

"You have my word. Do it."

Your wish is my command. A searing, burning pain shot through her body, making her shriek in torment. Her shoulder felt like it had been stabbed and was on fire. A tornado of white-blue flames coiled around her family members and everything started moving again. The fiery tendrils forced her family to faint away and then the tornado deposited them gently on the shore. The water column threw Blaze down at an alarming speed, and she landed with a sickening thud on the beach. Her shoulder was still burning uncontrollably. Surprisingly, none of her bones were broken. She got up groggily to realize that the thief was laying a few feet away from her, withering in pain from his broken bones. She stumbled over to him and grabbed him by the collar. His eyes were wide with terror as he uselessly tried to push her away.

"If you're going to be treacherous to someone," she said, her voice dangerously soft, "be prepared to have the favour returned." The wrath unspooled from within her and soon she was holding a flaming body. She felt no pain from the fire. She watched him go limp and then disintegrate into ash, the smell of burning flesh lingering around the remains. She felt no remorse as she stood up and turned her back on the char. She sprinted to her family to check if they were alive. They were all perfectly dry and healthy looking, appearing as if they were taking a peaceful nap. She clutched her shoulder and winced, and then used her other hand to shake Phoenix. *Wake up, please.* Phoenix's eyes opened slowly as she took in her surroundings.

"Ugh… where am I?" she turned to look at Blaze and backed up a little. "Who are you?" Blaze felt like her heart was being torn in half. The sister she had raised since she was born, the one she had taught to walk, ride a bike, and read, didn't know who she was.

"You…You were asleep here. I just came to see if you were okay. Is… is that your family?" Blaze's voice trembled. Phoenix got up and ran to Sabrina and Jax, yelling at them to wake up. They all got up unsteadily, rubbing their eyes. A wave of relief passed through her. They were all okay. Phoenix came back to her and tugged on her hand.

"Thanks for waking me up." She turned her head and gasped.

"What happened over there?" Blaze saw that she was pointing to the crater full of ash and char where she had burned that thief alive. She could see the fright in her sister's eyes. "What kind of monster would do something like that?" Nothing could compare to how wretched Blaze felt at that moment.

"Phoenix!" her mother called. Phoenix left Blaze's hand and went to her mother. Blaze realized the bag of stones was hanging around her wrist. Her parents and siblings were in a confused daze, trying to figure out how they managed to fall asleep on the shore. They hadn't noticed her. She placed the bag in the sand and said a tearful goodbye in her head. She turned and limped away with her tears stinging her cheeks as she silently prayed that they didn't notice her. She didn't need any more reminders of what she had lost. She had walked quite a distance when a cold, sharp laughter echoed through her mind. She fell to her knees as her shoulder erupted in pain, a searing agony that almost caused her to black out. She heaved against the sand, wishing she could die to escape it. She could think of nothing else but of the anguish that was wrecking her body. She heard a noise but was too weak to care about what it was. A black shadow loomed over her and then wrapped itself around her. She could feel a heartbeat against her back. The pain subsided, like someone had placed a freezing sheet of ice on her wounds. It wasn't exactly respite, but she wasn't close to dying either. She held onto the shadow for dear life, until there was no trace of the fire in her veins anymore. She could feel muscles and coarse hair under her hands. She pushed herself up to see who had come to save her. She found herself looking into the shinning black eyes of a stallion, with a gorgeous night sky coat. She was strangely attracted to him as he radiated a comforting and tranquil feeling. He nuzzled her affectionately placing his head in her lap. She stroked his snout gently. Only then did she notice the leaping white-blue flames had made up his tail and mane. She could feel nothing when she ran her hands through them.

I am your darkness, Blaze. She jumped, looking down at the horse. *I now carry the majority of the darkness inside you. Your evil, the evil of the demon flame, desire, impulses and emotions. As your name states, I am created of dark fire, the fire that is powered by the worst ambitions of this world.* Blaze slumped against him.

"Is this what I am now? An instrument of darkness?"

Darkness, does not always have to be bad, Blaze. It is what you use it for. Just like light, darkness is a means of power. Use it as reminder, as motivation and as a line of magic to do the right thing, for the right reasons. I am your companion now and I will help you.

"Shall I call you Darkfire then?"

I like it, he replied. She felt a shudder go through her and the voice of the flame returned.

Ah love, it said mockingly. *You were right my dear, it is the biggest weakness one can have. You accepted so much pain for your loved ones. You became help-less because of it and now will suffer for a lifetime. You performed wonderfully. Burning that thief alive is a show of what powerful levels of wickedness you can succumb to. Your darkness will be parallel to your love for your family. You love them greatly, so your dark power shall be as so. You no longer have a family who knows your love, or anyone to love you. You will die with no one of your blood to mourn you, to remember you, as if you never existed. You will always be weak in this area my dear. You may be strong in every other aspect, but love will bring anyone to their knees.* Just like that, the connection severed, returning her mind to herself. She buried her face in Darkfire's side and wept uncontrollably for hours, alone, under the pale light of the moon.

Jett gasped as he was tossed back into reality. The vision fell away from him, and he opened his eyes to the coffee table back in the Darkfires' hotel room. His head was aching and swarming with bits and pieces of the memory he just saw. The disk around his neck was burning, becoming a coin of glowing red metal. He barely noticed. He was holding on to the edge of the table, his knuckles white. Azura was observing him with a depressed expression.

"Now," she said quietly, "Do you understand?" Jett felt miserable for what he had assumed about Blaze, and how little faith he had in her. She had saved him, taught him how to walk again and though they were unconventional methods of doing so, he still he couldn't look past her cold exterior. The fire that he saw destroy that area of the chasm was a curse she had to carry. A curse she received to save her loved ones. After going through something like that, Jett felt like Blaze had experienced the dark side of love. He didn't blame her for being stonehearted or negative now. If he had to make that kind of sacrifice, would he have been able to live with it? He grabbed Azura's hand tightly. Jackson's promise echoed in his head. *In a week,* he had said.

"Azura…" Jett said urgently. "I've made a horrible mistake."

℃

Ace and Blaze sat together on beanbag chairs in Ace's room. The *Lapis Serpent* was his home and business, so he chose to reside there. Blaze regarded him fondly. The idea of Ace was surrounded with warm and exciting childhood memories. They were often told they were girl and boy versions of each other. Blaze agreed most of the time. They were incredibly similar, with the same ambitious drive, value for strength, and general coldness towards other people. Love had always been an evil to both of them, and they carried the same spark for adventure and combat. He was comfortable; the closest thing Blaze had to family. There was something different about the way he understood her. It was clear and concise, and she didn't have to explain herself. He got it, because he was just like her. He had been the one she called after the incident that ruined her life, and he had grabbed the next flight to come and get her and Darkfire when she thought she might have died from grief. Ace Ryder, her other half. They butt heads too because they were both unyieldingly stubborn, and had moments where they were best friends because of it as well. He leaned forward intently to listen to her as she explained everything that had been going on. The intense, shocking, blue eyes never wavered from her face.

"Well damn," he said when she had finished her story. "I never thought I'd live to see a *permotionem* return. He didn't come with you?"

"Nah, he's with Azura where he'll be safe. It would have been too risky to let him come with us." She leaned back in her chair. "Do you think you can find Mavis?"

"I'm not sure Blaze. Finding a missing person is one thing. But when magic comes into the mix, it makes it a lot harder. We don't even know if she's alive."

"I have entertained that idea too, but Jett is too much of a loose cannon for us to tell him that. Who knows how he would have reacted when we imply that instead of rescuing her we're now looking for a body?"

"True, it may be too much for him to bear. Is his twin not gifted?"

"Yeah, as far as we can tell, which is strange, but not unheard of. He's quite the pain in ass too."

"Isn't everyone to you? Besides me of course." A playful smile rested on his lips.

"On the contrary, you're the biggest one I've ever had to deal with. I don't know how I let you live for this long," she joked. Her expression turned serious. "I didn't come here just for Mavis. Like I told you, some of your little pets were involved with Kaitlin's murder. I want to see them."

"Blaze, I own thousands of them. There's no telling which ones were summoned." Blaze thought for a second.

"Then take me to the mother."

"Are you sure?"

"Now, Ace." He held his hands up in surrender.

"As you wish." He held her hand and pulled her up against him, cradling her head lightly. Darkness swallowed them. All Blaze could feel was Ace's leather jacket against her cheek while she held on to him as they spun in blackness. Slowly, light started to softly illuminate the space they were in. They were in a dimly lit corridor facing a steel door. The door had a large protrusion of a cobra head, covered in millions of small, blue, sparkling jewels. Two large rubies made up the eyes, while obsidian formed the slit pupils. It was a splitting image of the snakes that had circled protectively around Opal when she was trying to get to Kaitlin. Ace placed his hand on the steel and a black circle of light pulsed through his hand. The door swung open and millions of hisses and slithering sounds filled the air. They walked in together to an open oasis. In the moonlight, the water was a glossy black colour, rippling with movement under the surface. Large, sturdy trees rose up towards the sky, blanketed with moss and leaves. Her ears picked up a hiss that was close. Too close. She whipped around to see a cobra hanging near her ear from one of the tree branches. She gazed at it steadily. When it hissed again she reached out and grabbed it right at the beginning of its throat. She could feel the muscles in the neck trying to expand and contract to escape her grasp. She could also sense it trying to recoil in fear, now that it was close enough to sense the darkness in her. She let the snake go and it slithered away into the shadows of the treetops.

"Easy with my babies there," Ace said.

"It wouldn't have killed them."

"I know, and it's good to establish your strength over them. I still do need them though so I'd rather you didn't strangle them."

"Fine. For you." She punched him in the arm. As they walked towards the water several snakes crossed their path. They were docile to Ace, coming up to greet him or peacefully letting him pass by. For Blaze on the other hand, they had cleared a path for her, staying at lengthy distance. Once they had reached the oasis, Ace kneeled at the water and ran his hand through the waves a few times. The water began to shake and the ground rumbled. There was burst from the surface and an immense serpent rose out, towering several feet over them. Its forked tongue was easily the size of Blaze. It was an enormous version of the snakes that wandered around them. Reptilian fangs dripped with venom, sending steam rising up where it touched the water. Her eyes glowed like red jasper stones, framed by electric blue scales.

"I present the Lapis serpent," Ace announced. The mother of cobras lowered her head and curved her neck around Ace as he gently rubbed the scales at the side of her head. She nudged him affectionately. Ace took Blaze's hand and guided her towards the snake. The snake backed up and hissed at her, baring her fangs. Ace consoled the serpent with his free, hand, coaxing her to come back. She approached cautiously and bobbed her head around Ace's back.

"She won't hurt you," he soothed her. He slowly advanced Blaze's hand towards her, murmuring to the snake the entire time. Her hand came in contact with the cold slippery surface of snakeskin. They stood at a stalemate, facing each other warily.

"Now Blaze." Blaze took a deep breath and let her darkness float out in waves, searching for a matching pattern of energy in the serpent's memory. All of the blue cobras were linked to her, and every summoning and spell they were a part of was retained in her memory. They all carried entrails of the mother's heart, which beat as one when they were in close proximity. Blaze could feel it against her palm, the thrum of a million tiny heartbeats unifying in to a steady pulse in the earth beneath her. Nothing reached out to her as she navigated through the serpent's memory. It was like giving and electric shock to a patient and receiving no response. She could feel a strain in her head, which meant the mother was resisting, holding back access to parts of her mind. Blaze pushed back, forcing out more powerful waves of darkness. She didn't want to force the serpent into submission, but it was giving her little choice otherwise. *Weaken,* she urged the cobra. The strain slowly disappeared as Blaze worked her way through. She was also beginning to tire but she couldn't stop now. A tingle ran though her mind, a matching memory. Blaze mentally latched onto it. She reached out and squeezed Ace's hand, indicating she was ready. Ace had a handful of poppy seed powder, ready to push them both into sleep. He sprinkled it over them and the world slipped away.

Blaze was holding Ace's hand in Opal's apartment, where Opal had swung up warily from her bed. With Ace being a *hyponos,* he could take her into the dreams of the cobra and witness a rewind of what happened. Ace was far more advanced in his skill than Jen was and could access memories as well, which is what Blaze had managed to latch on to. She heard the raspy voice that gave the snakes their command. *Protect the messenger.* Opal's eyes were glazed over as she swayed towards the door. The snakes followed her obediently, upholding their orders.

"The caster is giving them messages through Opal's mind. She's in an unconscious possession!" Ace exclaimed. "That's not possible."

"With magic, there are few things that are impossible. It takes the right magician to figure it out," Blaze replied. They followed Opal to the Chronicles, watching her pick up a rusty chain from the junkyard along the way. *Make sure the message is delivered,* the voice rasped. The snakes became open and alert as they zoned in on anyone who came close, snapping their fangs out. *Retrieve the items.* One cobra shifted away while the others circled Opal. When Opal grabbed Kaitlin, the snake slithered up her desk and grabbed a scroll off of a pile of documents. Its ruby eyes flashed and the scroll vanished.

"There!" Blaze exclaimed. Ace focused his thoughts on the cobra, tapping into its memory. *Location,* he urged it. *Location.* They shot through a whirl of swirling landscapes until a ruby red cavern came into focus. Mavis lay unconscious on the ground and the scroll had materialized beside her, laying open.

"That's Mavis, isn't it?" Ace inquired. There was a claustrophobic feel to it all, as if they were trapped in a spider web.

"That's her. Someone has trapped her here; you can feel the aura of the barrier spells. But what is this place?" Blaze rushed towards the scroll, scanning the contents quickly. *Dreams, the eye of the soul, Blood, the vital of the goal,* was scrawled in scripted cursive as the title. Ace was looking over her shoulder, reading along.

"This is about necromancy… and resurrection?" Blaze asked.

"You're telling me someone is trying to bring back the dead? Don't they know that is in fact, impossible? It's a law of magic."

"There have always been those who try to challenge laws and find ways around them. They have never succeeded, but have in turn, found all sorts of alternatives to achieve something similar. You can't raise, resurrect or communicate with the dead. But you can deceive yourself into thinking you did.

241

Illusion magic. That doesn't stop crazy people from attempting to challenge the supernatural."

"According to this spell, it needs the blood of a soul once loved and broken," Ace looked at her wide-eyed. "Oh God. Mavis is the sacrifice. Has she had her heart broken?" Blaze recalled the sorrow and loss she had sensed from Mavis when she spoke to her in the hallway of the infirmary for the first time. She knew she had experienced something of the sort. This just confirmed that her gut instinct had been right. She nodded.

"Ace, no matter what, this spell will not work. We know you can't resurrect anyone, but you know what happens when a spell doesn't work? It backfires and poisons anyone who's involved. Whoever is doing this won't achieve anything, but they're going to kill a lot of people, and themselves, in the process. We have to find her!" The memory continued to play out before them as a small black dog came running out of the shadows and gently picked up the edge of the scroll with his mouth. The image began to fade as they reached the extent of the cobra's memory. The last thing Blaze saw was the tag that hung from the collar around the dog's neck, glittering in the red light of the cavern. A silver scorpion.

Blaze reeled back, stumbling away from Ace and the mother of cobras. Ace stroked the serpent's nose and thanked her for helping, just as she sank below the surface of the black water once again. With a snap of his fingers, he had brought them back to the lounge where Opal lay asleep. Blaze unsheathed her dagger and stared at the matching scorpion.

"Shadow Swarm…" Ace trailed off. Opal moaned and shifted to her side. Ace lowered his voice to a whisper. "They're behind this? What happened to laying low? Especially after that last incident…"

"I don't know. But I say now it's time I reunited with the Lady Scorpion."

"Blaze the Lady Scorpion…"

"Used to be my mother. Not anymore. I'm talking about the new one. Scarlett's… friend. The one who created this beauty for me." She twirled her dagger between her fingertips and ran the edge lightly down Ace's check. "Time to reclaim the family throne, don't you think?" she asked.

Ace smirked mischievously.

"There's that evil spark. Let's make it a team effort, shall we?"

Blaze pinched his cheek gently.

"Let's," she said. Blaze's phone went off at that moment. It was Scarlett.

"I have Mavis' location!" she exclaimed.

"What? How? Never mind that for now, where?" Blaze was about to leap out of her seat with anticipation.

"The Devil's Den cove in the Ring of Fire." Blaze's jaw dropped.

"In the middle of the Pacific Ocean?"

"Unfortunately."

"This information is to be trusted?"

"Yes. From a man who never breaks his word."

"Jackson?! You took this from Jackson?"

"Blaze..."

"Hold on Azura's calling me I'm going to add her in." Blaze merged them into a three-way call.

"Blaze you need to leave now!" Azura shouted over the line.

"Why?" Even as she asked this, Blaze motioned to Ace to prepare to run. She knew if Azura was telling her to do it, she would have to. Ace bolted to Opal and shook her awake. Once she was up he disappeared, probably going to find the boys.

"Jackson is coming. He knows where you are."

"How?"

"Someone told him. I don't have time to explain, you need to go!"

"Fine, but we have a lead. Scarlett, make an appointment with your friend Jinx. We're going to have an audience with the Lady Scorpion. I'll fight my way through until then."

"No! He's armed. Don't-" Blaze hung up the phone, cutting Azura off. Ace appeared with Adam and Joe in tow. She flipped up the couch cushions to reveal Ace's stash of immediate weapons. She tossed Joe some brass knuckles and Opal a steel staff. She then, with some hesitation, handed Adam a crossbow and arrows.

"I can't use this!" he exclaimed. Blaze, to be honest, wasn't sure he could either. But there would be too much opposition to have one of them protecting him at all times. His best chance would be to fight for himself. She put her cold mask on and stared him down until she felt his fear intensify.

"You better learn. Because now it's fight or die, so grow up and get used to defending yourself. String the arrow and fire. We don't have ti-" A loud explosion resonated through the building. She sighed. "The man couldn't just ring the doorbell, could he?"

"Who exactly is he?" Joe asked.

"Jackson. Don't ask me how, I don't know. We need to fight him off."

"For how long?"

"Until my reinforcements arrive."

"Blaze what-" another loud crash came from a few doors down.

"Fine," Joe said. "Let's kick some ass."

"That's what I like to hear," Ace said. He winked as he fired a hole through the wall.

CHAPTER 17

What's in a name?

OPAL STEADIED HERSELF MENTALLY AS THEY RAN THROUGH THE CORRI-dors of the building. Jackson. Again. Last time she had faced him one on one and almost hadn't gotten away. Now that bastard had probably brought six of his soldiers along for the ride. She followed at Ace's heels, keeping close as they sprinted through the maze of hallways. They jogged up the fire escape stairs that lead out to the rooftop terrace. She raced for the edge and looked down to see what they were up against. Myra guards were patrolling all sides of the building for any potential exits as the last of the *jaculus* stormed their way inside the lobby. She twirled her staff out and braced it in front of her. Blaze had her dagger and throwing knife ready while Joe's brass knuckles glinted beside her. Ace was on her other side and produced a leather whip from his jacket. Adam stood nervously with his crossbow notched at the terrace door. Opal felt nothing but pity for Adam at this point. The boy had never been up against anything more than a mundane fist fight and now he was going to face down Jackson and his crew with a crossbow he didn't know how to use. She promised herself she would protect him. But could she? *Shut up. You don't have time to doubt yourself right now.* Nervous energy thrummed through her as her legs yearned to pick up speed. She kept them at a standstill.

"So, are we just going to wait to die?" Adam asked sarcastically. Opal groaned on the inside. Adam would be getting an F in battle attitude.

"Trust me. We've just got to last," Blaze said. Before Adam could respond she and Ace leapt onto a chimneystack and crouched, waiting for Jackson to arrive. A few seconds later the door went flying across the roof as the combat expert jumped out, followed by Jackson and the rest of his posse. Six well-armed fighters stood before them, staring down Joe, Opal and Adam.

"Opal my dear," Jackson said dusting off his suit jacket. "Nice to see you out and about again. Afraid I'll have to cut it short. Pity. I was beginning to fancy the welt on my head that you left me with."

"Oh, you liked it, did you? I'd be more than happy to give you another one."

"I'd like to see you try."

"Enough," Joe interrupted. "Get out now Jackson, and we'll pretend like we didn't see you."

"Mr. Starks. You've returned." Jackson began to walk towards him. Opal pointed her staff out at him. He put his hands up. "Easy there. What happened with you exactly, Joseph?" Joe gave him a pointed look. "Useless question I see. Where is Miss Darkfire if I may ask? Not like her to chicken out of a fight. I heard she was here with you."

"From who exactly?" Opal prodded. Jackson laughed, smooth and musically.

"Why, from Jett of course." Opal's jaw dropped. Adam lowered his crossbow.

"You must be lying," Adam quavered. "Jett would never…"

"Never say never," Jackson smirked. "There's no telling what a person can do for the right price. His, was the location of his precious little friend, Mavis. I told him I would find her in under a week." Blaze dove down from her perch on the chimney, flipping down and slamming Jackson face first into the ground. Opal was in awe of her friend's reckless move. What was she doing? More importantly what the hell was Jett thinking? A feeling of betrayal was beginning to twist around her heart. Blaze flipped him over and rested the dagger against his neck. The *jaculus* surged forward but Jackson held out a hand to stop them.

"Not yet," he said under the strain of the blade. Blaze's eyes glittered darkly. "You knew where she was beforehand. Why lie to him about a week?"

"So I'd have something to offer Scarlett. She and I have some unfinished business and I needed leverage. It was splendidly perfect." Opal screamed internally. Not only had Jett given them up to Jackson, he had also been played in the process. Adam still looked like someone who had been kicked in the gut.

"He wouldn't..." he mumbled.

"Enough chitchat," Jackson said. "Attack!" He sent a flying uppercut towards Blaze. She jumped off in time to avoid his fist hitting her throat. Ace leapt down, cracking his whip, grabbing a *jaculus* by the hand and yanking him forward. Joe launched his first punch at the combat expert while Adam was stock-still. Opal jumped in front of him and hit the sword fighter square in the chest with her staff. She twirled it, deflecting his advancing blows. She felt a shove from behind and landed face first on the concrete. She had just turned over when Jackson pinned her down, clasping a metal brace on to her wrist and smashing it into the ground. She struggled against the brace but her arm was immobile. He had a gloating smile as he pressed her down, breathing heavily.

"This time," he breathed. "It'll end differently."

"Don't count on it," came a voice from her left. She heard a whoosh and crack as Jackson growled, stumbling to the side. Opal could see the cruel grip of a leather rope cutting into his arm. The whip cracked again, hitting Jackson square in the face, sending him sprawling across the concrete. Ace's luminous blue eyes hovered over her as he snapped the brace off to free her arm. His hand was soft and firm as he hoisted her up, his whip lashing out around them like lightning.

"Perhaps," he said between strikes, "now would be a good time to perform that little speed trick of yours." Opal stared blankly at him for a second, trying to process what he was saying. She mentally face-palmed herself. *Of course.* Her muscles began to twitch with the excitement to run, to make use of their incredible working power. She flew straight towards the *jaculus* who was attacking Adam and delivered a well-placed blow to his knees. As he crumpled her eyes took in every single movement of his body, the descending of his legs, the sagging of his arms and his weakening hold on the sword in his hand. She was aware of it all. She twisted his arm, causing his weapon to drop and began to thrash him with her staff at light speed, hitting every weak point as she saw it. Within minutes he was too beaten to move. Her blood was singing in her veins, burning from the high that using her speed triggered. Adam, having gotten over some of his initial shock, was firing terribly aimed arrows at Jackson's companions. The good news was that if he didn't hit the one he was aiming for it usually hit another. Opal just prayed that none of them would be in his line of misfire. Ace was beside her once again, standing back to back.

"Nice work," he said. He leapt away, flipping upwards with the utmost grace and knocking the lights out of another *jaculus* with a tight pull of his leather coil around his neck. Watching him fight was like watching Blaze, moving and fighting with effortless coordination, being as graceful and deadly as a panther and fierce as… well… fire. As if they had been trained to fight by each other's sides. Blaze was now facing Jackson, who had turned his attention to her. Blood spilled from several knife cuts along his arms, staining his shirt with patches of scarlet. Blaze had purpling bruises on her cheek and legs, her cargos torn from the left leg. Opal sometimes had to remind herself how powerful Jackson really was. Blaze was a magnificent fighter, good enough to be a *jaculus*. Jackson though, *was* one and had been for several years. They were close to parallel in strength and strategy, neither willing to back down. Ever. Joe's figure flashed in the darkness like a burning copper coin, his brass knuckles shining in the dimness. He now had taken it upon himself to protect Adam, who had given up on arrows and had started using his crossbow as a battle-axe. Joe's eyes glowed with a dark chocolaty sheen as he lashed out at the approaching *jaculus* and was slowly inching his way toward Blaze at the same time. Opal's heart could not help but ache for them. They would die for each other. But to die for someone was one thing, and to live and love them was another. Joe had chosen to love someone who may have lost the ability to love altogether. Blaze had never said a word on the subject, but Opal knew her friend well, and could see in the permanent exhaustion in Blaze's eyes, that she had ceased to try. Jackson's scream shattered her thoughts.

He was pressed against the edge of the roof, pale as the moon with the colour draining from his face. Opal had to stifle a cry herself when she saw what he was retreating from. Hundreds of black scorpions had spilled out around them and were crawling towards him steadily. Blaze stood in the centre of them, unaffected. The scorpions, in turn, respected her space and kept about a foot of distance from her. Jackson gave Blaze an expression of pure loathing.

"This not over you little devil spawn. Whatever fire burns inside of you, dark or otherwise, I will extinguish it and never let it burn again," he hissed at her. Blaze merely pointed at him and the scorpions rushed forward, stingers ready. Jackson leapt backwards and murmured something under his breath. His eyes glazed over and he began to fall apart, his body dissolving into sand, as did his companions. Within seconds they had dissipated completely, the particles lost in the wind. Joe threw his hands up.

"And he wants to arrest us for using magic. Bloody hypocrite."

"Nothing we didn't already know," Blaze said. The mass of scorpions pooled together around Blaze's feet, like an obedient little army waiting for their general's commands. Blaze smiled at them with silent gratitude. Although it was extremely odd and quite disgusting to Opal, the scorpions had forced Jackson to retreat. She supposed she could cut the deadly little things some slack here.

Suddenly, there was the sound of a million little legs shuffling around as they parted to make a path. Out of the shadows Opal could make out the shifting of a silver dress. The fabric rustled and began to move like a liquid mirror as the figure walked forward. A woman stepped out of the darkness, smiling sadly, as if she knew some terrible secret. Caramel curls tumbled down her back, framing her face like a fairy. Her facial features spoke to Opal of an extensive Grecian heritage. Silver streaks, not greying silver but shining silver, ran down the left side of her head. She was elegant, with prominent curves. The dress draped gracefully over her figure to give her a stately appearance. Only her eyes ruined the picture. They were red, red as rubies, with a layer of black that shimmered underneath the iris, giving them a dark tint. Because of that she appeared almost sinister. Blaze nodded at her and then turned to her friends.

"Everyone please meet Jinx. Leader of the Shadow Swarm, the Lady Scorpion and the creator of my faithful blade. The image of Blaze's scorpion hilted dagger flashed through Opal's mind.

"It has been many years since I have seen Blaze. Have you kept her under suitable care?" Jinx asked.

"I assure you, Blaze is safe and in top condition." Blaze said. Opal's confusion was reflected across everyone's faces. Why was she referring to herself in the third person?

"Of course she is, she's standing right in front of you," Joe said. "Can't you see that? And why are you referring to her as if she is some type of object?" Jinx laughed, tossing her hair back. Her blood-red eyes came to rest on Joe with a mix of amusement and sadness.

"My dear boy, Blaze is not a who. It's a what. It's the name of that lovely dagger."

"You named it after Blaze?"

"Quite the contrary. Until a few years ago, the only thing in this world named Blaze was that dagger." Joe whipped his head around to stare at Blaze in astonishment. Blaze gripped the hilt firmly in her hand, like she was holding on to a lifeline.

"This doesn't make sense... how..." Joe began. Blaze gazed at Joe with the rawest loneliness that Opal had ever seen. Opal averted her gaze quickly.

"Because," she said, "my name isn't Blaze."

༄

Joe sat in the back seat of a Lincoln navigator, looking miserably out the window. Ace and Opal sat beside him in uncomfortable silence. He couldn't care less; his mind was a million miles away. Blaze and Adam were riding in another car with Jinx, probably discussing Mavis and Jett. Part of Joe was relieved, and the other part was crushed. Blaze had refused to speak further about her name, insisting they get to a safe location first. She had not looked his way once through any of it. It wounded him internally. Here he was, claiming he loved a woman and yet he did not know her real name. Joe's mind was whirling with questions. *Why didn't she tell me? Why the dagger? Who is she?* Joe had hoped with every fibre of his being that Blaze cared for him enough to break down her walls and tell him the important things. Clearly, he didn't mean as much to her as he had thought. He had shared his life with her, his thoughts, innermost feelings and secrets. Foolishly, he had assumed she would do the same. She was still keeping secrets from him while he had lain himself down as an open book. Despair gripped at his heart. She would never love him, would she? He would never truly know her, as one should when they were in love. She was an illusion, a beautiful illusion that he could not see the reality to.

"Don't be so hard on Blaze," Ace said, finally breaking the silence. Joe sighed.

"And why is that?"

"A rose by any other name smells just as sweet. Do you think something as trivial as a name, changes who a person is? Blaze is still the girl you have always known. She never puts up a pretence, with you of all people."

"It's not just that, Ace. I don't want her to hide anything from me. Important things, like this. She didn't bother telling me for seven years that her name was not Blaze. If she doesn't consider that important, God knows what else she's keeping from me. I... I just wished that I could get through to her. To the real Blaze."

"She has never been artificial."

"Selectively leaving out details counts as deceit."

"Everyone is entitled to his or her secrets Joe," Ace put a hand on his shoulder. "Besides, it's futile to ask her."

"Because she wouldn't tell me?"

"Because she can't. She doesn't know what it is." Both Opal and Joe bolted upright.

"What?" Opal exclaimed. "She doesn't know her own name?"

"It's not so much not knowing as it is not remembering. Back when her umm... incident occurred, she asked me to remove the memory of her name from her mind and I obliged. Any memory, in her mind, in flowers and *ankh*, was rid of any trace of her real name. Even as an experienced *hyponos* I needed help of course, and I vowed to see her request through." Opal shared Joe's absolutely stunned expression.

"Why?" she asked softly. Joe was watching Ace carefully, reading his crystal-blue eyes, which held a shielding sadness and a burning desire to protect his friend.

"She didn't want to remember or be the girl who had failed to properly save her family. She thinks the whole nightmare was her fault, and she deserved every last blow that demon fire dealt her. She didn't want to be reminded every time she heard someone say it that it was the name of a failure."

"She didn't fail them! She saved them!" Joe protested. How could she possibly think otherwise?"

"You're preaching to the choir. I desperately tried to talk her out of it, but because we are so alike, I could understand her motivation. It also severed the last personal connection with her family; not knowing her birth name gave her less that she could mourn over, less to pull her back to them."

"Doesn't that mean you know her name?" Joe asked. Ace shook his head, running his fingers through his inky black hair. "At one time, you all knew her name too. She made me remove it from everyone's memory, not just hers, and replace it with Blaze. Even mine. Whatever I could do to ease her pain at the time, I did. Whoever she was before ceased to exist. Now there is just Blaze, and there's no return." Joe was gripping the leather upholstery of the seats so tightly that it left imprints on his palms. He remembered Blaze, bright as the sun and full of life, years ago. Now she has transformed into a barricade of ice and stone. He refused to believe that girl had ceased to exist. Ace had the same sort of heat that Blaze did, that cold negativity but prevailing emotional strength. He felt like if Ace looked into a mirror, Blaze would be his cracked reflection. A slight lump of jealousy formed in Joe's throat. Ace seemed so much closer to Blaze, knowing her like he did not. *It's only fair,* he chided himself. They had known each other from childhood and it would be weird if Ace wasn't as close to her as he was now. That didn't make the jealousy fade, but released some of the pressure in his chest. Opal pushed her maroon hair back, twisting a strand around her finger. She met his gaze and held it steadily. Her expression said *Now what are you going to do about it?* He shook his head at her. *I don't know.*

Joe's head spun as he tried to steady himself after Jinx's teleportation spell. It had deposited them in a dark arena-like area with only a few flickering torches that burned along the walls. Blaze groaned and cursed when she hit the floor, since Adam had landed on top of her when they arrived. She shoved him off in annoyance. Opal whispered to Adam quietly and managed to get a weak smile from him. Joe held a grudging respect for Opal for taking such excellent care of her charges. Both of them had been tasked with looking after the twins, but Opal had gone the extra mile to comfort Adam in every situation. Joe remembered watching and analyzing Jett's progress when he was on the hover pads. Adam was a steady anchor for his twin, always by his side. It seemed now Opal would be doing the same for him. Azura, he felt, was closer to Jett.

Jett. Jackson's taunt echoed through his mind. He knew Jackson was not to be trusted, because he was a cunning psychopath, but he was also known as a man of his word. Was it true that Jett had given them up to him? Jinx snapped her fingers with a crisp pop and glowing rows of torches lit up with hot white flames, illuminating the room. The ground sparkled under his feet and he realized he was standing on a huge insignia of the silver scorpion. The rest of the arena was furnished like a lounge, with sofas, entertainment systems and glass pool tables. Along the walls there were benches covered in papers, maps and writing. A weapons wall protruded out like a trophy case on the other side of the room.

Jinx seated herself on a silver loveseat and motioned for the rest to join her. Immediately, platters of food and drinks came out, hovering an inch or two in the air as they glided towards them. It was only when Jinx lifted a plate of finger sandwiches up that Joe saw the group of scorpions that had been carrying it underneath. Opal seemed like she was going to be sick. Joe knew insects were not one of her favourite creatures. Ace had noticed and quietly picked up the incoming food from the bugs and offered it to Opal. Blaze on the other hand, would thank the critters as they came by. They seemed to recognize her and scurried forward to approach her. Joe gathered his wits and went to sit beside her, trying not to cringe at the approaching scorpions. He slipped his hand into hers, lacing his fingers through. She regarded him with mild surprise. Although he still felt torn about what had happened, he could discuss that with her later. Right now, he would just be Joseph, Blaze's anchor. He smiled at her and her face softened. He felt her squeeze his hand. Warmth spread through him, making him feel ten times lighter.

"Where is everyone today?" Blaze inquired. They were the only people present in the arena.

"I ordered the rest of the Swarm out for this meeting. They've dispersed to our other locations."

"Shame. It would have been nice to have a reunion," Blaze said. Jinx raised an eyebrow at her.

"Not everyone would feel that way, mind you," she responded.

Blaze waved the comment off with a flick of her wrist.

"Water under the bridge. Anyways, thank you for appearing when you did."

"Anything for Scarlett. Her call was all I needed to round up my forces. Not to mention how much we all despise Jackson and his company." She crossed her legs and leaned back in her seat. "Now then, why has the former heir of the Swarm graced me with her presence?" Jinx's voice held a note of sarcasm and amusement.

"I have no interest in reclaiming the Swarm, so you can relax. Not after what you've done to it." Jinx's eyes narrowed and her amused expression turned into a tight mask of suppressed anger. Joe tensed, locking his eyes on Blaze. She was perfectly poised, like she knew the ball was in her court, smiling wickedly. He had wished one too many times that she wouldn't provoke people like that. If you could sense danger, you would know that it radiated off of Jinx. Then again, it radiated off of Blaze too.

"As for why I'm here, I'm currently on a mission to retrieve a lost soul and clear my friend's name. I explained that to you in the car."

"You were quite skimpy on the details."

"Well the only thing of importance to you is that when we followed the snake's memory for the location of that scroll, a small dog with the Swarm's symbol took it. Any idea on how that would be possible?"

"Perhaps you shouldn't speak of your situation in terms of possible and not possible. A lot of what happened has defied your understanding of 'possible'. All of that aside, you're out of luck. I have no idea why that little dog would have our tags. We use those on some scorpions occasionally and we never operate with dogs. Hasn't your mother told you that?" Joe blinked back his surprise. Storm had been right about Blaze's mother having a connection with the organization. Yet another part of Blaze's life she hadn't told him about.

"She did, but she also mentioned that under your command the Swarm had on occasion turned to… unorthodox resources before."

"Are you accusing me of something?" Jinx asked in a low voice.

"Not at all. Unless you're getting defensive because you have something I can accuse you of."

"Let me remind you, that you are in *my* domain right now. It's a courtesy that my little pets aren't eating you alive right now. It's not your place to interrogate me."

"My, my, touchy, are we?" Blaze leaned forward, locking her eyes with Jinx's ruby ones. "It's actually my domain. I'm still the blood heir to the Swarm, don't forget that. Your little pets, as you call them, will always obey me before they obey you. I can just as easily have you eaten right now and you know it, so don't try to test me." Blaze stood up and began to circle around Jinx's sofa slowly, like a panther circles its prey before deciding which angle to strike at. Joe had seen Blaze do this countless times before, trapping someone in a mess of their own words or implied threats. She was the powerful one. At least that's what she came across as. Joe wondered what it was like, to be so sure of your own strength, that no matter what, you never second-guessed yourself for it. It was one of the many things he had initially fallen in love with. Jinx though, to Joe's judgement only looked offended.

"Now," Blaze said, "I do believe in a fair trade. So, what is the price for your information? What do you want out of this?" Jinx stood up and turned to face her.

"Don't have much choice, do I?"

"You don't, but I'm giving you a chance to get something in return. Call it a gesture of good faith." Jinx rolled her eyes and then stood thoughtfully. Slowly a dreadful grin spread across her face. Joe was suddenly very aware that Jinx might make a terrible enemy. Those merciless red eyes rested on him for a brief moment and his insides froze. He shivered.

"Here's my offer. I will tell you what I know, and teleport you to the Devil's Den where Mavis is, in exchange for a small token you must get for me."

"And that would be?" Joe asked pointedly.

"Some memory flowers. Not just any, specific ones. I will provide you with their location. You just need to go and get them."

"So, steal them I'm assuming," Blaze said.

"Borrowing may be a better term. Without permission."

"Of course."

"They will be tied together with a gold ribbon, so look for that. They'll be in front of a tombstone."

"You want us to steal from someone's funeral?" Opal asked.

"Quite the contrary. I'll be sending you off to a restaurant that offers a dinner show. You'll have to perform there to gain access to the employee areas. One of the walls is a doorway to a garden with a cemetery beside it. Quite well sealed off from trespassers, and the only entrance is through that door."

"Why can't you get it yourself?"

"Because the owner and his staff recognize me. They will not recognize you." Blaze cocked her head to the side, considering Jinx's offer.

"There will be a catch. I know it," Blaze said. She sighed. "But I accept." Jinx's cat-like grin continued to light up her face.

"Excellent," she said, almost in a soft hiss. "You'll find the full details in the study. You know where to go. In the meantime, I'll gather my resources. When you return, we shall speak further." They shook hands on it.

"Come on guys, let's go," Blaze said. Opal, Adam and Joe got up to follow her. Joe turned around to look at Jinx one last time but she was no longer behind him. He turned his head back to see her standing right in front of him, like a ghostly spirit. He jumped back, landing in a fighting stance with his fists up. Jinx laughed.

"I don't know what Blaze sees in you *changjo*. How she came to admire you I will never understand." Joe bit his lip. Jinx knew that he was a creator. Like Jen and Ace were *hyponos*, he was a *changjo*, someone who was skilled at creating. When he had the flame channel sword made for Blaze to control her darkness, he had fashioned the majority of it with his own hands. He looked up to see if the others had noticed that he was talking to Jinx. They appeared frozen in front of him, unmoving.

"Don't worry about your friends, they don't know we're having this little chat." She grazed his shoulder with the tips of her fingers, the warmth of her breath close enough to affect the heat of his body. "It's been a while since I've met a fellow creator." That made sense to Joe, since she was the one who had made Blaze's other blade. "Never met one quite so handsome," she giggled. Joe resisted the urge to throw up. Her dress moved around her like molten silver, moving like she was gliding across the floor.

"What do you want from me?" he asked.

"Oh dear, I don't want anything from you. I was actually going to ask you if you wanted anything from me."

"What do you have that I could possibly want?"

"Think about it. I'm a big gateway into the hidden portions of Blaze's past. A history you have no part in. I know longing for knowledge when I see one, especially when I see a tender attachment between two people. Yours seems quite one sided, but nonetheless it is an attachment all the same." The truth in her statement stung and Joe couldn't deny he had a burning desire to know more, but he was no fool.

"I'm not going to make a deal with the Lady Scorpion for some buried history on my girlfriend."

"Your girlfriend is the true Lady Scorpion if you haven't realized that already. By blood, that title is hers."

"A title is just a title," he said defensively.

"Like name is just a name," she taunted him with a knowing smile. "Our titles define us in some way or the other, if we choose to accept them." Joe felt a flash of hurt when Jinx mentioned the name issue. That still bothered him. "I know you want it," she teased him "And as a show of 'good faith' as Blaze said, here's a tidbit of information for free." She tossed her hair over her shoulder, the silver streaks glittering brightly in the soft light of the lounge. "You want to know why I created that dagger for her in the first place?" Joe motioned for her to go on. "This was before she went dark, so you cannot blame this on the demon fire. I was asked to make it because she wanted to use it to kill someone. She was going to murder you." Joe's blood ran cold and his heart began to race in his chest. Jinx's laughter rang in his ears. He couldn't comprehend what she was saying. *Kill me? Why?*

"Why should I believe you?" he stammered.

"It doesn't benefit me in any way to lie. When you receive those memory flowers, take the black one and have ah, Jett is it? Have him look into it for you."

"How do you know about Jett?" he said, alarmed. Jinx just shrugged.

"I know many things. I make it my business to be well informed. It comes in quite handy as leverage. Things that you would never expect me to know, I probably do. If you want to hear the rest of the story…" she swiped his bangs aside with her fingers and traced a line down his ear to his collarbone. He grabbed her wrist and threw her hand off. She smiled coyly. "…I'll be waiting right here." Joe stepped back as Jinx began to spin, sending the flared edges of her dress twirling out like silver flower petals and then vanished in a flash. Joe swayed back and forth, reeling from what Jinx had just revealed to him. He knew Jinx was a dangerous person to trust. She could be doing all of this to mess with his head. But she *knew*. She knew Blaze, her family and God knows what else. He took a deep breath and unclenched his fists. With an uncertain conscience, he resumed following his friends out of the lounge.

CHAPTER 18

List of Broken Hearts

ACE FELL INTO STEP BESIDE BLAZE WHO WAS UNUSUALLY QUIET. OPAL and Joe were walking a little further behind them, so he took this chance to talk to his other half. He nudged her and locked gazes with her shimmering black eyes. They were hypnotic to look at, as dark as the night sky. The ones he had grown up looking into. They fell into a silent conversation, communicating with their pupils and shakes of the head.

Are you okay? he gestured. She flicked her eyes up, which meant *I don't know.*

"How is Joe holding up?" she whispered.

"Not great," Ace admitted truthfully. Her shoulders slumped slightly with defeat.

"I knew he wouldn't understand."

"It's not that he doesn't understand, it's more about why you hid it from him."

"You know why I did it." Ace did know. He knew what it was like, to feel that shame, that sense of weakness and failure. To know that you were never strong enough to do what you should have done. Remembering was a curse. The Darkfires had forgotten their daughter, but felt no pain because they did not remember her. Blaze felt it. All of it. No one could reverse demon flame and the psychological warfare it had done. Ace had always accepted her for who she became, because her heart had not swayed. He took her darkness and her light, her secrets and her motives. He was just afraid Joe wouldn't be able to do so, and a beautiful friendship would go down in flames.

"Do you want me to talk to him?" he asked placing an arm comfortingly around her shoulder. She sighed.

"No, I'll talk to him. He needs to understand that I can't live like an open book."

"Speaking of books..." Ace said as they turned into the study. Neatly lined rows of books ran around the room in floor to ceiling bookshelves, illuminated by low lamplight. On a side table, there was an envelope with a silver seal on it. Pressed into the wax was the scorpion insignia. Ace turned it over in his hands and pried the flap open. *Palo's* was written in loose cursive with the address underneath. A golden key was attached to the paper.

"What's that for?" Adam asked.

"Keys to the wardrobes. We'll have to get dressed up for the performance." Blaze said. "Can you still sing?" she asked Ace. He shrugged.

"I might be able to pull off a thing or two." She nodded. "Sounds good. Joe, you can play guitar and Opal you can do a keyboard set."

"What will I do?" Adam asked.

"Don't get in the way," was Blaze's response. Ace shared her sentiments. Adam frowned.

"So, I'm going to do nothing?"

"We'd prefer that. Your twin has already caused us enough grief as it is. We're going to try to minimize the damage." Adam's cheeks were slowly beginning to heat.

"Jett would never do that! I don't believe it"

"And yet Jackson found us, when the only other people who knew where we were, was him and Azura. Azura, who called me in advance as a warning. Even though Jackson is a monster, he is a man of his word, as much as I hate to admit it. At least he has some sort of honour, unlike Jett."

"He wanted to find Mavis! Who wouldn't be tempted?"

"So tempted that he would sell out the people already searching for her in the first place? Sell out Opal who has been taking nonstop care of him?" Ace turned to look at Opal who had a sad exhaustion in her eyes. Her dark red hair waved down her shoulders, framing her face attractively. If she had been smiling, Ace's heart might have fluttered a little.

"Adam," Opal began, "I have been running for my life over the past few days and have not had a moment to breathe. Now I find out the reason I couldn't is because Jett does not have the ability to make judgements properly. Even after we had done all we could to help him. Forgive me for saying so, but he has betrayed us. Betrayed me." Her voice carried a note of misery, pushing Adam to shame. Ace watched as Adam went silent, his eyes downcast. "I don't blame you for what Jett did. You seem to be a better person than him. But I would rather that you are not used as a pawn against us like he was. So, listen to Blaze, and stay out of the way." Ace looked at Opal with mild surprise. She did not strike him as the type to say such things. He supposed that enough stress could push anyone to that point eventually. Adam turned on his heel and stalked out the study door, slamming it behind him.

"Joe will you go after him, please?" Blaze asked him. He came over and gave her a quick kiss. She smiled against his lips. A twang of jealousy shot through Ace.

"Of course." Joe said. Ace watched him leave with envy. Joe had found someone who truly made him happy. Despite whatever problems he had with Blaze, he had found someone he could love. Ace looked at Blaze, a dreamy smile still on her lips, staring after him. Another jealous twang. All he had ever wished for was to be like Joe, to have someone he could love like that too. After the darkness took over, Blaze had such an issue with loving back, but he didn't, at least not to the same degree. He just couldn't find someone he could start that spark with. Women came and went in his life, nothing more than a pass time to him. He never fell for any of them. If they fell for him, eventually they would leave on their own because he was a difficult person to love. He supposed the problem ran both ways here. He couldn't find anyone, and no one could love him for long. He shook the thought out of his head. He shouldn't be jealous he chided himself. Love was a weakness after all. It would leave him scarred. He knew that from experience already.

☙

Ace helped Opal out of the Lexus that they had traveled in to reach Palo's. Her fingers were warm against his skin and she smelled like jasmine perfume. They had gone to the wardrobes to get ready and had outfitted themselves in eveningwear. Blaze had curled Opal's hair and put it up with white pearl pins and shaped her eyes with some silver eye shadow and liquid eyeliner to match her silver spaghetti strap gown. Ace remembered placing a delicate silver chain necklace around Opal's throat as Blaze went off to get Joe ready.

"Can you move your hair aside so I can fasten this?" he asked.

"Yeah, sure." She lifted her red locks over her shoulder to reveal the back of her neck. As Ace worked on joining the clasps he saw her shoulders sag.

"Anything bothering you?" he inquired.

"Where do I begin?" She gave a bitter laugh. "Right now, I feel like a child trying to play dress up. This isn't me. Elegance, poise, posture, not my cup of tea."

"You certainly look the part. Your perspective is the only thing holding you back right now. Not that I blame you for it."

"I just feel like this entire mission is pointless. Whatever magic was involved, is so far beyond us. Why are we even trying?"

"I'm assuming it's because your friends would rather not see you executed, but that's just my guess."

"It's not worth the pain I'm causing them. Blaze is taxing her resources and taking on unnecessary wrath from people like Jinx and Jackson. If in the end it's futile, all of this will cave down on her." Ace caught a watery shine reflecting off of Opal's eyes in the mirror in front of them. He clasped the necklace shut and walked around to face Opal. He placed a hand gently under her chin and titled it up to so she would look directly at him. Her eyes shone with a dark gleam, a forewarning of the tears that threatened to spill over. He made his voice soft.

"Don't you think she knows that?"

"Of course she does! But I know her too, and she will continue to tax herself even if I tell her not to. There's no stopping her!" Opal said, exasperated.

"Opal, Blaze knows what she can and can't handle. If she's brought something onto herself that she cannot handle, I assure you she's arranged for a way for it to be dealt with. She's always one step ahead."

"Do you know something I don't?" she asked curiously. He smiled mischievously.

"Of course, I do. I know so much more than you could ever imagine." His expression turned serious again. "Don't worry about Blaze, she will be fine. Right now, we're all more concerned about you. I acknowledge this could fail, but if you've come this far, you have nothing to lose by seeing it through to the end. Don't overthink it." He could see the curve of her mouth quirk into a small smile.

"Thank you, Ace." There was a small pause of silence that seemed to stretch out between them. It was as calm as it was electrifying, and for a moment it was just them, alone in the wardrobes where everything else slipped away.

"Well," a smooth voice jostled him out of his trance. Ace snapped his head up to see Blaze smiling like a cat through the doorway. "It's time to go." Ace groaned on the inside. He may have been Blaze's other half but she had something he didn't. The power to read emotions, and right now that's what he feared the most.

Ace pushed the thought aside and pointedly eyed Blaze up and down with admiration. She was in a strapless black evening gown, with two bands of fabric that wound around her upper arms to connect with the sweetheart neckline of the dress, leaving her shoulders prominent and bare. It hugged her figure all the way down to mid-thigh where it opened up into a slit and flared out. Her dragonfly necklace was around her throat, but otherwise she had left her hair straight and had no makeup or jewellery on. She was stunning, in the way fire was beautiful as it was deadly. He had always admired her for it, but since he burned the same way, he sought a beauty that opposed his. He and Blaze were both harsh beauties that made those around them disappear. But he needed someone who shone like soft twinkling light of innocence and grace, perhaps with pearls in her hair... *Snap out of it*, he scolded himself. He strode away from Opal, with an adoring smile aimed at Blaze. He drew her close to him and nodded appreciatively.

"Someone knows how to reel them in. You look beautiful." Blaze gazed back at him evenly. He knew she could see right through his bullshit. She was asking silently if he wanted her to play along. *Yes*, he signalled with his eyes. Her dark pupils gave him a disapproving glare before transforming into seductive look.

"Not bad yourself. That suit does not do you justice." She pulled on the lapels of his jacket and brought him so close their noses touched and ran a hand through his hair. Out of the corner of his eye he could see Opal flushing awkwardly, unaware of whether to leave or wait out the encounter. Blaze undid one of his buttons slowly.

"Giving us a little sneak peek at the real show wouldn't hurt, would it?" she asked in a low voice, but loud enough for Opal to hear. That did it, and Opal bowed out of the room quickly after that, lifting her silver dress up as she went. Once Ace knew she was gone, Blaze's eyes renewed their glow, but now with a burning fury.

"Ace Ryder. What on earth is wrong with you? Could you find no other way to imply what you wanted without dragging me into the picture?"

"I had no other option at the moment. You're the one who interrupted us, it would seem fitting."

"Don't give me that crap. You know that I know that you have started to like Opal, past what you deem you should. I felt it rolling off you. I was not expecting that mix of emotions when I walked into this room."

"Mix?" he asked tentatively. Blaze rolled her eyes.

"You know I can't reveal much about what I felt Ace, but you still have a long way to go in her eyes if that's what you're wondering." Ace's heart sunk a little.

"I don't want it. It's better this way. She'll end up like the others eventually, so it's better that we cut it off here," he said.

"I agree. She's a good friend of mine and the expression 'if you break her heart I'll break your face' will become all too literal to you if you treat her in any such way. Do you hear me?" Ace swallowed.

"Yes."

"Good. Now we have a performance to do, so get your shit together." He nodded silently and followed her out the door, turning only once to look back at where he had shared that moment with Opal, wishing he could relive it again.

❧

He was now arm in arm with Opal leading her to the doorway of Palo's. Blaze and Joe walked ahead of them, murmuring softly to each other. Adam trailed behind him and Opal, so Ace was forced to use his peripherals to keep an eye on him. Adam had returned with less anger in his cheeks after Joe had spoken to him, but remained silent the entire way. At least he had come without complaint. Ace wondered what wizardry Joe used on others to get them to calm down or understand. Since neither he nor Blaze were empathetic on any measurable level, that skill was like a wonder to them. Azura had called Blaze once again to let them know that they would arrive at the restaurant in about an hour to join them. Ace hoped she would arrive with Jett's mouth gagged. He still felt a bitterness in his throat from when he thought about what Jett had done, and how much it had hurt his best friend *and* Opal on top of that. He was fearsomely protective of his loved ones, especially Blaze, and would have to go to great lengths to restrain himself from strangling Jett on sight. Though Ace acknowledged the fact that Jackson had tempted and tricked Jett, Adam had not been fooled. Why was he? *Permotionem* or not, there was no excuse for what he had done.

They were greeted at the door by a smiling waiter in a crisp white uniform, who led them inside. He directed them around elegant, round, mahogany tables and paper lanterns to the backstage area near the back of the restaurant. The stage had an electric keyboard, acoustic guitar and microphones set up for them on a laminated ebony floor. The waiter motioned to a reserved table by the front of the stage.

"These will be your seats for tonight, where you can rest and eat between performance. Meals will be courtesy of the chef."

"Give him our thanks, it is much appreciated," Joe said. The waiter bowed and made way for the kitchen, where the smell of barbequed meat, fish stews and fresh baked bread wafted out. "South American cuisine huh? In Spain?" Joe wondered. "Smells just like a market I went to when I was in Venezuela with Azura."

"Who knows? It could be from Peru, Brazil or Argentina for all we know," Ace responded as he picked up a menu from the table and gave it a quick scan. "Seems like Brazil from the looks of it. Even have the flag on the corner of ever page." Blaze's eyes narrowed.

"Brazil, you say?" she asked.

"Yup, family owned since 1944."

"The Palo family I'm assuming," Opal said, her eyes widening.

"Yeah why?" Ace asked. Opal's dark eyes flashed. Ace looked at her with apprehension. "You've gone white, what's wrong?"

"What's Jackson's last name?" she asked quietly.

"No one knows that," Joe said confused.

"Think about it, Jackson is Brazilian, and his mother and grandmother were known for their culinary arts, running all of the cooking operations long before the Myra appointed staff came around. They left to start a restaurant chain remember?"

"He had a J.P embroidered on his handkerchief when he talked to me and Jett," Adam added, slowly realizing what was happening. *J.P. Jackson P. Ace* thought. *Jackson…Palo. Oh God no.*

"We're in Jackson's family restaurant? Jinx wants us to steal memories form him?!" Joe exclaimed. "She said the owner wouldn't recognize us!" Blaze sighed.

"He's technically not the owner, that would be the head chef, so she didn't lie but it still falls under his family name. Jinx wanted to trap us."

"No," Joe countered. "He's not here, he wouldn't come by without reason and Jinx still wants something from him. She's probably arranged it so we can have enough time to snag those flowers before any real trouble starts. She's not one to set people out on fruitless quests. She always plans to gain something form it, material or otherwise."

"How do we know that this hunch is right?' Adam asked. "It could be a different Palo family, it's a common name, I'm sure there are more of Myra's people that have the last name Palo."

"Not too many that would have something worth stealing, or a grave site gateway from their restaurant," Blaze pointed out. "Jinx hates him like the rest of us, so it would make sense for her to set us on a mission to steal something from him."

"Guys, the dinner rush is starting to come in," Joe said, pointing to the ever-widening stream of people coming through the front doors, slowly trickling in to fill the tables around them. "We'll have to discuss this later. Blaze and Joe, you're up first." Ace gave Blaze a quick kiss on the cheek.

"Knock'em dead," he said. She grinned.

"Don't I always?" Ace rolled his eyes but pushed her forward encouragingly. Joe took Blaze's hand gently and led her to the stage. He grabbed the guitar and swung it around his neck while positioning the microphones for both of them. Everything Joe did was laced with a gentle tenderness, as if he took immense joy in performing with Blaze. Blaze tapped her microphone to get the room to quiet down. She stood confident and assured, embracing the audience with her stage presence.

"Tonight, we are going to perform a song for all those who started over in some aspect of their lives. A toast to your efforts and a cheer to the continued success of them." The audience clapped politely. Joe strummed the guitar and began to play the opening chords. The sound vibrated through the restaurant with a melodious harmony. Blaze began to sing. Her voice was soft but firm.

> The night is young,
> And we start anew,
> A fire's begun,
> When I sing with you,
> It's just us two,
> Side by side,
> Stronger than the demons we that we try to hide

Ace felt a grin spread over his face. It was his and Blaze's favourite song from their childhood. He remembered them singing it at the top of their lungs over and over in the Darkfire's living room and his basement, often warranting complaints from the neighbours. The song didn't mean much to them back then, but now it meant more than they could say. A testament to their friendship, and the day he helped her start a new life, one that didn't include her family. It was bitter, but they had pulled through together and for that, this song would remain his anthem for her. Joe joined Blaze for the chorus. He picked up the speed of his notes on the guitar and built up the beat into the opening bars.

> Fire, Ice, it's all the same,
> Sink in the ocean or burn in flames,
> It's not which force is holding you down,
> It's the way you get off the ground,
> The devil told me I couldn't survive the tempest,
> That I would go down tattered and torn,

But today, Because I was relentless,
It turns out I was the storm

Blaze's eyes came to rest on Ace and she began to smile between words. He gave her thumbs up. Opal nudged him softly. As he turned to face her he realized he had been squeezing her hand and swaying her wrist to the beat of the music. His cheeks began to heat like someone had lit a match under them. He let go quickly, mumbling an apology under his breath. Opal grinned at him and gave him a playful nudge brushing her bare arm against him. "I love this song too," she whispered quietly. "Blaze would play it until I memorized it."

"Sounds like her," Ace chuckled while averting his gaze. He focused on Joe, whose hands appeared to be on autopilot as they ran over the strings.

Tonight, we make our dreams come true.

As Blaze and Joe's voices faded out there was a rupture of cheers and applause from the crowd. They bowed politely and walked off the stage. Adam inclined his head toward Joe.

"Nice work man. You can really work a guitar. You both sounded great."

"I can second that," said a voice from behind them. Ace's gaze landed on Azura, who walked out from behind them with Jett trailing beside her. She wore a simple black skirt and white top which was unexpected, since Azura despised dressing up. He was just glad she didn't come in jeans and sneakers. Despite that, she had managed to force Jett into a tailored navy-blue vest and pants with a white dress shirt. His pocket square had a *B.D.* embroidered on the side and his hair had been combed over. Jett looked worn and uncomfortable, trying to disappear behind Azura's small frame. Ace knew he was probably getting death stares from everyone and still did not feel the least bit sorry for him. Blaze hugged Azura.

"Glad you could make it." Blaze peered behind her shoulder and scanned the room. "We have some time before the next performance. What did your collector say?"

"Well, we do have a bit of shocking news," Azura lowered her voice. "A possession while someone is asleep is possible, if the caster is a *hyponos.*" All eyes turned to Ace. He held his hands up.

"Don't look at me, that's well beyond my abilities."

"It does take a highly skilled individual to pull it off, but that's why it's possible. My source told me that dreams create enough active brainpower to distract the subconscious and allow for a possession to affect the nervous system. The visual portion of hypnotizing, can be done because..."

"*Hyponos* can appear in dreams," Blaze said slowly, with a calculating expression on her face, "and then the victim can see them or their trance symbol." Everyone was struck with a moment of awe. "Opal," Blaze beamed, "You're truly innocent. The heads can't even argue that. But we have yet to trace it back to the caster, we can't prove anything until then."

"He said that if the caster and the victim are in close proximity, an *ankh* would be able to pick up that connection. It should glow with the aura of the caster." Azura informed them.

"So, we're going to have Opal go around to every *hyponos* in Myra, looking for a connection? That's impossible. There are millions of us," Ace pointed out.

"Better than nothing. How did he figure it out by the way?" Joe asked curiously.

"Several hours going over the missing titles in the seal. He had them, and managed to connect common topics that resurfaced. Which brings up another thing."

"Someone is trying to resurrect the dead?" Blaze asked. Azura raised an eyebrow at her.

"How did you know that?" Blaze recounted her and Ace's trip into the memory of the mother cobra. Adam and Jett snapped to attention at the mention of Mavis being sealed inside the cavern.

"A sacrifice?!" Adam exclaimed.

"Yes, she's a key to whatever spell that scroll entailed. She will be used to either start it or amplify it. In that case, it will burn away her mortal essence and reduce her body to charcoal," Ace informed them. Both of the twins responded with an expression of absolute horror.

"Then we have no time," Blaze said. "Now that it's confirmed that this is what is being attempted, we need to reach her first. They won't succeed in resurrection, but they will kill Mavis and themselves trying to." She spun to face Ace, eyes blazing with determination. "You still need to perform so stay here with everyone else," She zeroed in on Jett, and Ace could see him visibly trying to make himself shrink into Azura's back. "You will come with me. We are going after those memory flowers. Request from Jinx," she said in response to Azura's confused look. She grabbed Jett by the wrist and dragged him away into the crowd. Adam was staring desolately after his twin, but didn't lift a finger or say a word as he disappeared. Opal put a hand on his shoulder silently. Ace sighed to himself. Blaze was unforgiving and merciless, and didn't believe in second chances. She had a scorching fire in her gaze when she reached for Jett. Ace probably had the same in his. Jett had no hope of redemption from either of them.

☙

Jett let himself be dragged through to the employee area of the restaurant. He had expected as much to happen and supposed Blaze was dragging him outside to bury him in the entrance garden. Telling Azura had lifted a massive weight off his chest, but now everyone knew he had sold them out. She had initially been stunned to silence and then flipped out her phone to call Blaze. After setting the phone down she gave him the silent treatment, which Jett loathed. He wished she would scream and shout at him until she was blue in the face, so at least he would feel like he had received part of the punishment. Right now, he wished that Blaze would beat him or something so he could pay the price already and leave the guilt behind. The holding out was killing him. The pin drop silence that Azura pushed him into just let his own mind eat away at him, leaving him unable to say what he wanted to. The Darkfires had come back with an armload of books and papers and Azura immersed herself into the research. Jett sat quietly and only opened his mouth to politely respond to Ms. Drakfire's questions. He watched them go through book after book and finally draw a connection between the possession and a *hyponos*, and the reoccurring topic of bringing back the dead. Azura had asked that Benjamin lend an old suit of his for Jett to wear for their "meeting" as they had called it, and he had obliged. Ayesha whipped together some care packages for them and handed the parcels to Jett as they left, wishing him good luck. She ruffled Jett's hair and told him to take care of Azura. If only she had known how incredibly incompetent he would be at doing that. Nonetheless he smiled and nodded his head in acknowledgement. He remembered seeing Benjamin gently twirling the white memory flower that Jett had left on the table between his fingertips, just before the door swung shut. Then he and Azura ran for the train. Upon his arrival, his own brother wouldn't even look at him, causing Jett to deliberate if he had ever felt this low before. Adam was always on his side, he understood him in a way only he could, able to see through Jett like he was piece of glass. He knew Adam still understood why he had done it, but did not approve that those reasons had overridden his judgement. Opal had not bothered to turn around, and for that he felt even more wretched.

Blaze's grip on his hand was firm and he could feel the pulse in his wrist beat against the skin of her fingertips as she yanked him forward with an urgent grace. She never broke a stride as she sashayed past the waiters, ducking into the back room for performers and closing the door with a flick of her wrist. They were in a softly lit space with a couch and some vanities covered in makeup supplies and magazines. Paintings by Da Vinci and Claude Monet lined the walls and eighteenth-century lamps were placed at every corner of the room. She turned and fixed her unreadable gaze on him and slowly began to walk forward. He involuntary began to step back until he was pressed against the wall under a portrait of Bacchus. She was gorgeous in her evening gown, but the reason Jett's heart was beating faster was probably because he could see the glimmer of her dagger against her thigh when it came out of the slit of her dress. He closed his eyes, breathed deeply and prepared himself for whatever could happen. He opened his eyes to see her nose almost touching his, her large black eyes glittering in the yellow lamplight. He could see the heartbeat at the base of her throat, the soft curve of her mouth that twisted into a small smile. *Smile?* He thought bewildered. He had expected her to start breathing fire. It wasn't a malicious grin and she seemed amused.

"If you're going to maim me or whatever, I'd rather you do it now and get it over with," he breathed. Her hands went to his shoulders and grazed them gently. He felt pinpricks of heat wherever her fingers left his skin.

"Oh Jett. What are we going to do with you? Little troublemaker, aren't you?"

"Look, I know nothing I can say can express how sorry I am, but I'll do whatever is humanly possible to make up for it. Go ahead, do your worst."

His heart was pounding like a drum, waiting for Blaze's expression to turn deadly or for her whip to ignite and scorch him. To his surprise, she traced her fingers up his cheeks gently and held his face in both her hands with an unexpected tenderness. Her eyelashes brushed his skin as she blinked, sending a strange feeling lacing up his veins. Was she going to hurt him or not?

"Do you feel it?" she whispered. Her hand slid over to rest on his racing heart.

"F-Feel w-what?" he stammered. It was petrifying and intoxicating to be this close to her. Her body radiated a warmth that he had the strange urge to embrace.

"The connection. Between us."

"Us?" he asked warily.

"Come on, reach out for it. I know you can sense it too." She took his hands and placed them on her back and pressed herself against him. His shaky hands welcomed the warmth from her body heat but his head swirled with confused emotions, and they were clouding his thoughts.

"Jett," she whispered, letting hot air brush by his neck, causing the hair on the back of it to stand up. "Show me. Show me you feel it too. The rushing blood, the adrenaline pumping..." her hands slid down his sides, playing with the bottom of his vest and popped it open. He gasped and shuddered, staring at her wide-eye. He could feel it. His body responded to her words. As soon as it he realized it seemed to amplify itself to be ten times more overwhelming.

"Don't you?" she asked again. She looked up at him and tilted her head so for the briefest moment their lips brushed so lightly he could barely feel it, but that didn't stop the tremble that shook his body in response. Her expression changed in the blink of an eye and she pushed his hands off her and backed away.

"What is it?" he asked, dazed. Her brows were drawn together in a focused squint, staring at the painting above him. It was glowing with an eerie lavender light.

"Excellent, it worked. We found it."

"What?"

"The doorway to garden grave. Your enhanced emotions right now resonated with the *ankh* pieces in the room to reveal where it was. Anyone from Myra can create a sort of lock with *ankh* to guard personal areas. You though, as a *permotionem* can first of all, reveal them because it will pick up your energy and two, overpower the lock to get in. It saved us a lot of time not having to search the room." Jett felt like an utter idiot. Blaze had just hyped him up to get what she wanted. She didn't truly feel anything. He should have known better, she was with Joe after all. He wondered what part of his brain was stupid enough to believe it, or wanted it to be true. He was aware that his cheeks were probably the colour of a tomato as Blaze got to work, lifting the painting off of the wall. She had returned to her cold norm, leaving no trace of what had transpired, while Jett had it stamped all over his face.

"Don't worry," she said. "No one will know about this little experiment."

"Is that what it was?" he half squeaked. He blushed even harder and clamped his mouth shut. He could hear her laugh quietly, which did not help matters.

"Yes. All there was to it. Do you really think after what happened I could even want to do anything remotely of the sort? Don't be ridiculous." That about summed up Jett's feelings right now. Absolutely ridiculous. He didn't even like her, so how come he had responded that way? He watched the way her long hair fell like nighttime waterfall down her back, smooth and glossy in ebony layers. He thought of the memory Azura gave him. Blaze's genuine smile while racing up the cliff and her pure agony as she looked into the eyes of a sister who did not recognize her. He supposed he could argue that the memory was what caused him to react, but it had not crossed his mind since they arrived. Azura had forbidden him to say a word on the matter, so he kept his peace and let the events settle at the back of his mind. Not that it lessened his embarrassment in any form.

"No, it does not mean you have started to like me anyway. It was a reaction that was drawn out by the element of surprise. You reacted to it because it was new to you, uncharted territory. Besides, I don't want Jen to get on my bad side, so I didn't do anything major." *Jen*, Jett thought. Jen who had been visiting his dreams a lot lately. Jen, who he had been thinking about constantly. Of course, Blaze knew about it. She had revealed a pattern of *ankh* pieces pressed into the drywall, spread out in a spiral and pulsing with a vibrant purple light.

"Touch it and focus on any single emotion to break the lock." Jett placed his hand in the middle of the spiral and focused on his current humiliation. He was quite sure it was strong enough to overwhelm the *ankh*. Sure enough, the wall slid open to reveal an arched doorway. He could see a faint dot of daylight in the distance. Blaze stepped through and held out her hand for Jett to take. He held it gingerly and let the darkness envelop them both.

❦

Opal stared up at Ace, who was singing up on stage in a deep, honey-like voice. He had chosen to sing something she had never heard before, and was reaching the final verse of the song. His eyes locked with hers often and Opal couldn't help but think in the back of her mind that he might have been directing the lyrics at her. She shrugged it off, because she didn't want to think about what it meant if her hunch turned out to be correct. She sat back and enjoyed the music, letting it wash over her. She rubbed her wrist softly where Ace had grabbed it, while listening to Blaze's performance. *Blaze*, she thought. A flash of the scene in the wardrobes came back to her and she looked down at her lap, biting her lip. If Ace was into Blaze she wasn't about to interfere with them.

> *Twice the thunder, twice the fright,*
> *Twice the power of a tiger's might,*
> *I may be cruel,*
> *and my words will sting,*
> *but I know what melody the devil sings,*
> *She may make me glow,*
> *She may make me buzz*
> *But I'll never show her,*
> *No matter what she does,*
> *Best to leave,*
> *Best to forget,*
> *Rather than dream and live with regret,*
> *I'm stone cold,*
> *You can't melt the ice,*

The jaws of love are like a vice,
So stop yourself, before it starts,
Or you'll be another on my list of broken hearts

Ace finished his song to thundering applause and he bowed politely before making his way off the stage. Joe clapped him on the back while Azura and Adam praised his composure. Opal found it a little odd that Joe and Ace were so comfortable with each other. Did either of them know they were both vying for the same girl? *Man, this is awkward,* she thought. She debated asking Joe, but didn't want to raise an issue if there really wasn't one. Blaze had never shown any interest in Ace until tonight, and it brought up a torrent of confusing emotions in her head. It had always been Joe for Blaze, Opal had thought. Her head hurt just thinking about it. She guessed that part of the frustration was because she had hoped that Ace would be free for her to pursue, but if he truly had feelings for Blaze, even if Blaze did not return them, did Opal stand a chance against their years of friendship?

Adam snapped her out of her thoughts by offering her a breadbasket that had arrived at the table. She nodded her thanks and bit into the bun. A warm buttery flavour exploded in her mouth. She smiled and took another bite, and then another. She turned to look at Ace with a dreamy expression. He was so handsome, she thought. Ace caught her gaze and frowned. *He's even cuter when he's frowning,* Opal thought with a giggle. Ace took a bun and sniffed it. His eyes widened and he slapped the rest out of out of Opal's hand and Adam's before he could take a bite. Joe sprang up and ran towards the kitchen. Opal was so giddy that she couldn't talk. She was mesmerized by Ace, and nothing he was doing made too much sense to her. But God, did she want him. She saw Azura slump down beside Adam, the half-finished bun falling out of her fingers. *Poor thing, she must be so sleepy after that long journey here.* Ace was shaking Opal by the shoulders, saying something, and all she could do was relish the fact that he was touching her. His magnificent blue eyes were the last details she saw before curling into his arms and losing consciousness, his irises as fearsome as a supernova.

CHAPTER 19
Gateways to the Soul

JETT FOLLOWED BLAZE THROUGH THE GARDEN PATHWAYS BLINDLY, SINCE she appeared to know where they were going and he didn't have the slightest clue. If he had been in here alone he would have gotten hopelessly lost. Blaze hadn't let go of his hand, claiming that Jett was guiding them towards the flowers. Jett felt the push and pull of some kind of electrifying energy. Something was calling out to him, but he could not pinpoint where or what it was. So, he let Blaze pull him along through the twisting maze of roses, petunias, tulips and thorny vines that formed a huge stretch of the garden's walls. Jen's favourite flower was a yellow rose, he recalled, as they passed by a towering hedge of them. He had spoken to her on the train ride to Palo's when he had drifted off, and they had been sitting on a park bench in his dreamscape. It was a strange experience, because he could feel her and not feel her at the same time. She was like a ghostly wisp of reality that kept slipping through his fingers. Although she appeared in full, emerald eyes and all, the dream missed the warmth that her normal presence would have given him. His heart weighed on him heavily, since he had decided that he wouldn't tell Jen about how he sold out his group to Jackson. At least not yet. He had told her about going to Palo's as their next step, while she smiled at him, twirling a strand of her tawny hair around her finger.

"So how was Azura's trip? Did she find out anything useful?" she asked.

"Yeah, they had a breakthrough," Jett tried to act excited about their new-found information. He told her about the *hyponos* and the resurrection and how Azura's source was Blaze's father.

276

"Oh my God, I've never even thought of it that way and I'm a *hyponos* myself. Then again I'm not a very skilled one either so it makes sense."

"Neither did Ace, and he's a lot more experienced. This took someone really powerful apparently."

"No way to know who did it?"

"Not at the moment. It's frustrating the hell out of everyone."

"I'll say. They're racing against clock and their time runs out when the heads catch them," Jen said. At the mention of the heads, Jett felt sick to his stomach. Jackson's face flashed before his eyes, his promise echoing in Jett's ears. "They're scared of Blaze more than anything else. Storm told me they found out she was a slave to darkness. I don't want to judge her, but are they right for pursuing her like this? If she's that dark, what are her real motives here?" Joe felt another shudder of guilt. He had questioned Blaze the same way before and it had led him to do something that had landed them all in disaster. He didn't want Jen to make the same mistake. He took her hand and focused on his memory of Blaze's darkening. Jen had slowly trained him to do this each time she visited his mind, and he had gotten quite adept at sharing his memories with her. He let the memory unfold itself and play through like an unconscious motion picture. He could see Jen's shock and sadness as the memory progressed. Her hand flew over her mouth as she watched Blaze struggle in the current. As the memory faded out, with Blaze weeping into the side of her horse, Jen's lip had begun to tremble.

"Dear God…" she whispered. "I…I… I had no idea." Jett nodded sombrely.

"No one did. I felt awful when I saw the truth. Before I was asking the same questions that you did. Don't make the same mistake." Jen curled up against him and nodded. Even though he couldn't feel her, Jett felt a wave of security and peace wash over him. Jen had a way of tapping into the root of his stability, slowly wedging a place for herself there. He began to see the scene dissipate around him, a sign that he was waking up. "Good luck Jett," Jen's broken voice said before he opened his eyes.

Blaze picked up her pace and dragged Jett around a corner where a small gravesite came into view. Sure enough, adjacent to the tombstone lay a bouquet of memory flowers tied with a golden ribbon. There were various colours and Jett could feel the pulsation of emotions that were contained inside. Blaze approached the site cautiously, scanning for traps, Jett assumed.

She knelt and picked up the flowers gently, handling them with great care. Jett walked around and took a look at the tombstone. It was blank, with the exception of a golden snakehead inscribed in the middle.

"Symbol of the *jaculus*," Blaze said.

"No name or anything?" Jett asked while examining the front and back of the stone. She shook her head.

"Once you become part of the *jaculus*, their mandate states that you are an integral part of them, just another functioning limb of a bigger organism. When they die, all people have to remember them by is their status in the group. They forgo their name to death in commitment to the team. There is no concept of 'I' or 'you'. It is just the *jaculus*." Jett wondered what that would be like. To be forgotten as an individual but held in the memories of millions as a symbol of a greater organization. He didn't know how to feel about that. Whoever was buried here, their personal life meant nothing anymore. It was just their commitment to the *jaculus* that remained. Then again, was it better to be forgotten and become a number or statistic if you had something you wanted the world to forget? He could only ponder for a moment before Ace ran into the garden, carrying Opal in his arms. Adam was right behind him, carrying Azura. Blaze jumped to attention, automatically checking both of their vital signs.

"Bread...poisoned...leave...now," Adam wheezed. Blaze took the dagger from her thigh and slashed her dress, making it into a short skirt that she could easily run in.

"Let's go!" Blaze took Azura from Adam and shifted her on to her back. She kicked of her heels and took off, with Ace racing behind her and the twins hot on their trail.

"Where's Joe?" Blaze yelled.

"Fighting off the staff at the doorway!" Adam yelled back at her.

"You two go get him, I'm going to cut our way out!" Blaze held her dagger out and began hacking through the roses.

Jett ran as fast as his legs would take him, blazing a trail back through the tunnel. He could hear Adam thundering beside him. They burst into a room where Joe was wrestling an older man with a butcher knife. He had bloody marks on his face where Joe's brass knuckles had hit him. Adam and Jett split off to either side and simultaneously soccer-kicked the man in the ribs. He doubled over and Joe tossed and slammed him into the ground so violently that the floorboards shattered from the impact. The man was now knocked out cold, and the twins helped Joe to his feet. His suit was in tatters and splattered with blood. His face wasn't much better, as he sported a rapidly purpling black eye. Joe only had time to shakily breathe a thank you before they all made a beeline for the garden and the impressive pathway Blaze had cut out of the hedges. The path led out to a parking lot where Blaze and Ace had positioned themselves and their friends on motorcycles. She had Neal's remote in her hand and pressed the top button. The engines roared to life. Joe got on his own motorcycle while Adam and Jett got on another. Jett grabbed the handlebars, revved the engine and took off, following Blaze's lead. They roared down the road, swerving through cars at breakneck speeds. Jett looked behind him only once to see the group of angry staff hollering at them in the background. He steeled his nerves and shot forward, leaving the murderous mob behind.

❧

"Dammit," Jackson seethed. His restaurant cameras had picked up every-thing and he had watched Blaze and her friends escape. He paced back and forth fruitlessly. That girl was always one step too many out of his grasp. He thought he really would have gotten her this time. A small drawl of fear was starting to pump through him. He knew he was playing with fire. The more he provoked Blaze, the more anger she would build, and extract on him if the opportunity ever arose for her. The incident at the Seal had seared itself into his mind, and his nightmares now contained her burning eyes and whips of blue-white fire. He had faith though, that he could catch her before she could catch him. He had the city on his side after all and a secret weapon. He walked to the back of the room where a section was blocked off by a glass wall. Inside, a girl was suspended in the air, her eyes wide open, struggling to move.

"We almost had her," Jackson said smoothly, watching her fight against her constraints. "We need more though. I know you have more information that you've been holding back. My sensors have told me. I need you to relinquish all of it." Jackson could see her mouthing profanities at him. "No? That's okay.

I'll get it out of you one way or another, Jennifer dear." Jen thrashed back and forth but to no avail. She was bound inside. "You will do as I say and reveal whatever I desire. Visiting Jett's head has proven extremely useful for me and you will continue to do so. Until I get what I *want*," His hand hovered over a lever. "Now will you cooperate?" Her mouth shaped incredibly obscene insults. "Guess we'll just have to do this the hard way." He pulled the lever down and a terrifying tremor went through the glass, electrocuting Jen. Once she lay unresponsive, Jackson began to work his machine.

"Lea," he ordered, "Analyze her memories." Lea was Jackson's assistant and, quite conveniently, a *hyponos* as well. She entered the room from Jen's side of the glass barrier. Her small, birdlike figure was prominent through her blue security uniform. She leaned over Jen intently as she worked on surpassing her mental boundaries in silence. Jackson very much enjoyed having Lea as his assistant for this very reason. She never asked questions, did as she was told, and didn't disclose anything to anyone else. A perfect accomplice that he could keep in the dark. While Lea was busy, Jackson turned his thoughts to Scarlett. That woman had truly shredded his heart into pieces.

Jackson had a lifetime full of regrets and actions he wasn't proud of, and he had struggled so hard to hide that part of him from Scarlett. He had wanted to leave it, bury it so deep inside himself that they never resurfaced again. He just couldn't. His job, his life, the circle of the *jaculus*, he was afraid of losing it. He had been equally afraid of losing Scarlett. Now, he had lost her, and the day she left him was the day his worst fears were realized. If he became a better man, he thought, he could win her back. His definition of better and hers were vastly different, he had come to realize. He thought being better was reaching for the stars and becoming powerful. He clawed his way to the top of the city and gained unlimited control. He had thought it would have been more than enough, because wasn't power the symbol of a strong man? Scarlett apparently didn't think so. His hand made its way to his cheek, grazing over the area where Scarlett had slapped him. The sting revived itself as he recalled the encounter.

"*How could you have given me Lilith's curse?*" she had screamed at him. His heart wrenched with guilt. He had tried to erase that night from his memory but it was impossible. It came back to him in deadly flashes.

He and some other *jaculus* stealing the vials of fluid from the vaults. The sickly green liquid shimmering in his hands. He had felt wrong, mixing it into drinks, but went along with his fellow warriors to do it anyway. They had convinced him that it was, in some twisted way, the right thing to do. He could no longer recall why. He remembered the feeling of absolute terror when he saw Scarlett drink from the glass meant for Maya. He had wanted to scream at her to drop it, but his inner coward kept him silent and he watched wordlessly as she finished the glass. He had gone home and punched a hole in wall that night. He had kept the secret to himself and prayed that when the time came, it would just be explained as some kind of infertility. Somehow, she had found out and he felt like he had fallen down a cliff into a bottomless pit, from which he could never return.

I truly am damned, he thought. *I'm wicked by choice. No magic was needed to blacken my heart. I did that on my own.*

A single tear rolled down his cheek. He brushed away immediately. He had to capture Opal and Blaze. They had broken the law, but that was just a front for why Jackson really wanted them. They were going to help him win Scarlett back. He clenched his fists together. Lea came to his side of the room and tentatively placed a hand on his shoulder. He jerked away from her touch.

"Are you alright, sir?" she asked.

"Ah, yes Lea, I was just thinking. Go ahead." Lea nodded and sprinkled some powder under his nose. The overpowering smell of chloroform succumbed him to sleep and Lea's soft voice resonated in his thoughts.

"Brace yourself," she informed him. Jackson relaxed and let Lea flood Jen's memories through him.

☙

Adam struggled to keep a wild Azura under control in the backseat of the Lincoln navigator. They had driven to a rendezvous point where Jinx's drivers were waiting for them. They had discarded the bikes and urged the drivers to go as fast as they could. Once they were going over a hundred and forty kilometers an hour, Adam started to relax. Ace was having an equally difficult time with Opal in the seat across from him. Both had woken up but were clearly not sane. It was like they were high on some drug and would not come down from the exhilaration. Opal kept going on about how she felt so free and light. She would giggle and shriek every time Ace tried to keep her in her seat and would try and get up just so he would wrestle her down again. Azura was pulling Adam towards the window to gaze at the sunset, insisting that she had never seen lovelier colours splayed across the sky in her life. "It's so, so, so beautiful!" she wept with joy. Adam pulled her back by the arms, insisting that they admire the colours from a distance.

"Your voice is so pure and perfect," Opal crooned at Ace. "Never stop talking."

"If it means you'll shut up, then I'll read you the Bible," Ace mumbled.

"Oh, I'm leaving behind my grief!" Azura sang. Opal grinned at her.

"I feel the same way. No loss. No heartache. I'm finally *happy*."

"Happy, happy, happy!" they both sang together and burst into a fit of laughter. Adam let out a tired sigh. He wondered if this is what Azura felt like when she was taking care of them. Never had he thought the tables would be turned. Azura would never act like this in her right mind and neither would Opal. Ace took his Rollex off his wrist and tossed it to Adam.

"Give Azura that. She has a fixation for shiny stuff. It should keep her occupied." Adam raised an eyebrow at him, but handed it over to Azura after pulling her away from the window again. She squealed when she saw it.

"Thank you, Adam!" she chirped. Adam eased his arm around her as she lay down on her side and began to play with the watch.

"How did you know it would work?" he asked Ace.

"Something I learned from Blaze. She would always joke about Azura's fancy of shiny objects, and how all their friends strived to get her these types of items for her birthday. If nothing else, they would wrap her presents in tinfoil for the same effect. I figured the principle still applied here." Adam couldn't help but laugh.

"Tinfoil?"

"Don't ask me how it started, it's some inside joke." Adam wondered what could have possibly started that.

Soon he and Ace were collectively struggling to get the girls back into Jinx's lounge. At one point Blaze and Jett came to help when they tried to run away. It was almost funny to see Blaze running in a torn evening gown after Opal, who zoomed around like a shooting star. Blaze could only use the fact that Opal couldn't change directions to stop her. Joe held the bouquet of memory flowers and was summoning Jinx to come meet them. It appeared that Blaze had cleaned his cuts and bandaged his wounds in the other car to the best of her abilities. Pieces of her dress and shreds from Jett's suit were tied around his injuries. Adam and Jett held onto either side of Azura, and dangled Ace's watch in front of her every time she dropped it to keep her under control.

"Are you ready to go?" came Jinx's voice. She materialized in front of them. Her eyes furrowed when she saw Azura and Opal being held down by their friends.

"What happened to them?"

"Shouldn't you know?" Ace spat at her. "You set us up!" Jinx looked genuinely surprised. Adam could tell. Her expression was void of cocky assurance.

"What do you know?" Blaze said. "She didn't. Jackson found out some other way." Ace glared at Jett.

"Hey, I was with you the whole time! You can't blame me for this!" Adam wanted to jump in and defend his brother but stayed silent. He had lost his confidence in advocating his innocence.

"Jackson found out?" Jinx repeated. "How... I was so sure that he would not even know you stepped foot in there..."

"Well as you can see, his staff was not kind to us," Joe said shaking his injured arm. "Azura and Opal had their appetizer drugged." Jinx shook her head, her red eyes flashing.

"I don't understand... Well I apologize for that, truly. It was not how it was supposed to go. I see you did retrieve the memory flowers, so I will hold up my end now. It's time to go to the Devil's Den." She snapped her fingers and a swarm of scorpions began to crowd around her, carrying various items. Backpacks, water canteens and first aid kits were some of the items Adam could pick out after he got over his initial shock of the critters.

"We can't bring them with us in this state," Ace said. Opal was still holding onto his arm and giggling. Jinx thought for moment.

"That is true. I will take partial responsibility for this accident, so here's what I propose; I will teleport the five of you to the cove and take these two back to Myra with me. I'm going to pay Scarlett a visit anyway. There, they can receive proper treatment for their… current condition."

"Opal can't be in Myra. She's being hunted," Blaze reminded her. Jinx dismissed her concern with a wave of her hand.

"I have my methods. I assure you we will be undetected. That is a specialty of the Swarm is it not?" Blaze nodded grudgingly.

"Fine. Do as you must." Adam felt a wave of pressure push them back from Opal and Azura. Jinx touched their foreheads and they became drowsy and stable, barely moving a muscle or saying a word. She came up to Blaze and put a hand on her shoulder. "I truly wish you success in this mission, Lady Scorpion. The swarm stands with you." She bowed her head. Blaze seemed slightly surprised but clasped Jinx's hand in gratitude. Adam was equally puzzled. Jinx was incredibly hostile about her title before.

"Take care of them," Blaze said.

"Affirmed," Jinx responded. She stepped back and began the spell. Adam felt the power of the wind take over and the blinding white encompassed him as he dissipated. *Mavis. I'm coming.*

༄

Jinx prepared for another teleportation spell, using one of her drivers as the person to leave behind. She supported Azura and Opal on either arm. Azura was much easier because she was smaller, but Opal was almost her height and weighed heavily on her. As she prepared to leave, one of her scorpions came up to her with the memory flower bouquet on its back. Jinx picked it up carefully and examined it. Her mouth curled up into a smile as she turned it over in her hand. She truly did hope that Blaze rescued this young woman and returned safely. She had meant that. Jinx though, still had a score to settle with Blaze and she had started by using Joe as her pawn. That's why, to her delight, she found that the black memory flower was missing.

༄

Joe felt himself hit slippery rocks as he came out of the spell. He fell over with a thud, wincing as his injured arm flared with pain. He shook his head to clear his vision and began to scan for Blaze. It was almost a reflex now, for him to look for her face wherever he happened to be. She had landed in a low crouch, unscathed, and had gone to help Adam who had landed straight on his back. Ace was pulling Jett to his feet behind some red stalagmites. Joe looked down at his hands. They were bathed in crimson light. He got up slowly, taking in the scene around him. Walls the colour of shimmering rubies sparkled everywhere. The ground underneath his feet was a slightly darker, more blood-like colour. The air was hot and humid, like they had landed at the mouth of a boiling pot. *Of course, you idiot*, he thought. *This is the ring of fire. We're in or near a volcano.* The thought shook him slightly. He prayed silently that they were just near and not inside a volcano. If they were inside, then please let it be a dormant one. He could see why they called it the Devil's Den though. The whole cavern, if given raging fire, would be a pretty accurate representation of Hell, as he had seen it described in many books and plays. There was something definitely *wrong* about this place. He could feel an undercurrent of evil dispersed through the air. From the look on Blaze's face, he could tell she did too. She was alert, wary, and stepping lightly around the dome, trying to gauge the potential danger they were in.

"This is where Mavis has been trapped all this time?" Jett asked. "Oh my god... Who knows what has happened to her while she's been here?!"

"MAVIS!" Adam yelled. "MAVIS! WHERE ARE YOU? MAVIS!"

"Adam, I'm sure that this cavern is part of a volcanic interior, so it is quite large. I don't think shouting will help right now," Joe remarked. "Let's get freshened up so we can plan out a strategy." He pointed to pile of fallen supplies that had come through with them.

"Joe's right," Ace said. "We've all had a long day and we should get some sleep. It will do neither Mavis nor us any good to go on exhausted." Jett and Adam began to protest when Blaze shot them a glare. It wasn't her normal glare though; her eyes were alight with an almost violet fire, the same one that burned before her whip ignited.

Joe felt his heart leap into his throat. Even Ace began to walk towards her, concerned. "Blaze..." he began.

"Sleep," she said, her voice dangerously soft. "Now." The twins didn't argue. Joe could read the horror written all over their faces. They silently picked up a backpack, went about fifteen feet away and began to prepare for the night. Blaze whirled around and sat down, her back to them. Joe locked eyes with Ace. Ace motioned for him to go to her.

"You guys can take first watch," he said. Joe understood his underlying message. *She needs you.*

Ace went over to help the twins with their gear. As Joe approached Blaze, he saw the two scars on her shoulder had turned from a dull maroon to angry red, like they had been reopened. He plopped down beside her and pulled her close, as he leaned against the cavern wall, feeling her breathing heavily against his chest. She didn't resist and just melted into him.

"Joe..." she breathed. "It's all coming back. The agony, the sadness, the pain. My...my darkness is swelling up. It's overwhelming me, and I don't know if I can stop it." She looked up at him, her black eyes burning with purple fire, reflecting the crimson light of the cavern. "I don't even have Darkfire, I don't think I can summon him here. You can feel it, can't you? The barrier spells? The blood locks? This place... it's bringing out the demon in me...what if I... lose control?" Joe looked back into the flaming eyes he had loved for so long. He had seen them burn with fury, light up with happiness, and focus with intelligence. Now they held something he had only seen once. Fear. Fear not for herself, but for him and the others. Joe's heart clenched. He hated seeing her like this. She was normally so confident that she reassured him. There were times when he would reassure her too. But for stress of this magnitude, he had didn't have the slightest clue about how to approach her. Her dragonfly necklace was still around her throat. He touched it softly. She kept her gaze on him, frozen with fear. *Eyes are the gateways to the soul.* His grandmother used to say that. Blaze's eyes didn't reflect her soul right now. It reflected what had been torturing it for so long. An overwhelming tenderness came over him and his heart began to hammer away in his chest, relentlessly. He pulled her up in his arms and kissed her. She widened her eyes in surprise, but returned it. He could feel the elevated heat in her body as he pressed her against him, welcoming the pressure. He kissed her again, more passionately this time, running his fingers through her hair and tugging on her bottom lip. She gasped silently. It felt like a breath of pure, fresh air. He wanted to tell her, tell her how much he loved her, how he would stand by her despite what had happened. He didn't care right now if she loved him back or not. He would anchor her darkness. *I wish she could give part of it to me. Just to ease the burden on herself.* They continued, intensifying the electricity between them. Blaze suddenly half collapsed on him.

"Blaze?" he said worriedly? She blinked a few times and turned to look up at him again. Her irises were once again as dark as the night sky. "I… feel lighter now," She said tentatively, placing a hand over her heart. "The darkness is suppressing itself somehow… I can still feel it, but it's like its banging at me through a glass wall and I can only feel dull thuds." Joe placed his hand tenderly over her scars. She flinched as he touched her there.

"You… did something," she mumbled softly. Joe had no idea what he had done or why it had worked. Either way, a weight had been lifted off of his chest, now that she seemed to be at ease again, for the most part. She would constantly be fighting the urges, even if he had somehow suppressed them.

"I don't know what happened," he admitted. "But you're okay now." They sat in silence for some time, staring at the glittering wall in front of them. Joe looked over at the twins, to find them asleep, with Ace curled up beside them. Just like Blaze, he looked more innocent and vulnerable when he slept, all the harshness vanishing from his face. Ace had that simple sort of angelic beauty, with a clear skin and symmetrical features. If he didn't have stubble, Joe would associate him with the boy angels he used to see in the Chronicles facades. Well, with the exception that angels didn't have hair streaked with blue dye or ear piercings. He had always been intrigued by the stories of Ace that Blaze would tell. He remembered at one point being insanely jealous of their relationship a very long time ago. Blaze had no patience for that when he voiced his concern. He hadn't said that he was jealous, but had asked why she wasn't with Ace if she loved him so much. She had laughed, but had then put on a serious expression.

"There's one thing you should know about me Joe," she had told him. "I always know myself. I know what my strengths and weaknesses are, and what I need. Although I do love Ace and I would die for him, I'm not in love with him. There is a difference. When I look at Ace, it's like looking into a mirror. I don't feel anything special because we are the same. He understands me, and it's peaceful to be together. We show arrogance by appearing emotionless as a measure to feel strong. We have trouble telling people how we feel, not wanting to embarrass ourselves or show weakness, so we appear cruel instead. That comfortable and peaceful feeling isn't enough to fill up what we're missing in life. Darkness and darkness, negativity and negativity would just lead to more of itself. Whenever I think of him, it's like looking at myself in the mirror and all I can feel is a piece of cold, sharp glass when I put out my hand." Joe had sat in stunned silence for a while after that. Blaze was tranquil as she explained this to him, as if she was telling him how her day had been. He had never questioned their relationship after that. Meeting Ace had just reconfirmed what Blaze had said. It was clear he loved her, but not the same way. It was a protective love, not a deep one. The same way Jett and Adam felt about Mavis, he assumed.

He felt the even falling of her chest against him. *She's asleep.* He placed a kiss on her forehead and intertwined his free hand with hers. She was still in the ripped evening gown she had worn to Palo's. Her legs appeared crimson in the light, and were covered in thorn scratches. He silently ran his hand over them, light with his touch. Her eyelashes fluttered and then closed again. "Joe..." she murmured.

"Hmm?" he responded.

"What does the future look like to you?" she said in a sleepy voice. He was slightly surprised by that question. He wasn't sure if Blaze was talking with her full senses. She did tend to get slightly dazed when she was tired. He thought about it for a minute. What did he see? He was twenty-two right now. He wanted to shift from being a *bellator* to being a healer, and hopefully he would become an accomplished one soon. He had already started studying, with Azura's help. He wanted to be grounded, have his own place and a stable life in one of the more natural areas of Myra. He had already told Blaze about all of that, so what did she mean? He had never told her that she had always been a part of those visions. Her smile greeting him when he came home, her voice cheering for him when he passed his medical exams. Blaze had slowly just integrated herself into those visions and now he couldn't separate her from his ideal dream anymore.

"It revolves around you," he said quietly. He began to panic when she didn't respond. Had it been too much?

"Tell me," she said. He took a deep breath.

"Someday, having you to come home to every night. Not having to hold back my feelings because you return them. Keeping you happy with the little things you like. Like books and chai tea. And... and..."

"And one day leaving Myra behind for a normal life with you," she said. Joe stared at her open mouthed.

"You think about these things?" he asked in disbelief.

"Just because I don't say anything doesn't mean it doesn't cross my mind. Recently it has been. It's just never been my area of comfort to discuss. Not now of course, but maybe five to seven years in the future, I could see that," she giggled. "I've never said that to anyone. Not even Ace."

"Do you really see that?" he asked.

"Yeah. I want to have a reason to fight against my bitter blood. I do it for myself and for my friends right now, but my will gets overpowered from time to time. Having a family again will give me a reason until death, to fight back as hard as I can, despite the fact that I can never see my birth family again." Blaze's voice was fading between breaths, as if she was falling asleep again. Joe could hear the lingering sadness in her voice. It truly was a curse, what she had to bear. It made him feel guilty about the black memory flower tucked away in his suit jacket. Blaze was drifting off.

"*Saranghae*," Joe whispered. *I love you*, in Korean.

"*Shyhad, mai bhi karthi hoon*," Blaze murmured. Joe looked at her, perplexed. He didn't know which language she was speaking in or what she had said. He knew that she didn't know Korean, so she couldn't have been responding to what he had said. She knew so many languages that he couldn't tell which one she was using. It was too late to ask her though, she was fast asleep and he didn't want to wake her again. He hadn't noticed Ace standing by him until he nudged Joe with his toe. Joe was startled, but regained his composure when he saw Ace.

"Sleep," Ace told him, "it's my turn now." Joe nodded and gently eased Blaze down on to the ground. As Joe settled down beside her, Ace turned to him. "Maybe, I love you too," Ace said.

"Excuse me?" Joe said, clearly confused.

"That's what she said, in case you were wondering. *Maybe, I do to.*"

"Blaze said that?"

"In Urdu, yes," Joe just stared at him. "It means that she might love you. I figured you'd be happier if you actually knew what she said." Joe couldn't comprehend what Ace was saying. *Maybe, I love you too. That's what she said.*

"She…what…?" he knew he sounded like a fool, but there was no judgement in Ace's expression. He gave him a weary smile.

"I have always been jealous of you Joe. Not because you had Blaze," he said when an air of alarm crossed Joe's face. "Because of what you two have. Blaze and I have had the same problem for years. The inability to fall in love. You, have given her that. I never thought I would hear her say those words to anyone. I feared that for both of us. Now I only fear it for myself. So, thank you, for getting her heart to beat again. Not because it has to, but because it wants to." Joe felt like Ace was exposing a very well concealed portion of his personality to him. Openly admitting he was jealous and how he feared the same vulnerabilities that Blaze did could not have been easy for him.

"Ace…" he raised his hand up so Joe would stop.

"I am happy for you, truly. Don't worry about me," Ace muttered. Joe felt a powerful drowsiness over take him. He knew Ace was using his *hyponos* abilities to lull him to sleep. "Goodnight Joe," Ace said. Joe barely heard it, his heart was as light as a feather and he went to sleep, smiling. *Maybe, I love you too*, Ace's words echoed in his head.

❧

Ace sat with his head resting on his knees, keeping a lookout. Joe and Blaze slept peacefully behind him. He sighed. His best friend may or may not be in love now. Blaze no longer shared one of his biggest sorrows and that feeling was frighteningly lonely. It did feel better when you knew other people struggled with the same things you did. He probably should have been thinking that if it happened for Blaze it could happen for him too. He didn't think like that though, and Blaze didn't either. They always would be happy for the other person, but internally agonize over the fact that it could never happen for them. Just because one was successful doesn't mean the other would be. Ace despised it because he could receive all the love he wanted, he could just never return it. He was tired of feeling awful about breaking the hearts of girls that just couldn't make it through to him, so he had resorted to flings to keep things simple. He didn't want to hurt anyone.

Blaze turned over and hung an arm over Joe's stomach. Ace couldn't help but laugh at the fact that Joe didn't even know that Blaze had learned Korean for him. She was going to surprise him by singing Happy Birthday in it. *I wonder when Opal's birthday is,* he thought. He quickly pushed the thought away. Unless he wanted to die by Blaze's hands he would have to keep his distance from Opal. Eventually she would get attached and he wouldn't be able to and it would be the same story all over again. Opal deserved better than that. Jinx better be taking good care of her back in Myra. It was now enemy territory.

CHAPTER 20
End of my misery

ADAM WOKE UP TO SEE BLAZE PLACING BREAKFAST IN FRONT OF HIM. AS she walked away he got up and rubbed his eyes groggily. There was no sign of the violet fire in her eyes anymore, which was a relief. He nudged Jett, who was still asleep beside him. He looked at his twin sadly as Jett moaned and turned over. They had barely spoken a word to each other since Jett had come back with Azura. Now they were so close to finding Mavis. They really should be working as a team again. Adam still couldn't shake the consequences of what Jett had done. It had nearly killed them all. He had done it out of love for Mavis though, which conflicted Adam. He kept telling himself it didn't justify what Jett did, but he wanted to forgive his brother since it had come from that. *Blaze was right. Love is evil. It's weakness.* Jett had told him about the way she had explained it to him. How love becomes a chain, so that no matter what the consequences, you would do whatever you could to get the person you love back.

"I'm usually right," Blaze said from behind him. "You read emotions long enough you can start to pick up patterns of human behaviour. That's why when I warn you, you should listen." She had changed into a new *bellator* uniform, looking exactly the same as the day they met her.

"I'm realizing it all too late," Adam said, defeated. "I'm sorry, for him."

"You should not have to apologize for your brother's mistakes. Come with me." She reached out a hand to help Adam up and began to guide him away from Jett. Adam saw Ace silently take a lookout post near Jett as Blaze left.

"Where's Joe?" Adam asked.

"Exploring the cavern more to see where we can start working safely. He'll be back soon." Blaze led him to an expanse of rocky wall that had shards of minerals jutting out of it. On one of them was a small piece of torn denim. The same colour as Mavis jacket when they last saw her. Blaze handed it to him.

"She's definitely here, if that's any consolation." Adam was beginning to feel the spark of new hope. It was quickly replaced by dread, incited by an awful thought that crossed his mind, time and time again.

"Dead or alive?" he asked gravely.

"That I cannot say," Blaze said, toying with her necklace. "This place has strong dark magic cloaking it. I can sense blood locks being used as barrier spells, they block me from sensing her. It's easy to get in here, but once you're in, it's getting out that's the challenge. It's designed to be a prison. It's why Fang couldn't track her, because she was being veiled, and the fact that this place is in middle of the ocean. Fang's nose can only work on land and across small bodies of water. Whoever's done this, has really thought everything through, unfortunately." Blaze patted the shimmering red wall. "This place, I believe, is an ancient crossover of several supernatural regions, so it has twice the invocation power than other locations. Legend has it that it was once a gateway to some portion of Hell. I believe that's why they brought Mavis here, so they could work the enchantment without interference and start it from merging fuel tanks of power."

Adam rubbed the piece of denim between his fingers. "Would you know who they might be?"

"Don't you think I would have told you by now if I did?"

"Point taken," Adam sighed. "We're racing against a clock that we can't see. We don't know when this person may come back and finish the job."

"Trust me, we'll all feel it when they begin to finish the job. All we can do is just look for now."

"I suppose that's better than nothing." They shared a moment of silence.

"How is Jett doing?" Blaze asked. Adam stayed silent.

"I see." Blaze placed a hand on his shoulder. Adam tensed up. Blaze's skin was burning hot. "A side effect of being here," Blaze explained. "You can feel it because you're ordinary. The rest of them cannot, their innate abilities shield them. It won't burn you though."

293

"Why am I ordinary?" Adam asked.

"And your twin isn't? It's because these abilities are not based on genetics. They are gifts you could say, and are randomly but rarely distributed through the world. There is about five percent of the world's population that is gifted and the majority of them do not know it. Myra does send out hunters to search every year for these individuals to bring back to train."

"What happens after they are trained?"

"They go back into the world and use their abilities to help others. Many great doctors, engineers and inventors have studied in Myra. Although recently we've become more secretive for some reason, and we just tend to send our undercover mentors to harness and develop these skills without revealing who they are or where they came from. Your chances of being born with a gift though are increased, not guaranteed, if either of your parents has a gift, or you have at some point have been exposed to raw *ankh* dust while in infancy." Adam continued to toy with the denim in his hand. Blaze let him take in the information quietly.

"Where did Jett get his necklace from?" Blaze asked after a while. *That's random*, Adam thought.

"Our father gave it to him before he died," he said, "Why?"

"I saw it had a fire on one side and a wave on the other. That is usually a symbol of balance, used by *changjo*, creators. When they produce a blade or any other weapon, they shape the steel in a forge and then cool it in an ice bath. It represents how two opposites work together to design something beautiful. Normally fire and water destroy each other. But when metal is between them, they can create. I was wondering if your father had been a *changjo*, and that's how he came across it."

"I'm sure if my father was one, he would have had no idea about it. Just like Jett. He always told us one of his childhood friends had given it to him, as a goodbye present."

"Why did his friend leave?" Blaze asked.

"I'm not sure, I never really asked and he didn't tell us. Uncle Ben, as we called him, was always somewhat of a mystery." Blaze cocked her head to one side.

"Was that his name? Ben?"

"Yeah. Dad gave the necklace to Jett because Jett was never too good with the idea of balance. He said that Uncle Ben had taught him about that and now his necklace would help Jett understand it too. Does that mean Uncle Ben could have been a *changjo?*" There was a small waver in Blaze's smile. Adam wondered if he had imagined it. When he blinked, her expression was normal once again.

"It is possible. There are many of us dispersed throughout the world," she said after some deliberation.

It was strange talking to her now. Before it had felt like Blaze spoke through a wall of ice when she was addressing him. Now even though she wasn't in the least bit friendly, he felt like he could now sense her breathing, giving some indication that she was human. It was not much but it was something. Abruptly, a shriek echoed through the cavern and Blaze's dagger was out, her eyes alight and alert. She dashed back to Ace, pulling Adam along with her. Jett had woken up from hearing the scream and was rubbing his eyes clear.

"What's going on?" he mumbled. Ace's fiery blue eyes met with Blaze's. Adam watched an unspoken conversation take place. Blaze ran off in a flash while Ace grabbed Adam's arm with a grip of steel. "Don't move," he commanded.

"What's happening?" Adam demanded.

"I think Joe may have found Mavis." Adam's eyes widened.

"That scream was her?" He twisted his arm fruitlessly in Ace's solid grip. "Let me go! I have to see if she's okay!"

"We already have two qualified experts doing that. You need to stay here where you can't get hurt. Whatever caused her to scream probably would do the same to you." Jett's wrist was also being held in Ace's other hand, as he struggled to move.

"Try all you want," Ace said. "I'm too strong for you." Adam couldn't deny that. Ace's arms were lined with muscle and he could feel the crushing power of his hand on his wrist. Adam gave up and began to tensely bounce his leg in anticipation. Without thinking he clasped Jett on the shoulder, like he always did when he needed support. Jett held on to his hand. Adam could feel him trembling. It seemed like they had been trying to find Mavis for so long that they had given up hope of a successful rescue. Part of him was thinking it may be another false alarm and it would have been some other person's scream. But if it was her…

Joe appeared, carrying someone on his back. As he drew closer Adam could make out a heavy dusting of red, rocky powder covering the body. Joe was a few feet from them when Adam saw a hint of golden hair through the dust. His heart rose with excitement and he pulled himself towards them. Ace let him go and he shot like a bullet to Joe's side to help him lay her down. Joe backed up as Adam and Jett hovered and fussed over Mavis. Adam wiped the hair away from her eyes and rubbed the powder off of her face. She was in the same clothes she had left in and they were in tatters, leaving little to protect her already bruised and beat-up limbs.

"Mavis! Mavis! It's me…" Jett was holding her in his arms while Adam was holding her hands, checking for a pulse. He almost cried with relief when he felt it thump against his fingers.

"She's alive… She's alive! Mavis, please…" Adam said over and over. Jett clutched her to his chest. She let out a small groan, but her eyes stayed closed.

"Let her go," Blaze said as she came into view. "Give us space so we can work on keeping her alive." Adam and Jett backed up tentatively and let Joe and Blaze take Mavis. Adam's heart was crashing against his rib cage as his view was occasionally blocked by the movement of Joe's back. He could see Blaze and Joe working swiftly, taking the medical supplies in their backpacks out to bandage and apply salve to most of Mavis' legs and shoulders. Blaze put a liquid to her mouth and forced it down, making Mavis cough and sputter. It was one of the vials Adam remembered Azura holding when she was treating Jett.

Dear God please, I can't lose her too, Adam prayed silently.

"Jett," Blaze commanded, "come here." Jett went to her side obediently. "Hold on to Joe and focus on raising his strength. Think about times you felt invincible and empowered or the complete opposite, weak and powerless, and channel it. Let your body guide it to Joe." Adam watched as Jett closed his eyes to focus. He, for once, couldn't tell what his twin was thinking or feeling. Whenever Jett used his talent now, it severed the normal connection Adam had with him. The thought sent a ripple of sadness through him. This is where his brother was divided from him. It separated them in way that no matter what, Adam could not help Jett. In this area, Jett was alone. Joe's hand began to glow green as he ran it over Mavis' body. He could see her twitch every time he passed over a limb but as soon as he pulled away it lay unresponsive again.

"Any time now Jett," he said, his voice strained.

"I'm trying!" Adam could see sweat forming on their foreheads. Adam felt his feet draw him forward and his hand clasp Jett's tightly. Jett's head turned to stare Adam straight in the eye. Adam looked back at the reflection of his own face, the one that revealed the same anguish and stress that he felt right now.

"For all the times you felt like you could never learn to walk again. For all the times you felt useless when we were searching for her. For the regret you felt after you told Jackson about us. Remember that now. Don't try to remember when you were strong because it's hard to recall. People always remember their lowest points much more vividly, because that is the essence of what actually makes us strong. Bring it back, for Mavis." Adam said the last sentence pleadingly. Jett stared bewildered at him for a moment. The confusion in his eyes cleared and he nodded, focusing once again. The glow from Joe's hand was beginning to weaken and flicker. Adam held his breath as Jett attempted to awaken his power. The light winked out and disappeared. Joe dropped his hand in exhaustion.

"No..." Adam stammered.

"No," came Jett's voice, loud and clear. He gripped Joe's shoulder so tightly that the pale blue veins in his arms stood out. Adam gasped as he watched Joe's eyes turn as black as night, becoming identical to Blaze's. His hand came back up and had a bright green aura surrounding it. Joe hovered over Mavis' heart and let the pulsing light float above it. Jett fell backwards, heaving, holding his chest as he caught his breath. The light from Joe's hand faded, as did the black colouring from his eyes. Mavis lay still on his lap. For a terrible minute Adam watched as a death-like paleness settled on her skin, and slowly began to despair as her chest ceased to rise.

Unexpectedly, she inhaled sharply, startling them all. Her eyes popped open, showing their beautiful cerulean irises, as blue as Atlantic Ocean, as blue as the day he first saw them.

"Joe?" she whispered.

"Yeah, it's me," Joe said, relieved. "You're okay." He slowly pushed her into a sitting position.

"MAVIS!" Adam and Jett shouted at the same time. They both dropped to their knees and hugged her hard, almost knocking her back again. Adam buried his face in the dusted curls of her hair, feeling her heart pulse against him. He could feel her begin to tremble as she hugged them back.

"It's really you," she whispered. "You found me."

❧

Jett intertwined his fingers through Mavis', as Adam slowly fed her the concoction Joe had given them to help her strength return. Jett could see the hollowness in her face from malnutrition and dehydration. Her hand was weak and as her fingers struggled to grasp his. He wondered how she survived for so long. A huge weight had been lifted from his chest now that Mavis was beside him once again, but another had settled in its place. The others would surely tell Mavis about how they had found her, and in turn they would reveal that he had betrayed them. Jett didn't think anything could hurt him more than seeing his brother's reaction to his betrayal, but now it was quite possible that Mavis' would cut just as deep. He couldn't believe he had risked Opal's safety for a promise from a person he didn't even know. Opal, Blaze and the rest of them had helped him get here, to Mavis' side. He couldn't recall what on earth had clouded his judgement. He knew Blaze had hid her curse from them, but it was also for a reason. Jackson had lied to him too, by only showing him the partial truth. In that, he had given himself away to Jackson's manipulation. What would Mavis think if she knew about the type of person he been lately?

"Umm... who is this?" Mavis asked when Ace came over with a washcloth.

"Mavis, meet Ace Ryder. He's Blaze's good friend and a detective in a manner of speaking. He helped us find you."

"Oh," Mavis managed a weak smile. "Thank you, Ace." She held her hand out for him to shake. Ace gave it a brief shake before smiling at her.

"You're welcome. Don't overextend yourself now and just relax, you're in good hands." He began to rub the red dirt off her arms in gentle strokes. Blaze came and handed Mavis a bundle of clothes.

"Here, change into these when you're ready. It may be a little big but it beats the rags you have on now." Mavis nodded. She grasped Blaze's wrist, pulling her close.

"Thank you, Blaze. For everything," she managed through shaky breaths. Adam gave her another spoonful of medicine to help her with her voice.

"Don't thank me yet. We still need to find a way out of here."

"You reunited me with my family. That's more than I could ask for. I'm ready for whatever comes after that." Jett lifted her hand and put his lips against it softly. Her skin was still hot and feverish, even though it was drastically better than when they first found her.

"Then you won't mind answering my questions then?"

"Of course not. Ask away." Blaze motioned for Adam to move aside so she could sit by Mavis.

"Start from the beginning. What happened the day you disappeared? How did you get here and what have you done since then? It's important you don't leave anything out. If we figure out how you got in, maybe we can use it to develop a way out."

"Okay, so the day I disappeared. I came back from the Chronicles with Azura and found this strange message someone had left on my hand. I don't know why or how it got there. It said *knowledge is power, come back, alone.* I was too curious for my own good, I guess. I went back, and I can remember going through the general section at the front while I was waiting for something for happen. I talked to Jen for a bit and then she went out to lunch with Storm, who also happened to be in the Chronicles. Once they had gone, someone swung at me from behind, I clearly remember feeling metal hitting my skull and passing out. I woke up in this dreary place."

"There was an earthquake that day that nearly tore Myra apart," Jett informed her. Mavis' eyes went wide.

"Was everyone okay?"

"There were a lot of casualties unfortunately," Blaze said. "Joe disappeared that day too."

"How did you find him?" Mavis asked

"Jen has a pet wolf who tracked him down," Jett said. "It's a long story. We hoped that it would be able to find you too, but we are currently in the middle of the ocean and the wolf couldn't track over bodies of water."

"Hold up," Mavis held up her hand. "Where are we exactly?" Jett truly wished that this place had a more pleasant name than the one he was about to utter.

"The Devil's Den cove in the ring of fire."

"Ring of fire? You mean like the volcanoes?" she asked.

Jett swallowed.

"Yeah, and we're inside one right now." The horror in Mavis' eyes made Jett wish he could take his words back.

"That does make quite a bit of sense now I suppose," Mavis said after a while. "It explains the landscape."

"What happened after you arrived here Mavis?" Blaze prodded.

"Right, I woke up and this...this... voice started talking in my head. Telling me that I wanted this and that it was completing our deal. It was enough to drive me insane, and I had no memories of any type of deal. It led me through the tunnels and made me speak spells I didn't know, like it could possess my body and use my mouth. A vial of... blood, I think, was used to open a doorway and I fell through to this marble room. It gave me the feeling of being at peace, as if I had my memories back but I still didn't know anything. That room or that feeling somehow sustained me. I didn't feel hungry or tired in that state. Then the voice suddenly took that feeling away. When you heard me scream it was because I could feel all of the necessities I was lacking again. It overpowered me and I fell from the ledge of the marble room into the opening where Joe found me."

"A voice you say?" Ace mulled over. "Does it still try to contact you?"

"It hasn't for some time now. The last thing I felt was just its presence recently, when the peaceful notion was ripped away from me. The last thing I told it was that I'd like to be left alone when it first gave me some serenity. I'll let you know if it tries again, but I'm not sure it will."

"Mavis, you need to understand something," Blaze said. "When I was working with Ace to discover where you were, we saw a vision of you lying unconscious here, but there was a scroll beside you. The enchantment involved using a sacrifice, and I think whoever brought you here intended for you to play that role. This area is very powerful in terms of magical potential and it would be a great place to start unusually powerful sorcery. They may come back at any time to kill you and complete the job. So, tell me honestly, is that all you remember?"

"I'm sorry, but that really is all. I wish I could tell you more. But… someone really wants my life?" her lip trembled. Jett nodded painfully. "This means that we have to leave, as soon as possible right?"

"Yeah," Blaze agreed. "Have to work on an escape route though."

"Maybe if you guys go to the marble room, it will have some answers. I fell from it, so there's definitely a way back up. Maybe if the voice contacts me there again, you guys can help me force it to guide us instead."

"A long shot, but worth a try. Rest up, and we'll head out when you're back on your feet." Blaze left with Ace to join Joe by the sleeping bags.

"I can't believe you survived that. With a strange voice in your head too." Adam pulled on Mavis' curls affectionately.

"I'm sorry, guys. I must have caused you so much pain and panic. All this time you guys were exhausting yourselves looking for me. This time, curiosity almost literally killed the cat. That teaches me to never go off alone to entertain mysterious messages." Jett managed a small grin.

"We'd prefer if it stayed that way, that's for sure. All that's left is to get out."

"I really wish I knew how," Mavis said sadly.

☙

Adam, Jett and Joe took turns every few hours to looking after Mavis while the others explored the cavern. Ace kept a wary eye out for Mavis. He could see that Adam and Jett cared for her immensely, but leaving them alone wasn't the best idea in his mind. The fact that Joe came by routinely eased his stress. They had worked so hard to find this girl, and he didn't know if he had it in him to find any of them again if they went missing or fell through a hole. He and Blaze had probably walked through fifteen tunnels, each of them either leading to a dead end or connecting with one they had already been through. They were both getting frustrated as the day wore on, and more and more red dust collected on their boots. The marble room Mavis had mentioned was nowhere to be found. He supposed that Mavis would be able to lead them to it when she was well enough to travel. Ace sat down on the crimson earth and took a deep breath of humid cavern air. Blaze settled down beside him, ruffling his hair as she crossed her legs, an affectionate gesture she had done since they were kids. She rested her head on his shoulder, sighing. He knew exactly what she was feeling right now. It was evident that Mavis had been transported here through magic. That being said, there may not even be a physical path out of the volcanic interior. The barrier spells that had been cast around this place did not give them the option of teleporting out, nor did they have anyone they could leave behind even if the spell could work. They were trapped.

"I know Ace, I know," Blaze said softly. No matter how long Ace had known Blaze, her uncanny ability to predict what he was thinking still threw him off. Ace turned to see weak flames dancing in her eyes. They flickered and then winked out again.

"Is your darkness stable?" he asked, concerned.

"Yeah it is. That was me intentionally trying to see how much of a power reservoir I could manage without losing control. Apparently, it's not much."

"There's something certainly *wrong* about this place. It's like I have a pit of uneasiness in my stomach that refuses to go away," Ace said.

"There is a very heavy veil of dark magic cloaking the area. I feel that much," She kicked up some red dust. "Our supplies won't last forever. If it comes down to it, I'll have to channel my power to blow a way out for you guys." Ace gripped her hand tightly.

"We can't leave you! You're not going to stay back while this place collapses on top of you." Blaze shrugged.

"If I do use magic, my darkness will swallow me first, so it doesn't matter. If all else fails, it's the only way. I'd rather you all get out alive. It'll finally be the end of my misery."

"Blaze by ending your misery, you'd subject the rest of us to misery. Can you imagine the damage it will do to Joseph? To me? To Opal? Opal already hates the fact that you're sacrificing so much for her. She'll never be able to live it down if you died that way." Blaze cupped his face gently. "That's why I'm telling you. Because you know why it must be done. Why I want to do it." Ace felt tears beginning to burn against the back of his eyes. He didn't think he could stand to see her die. There was too much history, too much love that Blaze's face carried, too much compassion that was reflected when he looked into her eyes. He knew that if it were him, he would have made the same request. His heart wrenched with grief.

"Promise me Ace," Blaze whispered, "if it comes down to it, you will get everyone to safety, no matter what it may cost me. Promise me!" Ace swallowed hard. His eyes were shining as he pulled Blaze into his arms.

"I promise."

&

Blaze was keeping watch as the others slept soundly behind her. Joe's hand covered hers loosely and she used her other one to gentle caress his hair. It had to be the most peaceful thing she had done since getting here. For a just a moment in this wretched cavern, she felt happy. Her mind wandered as she thought about what Ace said. *Can you imagine the damage it will do to Joseph?* Blaze gazed down at Joe's sleeping face. He looked carefree and relaxed, as if he was dreaming of something pleasant. She wondered often, what it was like to be mundane. Mundane like Adam and Mavis were. They had no powers so they paid no price for it, living in blissful ignorance of the supernatural energies that encompassed the Earth. The ones Blaze could touch. The ones that had given her gift and the same ones that had cursed her. In her opinion, it was better to have neither. Don't ask for pleasure, don't ask for pain, because having one would give you the other. It was never a deal you wanted. Alas, she couldn't escape it. She had silently observed the twins with Mavis, with much envy, as they tried tirelessly to keep her optimistic and happy, distracting her with positive stories of what had transpired since she was gone. Jett had filled her in on his budding romance with Jen and Mavis had laughed and teased him for a bit. Then she had given him some advice on how he should handle it. Adam told her about the new dishes he was planning to make on their return home, emphasising Mavis' favourite ingredients. They truly cared for each other a lot; she could feel that radiating off of them. They would be able to return to their ordinary world and forget about all of this. No more magic.

She couldn't escape it, and that's what made her so jealous. She was cursed to remember, until she died. *Which may not be far off.* She also felt an undercurrent of strong tension too, although she couldn't pinpoint who or where it was coming from. It had been here since she had arrived, so she had temporarily attributed it to the dark magic that had imprisoned them here.

Something moved in her peripheral vision and she swung around to see a haze of white smoke coming towards them. Her eyes widened in alarm and she shook Joe as hard as she could.

"Wake up! Wake up everyone! NOW!" Everyone bolted up right. Ace was by her side in a flash.

"What is that?"

"We're not waiting to find out."

"MAVIS!" came Jett's terrified voice.

"AAAAHH!" she screamed. The smoke had curled into a rope-like form and had latched on to Mavis' leg and was dragging her away from them. Mavis clawed at the ground to no avail and the smoke continued to turn thicker and pulled her back faster. "HELP ME!" Her eyes were wide with terror. Blaze ran after her with Joe thundering behind her. Even though Blaze was sprinting, she could barely keep up with Mavis as the smoke zipped through the cavern tunnels. Mavis vanished from view. Blaze couldn't stop herself from falling over the ledge that had appeared. She had run off of it and plummeted downward. She twisted her body and prepared for an impact and roll. Her shoulder slammed into the rock and she flung herself over to avoid creating a crater in the ground. Her arm still erupted into pain, but she hadn't broken any bones. The boys fell beside her. Joe and Ace managed to catch Jett and Adam to minimize their bodily damage. Blaze sat up and looked around. Her voice hitched in her throat. The ground was made of marble. White, shining marble just as Mavis had described, inscribed with symbols crafted from reddish-pink sandstone. Mavis lay twenty feet from them, unmoving. Blaze was about to go to her when she felt the searing heat on her back. She whipped around to see boiling red lava flowing in a steady stream about a yard away from her. *This must be near the heart of the volcano,* she thought. Ghastly hot steam rose from the liquid fire as it bubbled and ran by her. She quickly backed up as dry air seared her lungs. She took another step back and was able to breathe again. It seemed like someone had created a bubble of protection around most of the room to keep the magma from killing them. Not that Blaze wasn't grateful. But a few steps out of the perimeter and she would become charcoal. Joe grabbed her arm.

"Are you alright?!" he exclaimed.

"Yeah I'm fine. Get Mavis up," Blaze said. The white smoke had disappeared and Adam and Jett were making their way to Mavis.

"Mavis are you okay?" Adam reached out to her. Mavis looked up unsteadily.

"Adam…Jett…" A strange look came across her face. She got up slowly. "I'm fine…" She straightened up and dusted off her shorts. Alarm bells went off in Blaze's head. Mavis was beginning to glow. "I'm more than okay." She pushed her hand out and Adam went flying into the cavern wall. He landed with a sickening thud.

"Adam!" Jett said in horror. Jett tried to go to him but was jerked back. He tried to move his feet but it was as if someone had cemented him to the ground.

"I can't move! Mavis, what's going on? What's happening to you?" Mavis took a deep breath and closed her eyes. Her clothes were replaced by a floor length, spaghetti strap, white silk gown. The exhaustion washed away from her face as did her injuries, as if she had just woken up form a peaceful night's sleep. Blaze stood frozen in her place.

"That was magic… but you're mundane, that's impossible!"

"Blaze, you out of all people should know by now that nothing's impossible. Not when magic is involved." Mavis' grin was now wicked and cold. "I have spent my life preparing for this moment. You all get to witness my grand finale. My revenge will now be complete."

"Mavis…" Jett said, horrified. "What are you talking about? What revenge?"

"Revenge for the love I lost so many years ago. Revenge against the person who killed him."

"And who would that be?" Blaze asked. Mavis' icy blue eyes scanned the room until they came to rest on Blaze again. Blaze returned her gaze with a level look of her own.

"Why you of course, Miss Blaze Darkfire."

CHAPTER 21
Revenge

SCARLETT COVERED AZURA AND OPAL WITH THICK WOOLLEN BLANKETS as they slept off the influence of the drug. Jinx had shown up at her apartment with the two of them, and they had been in quite a crazed state. While Jinx kept the two occupied Scarlett had run to infirmary for a counteractive drug. Luckily, she had visited Azura at work enough times to know where she kept them, and there were still a few bottles left. It did leave the two heavily sedated, and they had fallen asleep almost immediately. She and Jinx now sat on her couch, watching over Azura and Opal. Jinx had filled her in on what she knew. Blaze had really done it. She was in the Devil's Den. Scarlett could only hope that Blaze's quick thinking and power would lead her back to Myra again. As far as Jinx had confirmed, they had not mentioned a way to return.

"They'll find a way," Jinx said. "You don't bet against Blaze."

"This may be the challenge that is her match," Scarlett said. She knew Blaze was strong, but everyone had their limits. She always worried if Blaze would one day overextend herself. She was afraid now that she had. She and Storm had looked up whatever they could find about the Devil's Den, once Scarlett had called Jinx to go help Blaze. There wasn't much that could be found. Apparently, it was a very ancient crossing of magical realms and was rumoured to be a former gateway to Hell that had been sealed off. The legend had stated that anyone who went there never returned the same, if they returned at all. The thought made Scarlett shudder. *Please let it just be a legend.* Jinx put a comforting hand on her shoulder.

"Tell me what is really bugging you Scar," Jinx said. "I know you're worried for your friends, but I know you well enough to see that it isn't the whole story." Scarlett sighed.

"When Jackson gave me Mavis' location, it was in exchange for a conversation. He tried to convince me that he missed me, and wanted me to come back to him." Jinx blinked slowly and then scoffed.

"How dare he even attempt to ask you that after what he's done."

"That's exactly what I thought. Now though, I can't help but feel that he's getting involved with all this drama just to try to win me back. If he's hurting people for that reason, I should go to him just to have it stop. It not worth the havoc he's creating."

"If that's true, he's just damning himself further. You won't really love him for these horrendous things and he will know it. Then he might continue in the futile attempt to win you over. It's also not worth risking *you*."

"I don't know," Scarlett sighed. "I still don't understand how he found out about your Palo's mission," she mulled, "You're excellent at keeping things hush and undetected." Jinx shook her head.

"It still baffles me. Unless one of them told him, which they didn't, and it's the only way I could think of that Jackson could have known. Even my drivers and guards were kept in the dark about it." They sat in silence over the thought until a loud scratching noise came from Scarlett's front door. Jinx was up in flash, moving soundlessly towards it. Scarlett also approached cautiously. If it was Jackson, she would have to rely on Jinx to smack him upside the head. She twisted the knob slowly and opened the door. A pair of glowing eyes looked up at her. *Help me*, Scarlett translated. She swung the door open to let Fang come inside.

"That is one *massive* wolf," Jinx said in awe. Scarlett stroked the fur around Fang's neck to sooth her. She could feel the canine's agitation.

"What happened? Shouldn't you be with Jen right now?" Fang whined. *Missing. No trace. Help locate.* "Missing?" Scarlett exclaimed.

"Yes, missing," came a voice from the corridor. Neal had appeared in the doorway, panting. "I went to talk to Jen in the Chronicles today and found her wolf pacing the office in distress. She dragged me over the door and showed be that the lock had be forcefully broken. Something had happened. No one has seen Jen for days. I brought Fang here so she could tell you more than what I could get out of her." Fang growled. *Tracking item.* Scarlett nodded.

"Fang is a tracker, we need to get something of Jen's so she can sniff her out.

"The books and offices in the Chronicles have been touched by so many people that nothing in there would suffice," Neal pointed out. "We need something that is exclusively hers."

"You said Jen was in the infirmary for some time, right Scar?" Jinx asked. "Yeah why?"

"Her hospital gown would still have her scent on it. As far as I know, they aren't reused. I don't believe they would have been thrown out yet."

"That's perfect Jinx! We need to get it as soon as possible."

"Leave that to me." Opal had woken up and was gazing intently at Fang. "I'll be back in a flash." Before the others could say a word, Opal was gone.

"Seems like she's recovered," Jinx observed.

"It seems so," Neal responded. "Azura is still asleep though."

"It may take her longer to fight off the drug. Everyone differs in that." Opal returned with the gown in hand.

"Thanks." Neal took it from her and held it out for Fang to smell.

"Are you feeling alright?" Scarlett asked Opal.

"Yeah, I remember everything. Thanks for helping me out Scar. You too Jinx, it was much appreciated." Jinx nodded at her. Fang's nose twitched and the wolf turned around to dart out of the apartment building.

"You guys follow her," Neal said. "I'll take care of Azura." Scarlett tossed him the keys.

"You better," she said before speeding down with Opal and Jinx. They tore through the streets to keep up with the racing canine. The only reason they hadn't lost her yet was because only Opal's speed could keep up with the leg muscle of a wolf, especially one of Fang's size. They slowed down when Fang stopped and growled at a pristine white door.

"That's strange, this is one of the entrances to the experimental labs that Neal works in," Scarlett said. Fang bared her teeth.

"She's really upset," Opal pointed out, "Jen must be nearby."

"We can't get in without clearance," Scarlett responded. She had to jump back as Fang slammed into the door. "Fang! Stop!" The wolf pounded against the door again and again. "You can't get through! Those doors aren't ordinary! They're meant to keep threats out!" Scarlet wished, not for the first time, that her power would extend so animals could understand her too. She was about to grab on to Fang's fur went she slammed into it again, and the doors cracked. Jinx quickly jumped in front of Fang and performed a well-placed spin kick on the door. The material shattered, leaving a hole just big enough for them to duck through.

"Apparently," Jinx said slowly, "Fang is not an ordinary wolf." *Follow me,* Fang said and wedged herself through the hole. They followed suit and raced after her. A scream vibrated through the building and they trio turned the corner to find Fang snarling at someone. The figure was backed up against the wall, their face hidden in shadow. To the left of them Scarlett could see Jen suspended on the other side of a glass wall, unconscious.

"Show yourself!" Jinx commanded. The person took a shaky step forward, allowing light to illuminate their face. Scarlett felt the blood in her veins run cold. It was Jackson.

Something inside Scarlett snapped. "Fang," she said icily, "Attack." Somehow Fang understood what she had said. She leapt at Jackson with her claws out, ready to cut his throat.

~

"Me?" Blaze said in the most even voice she could muster. Inside she was astonished. "I didn't even know you existed until you came to Myra. You said this love of yours was lost a long time ago. How on earth would I know him, let alone kill him?"

"That's the thing Blaze, you did. You murdered him in cold blood. Burned him alive and left his charcoaled body on the beach to find," Mavis spat at her. Blaze's eyes widened.

"The thief…"

"I see you remember," Blaze felt the weight of everyone's astonishment as the tension rose in the room. "His name was Ashton Kyle. He took those stones to try and heal his dying mother. Until you got in the way. I remember waiting by her bedside, assuring her of the return of a son who would never come. She died waiting for him, and my heart died when I found out what became of him," she said with her eyes shining. Blaze felt a cold numbing go through her, like her blood was freezing into ice in her veins. She stood up straight and twirled her dagger in her hand, staring Mavis dead on. "That thief tried to kill my entire family, and because of it I had to choose to become *cursed* to save them. That curse gave me the power to kill him. If he hadn't put my family in danger in the first place, it would never have happened." The ice in her blood was prickling inside of her. "Your lover was so stupid, that he couldn't have even tried to ask for help before deciding to steal from the most accomplished professor of dark magic? If he had, I assure you my father would have tried to help him. But because of him I lost my entire family. So no, I don't regret letting that little weasel burn to death in front of me. He. Deserved. Every. Last. Bit." Blaze wished her words could spit venom. Anger was starting to boil from the wounds that her family had left her with. "And you have the audacity to say you suffered," Blaze shot at her. "You don't know what true pain is." Mavis' face was red with fury.

"I don't know what pain is?! He was the love of my life, and every day without him burns my very soul. I have spent years hurting, weeping and grieving over his death. He was the only real family I ever had. You ripped all of that away from me. Why couldn't you just let him go?"

"Are you kidding me? From what it looks like, your boyfriend didn't know shit about the magical arts. All those stones were infused with dark emotions, very dangerous ones. If he used one on his mother it would have killed her anyways. The price for those enchantments are too steep. There is a time when a life is beyond salvaging. Everyone must face death. Disrupting that always has a dire cost, and it usually fails. You don't mess with nature."

"Liar. Didn't you save your family from death with magic?"

"Only because it was magic that was trying to kill them in the first place! It was not from a natural cause! It was because your pathetic excuse of boyfriend didn't know what he was messing with!" Blaze held out her arms. "You want to kill me? Go ahead."

"Blaze no!" Joe exclaimed. He ran to her side.

"I won't let her do this," he said. Mavis threw her head back and laughed manically.

"Isn't that a wishful thought? Don't worry though dear, I'm not going to kill Blaze," she grinned diabolically, "I'm going to kill you." The words didn't even register in Blaze's mind when Joe began to choke and started to rise slowly in the air. She could see his body following Mavis' hand movements. *NOOO!* her mind screamed. She would cut off Mavis' arms if that's what it took to keep Joe safe. She flipped out her dagger just as a leather whip cracked and coiled around Mavis' arm, yanking her forward. Joe dropped, gasping for air as Mavis struggled with the cutting edge of Ace's whip. Ace cracked it again, striking Mavis across the face, leaving a long red mark on one cheek. He leaped and landed in front of Blaze as she helped Joe get off the ground. Her heart eased when she saw that he was okay.

"You couldn't expect it be that easy," Ace said. The annoyance was clear in Mavis' eyes. She felt her face; lightly touching her newly inflicted injury.

"I didn't expect it to be," she replied.

"MAVIS!" said Jett as he fruitlessly struggled to move. "Why? Why are you doing this? Why did you never tell me about Ashton?" Blaze felt the hurt rolling off of Jett.

"Yeah, Mavis why? Why didn't you?" It was Adam, who had finally gotten up. "We were family," he trembled. It appeared only for a moment, but Blaze felt guilt and remorse come from Mavis. The wheel in Blaze's mind turned at lightning speed, fitting all the pieces of the puzzle together.

"Because she knew you were a *permotionem*," Blaze breathed, "all along." Blaze slowly began to circle towards her. "Your boyfriend knew something about magic. I'm assuming he taught you as well. Once he was gone you probably did some digging in that area." Blaze gripped Ace's shoulder. "That vision we had, we thought she was a sacrifice when we saw that scroll beside her. We were wrong; she's the one who was going to cast it. It was about resurrection. You're going to try to bring Ashton back from the dead," Her voice caught in her throat. "And you're going to use Jett to do it."

Mavis straightened up and dusted off her gown. "You're a smart one Darkfire, you figured that out. But you aren't smart enough to stop me. I've been formulating this for years."

"I'm smarter than you think Mavis." Blaze was recalling every interaction she had ever had with her, and how her subtle suspicions about Mavis had become true in a way she couldn't imagine. "You say I'm the bad guy? The murder? At least I killed someone who was guilty. What about you? Your hands aren't clean of blood either, are they?"

311

"What are you saying Blaze?" Jett asked in small voice.

"When I initially met Mavis, I...I... Ugh I can't say it! My powers are holding me back," she said, frustrated. "I felt emotions coming from her that I concluded had meant that she had done something horrible in her past. I knew it was from a broken heart. They only happened around you and Adam. At first, I paid no mind, but now I know which spell she's using and what she needs for it. There is only one thing she could have done." Even Ace was looking at her confused. Blaze took a deep breath. She knew that what she was about to do would only help Mavis' enchantment along, but they had to know. Blaze turned to Jett.

"She killed your father." There was pin drop silence in the room.

"What? No! I refuse to believe it!" Adam looked at Jett. Jett fixed his eyes on Mavis.

"Tell me it's not true." Jett was on the verge of tears. "Please."

"I take back what I said about you being smart. You just made this spell a lot more efficient," Mavis smirked, "yes, it's true." Mavis shot a black jet of smoke out of her hand that began to engulf Jett. Blaze's heart wrenched as she felt the one thing she feared to feel, Jett's emotional response to betrayal. It was so overpoweringly strong that Blaze's senses were overloaded, making her dizzy.

"Jett! Stop! Please! She's using the emotion to power her spell! Don't let her have it!" Ace yelled. Blaze felt the tiniest flutter of relief. Ace had figured out what was going on.

"It's too late," Mavis gloated. The smoke cleared and Jett was trapped inside an orb, fashioned from black flames. He banged the barrier to no avail. Red smoke was starting to collect at the top of the dome. Mavis flicked her wrist and the ground shot up, grabbing everyone's arms and yanking them down to their knees, keeping them shackled with earthen chains. Blaze could feel the rocks cutting into her skin as she wrestled against it.

"I will admit I didn't think you would be able to piece that together, Blaze. You did save me from having to tell him though."

"You killed our father..." Adam said, the despair creeping into his voice. "How could you? He treated you like his daughter! You were our best friend. How *could* you?!" A genuine air of regret flashed over Mavis' face.

"I truly cared for your father, as I still do for you two. That's why Blaze could pick up my guilt and sadness because I felt horrible about doing it. I poisoned the tea I gave him every day while he watched his sports matches. He had to be killed over time so the doctors could attribute it to a chronic illness. When he finally did pass away, I did cry for him. But it had to be done if I ever wanted to see my Ashton again." Adam was shocked to silence as Mavis gazed at him with true regret in her eyes. "If it could have been anyone else I would have spared him. But he was the only one. Jett is the only *permotionem* alive. You see, killing Joseph Davis had two purposes. One was so that when Jett realized it, the betrayal would be so strong that his *permotionem* spirit would be able to provide the massive power I needed for this spell. Which is currently happening," They all turned their eyes to the orb, where the red smoke cloud was steadily increasing in size. "That's why I became friends with Jett. I need to be close enough to him that my betrayal would cut him deeply."

"Mission freaking accomplished," Ace spat.

"Indeed. The second reason was so he would give Jett that disk necklace he wears all the time." Blaze saw Jett's hand close around the silver disk that hung at the hallow of his throat. "He always said he'd give it to Jett when the time was right. Death I suppose was that time. Your father didn't know it, but it's a powerful relic. The *permotionem* in Jett activated it. I altered the charm so that it would keep Jett safe and alive until I needed him. That's why nothing has been able to kill him yet, even your deadly memory flowers. It was like a guardian or protection spell in a way. I knew that Myra was somewhere in Costa Rica and I made sure I was granted the trip here so I could find it. Initially I thought it would have taken me years, but I was lucky enough to stumble upon it within my first few days. Since then I've accelerated my plans. His father's charm will protect him no longer."

"Mavis!" Jett was clawing at the flames that separated him from the group. "You have me now! Let the others go!"

"I'm sorry Jett, I can't do that. I can't have anyone revealing my plans."

"You caused the earthquake, didn't you?" Joe asked. "You had Opal possessed to kill Kaitlin so you could get the books you needed from the Seal. You're probably the one who sent me to those quartz mines."

"Correct, Mr. Starks. I needed your blood to put the barrier spells on this place. Mixing it with shards of quartz did the trick. I knew they would find you though, I counted on it, so you could be here for this." Blaze's heart seemed like it had stopped beating. She hadn't known that, and a horrifying truth revealed itself to her.

"Why my blood?" he asked.

"Because she wants to bring her love back from the dead," Blaze said in a shaky voice. Tears burned at the back of her eyes. "So, she has to give up someone else's love in exchange. That is the price. Who better to take it from than the one who killed him in first place?"

Joe's jaw dropped. "You're going to kill me because Blaze loves me?" Mavis grinned.

"Fitting, isn't it? She'll finally be punished for what she's done."

"How can that be?!" Blaze shouted in exasperation. "I should have been able to feel your emotions and predict this when I came here!"

"I knew that pesky little power of yours would get in the way, so I altered the spell so I didn't remember what I was doing until my magic brought me back to the marble room, where my memories would be returned to me. All the emotions you felt were filtered, because I had no memorable trace of my intentions."

"You crazy bitch!" Blaze roared. "No one can be brought back from the dead! It's a law of magic! You're just going to kill us all, including yourself!"

"The laws of magic are subject to several interpretations. Things always seem impossible, until someone comes by and does them. I plan to be that person."

"It will never work."

"Let's find out, shall we?" Jett gasped and fell to his knees.

"What are you doing to him?!" Adam yelled.

"The spell is burning away his soul. He may not survive this!" Ace yelled back.

"Mavis please, stop this insanity!" Tears flowed freely down Adam's cheeks. Blaze felt daunting waves of desperation from him.

"I'm truly sorry Adam, but my love for Ashton is still stronger than my love for your family," Mavis was glowing brighter with every passing minute. Blaze stopped her desperation from surfacing. She should have known.

ev

Mavis' cold blue eyes settled on Joe. "It's your time now." The earth shifted and Joe was dragged forward to Mavis' feet. Despair rose up in Blaze's throat like bile. Mavis would not stop, she could see that much. Blaze could not lose Joe. She just couldn't. Mavis yanked him up and pulled him towards the river of lava. They stopped a few feet short of the bank. Mavis began to twirl her hand in the air and the red smoke followed suit, travelling to the surface of the lava and forming a spinning vortex. Joe tried to fight her but the earth still bound him. Blaze was using all of her strength to break free.

"NO! JOSEPH!" Her dagger suddenly disappeared from her hand and appeared in Mavis'.

"This should work well for a sacrificial weapon. It was originally created to kill you anyway. Today it'll fulfill that purpose." Blaze was awestruck. How did Mavis know that? That was beside the point, and her focus returned to her wrists that were still in chains and bloody from struggling. A powerful current ripped through the air, knocking everyone down to the ground. Blaze could feel the pulsation of pure, raw anger. She looked up at Jett to see his eyes glowing red with power through the wispy black flames that imprisoned him. She quickly latched on to the emotion he was passing on to them. Any emotion was strength. She linked the anger to her own and focused it into the shackles. With the energy flowing through her she ripped her arms upwards with a yell, shattering the chains into pieces of clay. She shot her arms out and blew off the others' chains too.

Before Mavis could put her head up to see what was going on, Blaze took off and flipped up and over gracefully, and slammed down on Mavis' back, knocking the wind out of her. Blaze took a fistful of Mavis' blonde hair and yanked her head back until Mavis yelped with pain. "No one..." Blaze said dangerously, "crosses the Lady Scorpion."

"First time for everything," Mavis breathed. Mavis grabbed Blaze's hand and flipped her off her back. Blaze felt herself being thrown backwards into the ground, landing with a thud. Mavis had rolled on top of her, holding Blaze's own dagger at her throat. She had just locked eyes with her when Joe tackled Mavis from the side. In a flash Blaze was on her feet again. Joe and Mavis both lay sprawled in front of her. Joe made a desperate grab for the dagger. Mavis caught his hand before he could reach it and they began to wrestle each other. Blaze's peripherals could pick up the chaos that was taking place around her. Adam and Ace were frantically trying to free Jett from the orb that was draining his life force. The effort of sending out his anger had taken its toll on Jett, and he was clutching the ground while he tried to fight the sapping of his energy. *Good, if they can get Jett out, the whole thing will fall apart.* Blaze turned just in time to see Mavis blast Joe backwards with a shove of her hand and pick up the dagger. Joe landed a few feet away from her. Blaze's hand closed around a throwing knife on her belt and let it fly. Mavis quickly deflected it with the dagger but yelped as the knife instead of hitting her heart, slashed her arm. Blood bloomed from the cut and began to drip down.

"Nice try Darkfire, but you just delayed the inevitable. The spell is almost complete." Blaze could hear Adam yelling Jett's name, she assumed because Jett was close to death by now. Mavis funnelled the last bit of red smoke into the vortex and it began to whirl at twice the power, sending dust and magma flying. Everyone except Mavis struggled against the pull of the wind, as it threatened to pull them into the vortex. Blaze was forced down to keep herself from flying, the torrents cutting at her like millions of tiny spikes. She felt the cold metal of her dagger push her head up to face Mavis. "I wanted you to see your lover die and mine be returned. I guess I can't afford to have you getting in the way, so I'll spare you that and kill you first." Blaze's breathing was even and steady. She managed to sit up straight on her knees and tossed her hair back. She didn't fear Mavis. She didn't fear anyone. She only feared what she would do to her loved ones. But Blaze knew better than that. She knew more about dark magic than anyone, even more so than her father. She always knew herself inside and out, even after the darkness took over. What Mavis didn't know though, was that killing her would release her darkness into in the cavern and it should be able to annihilate her and her spell, leaving her loved ones safe if she cast a small protection spell before she died. Her friends and Joseph would never have let her sacrifice herself if they knew, so she had kept quiet about it. There were some things that just had to be done. She gazed at everyone one last time. Jett, Adam, Ace and lastly Joseph, who was also struggling to move towards her against the wind currents. *Joseph Starks, my fire,* she thought. She braced herself and accumulated the strength inside her to start the protection invocation. "Do it," Blaze taunted Mavis.

"Gladly." Mavis raised the dagger and Blaze cast her protection spell silently. She looked up defiantly at Mavis as she brought the dagger down. Blaze never felt the metal go through her chest. She was propelled towards the river, landing at the edge as her side erupted in pain. She rolled over to see the dagger going through Joe's skin. Joe's eyes were wide as Mavis yanked the knife back and he crumpled to the ground. Blaze felt time stop and all she could see was his body hitting the ground and the blood beginning to pool around him. Her heart felt like it was burning, scorching the blood in her veins, cutting at her soul with edges of jagged blade.

Blaze found herself leaping up and running to his side, lifting his upper body into her embrace as Mavis stepped back, astonished.

"Joseph! Joseph!" Blaze cried. Her salty tears flowed freely, falling on his shirt, dampening the reddening cloth. She could feel him shuddering, his chest jerking with shallow breaths as the life left his body. She cupped the sides of his face. "Please," she wept. "I can't lose you! That should have been me!" Joe's eyes fluttered open and he placed a weak hand on her arm. "I love you. I always have, and that's why I did what I just did. That's why you did it too. I knew you would try to sacrifice yourself and I couldn't bear to see you do it," He coughed, spitting up blood. "Call me selfish, because I know you can't bear to see it either, but believe me when I say I don't regret doing it, and you cannot blame yourself." Blaze felt like she was being cleaved in two.

"Joseph…" she begged. Her clothes were sticky with blood. Joseph's blood. His voice was fading.

"Angel," he breathed, "my dark angel." Blaze watched in terror as his chest ceased to rise.

"No," she whispered. She pressed her ear against his chest, urgently trying to listen for a heartbeat that would never pulse again. "He's gone." Blaze gripped his body to hers, letting the tears splatter on the earth around her.

"Now you finally know how it feels! The agony of losing your true love," Mavis held the dagger out in front of her, still stained red. "Now I have what I need. Joseph's blood. It will return my Ashton and we will finally be reunited once again." Mavis started making her way to the vortex.

Looking down at Joseph's lifeless body in her arms sent a jolt through Blaze. Her nerves turned to steel and her blood began to boil. She lay Joe down gently and then stood up to look at Mavis' retreating form. She would not hold back this time. When Joseph died he broke the barrier he had placed on her darkness and now it came rushing up like a tornado building its way towards the sky. This was the Devil's Den. The fire of Hell flowed through her and it would be ten times more destructive here. The anguish built itself up, adding whirlwind after whirlwind of scarring memories and feelings. The most prominent one glowed in her mind's eye, watching the dagger going through Joseph's chest. The pain tortured her mentally, but she could fell every fibre of her body and soul being supercharged with energy. Her eyes held their deadly violet flames once more and she let the blackness wash over her. She yelled as her scars ignited and her whip burst forth, coiling down her arm in a long rippling wave of pure demon fire. The light from it was almost blinding and she could see the ground around her starting to steam from its heat, but Blaze barely felt a thing. Her whip swung out, cleaving the ground in two, allowing for magma to come bubbling up and separating her and Mavis on a rocky island of their own. She cracked her whip again and it smashed against the orb, shattering it into fragments of black glass. She hit a wall, blasting a massive hole through it. At the other end, she could see the blue of the sea. The vortex vanished and Ace and Adam sprinted to get Jett out of the rubble. Her vision was red as she zoned in on Mavis who had turned around and was frozen in horror. *No mercy*, her demons urged her. *So be it*, she responded. She felt herself lose control and become engulfed in the fury of her powers. Her whip lashed out and grabbed Mavis before she had a chance to scream. It dragged her away from the vortex and pushed her to face Blaze, tightening around her in a frightening coil of fire. Blaze watched, detached, as Mavis shrieked in torment as the flames scorched her.

"Let me do *you* a favour," Blaze said coldly as she began to rise in the air, bringing Mavis along with her. "You'll get to experience what Ashton did before he died. After that you'll finally be reunited. That is, if Lucifer allows you to find each other. If I'm manifesting Hell's power on Earth, it has a fate much worse in store for you when you fall to its depths." Mavis' eyes bulged as she choked and thrashed. Blaze pulled the whip tighter and tighter until Mavis was ablaze, her body going limp. Blaze let the power surge through her until she was holding a charcoaled body once again. The rush slowly faded and Blaze was in a free fall, plummeting towards earth. Her energy was gone and weakness had taken over. A strong pair of arms caught her and held her close. The world was spinning around her and a pair of electric blue eyes spun with it. *Ace. My mirror*, she thought before she was swallowed into a void of blackness.

CHAPTER 22

Mirror, Mirror

AZURA DIDN'T THINK SHE HAD EVER WORKED HARDER IN HER LIFE. EVEN with Storm and Neal helping her. When Ace had teleported into Scarlett's apartment he had scared the life out of Neal. Not because he appeared randomly, but because he had brought one person who was traumatized, two people who were dying, and one that was already dead. What made Azura's heart jump even more was the fact that one of them was Blaze. In the back of her mind she knew there would be a day when she would have to properly heal her friends. There were no other healers around and she couldn't request help without the heads finding out. Not that they would help her anyway. As they had rushed everyone to the infirmary, the blood had pounded in her veins as she tried to mentally prepare herself for what she had to do. Unless you were a *permotionem* any emotions would only get in the way of proper healing. A healing hand had to be steady, not shaking with fear, or wavered by despair like Azura's were initially. She couldn't let herself feel the horror of staring down at her best friend's unresponsive body or the lack of a pulse in Joe's chest.

Jett initially had intense muscle spasms, and they had to tranquilize him so he didn't hurt himself further. Neal gave her the occasional hand squeeze when he saw her calm beginning to crack as they all worked as fast as they possibly could. Neal had brought some prototype pieces from the labs that could pinpoint weak and impaired areas on the body and was scanning for tissue damage. Storm was outside trying to keep Darkfire under control, after he had broken down the infirmary doors to get to Blaze. She supposed he had felt her return, and how something was incredibly wrong. As soon as Darkfire had gotten close to Blaze she had gasped and her eyes popped open, but they were engulfed in flames and she had screeched with pain. As much as it hurt to watch Darkfire cry for Blaze, Azura had to separate them. Without Scarlett there to calm Darkfire down, Storm had to rope him with a chain of water and pull him outside so they could continue to work. Jinx, Scarlett and Opal had not yet returned and weren't picking up their phones. Something must have happened, Azura reasoned with herself. Ace had taken Adam outside to clean him up and calm him down. She wondered how that was going, but couldn't think about what Adam could be feeling right now or even Ace, who knew how to hide it well. The lives of the people closest to them were in her hands now, and it shook her to the core. She pushed the thought aside and focused on the task at hand. Blaze's skin was burning, so much so that Azura couldn't touch her directly. She had gotten insulated gloves from the kitchen to wear whenever she had to turn Blaze over to examine her scars. They were constantly pulsing from a dull maroon to an angry scarlet red. Neal had managed to cut open whatever was left of Jett's shirt to reveal a pattern of interlocking, pointed spirals that seemed to be tattooed on to the skin just over his heart. When Azura had scanned him, it had seemed like someone had literally sucked the life energy out of him, she could barely register that there was any at all. She had to avoid the area with the spirals; anytime she scanned it she received a shock of intense dark energy. Azura crossed her hands over Blaze's chest, her hand beginning to glow with a green aura. She felt the darkness rushing under Blaze's skin and the damaged tissues right under the surface. The physical body was easy to heal, Blaze had almost no bruises or cuts now. But her mental spirit had been hit out of whack. Azura tried to clasp on to the path of rushing dark energy and was urging it to dissipate. Some of it weakened under her will but the rest was too strong for her to control, and she had to break away. Blaze gasped, her body jerking up. Azura jumped back. A violet fire still danced in her irises. "*Joseph,*" she rasped before collapsing again.

Azura could feel the strain in her muscles as the exhaustion of constant healing began to tear away at her. She kneeled by Blaze's side and put her head down, gripping the sheet so tightly that her knuckles turned white. After a moment a pair of long, lean arms wrapped around her. Neal pulled her close and she allowed it, slumping against him. They sat there for a minute in utter silence.

"Now should I use it?" Neal whispered softly. Azura shut her eyes.

"Do it," she answered. Neal let her go gently and began to assemble Azura's last resort. She had hoped she wouldn't have to use it, but everything else she had done had failed. This was the only sliver of hope she had left. Though it wasn't much of a solution. The apparatus that Neal had brought was something Azura had requested as a failsafe a long time back, when someone else she couldn't bear to lose was in danger. She had not needed it then, but had kept it safe in case one day she would need it again. Indeed, that day had come. Eight long white bars were placed around Blaze and Jett. Four of them underneath and four of them overhead. Once the last bar was set in place, both of their bodies were elevated, staying suspended in the air. All that was left was for Azura to kick-start the spell that bound the eight bars together. She took a deep breath. This involved magic, which was why it had been kept as a last resort. The bars were made of white *ankh*, to amplify her range of energies to put Blaze and Jett in a sort of suspended animation. They would remain as they were, not really living but not really dead. Until Azura could find a way to bring them back to consciousness, that's how they would stay. All magic though came with a price. She felt Neal's hand on her shoulder, asking if she really wanted to do this. She winced, looking at Blaze again. She remembered convincing Blaze to help Jett how walk again. How Blaze had said it would have been better if Jett died. She couldn't fathom her friend's stubbornness then. Now she cursed herself for not having listened to her. Whatever the situations may have been, Jett had the biggest part to play the tragedy that was unfolding now. Though she still stood by the fact they should not have let him die, but now she wished she had been more cautious. She owed her friend this. She nodded at Neal and placed her hands on two bars. She steadied herself, rocking slightly on the balls of her feet. If she went through with this, she would have to pay the price. The price being that if they ever managed to wake these two up again, they would be bound to her. If one of them died, so would she. It did not go the other way around. If she passed, the spell would break and everything would return to normal. It was cruel that way. Her friends would now have to live not just for themselves now, but for her as well. Magic had harsh consequences but Azura had trifled with it before and she would do so again. She knew if Blaze could see her right now she would have yelled at her, saying how magic had ruined her life and she didn't want it to ruin Azura's too. She would tell her that there was a time when a life was beyond saving. She would say to let her go. Azura also knew though, that if it was her lying in that hospital bed, Blaze would have done everything in her power to save her. So now, she was going to do the same. She had not mentioned that price to Neal when she had asked him for it. He would have tried to stop her too.

She gathered her remaining strength and sent a blast of energy through the *ankh*s. The stones began to glow an electrifying green and connected to form a glowing box around Jett and Blaze. Azura felt her heartbeat intensify, as if she had three hearts that beat in her chest. She felt the rhythm of both Blaze and Jett's stabilize and thump evenly. It was a strange sensation. She could separate her own quick paced rhythm from their steady ones. She stumbled backwards as the sensation disoriented her. Neal helped her stay upright as she regained her bearings. Jett and Blaze now looked as if they were sleeping peacefully, the green glow bathing their skin. Blaze's hair spread out around her like a black silk fan, the strands floating like wisps of smoky ribbon. Azura sighed. She had bought them time, but what use was it when they had no idea what to do with it?

☙

Fang left massive claw marks in the wall she had slammed into after Jackson barely escaped her grasp. He tucked in and rolled against the floor to avoid being sliced. Fang snarled and whipped around to face him getting ready to pounce again. Scarlett and Jinx had gone to the glass wall to free Jen. Opal could see Jinx and the control console and Scarlett pounding the glass with brute force. Opal pushed back her maroon hair and sped forward, tackling Jackson down. He managed to push her off and roll back onto his feet. Opal saw the twitch in Fang's hind legs and ducked as the wolf flew over her and caught Jackson square in the chest. Jackson's entire body slammed against the white marble title with a sickening thud. Fang stood over him now, her claws pinning him down and her snarling jaw inches from his face. Opal could see his body shake with fright. Opal had to think fast. She couldn't let Fang kill him. At least not yet, because they needed to interrogate him about what on earth he was doing. After that, Fang could use him as a chew toy. Opal slowly stroked Fang's fur to lower the wolf's current fury so she wouldn't attack while they worked on getting Jen free. Any time she felt Fang's muscles tense she had to restrain the wolf by the shoulders. Jinx and Scarlett were still struggling to break the glass.

"Screw it," Jinx said. She pulled her arm back and slammed it full force into the control panel. The buttons shattered and sizzled with electricity from the circuits underneath as shards of metal and plastic flew across the room. The panel began to flicker and buzz as the motherboard went haywire. Jen fell to the floor with a thud as the suspension that held her up gave way. She turned over and moaned. Opal breathed a sigh of relief. Jen was still alive. Now they just had to get to her. Opal coaxed Fang back just enough so that she could grab onto the collar of Jackson's shirt.

"If you value your face pretty boy, you're going to tell us how to get into that room," Opal hissed. She was surprised at the malice in her own voice. Opal had always considered herself more of a gentle soul but over the last few weeks Jackson had gone above and beyond to change that. Jackson's ear was dangerously close to Fang's jaw. He flinched as Fang growled. "B-b-back door, around the corner, code one, eight, seven, four." Opal yelled out the numbers to Scarlett and watched her and Jinx make a beeline for the door. As they turned around the corner Opal was left alone with Jackson, still pinned under Fang's claws.

"Opal…" he rasped. Before Opal knew what she was doing, her hand cracked as she hit him across the face, leaving a quickly reddening mark. She grabbed his collar and tightened her grip, staring him eye to eye. He was the reason she had to run in the first place. She had cooperatively been sitting in jail before he tried to attack her. Being on the run was the reason behind half of their obstacles on this twisted journey.

"Don't even start with me. You'll be dog food if you open your mouth one more time, understand?" Jackson's lowered his gaze and bit down on his lip in silence. Jinx appeared with Jen in her arms, who looked deathly and severely malnourished. The veins in her arms were visible though her pale skin. Opal resisted caving to the wall of anger that was climbing inside of her right now. She didn't know what Jackson had done yet, and was afraid if she did, she might commit a murder herself. Opal took Jen from Jinx and winced at how light she was as she carried her.

"I'll get her to the infirmary first. You guys can decide what to do with this asshole." Jinx raised her hand and two red scorpion-shaped chains materialized to bind Jackson's hands and feet together.

"Guys…" Scarlett said, as she slowly lowered her phone from her ear.

"We have to get back now. Like right now." The current of agitation was clear in the tone of her words.

"Why?" Jinx asked.

"Because Joseph… is dead." Opal's head began to swim. *Joseph…is dead. Blaze. Dear God, Blaze!* Opal was leaving a trail of smoke behind her as she went thundering through the city, while making sure Jen was secure in her grasp. In a few minutes, she was at the infirmary doors. Jinx and Scarlett would catch up when they could. They knew what had gone through her mind. Blaze was normally the one with the unbreakable armour. The shoulder that was leaned on. Today though, Opal would have to channel those qualities into herself. Because the day may have come, that Blaze Darkfire had finally been broken.

⌘

Ace watched Blaze float in her ghostly green container. The minute he had walked in he had realized what Azura had done. He couldn't even blame her. The poor girl was exhausted. Opal had arrived only minutes after Azura had finished with Blaze and Jett. She had to get Jen on IV fluids to repair the damage the lack of food and electrocution had done. Neal had visibly gasped when he scanned her muscles and tissues. No one had asked any questions about what had happened or how, and Azura had gone straight to work, tight-lipped, and got her into a stable condition. Ace could tell she was about to pass out at that point. Her hands had a visible tremble and the bags under her eyes were dark. He and Neal had gotten her to rest on the armchair in the room and Ace had slowly coaxed her to close her eyes, using his powers to lull her into a dreamless sleep. Neal had taken her to one of the other infirmary rooms so she could slumber in peace. He sighed. Azura would now die if one of them did. He remembered something Blaze used say; it was probably something all of her friends had heard before. *To die for someone is one thing. To live for them is another.* She would now have to live for Azura. She could no longer die for her, seeing as that would now defeat the purpose of the sacrifice. *You can bring as much pain as you want on to yourself. But when another is hurt because of your mistake, it's a feeling you never live down.* Blaze often found herself in dangerous situations. But she kept calm because she didn't fear death, and that calm is what normally would get her out of those situations. Now though, she might have to fear it. Because that death was no longer just hers. *Magic always comes with a price.* Indeed, it did.

Opal stepped into the room quietly, softly shutting the door behind her. She made her way to the bed near the back of the room, where Joe's body lay. Azura had covered him up with a white sheet up to his neck and shut his eyes. He still had a lifelike flush in his face that hadn't faded yet. It had only been a few hours since he had passed away, but to Ace it had seemed like eternity. He had bid him farewell silently, reading a prayer for a brother who had passed. In a strange way Joe had been a distant brother to him. He had loved Blaze as much as Ace did, but that aside, they had also defended each other in battle and had worked tirelessly to keep each other safe because they knew that if either one of them were to get harmed, Blaze would be the one who suffered. He remembered the musical happiness in Blaze's voice when she used to tell him about Joe. He didn't know what she had said to Joe about him, but he assumed it wasn't too bad considering how relaxed he was when they had met.

He could sense Opal behind him paying her respects to Joseph as she mumbled under her breath softly. Ace reached for the inside pocket of his jacket and pulled out a black rose. He started twirling it gently between his fingers, watching the black colour move and shift inside the petals. Joe had given it to him when they had tumbled into the Devil's Den. They had been exploring the cavern together at one point when Blaze had been keeping watch over the twins. He had handed it to him, telling him to keep it.

"Why?" Ace had asked.

"Jinx had a conversation with me before we went to Palo's. She told me that Blaze had her dagger made to kill me originally. If I wanted to know why, I had to take this flower from the bouquet of memory flowers we stole and have Jett look into it for me." Ace hadn't been surprised that Jinx had known about Jett. There wasn't much she didn't know about. Ace began to open his mouth when Joe held up his hand.

"I know she's dangerous, and was probably trying to bait me. But after the whole revelation about her name, I had the insane craving to know more. But as soon as I took it, I felt horrible. Because what good would it do me to know about something that no longer matters? It would bring up an unnecessary barrier between us. That's why I want you to keep it for me. So I'm not tempted to exploit the memory. I don't know whose memory it is. It could be someone who was seeing the event through a negative light and would give me a biased re-encounter because I would feel what they felt. That was most likely Jinx's goal. She's always been hostile about Blaze's birthright to the Swarm and probably wanted to attack her personally through me. If I'm going to hear this story, it should be from Blaze herself." Ace had taken it gingerly from his fingers.

"Black huh? The colour of strength." He wondered who in that memory had been the strong one. "I can't see any other reason for Jinx to hate Blaze. To my knowledge she has done nothing else against Jinx so far." Ace said. Joe shrugged.

"Who knows?" he said quietly. Ace was silent for a moment before slipping it into his jacket pocket. That had taken guts to admit, and even more guts to let go of the flower, and Ace respected that. Joe shot him a grateful look.

"Some things are better left unknown. I'm learning that slowly. Thanks."

"Anytime, man," Ace responded while clapping him on the shoulder.

Now Ace sat still, staring intently into the coal-coloured rose. He had known that Blaze had had a blade made for her by Jinx many years ago. He had not known that Joe had been the targeted victim for that weapon. Life was insanely ironic. Joseph had ended up dying by it anyway. The blade, now cleaned of blood was next to Blaze's bed on the side table, glittering in the evening light that was coming through the windows. He wasn't sure she would want it anymore now. He felt the light brush of fingers on his shoulder. Opal's hand rested there gently. The heat from her hand was warming the ice in his veins. He did his best to maintain his composure.

"How is she doing?" Opal asked him quietly. *That is a loaded question*, he thought. Blaze could be trapped in web of nightmares for all he knew.

"She's stabilized, as far as we can see. She'll stay like that until we can wake her. She channelled too much demon fire, utterly exhausting her power reservoirs. Azura has brought her back, I guess you could say. But not completely." His voice cracked slightly as he finished that sentence.

"So, there is still hope," Opal said. Ace assumed she had meant it in a reassuring manner, but a cold bitterness had taken a hold of him.

"Hope," he almost spat, "is an ugly thing". Opal recoiled at his words and he instantly felt bad. She had only been trying to soothe him, in her own way. But right now, he was stoking the fire that was raging away inside of him. A silent fury that burned him clean through and left him feeling like the densest of volcanic stone was sitting at the pit of his stomach. He softened his voice. "I can't bear to hope Opal. The disappointment from it will crush me." Opal turned her head to gaze at him with a weary smile.

"Are you sure you and Blaze don't share a mind?" she asked him in a half-teasing, half-exhausted tone.

"Heard that one before, huh?"

"A variation of it." She rubbed her arms together as if she was chilly. Ace, with his focus still on Blaze, peeled off his leather jacket absentmindedly and handed it to her without a word. She accepted it after a moment's hesitation. They sat in silence, both of them mourning over their departed friend, and distressing over their coma-encased ones, in their separate ways.

"Why does darkness cause so much pain?" Opal half-whispered to herself.

"Darkness does not cause pain, Opal." She arched an eyebrow at him. Ace pivoted so he could look her in the eyes. She seemed like a beautiful illusion to him as she looked back into his own, unwavering. So very close to him but so far out of his reality. He hid the hitch in his throat and assumed the confidence to speak. "Light and dark are two sides of the same coin. They are means of energy, of power. What differs between them is their sources I suppose. Darkness comes from unpleasant emotions like anger, sadness, and despair while light comes from happiness, love, contentment etc. They in themselves cannot cause pain nor can they diminish it. It is if they are used for good or for evil that makes the difference. Being dark is not the same as being evil, nor does using light mean you are good. That is an association, generalization that many people make. But it is an association, not an iron binding. You can use darkness for good, or light for evil. Actions determine what pain is dealt. Not the means that were used to enact them." He looked back upon Blaze's pale face, smooth and soft under the emerald glow of her container. "Blaze was given a heightened darkness, awful emotions that are easily triggered, releasing more power. An imbalance in light or dark can drive a person mad and make it very hard to control. It is not what causes the pain though."

"Do you believe in God, Ace?" Opal asked. The question threw him severely off guard.

"God? Uh… yes, I suppose. Why?" Opal wrung her hands together as if contemplating whether to remain silent or not. To Ace's relief, she spoke.

"If God does truly exist… why does he let these things happen? Could he not stop it and help us?" Ace didn't have to think twice about this question. He had wondered the very same thing a long ago, and with Blaze they had discovered an answer they were content with together.

"Opal, has Blaze ever told you what the most powerful force in the world is?"

"Choice," she said without batting an eyelash.

"No matter what you believe in, science, religion, Hades, whatever, there is the concept of a moral code. Actions that are good and those that are evil. My mother told me that angels were pure goodness. That they could do no evil. That was how God created them. So, I asked her if God wanted me to be good why couldn't He have just made me an angel? She then told me about the creation of man. Of when the angels were commanded to bow before Adam. They bowed to him because Adam was given something they were not. The freedom of choice, the power of choice. The angels were good because they had to be. It was not in any fibre of their being to disobey God. Man, though was given choice to be good or to be evil. To be able to choose was a power that no other creation was given, save some spirits if you believe in that. That was why Heaven and Hell were created. Because humans would obey God out of free will, even though they would be tempted by evil and could easily turn to it. Being able to choose, to resist, gave them power like no other. They were the masters of their fate. That is why angels *serve* Heaven and humans *achieve* Heaven. They can achieve Hell too of course."

"What about the Devil? Was he not an angel before?"

"In the stories I learned growing up, the Devil was not an angel, only a spirit ranked among the angels due to his devotion to God. When he disobeyed, he was cast down. That is a matter of speculation though." He raked his fingers through his hair, pushing it back. "If God kept things like a rose garden, Heaven would have no reason to exist. You need to earn good things, choose them. You cannot choose though, if you do not have two choices, the second being the opposite. Light cannot exist without the dark, just as love cannot exist without hate. You can't choose one without knowing the other. Otherwise what would we compare them to? Can you imagine though, since angels were not created with choice, they have never felt things like emotions? They have not felt relief or distress. They have no need to. They are noble and pure, in a way we cannot comprehend, but they, for sure are not human. That is why now, my desire to have been born an angel has significantly decreased."

"I have never thought about it that way," She twirled a strand of her hair tightly around her finger. "Is this why you believe?" Her eyes were now wide and curious as she searched for answers on his face.

"It is a major factor, yes. I suppose it's also because I like to keep faith that there is some type of justice in the world. In this world or the hereafter. It might be just my will to think this way but I'm content with it since it keeps my peace of mind." Ace got up and walked around to Opal, staring at her face to face. He reached out for her hand gently; afraid he might startle her and send her running. It was irrational to think like that, but he did anyway, he could not help himself. She tilted her chin to look up at him, her dark red hair cascading down her back. Her hand was cool, a reprieve from his own burning skin.

"It seems the world is full of mirrors," she breathed. "Love and hate, happiness and sadness, dark and light. All inverted reflections of each other. They are so similar in every way, with only a minor detail setting them apart from each other."

"That is the best analogy I have heard in a long time." Ace's mouth quirked up in a half smile.

"Blaze is your mirror. Eyes that burn with fire reflected as eyes that hold the storm of the sea," she said quietly. Ace quietly debated if that statement meant she liked his eyes or not.

"My mirror, that she is. How do you say we differ though?" Ace asked out of pure curiosity.

"I have yet to figure that out," Opal's eyes popped open, startlingly wide. "Mirrors! That's it!" For once, Ace was dumbfounded. What was she talking about?

She pulled him over to Blaze's bedside. "You can wake her!" Opal said in excitement. "It's a long shot, but I think it might work. You're a *hyponos* so it should make things easier too."

"Would you calm down and tell me what you're getting at? How can I do this?" Opal bounced with the vibrancy of an energized child. Her mind was working at a million miles an hour. "You're her mirror, right?" Ace nodded. "It means her mind and heart for the most part, work as yours does. Whatever would pull you out of a coma would pull her out too. You need to go into her unconscious mind, dissipate the extra darkness and pull her out. It may be the only way!"

Ace had nothing to lose. He wanted his friend back desperately and even though he had only ever gone into dreams, not into unconsciousness, he readied himself for the task. The unconscious was another level of the mind, much harder to enter, much harder to navigate. It could take him hours. He took a deep breath.

"Alright Opal. I will try. It may take me hours though."

"I will stay by your side the whole time, don't worry. If it means giving Blaze a fighting chance, I will support you in any way that I can." She led him over to a nearby infirmary bed.

"You must catch me when I fall," he told her. She nodded, her eyes fierce and determined. He exhaled and lowered himself into his own dream state. He felt himself fall, and in the last moments of his conscious thought, felt two arms catch him. Suddenly, Ace was in the comforting blackness of his own mind. He tried to steady his nerves. He had not mentioned this to Opal, but with her looking so hopeful he didn't want to bring her mood down. There was a reason the unconscious was only explored by few. It was because it was dangerous. If he could not return to his own mind, he would be stuck in a dreamless oblivion. He had read about it in books and scrolls when he was studying to master his powers, of how to enter and how to follow the thoughts as they race through intangible space. He supposed he was as ready as he could possibly be for this moment. *You can do it. You must,* a voice echoed through the blackness. He did not know who it was, or where it came from. He pictured Blaze in his mind and linked onto the pattern of her brain waves. They pulsed slowly and steadily, like a beacon. Following it like a trail of light, he let himself be pulled into her mind.

ᥱᤢ

Blaze was lost. She wandered around aimlessly, looking for something, anything. She felt nothing and saw nothing. All she could hear were whispers, too many to count that rushed by her ears in a jumble. Sometimes she would catch a familiar word and others that were foreign to her. Sometimes she heard names, other times she heard commands. *Jump, strike, move.* She didn't know it now, but they were her battle reflexes. Stored away, zipping around, ready to be used if they were needed. She heard her fears, her beliefs and the names of those close to her, although they made no sense when they hit her ears. Commands came for her heart to beat, for her lungs to breathe and for her immune system to be on alert. To her it was like a wind. A great, thundering wind that carried many secrets in its roar. Her secrets. She let herself be carried away with the current.

ᥱᤢ

Ace had read that the unconscious looked vastly different to each person that entered it. He would see something different than what Blaze saw inside her own mind. Her essence would tug at his brain, melding with his mind. He would understand as she does, while maintaining his own judgement. That took work of course. Blaze was stubborn and strong-willed, so her pull was intense, threatening to tear apart Ace's mind. But he was just as strong, so he resisted, latching on only enough to let the thoughts become known to him. First things first, the extra demon fire had to be put out. According to Azura, Blaze's physical body had healed itself. The problem was that her energy was not being replenished, like a long night's sleep would have done. That energy was needed as a barrier, so the darkness didn't consume her. The demon fire stopped this from happening, using up any energy that was created to fuel itself. It would reach into the darkest parts of her mind and feed from there. Ace saw moving tendrils of light that seemed to go everywhere and nowhere. Blaze's unconscious thoughts. He focused on a memory of his own strength. Black tendrils responded, shooting towards him. They hit him, and he saw a collection of the strength in Blaze's life. Her own, the strength of others and her ideas of what strength should be. Ace committed them to his memory. He then focused on his loss. White light moved towards him now and he grabbed on to it, letting it take him wherever it wished to go. It could have been minutes or hours before it deposited him in front of a churning vortex of almost blinding white light.

This wasn't like the other areas of her mind. The other emotions flowed freely, but the loss was restrained to this corner, building in its size. It over-whelmed Ace, filling him with torrents of events, memories and fears. He struggled to keep his sanity against the vicious pull of the vortex. He saw Joseph dying over and over through the whirlwind of memories. He felt the agony in his chest. There was a menacing laugh, bellows of a voice colder than Hell. The voice of the demon fire. Blaze had told him how it sounded, like ice gripping your heart, but nothing could have prepared him for the real thing. *Hopeless. Helpless. Worthless, Weak*, it chanted. Ace felt his own anger rise. How dare this monstrosity tell Blaze what she was? She was brave, strong and loyal. *That's how she always saw me. She is just like me.* Ace pushed himself into the middle of the vortex. He concentrated like his life depended on it. He imagined himself looking into a mirror. A mirror where the reflection he saw was Blaze. He stood confident and smiling and Blaze returned the look. Her eyes glowed with flames and he could sense his own showed the rage of the sea. He focused on the one memory he thought could bring her back. A time they were both fearless, strong, and steadfast. The voice got weaker as the white light dimmed in its intensity. He could see streaks escaping the vortex, joining into the orderly chaos of the other emotions. He held himself together until the only thing left was the voice of the fire. *I am not so easily overcome young one*, it chuckled. *She used me, she must pay the price.*

"She has paid enough."

Is that so? What are you going to do about it little hyponos? I speak from beyond Hell itself.

"Then I will have to strike you down with the hand of Heaven." Ace was exhausted, but this was the last step. The jump before landing on the other side. *No part of Heaven is in her, child. You are foolish to think otherwise.*

Ace smiled smugly. "Perhaps you forget, demon, that free will is what make us Heaven's chosen ones. She is human; her freedom is enough to crush you. I may not be able to rid her of your taint, but I will make sure you never whisper to her again."

He yelled Blaze's name. Not Blaze, but the one she was born to. He didn't know how he knew it, but it must have been buried in her unconsciousness. He did not remember it afterwards. "CHOOSE!" he yelled.

❧

Blaze heard her name, like clear ringing of a gong. *Choose!* came the command. It was the only one she understood. She blinked, as if seeing clearly for the first time. Along with it came the whispers of a memory, a memory she had buried so long ago that she couldn't have recalled it herself. As the memory ended, she saw herself looking into three mirrors. One of her reflections smiled back at her, prevailing and resilient. The second one was a black outline of herself, like looking at her shadow. Only its eye sockets blazed with violet flames, and the reflection clutched its shoulder like it was in pain. The third was not a reflection of her at all. It was of Ace. He stood there in a tranquil silence, with the sleeves of his t-shirt rolled up. As he turned to the side, Blaze saw that there was a pattern cut out of the skin on his arm, in the shape of a scorpion. Underneath, where there should have been flesh and blood, was dark fire. The black flames raged inside the cut, licking the edges of the skin. *Just like me,* she thought. *He understands the blaze in my blood.* Ace was calm as he passed his hand over the cut and it vanished. *That's what it means, to be strong,* Ace's voice whispered. He motioned to the first two mirrors. *It doesn't mean that you should become arrogant or that you should become nothing more than a shadow. It doesn't mean that you must be the hero or must be the villain. It means you fight the battles that no one can see. You prevail because the fire inside your heart burns brighter than the fire inside your veins. So, my friend, you must choose.* She put her hand on the glass, trying to reach through it to touch his face.

I choose, Blaze thought, *Strength.* She heard a faint scream, a voice of ice being carried away by the roar of the wind. Blackness was all she saw until she was pulled out through the darkness, through her dreamscape, into the waking world.

⁊

Ace was thrust back inside his own mind. He didn't know how. Maybe Blaze had guided him there. The familiarity of his brain soothed his tenses muscles. He worked his way back into his dreams and let them run wild. He would need to sleep before he could wake again. And when he did, eyes full of violet flames would greet him.

⁊

Opal nearly wept with relief when Blaze had opened her eyes, slowly but steadily as if she was waking from a long, restful sleep. They initially had glowing flames leaping in them, like when she lost control, but the look on her face was a peaceful one. "I have returned," she said softly. Opal squeezed her hand tightly and told her not to move. Once Blaze had awoken, she had dropped from the green container and it had resized itself to fit around Jett only. Ace was on her other side, sleeping soundly. It had taken him three hours to pull Blaze out. She had watched him as he slept, his face twisting occasionally, probably corresponding to what he was doing. He had done it. Once Opal had brought in some food and made sure Blaze was comfortable, she got down to talking. Not wanting to overwhelm her, Opal spoke slowly, and explained things in short fragments. The fire in her eyes had dimmed, but still flickered with a violet hue. Blaze had told her it was an after effect, and it would go away on its own. They had flared up again when Opal told her what Azura had done. Blaze kept her hands clenched in fists and didn't say a word. She didn't have to. Both of them knew what it meant for Blaze from now on. What she would have to uphold. Not for her sake, but for Azura's. She continued to talk, and it tore Opal's heart in two to see Blaze realize that Joseph was truly dead. Blaze's eyes went to the back of the room, where Joe's body lay covered under a white sheet. Her lips began to tremble and her eyes shimmered with unshed tears. Opal put her arm around her friend and Blaze leaned her head into her shoulder. For the first time in her life, Opal saw Blaze cry.

Opal let Blaze cry to her heart's content. Once she regained some of her composure, Opal went on to explain how Ace had brought her back. Blaze managed a small, sad smile.

"I heard his voice, telling me to choose. I always believed that the best thing anyone could be, was strong. Mentally, physically, emotionally. I remember my parents drilling that into me. While the demon fire urged me to be weak, to give in, the voices of my parents, of Joseph and Ace reminded me of what I wanted more than anything else. Strength. It cannot be given to you. You must choose it, and build into yourself."

"You chose it long before you knew you did," Opal said with surety. She glanced over at Ace, her eye following the graceful lines of his form.

"You sent my mirror in to remind me of who I wanted to be." Blaze said, watching her face intently.

"No, I sent him to remind you of who you already are."

"She's right," Ace mumbled sleepily as he pushed himself up. He swung his legs over the edge of the bed and made his way to Blaze, giving her a kiss on the forehead.

"Thank you," she said.

"You would have done the same for me," he responded. That was that. She would. They both would, a hundred times over.

Soon the room was full. Opal had led Blaze outside first to see Darkfire and calm him. The horse had almost stampeded them trying to get to Blaze. Once his neighs turned to happy ones, he had taken off. Back inside everyone gathered around her. Storm, Azura, Neal, Adam, Ace, Scarlett and Jinx. Jen was still heavily sedated and was recovering in the next room. It was a bittersweet occasion. They all said their goodbyes to Joseph. They would hold a funeral for him next week. Blaze was dreading the call she had to make to his parents. Adam though, despite being shrouded in anxiety for his twin, came to thank Blaze, mumbling that he would give her his apology when they were alone. Blaze nodded and touched his arm with a surprising softness. His gaze was downcast as he moved aside for everyone else. Jackson had been bound to the integration room with restraints that only Jinx could break. He was going to get a serious beating from all that were present. Blaze could still feel the darkness in her. It hadn't completely gone away. She could still feel the scars on her shoulder getting warm anytime she thought of her whip. She would still be able to summon it. But the voice that had taunted her for years, whispered to her no longer. The burden was bearable now. She had met Azura's frightened eyes with her own calm expression, silently reassuring her that whatever she had done was okay. Once everyone was up to date, Blaze held up hand so everyone quieted down.

"We have one last task before we can relax everyone. Jett is still trapped in a coma. Regardless of whatever else he has done, in the final fight, he lent all of us the power we needed. He did play a part in saving our lives. So now we are going to find his mirror so they can wake him." Before Neal could speak Blaze stopped him. "No, Adam is not his mirror. The mirror must match him in personality, not in appearance. Adam is quite different from his brother." Adam nodded in agreement.

"We may share the same body but that is pretty much where it ends."

"How will we find them then? It could take us years of searching." Storm pointed it out.

"I think we already found her. Jen," Blaze said.

"How do you know it's her?" Azura asked.

"I don't know for sure but some simple mental tests will help us determine that. From what I've seen though, she exhibits many of the same characteristics as Jett. When she's fully healed, we'll discuss this further." Azura put a comforting hand on Adam's shoulder. Adam shot her a grateful look.

"For now, my friends, let all just be grateful to be alive." Azura said. Blaze leaned her head on Ace's chest and let the storm in his heart and fire in hers sing to each other.

഑

Blaze was alone later that afternoon, and she had gone to sit by Joseph's body. Azura knew Blaze had not said goodbye properly, and insisted that she should muster up the courage to do it. Suppressing it would just make it worse. Unexpressed emotions never truly died, they just clawed their way up again in an uglier form. So here she was, holding his lifeless hand as the tears dripped steadily down her cheeks. The last time Blaze had cried was when she became dark. She couldn't even remember the last time she had cried in front of another human. But when Mavis had stabbed him, her resolve had broken. It had been like a bullet to the chest, and now the lasting depression had left her hollow. There was a void, a hole in her that would never be filled. Her dagger was still on her bedside table, mocking her with its gleam. She couldn't bear to look at it now. It had fulfilled its purpose, and Blaze had a boiling self-hatred for having it made. Joseph had been her anchor to this earth and now he was gone, leaving her like an untethered kite in sky, threatening to be torn apart by the wind.

She kissed his cold, dry lips lightly, and broke down. She wept for what she had loved and what she had lost. She wept for the years of friendship, trust and secrets that would turn to dust. Most of all, she wept for the savage that was love. Mavis had gone to all the trouble of resurrecting Ashton, out of love. Blaze loved her family and that's why she was tortured by their existence. The reason they all suffered over and over again was because they *loved*. Mavis had targeted Joseph because she thought Blaze loved him.

Blaze swallowed hard, biting the inside of her lip. Mavis' spell didn't work because she was trying to achieve the impossible. The crueler fact was that it wouldn't have worked because Blaze didn't love Joseph. She hadn't fallen *in love* with him by the time they had been up against Mavis. She had told Joseph that she might have. It had turned out that she didn't, and Joseph had died believing that she could have. That hurt Blaze even more. The guilt crashed into her like stormy waves against a rocky shore. *I'm sorry Joseph,* she thought, *I couldn't fall in love with you.* She stood up, wiping her eyes and numbed herself to the point where she could feel her pain no longer. She was soulless and cold as she clutched her dragonfly necklace in her hand. There was a poem Blaze had read once in an old diary when she was browsing through the Chronicles, and it had stuck with her to this day. She wished she had heeded its warning.

> *A terrible beauty that shines,*
> *like the hand that controls the glove.*
> *Beware of this vicious malevolence.*
> *There is no evil angel but love.*

She repeated the words under her breath, squeezing her necklace so hard that it cut into her skin. She let the blood drip down her fingers. *I can never let anyone love me. It will destroy them.*

♔

Jinx watched, amused, as Jackson struggled against his chains. It was quite satisfying to see him squirm like a worm on a hook. Every now and then he would try and break his manacles with renewed energy, to no avail. He was dishevelled and dirty, with a noticeably bleeding lip.

"I know you like seeing me suffer, Jinx," Jackson said, pushing himself upright. "But I know you aren't here just to rejoice in my misery. Get on with it. What do you want to know?" Jinx let the silence play out, revelling in the moment. She didn't think she'd ever see Jackson this helpless. She took great pleasure from it.

"Why?" Jinx asked.

"Why what?"

"Why go to all this trouble? Risking your position as a head, your status in the *jaculus*, not to mention Blaze's wrath…" Jackson flinched when she said Blaze's name. He must be more afraid of her than Jinx thought. Yet he had tried to go against her anyway. "Was it for Scarlett? Because I don't see how of any of this would have done anything but lower her opinion of you."

Jackson let out a rattling cough that resembled a sad laugh. It was the laugh of a man who knew he had lost his gamble.

"Mavis came to me, asking me to apprehend Jen. Apparently, Jen was close to figuring out whatever Mavis was planning to do. I had no idea a mundane knew so much about us. She knew about sorcery that went beyond the laws of Myra, beyond even Blaze's and Benjamin's knowledge. She claimed she could do the impossible, bringing your love back from the dead."

"You believed her just like that?"

"Of course not. She struck me against the ceiling with the wave of her hand. That's when I believed her. She told me if I could detain Opal and Blaze, she could go through with her plan, and she offered me something I couldn't refuse in return." Jinx's eyes widened.

"Scarlett's love? You cannot make someone love you Jackson. No magic is powerful enough for that. It's a divine law," she said.

"It's also a divine law that you can't bring back the dead either but she was going to do it." Jackson responded. "The reason I agreed wasn't because she promised me her love. I knew magic too well for that. She promised that she would wipe Scarlett's memories."

"So, she wouldn't remember what you had done…" Jinx exhaled. It made sense now, why Jackson was hell-bent on capturing Blaze and Opal. In exchange, he would be getting a fresh start with Scarlett. Jinx had to admit, Mavis really knew how to tap into everyone's desires and twist them to her will. She knew just what to say in order to get Jackson to turn his back on his comrades. That was a talent in itself. Despicable, but a skill nonetheless.

"You played your last card foolishly Jackson. Scarlett would never love you, not truly, if her memories were stripped from her. It wouldn't be real, but you wanted her badly enough to settle for the illusion. Love made you weak, and your fellow heads and fellow *jaculus* will not stand up for you now. All that's left is to watch Blaze extract her revenge. After that, all you will do is burn." Jinx loved the viciousness of her own words, and the tears that rolled down Jackson's cheeks because of it.

☙

Blaze sat in the rubble of the Seal, playing with a shard of glass between her fingers. Fragments of metal and crystal littered the ground. Chucks of marble were tossed about, as if a wrecking ball had demolished the building. Not much had been cleaned up since her fight with heads. She continued to sit in the center of her destruction. She didn't regret this fight, but was mourning the fact that all the books had been destroyed as well. Her father's life's work, and the generations of knowledge before him, was now ash.

She heard Adam's footsteps before she saw him. She got up and brushed the ash and dust of her pants and turned to face him. He was hunched over in a hoodie, trying to brace himself against the heavy winds that blew over the river pathway to the Seal. Adam seemed exhausted and Blaze couldn't blame him, given the past few days. His so-called best friend was dead, Jett was still in a coma, and the one person who may be able get him out had been tortured severely.

"I got your message," he said. "What did you want to talk about?"

"I wanted to reassure you that we will do everything in our power to save Jett. Do not doubt that, as you have before." Adam flinched at the truth in her words. "We still have much that is unanswered. We don't know who helped Mavis control Opal or why, how she got into the Seal and how she had a dog with the Shadow Swarm's symbol bring her the scroll. We don't know if Jen is Jett's mirror, but a person can have several mirrors. We will find one. I promise." She meant it, and Blaze Darkfire never broke her promises. She took a deep breath and steeled her nerves.

"Have you ever heard anything about my father Adam?" Blaze asked. He shook his head.

"Not that I know of."

"He was a professor on dark magic. One of the best to ever teach in Myra." She stopped him before he could open his mouth. "We are estranged, that should answer many of the questions you were about to ask." He bit his lip and nodded. "When I was still in contact with him, I introduced him to Joseph." There was a hitch in her throat when she said his name. She coughed and continued. "He told me it was a lovely name."

"I'm not sure I follow," Adam said, puzzled.

"My father was a *changjo*. Before he came to Myra to learn about his gift, he lived in Manchester, where he met my mother. My mother was a Myra mentor that was sent to seek out people with our gifts and bring them for training. She revealed our world to him. He left England, and many of his friends along with it."

"I still don't see your point," he said.

"Where did your father live before he had you and Jett?" Blaze asked.

"Manchester... England..." Adam said with a slow realization. Blaze bit her words back, not wanting to say what she had to.

"Blaze," he asked, agitated, "What was your father's name?" Blaze sighed.

"Benjamin. Benjamin Darkfire. You would know him as Uncle Ben." Adam's jaw dropped open. "It wasn't hard to connect the dots when you told me your father got a necklace from an Uncle Ben as a farewell token. My father always used to talk about a childhood friend, named Joseph. That's why he loved the name. It's also why the necklace had been protecting Jett all this time. Because that's what my father had designed it to do. It protected your father until Mavis altered it, and now it protects Jett."

"So, our fathers were best friends?" he asked. Blaze nodded. Adam put his head in his hands. "This is a lot to take in."

"There's more unfortunately," she said.

"Is it good news?" he asked.

"More of a request." Adam motioned for her to go on. "I know my father would want to know that both of our Josephs died. I would like you to tell him for me, and invite him to Joseph's funeral."

"I know you are estranged and all, but couldn't you make an exception for this? Why do I have to go?"

"Because," she said, "my father doesn't know I'm still alive. I'd like to keep it that way."

෴

Am I dead? Jett thought. He was tossing and turning while suspended in the air. He saw flashes of gold and green and blue, along with a cool breeze that beckoned him. He saw torrents of orange and violet, sending him sprawling backwards as they radiated unearthly heat. He lost himself in the flux, twisting from side to side. One of the orange torrents landed in front of him, slowly shaping itself into the form of a man. Once he materialized, the fluctuating colours vanished. He was about Jett's height, with sandy hair and deep green eyes like gleaming jade stones. He was in loose linen clothing and he smiled sadly at Jett. Jett backed away.

"Hello Jett," he said in deep voice. "I am Ashton Kyle."

෴

Jen woke up, disoriented and dizzy. Her mind was weak and her memory was shaky. She was strapped into an infirmary bed. She struggled to roll over, her body aching with every movement. *Jackson*, she seethed, *you will pay.* Her head felt like it was encased in lead, heavy and dull. A steady ache throbbed in her temples. *Jett!* she thought, her eyes flying wide open. *I need to see if he's safe. I must tell him about Jackson. I must...* It was when she rolled over that she noticed something on her arm. There was writing that went from her shoulder to her elbow. In thick, black, sinister cursive lines, as if someone had inked a tattoo onto her, was a word. When she saw it, she gasped. *Proditor*, it said. *Traitor.*

THE END

Lightning Source UK Ltd.
Milton Keynes UK
UKOW01n1333070318
319055UK00001B/28/P